THE SILVER SPHERE

MICHAEL DADICH

ISBN 10: 1622536010
ISBN 13: 978-1-62253-601-6

Cover Art & Interior Illustrations & Graphics
Copyright © 2012 Mallory Rock

Formatting & Layout: Mallory Rock

Chief Editor: Lane Diamond
Contributing Editor: Kira McFadden

Evolved Publishing LLC.
www.evolvedpub.com

The Silver Sphere is a work of fiction. Names, characters, places and incidents are products of the author's imagination, or the author has used them fictitiously.

For Jenna and Jax;
when they smile my heart is whole.

"Hell is empty and all the devils are here."

William Shakespeare

CHAPTER 1

"Your world will be over soon, won't it, dear Bianca?"

The cloaked creature rasped out the syllables one at a time, and each sound pushed Bianca closer toward the cold stone floor. Moonlight splashed across the room from a wall of windows. Even if she could have yelled, no one would have heard her. Pain made her dizzy.

As the assault on her consciousness raged, she struggled to her feet against the heavy stupor overtaking her body. Her limbs shook. The long table in front of her provided only a moment of support before she collapsed upon the solid oak board.

Her vision blurred from the pressure, and a murmur gurgled from her throat as she tried to call out to the Assembly members hunched in their chairs. The maroon wine spilled across the table told of their downfall. Were they unconscious or dead? She couldn't begin to guess. Her goblet remained almost untouched.

"How easy this was...."

The din of his words made her gaze upward, where a hood surrounded his darkened features. Screams echoed in her head, though no sound broke from her lips.

He knelt beside her and whispered, "Dear Bianca." His hands caressed full chunks of her raven hair, and he started pulling the strands through his fingers.

Horror traveled down her spine and numbed her. She felt the escape of fainting descend upon her, fogging her mind; how she wanted to drift off and shun the maddening fear. Yet he would not let her. She tried in vain to pull away, but his power over her was too great.

"Don't." She must have said it aloud because his grip tightened and he jerked her head back, forcing her to look at him. She gasped as he pulled the cowl away.

Her tormentor had a pallid complexion and a high forehead. Long, wiry auburn hair framed his narrow face, at the center of which sat a nose snubbed like a snout. It was the piercing glare of his eyes that caught her, though. Their intensity made her skin crawl.

"Malefic," she mouthed, her breath releasing in a terrified wheeze.

He loosened his grasp and eased her to the floor. Then he stepped over her body and slithered to the head of the table, admiring his handiwork.

Bianca's legs and arms stiffened. Malefic oozed power, and as she watched him, her mind reeled. What had led to such laxness in their security? Where had he come from?

We were betrayed, of course, she thought, as unconsciousness bid her closer to blackness.

Malefic turned and glared into her eyes, a sneer twisting his expression into a grotesque mask. "The Aulic Assembly is mine." His harsh voice pulled her to the brink. "Father will be pleased."

CHAPTER 2

Shelby Pardow sat across the table from the beast. Her cereal rested on her tongue like paper, and she melted the particles to avoid any crunching. She planned every movement she made. Were it possible, she'd escape the beast without exchanging a single word with him.

Her father, Byron, had barged in from his night out. At eight o'clock that morning, the sickening-sweet scent of alcohol and cigarettes remained on his breath.

She needed to be cautious; after he drank gin, the devil possessed him. She glanced up at his rumpled clothes, haggard expression, and gray stubble along his jaw. His depression had worsened since Mom abandoned them.

He munched a slice of cold pizza left over from dinner earlier that week. His behavior turned her stomach sour. She needed him—well, except when she needed to avoid him.

Dang it all. How did I forget to set the iPod alarm last night?

The beast glared at her from across the table. "So, to what do I owe the pleasure, missy?"

The beast only called her "missy."

"Nothing, Dad. I just wanted to see you before I left for the library."

Her sweet reply was countered with a snarl. "Oh, really? Or did you oversleep before you cut out to your precious book cave, huh, missy?"

She took small bites of cereal and kept her eyes locked on the blue, flower-patterned bowl. Usually he ignored her when she did not look at him. She hoped today would be the same.

"Answer me!" the beast roared, jarring the table and sending her saucer crashing to the floor. The beast had consumed him.

Shelby winced. Maybe it believed she was her mother. Everyone always said she resembled Samantha.

She glimpsed her father in the beast's face. He scanned the ground with remorse, and for a moment, she thought he might return after all. Hope, however, was shattered.

The alcoholic creature rose with a howl.

Trembling, she stood and backed away. Her foot slipped on the cereal and milk now layering the slick linoleum, nearly tumbling her down.

"Look what you've done now, missy!" The beast growled as he whirled around the table and grasped her by the neck.

Her heart throbbed and her legs buckled.

"I'll teach you to respect food, missy. Children are starving in this world, some even here in town. Now you eat that food, missy. You eat it right off the floor."

"Daddy... please...." She managed to choke the words out in between gasps for air, and she sniffled in fear. On the ground, the dish wobbled and skidded a few feet.

"Go ahead, missy."

Shelby obeyed. Salty tears ran down her face to blend with the flavor of linoleum, low-fat milk, and cereal.

The second he gave an inch, she'd race for the front door. He'd never follow, but even if the beast did, Mr. Dempsey, the kind librarian, would protect her. She'd run straight to him.

The disgusting tang of the floor, and a sudden silence, snapped her back to the moment. The beast had let up, so Shelby stopped licking at the ground and eyed him.

He sauntered to the kitchen sink, poured a tall glass of water, and began chugging it.

Without delay, she got to her feet and charged to the front door. She ripped the deadbolt open, sped down to Bounty Lane, and ran toward Main Street, where the library waited. Houses flashed by, each fronted by a lovely yard, fenced in and tidy.

The beast did not follow.

Shelby halted, shivering in the morning sun, then doubled over and dry heaved. Sweat rolled down her brow and her hair clung to the back of her neck. She wanted to erupt into tears, but she sucked in a lungful of air and shut her eyes, forcing herself to calm down. Everything would be okay now, but she *had* to remember to set her iPod before the beast came home.

Shelby touched the back of her sore neck. Tears welled in her eyes.

What will I do if the beast never leaves?

She leaned against the rough brick wall of a store. Main Street spread before her with people bustling about their business. Children screamed and ran from a candy shop in droves, sweets in their hands.

Exactly what I need, she decided. *Something sweet to wash away the dusty linoleum.*

With a wad of money stuffed in her jean pockets, she strolled down the street to the drugstore that sold her favorite drink. She stepped in, but no one stood at the register.

How predictable. Someone made a spill in one of the snack isles, and Mr. Goodman is mopping up.

She called to him, "Hey, Mr. Goodman! Buying milk!" and left the exact change on the counter for the bottle of strawberry milk.

She swilled the ice-cold beverage down, soothing her throat and rinsing the gross linoleum taste from her mouth, and walked to the exit with empty bottle in hand.

Daddy *would* be back in the afternoon. And she *would* talk to him. He'd declare his resolve never to drink again, and profess his never-ending love for her. Everything would be fine. It had to be.

Shelby tossed the bottle in a wastebasket and stepped out onto the street. She scanned both sides of the avenue, though she knew he hadn't followed. Her body still shook from the beast's attack. No sign of *it* on either side of the boulevard. She closed her eyes and exhaled. Confident, she strolled to the library.

The beast may not have even realized she'd left yet; her friends had nicknamed her "ninja girl" for a reason. She'd escaped again, though not without some harm. She rubbed the back of her neck, trying to let it go. Her father would *never* hurt her, but the beast.... That's what had done this to her.

The important thing was she'd managed to get away. "Par for the course," she said to no one.

Shelby arrived at the Rutherford B. Hayes Library, longing for its air conditioning and calm setting to cool her sweaty brow and dampened tee-shirt. She ascended the stairs and breezed through the entrance, where a wash of cold air enveloped her. She paused at the front counter and stretched her hands up over her head, reveling in the cool tranquility of her sanctuary.

Mr. Dempsey gazed up from his notebook, twirling a pencil. In his mid-fifties, he was a sweet man, though stern when necessary.

Shelby's mind drifted to the time a surly gang of boys ignited the library trash bin with matches. Mr. Dempsey stopped them as soon as he spotted the

punks, barking at them like a drill sergeant. The thugs hesitated only a moment before bolting. Her confidence in him swelled after that. The gang had intimidated her friends many times over the years, but never after that.

"Top of the morning to you, young Shelby. Have you been running track? Don't tell me kids run track in their jeans these days." Whenever he spoke, he gave her his complete attention. He brushed some eraser residue off his crisp blue chambray shirt and khaki pants while maintaining his gaze.

"Awe, no, Mr. Dempsey, a crazy old stray over on Bounty Lane interrupted my path. I got a li'l nervous and ran over to Main. Hot outside." No reason to tell him the embarrassing truth. Anyway, private persons didn't share things that were... well, private. "Any of the computers open yet?"

She inquired as a matter of courtesy; computers were always open this early in the day.

"Take your pick of the four in the back right. I shut off the ones on the left 'til this afternoon to save power. Have fun and stay off the restricted sites."

The routine soothed her. She felt at home here, as if coming in and saying hello could be as normal as waking up and brushing her teeth. She grinned. Mr. Dempsey always reminded her that not all adults yelled at her or threatened her.

"Of course, Mr. Dempsey." Shelby glided to the back and slid into a cubicle. She flipped on the computer to study a site referring to magic spells she intended to use to cure her father.

An odd sensation raced up her spine, and she shuddered at the electric tingling. Without making an effort, she grew more alert as she peered at the screen. A dialogue box appeared with a clang.

She jolted. *How bizarre. I haven't even signed onto the instant messenger.*

It was different from other windows she'd seen, with a rainbow-colored border around a glowing box. Yet the sender's identity remained hidden.

She ran her fingers through her dark hair, her right leg rocking up and down.
You are needed.

Perplexed, she spied over her shoulder at the silent library. She stood on her chair and inspected the other cubicles nearby, but all of them sat empty, the computers still off. Maybe a virus had infected this machine.

"Is anyone here? I'm having a problem with my computer."

No answer. Her attention shifted to the glowing note. It was probably harmless.

She sank back down. "*For what?*" she typed, and hit the enter button.

At once, a sharp clang signaled another message.
The balance is in their favor.
Your Kin is our savior.
As she is missing,
Biskara is hissing.

An ancient evil has come.
Save us from thralldom.
Please answer our plea for help.

Did she know anyone named Biskara? It seemed vaguely familiar. Shelby had many friends on the Internet, most of them girls her age, in tenth grade. Some of them preferred quirky nicknames, so Biskara could have been one of their handles. Someone was probably playing a joke on her. Sometimes they did that to one another for simple fun, but this was just weird.

She typed, "*How?*" and hit "send."

A clang and a note followed.

File down the aisle to the storage room.
We will be there to greet you soon.

Mr. Dempsey might know what the message meant, or at least he could check its validity. She knew where the storage room was; last summer, she and some other kids had helped Mr. Dempsey clean the dark cavern. It was little more than a creepy closet near the back of the main section of the library. One glaring light hung with a chord in the middle of the gloomy antechamber. Just the thought of searching for that cord, in the dark by herself, sent chills down her spine.

A voice disrupted her thoughts. "How are we doing today, Miss Shelby?"

She jerked back from the monitor and gasped. "Mr. Dempsey."

"Oh, I'm sorry, Shelby. I didn't mean to sneak up on you. My silence is a curse sometimes. I thought I heard you call out."

"I did. I did." She tried to calm her panting. "Look at these messages, Mr. Dempsey. That one said they need help against an ancient evil."

She took a deep breath as Mr. Dempsey studied the dialogue box. Unlike the beast, he always listened to kids.

"Hmm, the storage room? I was just inside not twenty minutes ago, and nobody else is here except you. The O'Connor boys and some of their friends left right before you arrived, and that's been the traffic this morning. I suppose we ought to investigate, eh?"

"I do believe so." She relaxed, relieved to have his company.

She followed him over to the storage room. The entryway was solid oak, like all of the other doors.

Mr. Dempsey turned the handle and pushed it open. "Is anyone here?"

Silence.

He proceeded to the hanging light while Shelby tentatively strode behind him. A strange, damp chill hung in the air—colder than air conditioning should have made it. She shivered and rubbed her arms as goose pimples swelled over her flesh.

Mr. Dempsey tugged the chord, but the bulb did not turn on. He pulled the cord a few more times, but still no light.

"The bulb must be out. I have extras at the front desk in the bottom drawer. Why don't you grab one, Shelby?"

"Sure, Mr. D."

She turned and shuffled toward the door, which whirled shut with a bang. Shelby gasped and her heart jumped. Without light from the entrance, the room went pitch black.

"Mr. Dempsey?" she cried out.

CHAPTER 3

"Geek!"

"Loser!"

Zach Ryder halted and peeked around the corner of the school hallway. The final bell rang almost ten minutes ago, and the tiled halls loomed empty. Well, mostly.

Four massive brutes shoved one of Zach's friends into the row of metal lockers. One grabbed Adrian by the cuff of his shirt and walloped him.

Adrian whimpered. His small hands flailed in an attempt to cover his face.

Zach's guts churned. If he tried to assist, they'd pummel him. But he couldn't just hide. He and Adrian had known each other since third grade.

Zach glanced around in hopes of finding a teacher. No one appeared, and the teacher's lounge was on the far side of the school. If he bolted for aid, Adrian would be a bloody mess by the time he returned.

The fire alarm across the hall caught his attention. The little red box never looked so inviting.

Without hesitation, he scooted over and tugged the white handle. The bell reverberated down the corridor. He turned back to glimpse the bullies scrambling, yelling, "Fire drill now? Let's beat it before teachers get down here. We'll finish with you another time, wimp!"

Zach raced over to his friend and knelt beside him. "Adrian, are you okay?"

"Yeah, sure," his friend muttered through a bloody lip. A shiner already swelled over his right eye, his spectacles askew.

"Can you walk? We need to split."

Adrian groaned as Zach pulled him up and threw Adrian's arm around his neck. Zach realized how much smaller they were compared to their antagonizers, as he hefted Adrian's bag over his other shoulder and grunted.

"Geez! What do you have in here?"

Adrian didn't reply.

They hurried out the exit opposite the one the bullies had gone through. Zach sensed commotion behind, as teachers scurried around trying to figure out the cause of the blaring. Only a few of them had arrived at this end of the school, no doubt looking for any students left from band or soccer practice.

Zach shouldered the door open and he and Adrian slipped out of the building unnoticed. Once outside, he guided Adrian down to the green lawn. He dropped the heavy bag of books and wiped a layer of sweat from his brow.

"Did you pull the alarm?" asked Adrian, eying Zach as he fixed his glasses. One of the arms had been bent and he struggled to straighten it.

Zach nodded. "Yeah, I... I didn't think I'd find teachers quick enough."

Adrian smirked. The smashed lip looked only half as bad when he smiled. "Thanks. I'll have to remember that one."

Zach plopped down beside him, the grass cool and soft. "No problem. Is your mom on her way?"

"Not for another hour. Math club today."

"Wanna go to the five-and-dime?" Zach eyed the school. If Gordie and his gang found them out here, he wouldn't be able to pull a fire alarm to escape. "We can get some ice for your eye."

Adrian picked at the lawn, snapping blades and dropping them in a neat pile. "I dunno, Zach. I might just head home."

"I'll walk with you."

"You don't have to."

Zach noticed the tears welling in Adrian's eyes. The other boy wiped them away as his mussed brown hair whipped in the breeze. He looked miserable.

"I want to. You're my bro," said Zach. "I'm not going to have you go home alone. Come on, I'll carry your bag."

Adrian stood. Zach offered to let him lean against his shoulder, but Adrian shook his head.

"I'm good. Just a little freaked out."

Zach hoisted the book knapsack over his back. "No problem."

They paced in silence for a time. Zach considered teasing his friend, but nothing sounded right. Being beat up was terrifying—Zach had suffered his fair share of bullying.

Cars zoomed by on Harding Boulevard. They lived a good three miles from the school, but by the time they reached his neighborhood, Adrian started chatting again.

"I did buy a new fatpack," he said with a smirk. "I didn't think I'd do enough chores. Forty dollars down the drain!" He laughed.

"Did you open it yet?"

"Oh, of course. And you'll *never* guess what I got!"

"Which series?" Zach asked. He didn't immerse himself into *Magic* the way Adrian had, but he understood the game well enough. Sometimes they'd play together. Zach liked his Sliver deck. If he pulled the Sliver Queen out, almost nothing stopped it.

"New Phyrexia, duh," Adrian said with a snort. He grinned, then winced and touched his split lip. "Anyways, I got *Karn*! The *Planeswalker*! Can you believe?"

Zach shook his head. "I never understood Planeswalkers. They seem to break the game."

"Nah, you have the Eldrazi to balance everything."

They reached Adrian's place, a ranch style, red brick house with a sprawling front yard. A single cottonwood stood sentinel in the center of the lawn. The tree was already dropping cotton across the plot.

"We'll have to play a game. You gonna be okay?" Zach stuffed his hands in his pockets.

"Yeah." Adrian shrugged a frail shoulder and took his bag. "Thanks again, Zach. You're a good friend."

"No problem. Take care, bud."

"Hey, want to come in and play a quick game, like the old days?"

"Nah. I should have been home by now."

"You sure? Come on! It's not like they would even notice."

Zach glanced at him.

Adrian pushed his glasses back into place, but the arm was still crooked and they kept sliding down his nose. "Umm, I didn't mean that."

"Cool." Zach sauntered off and waved.

"See y-you tomorrow," Adrian stammered, then jumped inside his house.

The stroll to his house relaxed Zach. Late afternoon sunlight beckoned the rich gold of early autumn. Long, purple shadows cascaded across the sidewalk and street. A picket fence sent lengthy spikes over the tarmac of the road, spearing the lawns on the other side.

Soon, he left the smaller neighborhoods behind, and sighed. The homes where he lived stood too uniform, lacking character and warmth. His house appeared more box-like than all the rest. He hiked up the winding drive to the front door.

The spare key hid behind his mother's pot of azaleas. He fished it out and unlocked the door, carefully replacing the key before he went inside. The moment he entered the house, he wished he'd gone around back.

"No, I don't have *a clue* where your special mug is! Just use another one!"

"You're the one who always puts everything away! Where'd you place the dang thing?"

"I didn't put it *anywhere*! I bet you left it upstairs! Did you even check?"

Zach rubbed the bridge of his nose and sighed. He began to ease his way up the flight of elegant wooden steps when his mother shouted, "Zach, is that you?"

"Oh, smart, Sharon. Get the boy involved!"

"He might know where your stupid mug is!"

Zach retreated down into the kitchen. The tiled floor and marble countertops made the room feel cold. Even the dark wood of the cabinets didn't help warm the kitchen. He shivered.

"Hi, I'm here."

His mother stood with hands on hips. "Zach, where were you?"

"Adrian got beat up. I walked him home."

And, as usual, it went in one ear and out the other. "That's nice. Where's your father's mug?"

"I don't know. Didn't you hear me?"

"Of course."

Zach rubbed his temples and muttered, "You *never* listen."

"Zachy, if you know where my mug is, speak up," said his father, who patrolled the counter, tearing through the cupboards. "And, Sharon, be a dear and make me a snack. Some of those marshmallow treats?"

"Oh, and while I'm at it, should I wash your car?" Her voice rose in pitch.

Zach backed out of the kitchen. By the time they were both screaming, he had whipped out the back door and dashed to the guesthouse. The French doors beckoned him, promising to keep him safe from the tension of his family life. He trooped inside, locked the door, and breathed a sigh of relief. Now he could be a normal kid.

His computer—not the ones his parents used, but *his*, the one he had scrimped and saved for about three years ago—hummed happily on his desk. He slipped into the comfortable chair and switched the monitor on. The computer chimed to life. Once the loading screen had gone, he accessed the chat. Maybe Adrian would be online. He really wanted to talk to someone.

The sound of clanging swords made him jump. A message popped up.

YOU ARE NEEDED.

Zach paused. For such a small dialogue box on his computer, the brief text shouted in capital letters. Why did it appear so different from the usual exchanges? Had Adrian or another friend discovered some new technique? It couldn't be from his foster parents. Sometimes they messaged him after calming down, to coax him back inside for dinner—if they remembered he existed.

No, they were still shouting.

Mouth agape, he stared at the note: *YOU ARE NEEDED.*

The box flashed on his screen, awaiting a response. How curious. A joke from his friends? If it was Adrian, he would play along—or maybe not. He was tired of games right now. Zach typed in, "*Who is this?*" and sent it back.

A brief silence intensified the next loud bang. The jangle made Zach's skin crawl. Never before had an instant messenger ring resounded with such violence. The noise conveyed something unearthly in the dialogue box.

> *In a different world and another time,*
> *your alter ego will brilliantly shine.*
> *You and others just like him are very*
> *close to next of kin.*
> *These heroes gone and evil hissing,*
> *the sphere's power is now missing.*
> *The balance is quickly shifting.*
> *Please heed our call for help.*

Zach read the rhyme twice, and goose bumps raced over his skin. His conviction grew surer. Adrian had to be playing around with him. He and his friends would tease each other on instant message now and again—except the box offered no identity.

The queasy unease in his stomach worsened. His hands shook a little as he typed. "*How can I help?*"

The clang sounded the arrival of another memo.

> *Step outside and find us waiting.*
> *Promptly now, as we are fading.*

He swiveled in his chair. A noise he couldn't identify emanated from near the French doors—perhaps a bell or a whooshing sound. His blood surged. The pounding of his heart deafened him.

He turned to stare at the message for a minute before rising from the chair. The knot in his gut confirmed that it wasn't a game, and it wasn't any of his friends. Before he even touched the knob, both doors swung open and a cold, clammy burst of air whipped through the opening. Knocking knees made it hard to walk and tremors shook his body, but his resolve remained steady.

Zach pushed across the threshold. An unexpected, murky fog lay in front of him. His house loomed ahead, and he headed for the back door. The bay windows from the kitchen, only a short distance away, were a yellow haze as the mist became thicker and darker with each step, cloaking the outlines of his rooftop.

He squinted, trying to find his home. His uneasiness intensified as he hiked onward—no way it should have vanished completely.

On and on he trudged. Grass became compact and stronger, like the scrub of a marsh. Bald patches of earth sprang up where walkways and a trimmed lawn should have been. He continued stepping cautiously, even as he noticed the changing ground. His tennis shoes squished into its spongy, mire-like surface. Where had the well-kept turf gone?

Still, no sign of his home.

The mist grew heavier and his clothing became soaked. He longed for the shouting and anger usually emanating from the house. Even when he stopped and strained to listen, no sounds could be heard; their shouts too had been swallowed by the dense blanket of fog.

Only fear kept him from calling for help. Wherever he stood, this wasn't home any longer. He ventured alone in the murk, thinking he might have gone the wrong way and ended up near Willows Road, which wound around the back of his parents' property. Zach turned and began retracing his steps, hoping he could backtrack to the guest house.

No such luck.

He stopped at last by a bulky object that loomed from the brume before him, blocking his path. The mist dissipated. A tree trunk was recumbent in the mud, its girth as wide as he was tall. The tree branches traveled in both directions as far as he could see, and he pondered turning around. The coarse lumber offered several good footholds, so he decided to scale up its side and take a peek. He'd never seen a tree this big before.

Rough bark, sticky with honey-like sap, made the task much trickier than he'd thought. He climbed the immense growth, but hesitated when a voice echoed ahead.

Zach froze to listen.

"What do you mean we've lost him, Casselton? The poor lad doesn't even know where he is."

"Vilaborg, we do not quite have this down to an exact science."

"What science do you have down at all, Cassie? The science fair you attended at the fifth level? Don't you have an approximate idea where the portal opened, or are we to freeze to death looking for the Kin?"

"You know how things go, you fool. Stop behaving like this is your first time. This is not uncommon, Vilaborg. The portal must have opened somewhere nearby. He will turn up. Blazes that the Cark Woods needed to be used for a Kin intercept," vented a clearly exasperated Casselton.

Zach stayed rooted to the trunk as he processed the new information. These two had opened a portal without being in full command of the science? Adrian would have scoffed! Zach pondered approaching them, but decided to wait. They might be dangerous.

The voices traveled farther away, and he hoisted himself over and dropped to the ground below, landing in a squat. A tingling, like pins and needles, coursed through his body. Zach shivered and looked at his arms and....

His breath caught in his throat as he stared at his clothing. He ran his hands over the shirt and trousers, as if touching them might make them real.

His clothes had transformed. His blue vintage MegaMan top had disappeared. Now the linen doublet he wore made him itchy. Instead of jeans, his legs were covered with brown leather. Squires used to wear such clothing, he recalled from his readings, but that had been a long time ago.

Other things had changed. For one, he'd grown taller—now the trunk of the tree was a head shorter than he. He felt stronger, too. Cold despair quickly replaced awe.

He collapsed against the fallen timber and pulled his knees to his chest. A tear crept down his face.

I'm not Zach anymore, he thought.

CHAPTER 4

"Shelby, are you okay?"

"I'm right here. The door just slammed shut."

Mr. Dempsey bumped into a box as he stumbled toward her. "We're close to the exit. Let's get some light back, eh?"

His voice reassured Shelby and gently rallied her. "Yes, please," she said.

Mr. Dempsey guided her forward.

She expected to reach the door soon, but they kept walking. Ten steps, fifteen steps, then thirty steps later, and still they had not found the entryway. She pinched herself to check whether this was all a bad dream or not. The pinch hurt and she didn't wake up.

"That's strange," Mr. Dempsey said. "I can't see a darn thing, but I know this room like the back of my hand. We should've hit the door by now."

The temperature dropped further—or did her cold fear make it seem so? Shelby shivered even more and, in an attempt to stay warm, wrapped her arms around herself.

"Do you feel cold, Mr. Dempsey?"

"Right through my bones, Shelby. Let's go this way." He eased her in another direction.

They tiptoed forward one careful step at a time. The darkness remained complete.

"I can't understand this for the life of me," Mr. Dempsey whispered. "Walls don't just vanish!"

The ground underneath Shelby's shoes had changed. The pull of gravity seemed different. No longer did the familiar, even hardwood floors of the library support them; rough stone and loose gravel now made the walk bumpy. The smell of the air changed too, as old printer's ink and paper had been replaced with the scent of rock and water.

"Mr. Dempsey, the floor...."

"I feel it, too. This is so strange."

Her eyes adjusted to the easing darkness, and she could just make out the shadowy outlines of some type of corridor. As they advanced, Shelby strained her ears. The steady trickle of water echoed from somewhere far off.

An orange glow appeared up ahead. Every muscle in her body tensed, and her heartbeat sped up.

Mr. Dempsey stopped and touched her elbow, and Shelby halted as well.

"I don't quite know what's going on here," he whispered in her ear. "I actually thought I dozed off at the front desk and this was a dream. I even pinched myself."

"Me too," she said, glad he was present to protect her. If anything went wrong, Mr. Dempsey would help her.

"We're in some sort of cave. The message on your computer drew us here. We should proceed cautiously, so keep quiet."

Shelby nodded, calmed by his logical evaluation of their situation. Mr. Dempsey knew everything. As long as he was with her, nothing could hurt her.

The light guttered as they crept forward. The scent of fresh air entered the cave and Shelby sighed. Its essence was refreshing.

"Shhh...." Mr. Dempsey put his forefinger in front of his nose.

The murmur of voices rose ahead of them. She glanced at Mr. Dempsey, and he again pressed his finger hard up against the tip of his nose. She nodded.

They moved forward a few more paces and halted. The cave ended and bright light shone outside. Shelby examined her surroundings as she listened. They were in a forest, where thick trees and foliage encompassed them.

The voices sounded clearer, and she could make out the conversation.

"Now, now, we will find her, Sculptor. You worry too much. Only ten minutes have passed. Give her time."

"I can't understand how after all these years the great Achernar has not perfected the mobile portal. I mean, really now, Barrick. We should be right in front of the entrance, ready to greet our guest. They're always frightened as it is."

The first person, Barrick, said, "Many energies are at work in the portal, Sculptor, both scientific and arcane. Near impossible to perfectly harness such a force, no matter how much research Achernar and the mentors conduct."

"Maybe we should rely on Malefic to decipher the solution then. I hear he was quite the mentor trainee up in Catonia."

"Come on, Sculptor. All you do is gripe. We've been entrusted by Achernar himself to carry out this crucial task. Intercepting Kin is an honor, and you sit gossiping and grumbling as though a schoolgirl. ," Barrick bellowed. "As far as Malefic goes, you should join him if you're so impressed. A mixed breed like you would be enslaved on the spot. Don't you recall the number of lives lost in Hideux's camps on Andromeda? I'd lop Malefic's head off without hesitating." Hurt seemed to lurk under his angry voice, accompanied by fear. "But no, you constantly praise him like some lunatic."

Harrumph. "It's not clear if he's even Biskara's son," wheezed Sculptor. "Those are just rumors, you know that."

"He's still a renegade and a criminal."

A brusque silence followed, until insects chirped and their buzzing filled the air. An animal rustled in the underbrush somewhere in the distance. Shelby was sure she heard a bird quack above, but when she glanced up, there was nothing in the trees except leaves.

Mr. Dempsey's typically calm expression was strained, and he appeared about as confused as she.

He peered at her and motioned to lean in. "Seems these are our friends who sent you the message," he whispered. "From what they're saying, they don't sound hostile. They mentioned a portal of some sort, I guess like a teleportation device. It sounds inconceivable." He shook his head. "I want to talk to them. You hide here and listen. When I know it's safe, I'll call you in."

"No way! No way will I let you go by yourself."

"Now, Shelby, I would never forgive myself if something happened to you. This isn't a debate. Your safety is my priority, and that's that."

She nodded, but it still bothered her. After all, she'd stood up to the beast and managed to escape. Didn't he realize she was the *ninja girl*? She'd be more help to him if he'd take her with him.

He studied her a moment with a puzzled frown. "You seem different—older or something. Maybe it's just the light." They were still crouched at the mouth of the cave.

She shrugged.

"Okay, wish me luck." He walked toward the flickering titian.

She crept forward, straining her ears as the two strangers spoke.

"We'll wait a little longer," Barrick said, "and then we should spread out. I don't want to be the only Meridian soldier in history to lose a Kin," he hollered. He seemed to have a bad temper.

Shelby repressed a shiver. The shouting man reminded her of the beast, but she forced herself to stay calm. *I'm the ninja girl,* she thought, mouthing the words. Her fingers tightened around the cold rock of the cave. *I can do this.*

She squinted and tried to view what was occurring ahead. Mr. Dempsey still shuffled forward through the foliage. She watched him for a moment, but spotted little else. While she strained to see, she heard the other man use that word again—*Kin*. What was a Kin, anyway? Could *she* be a Kin? Maybe Mr. Dempsey was right, and these two were waiting for *her*.

She snuck closer and hid behind a tree to get a clearer picture. As Mr. Dempsey approached a campsite, she crept beside a wide, short evergreen.

Pine needles dug into the palms of her hands and scraped against her pants while she crawled. As she ducked under the tree, branches grabbed her hair. She pulled her strands free, careful not to make a single sound. Once settled, she poked her head around the trunk.

Her jaw dropped and her eyes bulged at what she witnessed. Nothing could have prepared her for this.

Mr. Dempsey stood speechless before two figures crouched beside a campfire. Dusk was falling, bruising the twilight above. It had been sunset when she and Mr. Dempsey arrived, but night was truly upon them now.

"Who goes there?" Sculptor demanded, jumping to his feet.

She blinked hard. The voices had sounded ordinary, but these individuals weren't normal. They had typical skin and hair, yet they were built for war. Even the football players at her high school seemed scrawny compared to the two troopers—especially the one called Barrick. They resembled characters in a movie about Camelot and King Arthur, not people from modern-day Earth.

Barrick rose, his muscles bulging through the studded armor and boiled leather he wore. His beefy forehead was almost absent in an untamed jungle of eyebrows, and his neck seemed as thick as a ship's mast. He eased a large sword from his scabbard. The blade gleamed in the flickering light of the campfire.

Mr. Dempsey stood motionless while Barrick glowered at him.

In one swift motion, Sculptor stepped toward Mr. Dempsey and aimed a pistol at the librarian's head. Sculptor's lean, abnormally long face expressed little. Shelby thought she glimpsed a glimmer of fear cross his eyes, but it was gone in an instant. The dark blue cape strapped to his shoulders stirred in the breeze. One portrayed a medieval warrior and the other some sort of futuristic policeman in Arthurian armor.

She wanted to dart out from behind her tree to keep them from hurting Mr. Dempsey, but fear froze her to the spot. Barrick, the short one with the sword, wore a fierce sneer, and for a moment, she thought she saw the beast in him. A whimper escaped her. Her nails dug into the tree's soft bark, and cold sweat rolled down her temples. If she allowed them to hurt Mr. Dempsey, she'd never forgive herself.

"Speak up, dear sir," Sculptor snapped, "or I will unleash Barrick upon you. They say his people are closet cannibals."

"Shut up, you raging idiot," Barrick said, his glare still focused on Mr. Dempsey.

"I, uh-um, w-well, I, I..." Mr. Dempsey stammered.

"Well, well," Sculptor said. "You are quite the vocalist, my dear sir. Perhaps you should audition as an announcer for the games at Fornax. You would do just fine, better than the biased gibberish Jeb Rooza and his sidekicks regurgitated at last year's events, eh, Barrick?"

Barrick seethed with anger. "Shut up, you blasted fool. This is serious. He resembles a citizen of Earth, yet he may be Malefic's spy." The brute trudged forward a step, his long sword raised, the sharp blade glittering like magma.

Shelby shook with terror.

"Identify yourself at once," Barrick said.

"How original, my dear Barrick," Sculptor scoffed, throwing his partner a weary glance. "I didn't suspect you were an avant-garde man. Such a progressive demand merits your potential as a poet."

Mr. Dempsey snapped out of his stupor. "Hold on now," he called. "I presume I'm present due to something about a portal you opened. I was in the library, and went to the storage room for supplies, and then I was here."

Sculptor cocked an eyebrow. "The Rutherford B. Hayes Library?"

"Why y-yes, actually. I-I'm its curator, Walter Dempsey."

"Please tell me, how'd such an average president manage to get an athenaeum named after him?" Sculptor offered a wry smile. "Why not a school, or better yet, a stadium?"

Barrick huffed. "Stop jesting! We need to learn if this person knows anything about Shelby Pardow."

He sheathed his sword and prowled closer. Though Mr. Dempsey towered over him, Barrick appeared a formidable figure. The stout man looked much stronger than Mr. Dempsey, and twice as mean as the beast.

Shelby ducked lower to the ground, trembling. She prayed Barrick wouldn't hurt poor Mr. Dempsey.

Barrick bowed on bended knee. "Forgive me, my friend, and trust me. We'll not harm you. Seems to be a miscommunication. We were looking for a girl named Shelby. But now that you're here, you must come with us so Lord Achernar can resolve the issue. We apologize, sir, for any inconvenience we have caused you."

Sculptor holstered his gun. "Yes, we're sorry, sir. My personal apologies that I was placed on this all-important mission with a bumbling buffoon like Barrick. Why, he can't even open the mobile portal at the right place!"

Barrick, still on his knee, grimaced at Sculptor and discharged a low growl.

Such odd cohorts. Shelby exhaled. Some bark of the tree remained stuck in her nails as she released her grip. Barrick, though a fearsome person, seemed more easily tempered than the beast.

"What do you need Shelby for?" said Mr. Dempsey.

"Well, sir, the situation is complex. Let's just say our destiny sways in the balance without her help and the rest of the Kin. Always the case when Biskara is involved." Barrick rose from his knee. "The Kin are the only ones who can locate those on the Aulic Assembly, who have gone missing."

Mr. Dempsey looked lost in thought as he tapped his chin with his forefinger. "Lord Achernar... you said before. Hmm, if I do recall, Achernar is the brightest star in the constellation Eridanus in the southern hemisphere of the universe."

"Oh yes, sir, you are absolutely right." Barrick beamed. "He is the brightest king of all, Achernar is."

"A king, you say. Pray tell, where on Earth are we?"

Sculptor belted out a high-pitched laugh as he strode closer to the librarian. The sound startled Shelby, and she drew farther behind the tree, ignoring the tingling sensation running through her like an electrical current. Crouching for so long must have put her limbs to sleep.

"Earth? My dear sir," Sculptor said, "you aren't listening to us. We are on Azimuth, over two hundred light years from your planet."

Shelby leaned back around the trunk, examining Barrick and Sculptor. The unsettling pang in her stomach was fading. Barrick still made her a little uneasy, but she really liked Sculptor. He was funny and kind to Mr. Dempsey so far.

"Nonsense. Where are we? Traveling that distance isn't possible, especially without the proper... uh... a ship or... or...." Mr. Dempsey fell silent.

Shelby frowned. The two men were pokerfaced.

Mr. Dempsey must have seen it too, because he whispered, "You're not kidding about this portal, are you?"

"'Tis a shock, sir, always is. Methinks I'd react the same way if the tables were turned. Thank heavens the portal makes it so we speak the same language."

Barrick held out his water canteen. "Thirsty?"

"No. I mean... yes." Mr. Dempsey sounded parched. He accepted the container and guzzled. After returning it, he walked several steps from the side of the campfire and gazed up into the darkness.

By now, the sky was black and Shelby could make out a few stars.

Mr. Dempsey was silent for a few long seconds.

Shelby held her breath, waiting to hear his next words. She yearned to know what a Kin was and why these two wanted to see her.

"You don't mean to harm me in any way?" Mr. Dempsey asked at last, and turned toward Barrick.

"On my honor as a Tuskarian, sir, no. I wouldn't let you wander around and get yourself killed, either, considering it's my fault you're here." Barrick walked over and extended his hand.

Mr. Dempsey hesitated briefly before raising his hand, and Barrick grasped his forearm. Mr. Dempsey returned the gesture, and they nodded to one another.

Releasing his grip, Mr. Dempsey said, "Now, Barrick, how do I get back to Earth? Can you reopen that portal gizmo?"

Barrick shook his head. "Alas, it only accepts guests from Earth. Yet all is not lost. Lord Achernar will be able to transport you back. I'm sure of it."

Mr. Dempsey nodded, holding his chin. "What do you intend to do when you find Shelby?"

"Why, we're sworn to protect her with our lives, and take her to meet the rest of the Kin and Lord Achernar."

"So your mission involves others? Other children?"

"Children? I guess on Earth they're considered children, but the Kin are fierce adversaries on Azimuth."

"What are these 'Kin' you speak of, Barrick?"

Sculptor stepped forward. "We have to take you to Achernar, Mr. Dempsey. We can discuss as we ride. Malefic's soldiers are combing the woods, and we need to move out. Our first priority is finding Shelby. She's mincemeat if Malefic finds her before we do." Sculptor's tone had gone from playful to serious. His expression had changed, too. He rubbed his temples and his brow contorted.

"Well, I don't think finding her will be much of a problem at this point." Mr. Dempsey walked in Shelby's direction. He paused and glanced around, rubbing the back of his neck, then shouted up the path. "Hey, Shelby, you can come down now."

"I'm right here," she blurted, stepping from behind the tree. A few pine needles stuck to her hair, and she picked them out as she edged toward him. She was careful of the underbrush.

The glare of the campfire illuminated her arrival.

Mr. Dempsey gaped. "Shelby, you *are* older. I thought it was just the light! And your clothes...."

She stared down and gasped. Similar garb to Sculptor and Barrick replaced her old attire. Now she wore brown leather pants and a matching shirt. She expected such fabric to be stiff, but the outfit fit like a second skin. Around her waist was a boiled ox-hide belt with studs and a gold buckle.

"I... I'm t-taller," she stuttered.

She then inspected Mr. Dempsey. In the dark, it had been hard to tell, but now she viewed him clearly. The lines under his eyes and around his mouth had gone. "Mr. Dempsey, you're younger!" Despite his transformation, he still wore the same khaki pants and sweater vest from Earth.

Mr. Dempsey studied himself and then placed his hands closer to the fire. "I do feel better than I have in years. Remarkable."

"Well, thank the stars and all our mothers," Sculptor said, sounding relieved. "Something good! Now I can go back to Meracuse with pride and not have to report to Achernar that we lost a Kin. Not to mention this Tuskarian brute! He's so hard to work with!"

Mr. Dempsey began, "Shelby—"

"I listened to everything. This is crazy."

"I know. I can't explain it—or believe what happened."

She turned to Sculptor and Barrick. "Lord Achernar sent you to retrieve me?"

"Yes, milady. Captain Lazzo Barrick of the second brigade, third division of the alliance of Meridia. I am also your designated interceptor. Nevertheless... at your service." He bowed.

"I've been stuck with this raving brute from Tuska before, madam," Sculptor said. "So no need to fret. For a fortnight, I have traveled with this savage, and I'm accustomed to his eccentricities. Please, forgive him his lack of manners. I'm Sculptor Luten. Charmed to meet you." He swirled his arm in a flowery bow, then straightened again and studied the dark trees. "Since the introductions have been made, we must be off. Malefic is roaming through these parts, and it is important we return to our battalion."

"Malefic?" asked Mr. Dempsey.

"We'll have plenty of time to discuss everything, sir, but questions will need to be answered on the road. For now, we, my merry group, are off." Sculptor spun on his heels with a flourish of his cape.

Shelby and Mr. Dempsey eyed the splendid steed Barrick brought before them. The Clydesdale had a shiny, chocolate-colored coat with a honey-blonde mane. A feathering of long, cream-colored hair gracing the back of its legs flapped as it trotted over. The horse snorted.

"This is Lenore," Barrick said, and fed her a sugar cube. "She's very well trained, so don't fret if you've never ridden before. We have only one additional mount, as we didn't anticipate Mr. Dempsey's arrival. Both of you can share her, if you like. She's a sturdy girl."

Mounting a horse turned out to be more difficult than Shelby had imagined. Though she had grown, the Clydesdale still towered over her. She managed to put her left foot in the stirrup, but couldn't quite pull herself over. Barrick offered his hand, and she used it as a step to mount. Once in the saddle, Shelby fought retreating to the ground, uncomfortable with the way Lenore swayed beneath her.

"Use the reins to direct her. Just the slightest tug will tell her which way to go. She'll follow us without any direction, though." Barrick smiled up at her.

She nodded. "Thanks."

Mr. Dempsey mounted behind her with Barrick's help. He seemed more at home on the enormous horse than she.

Sculptor put out the fire by emptying a bucket over the flames and kicking dirt onto the ashes. Once the pit was smoking white, he said, "We should go. Malefic's men may soon find our camp."

Barrick and Sculptor mounted their steeds with the elegance of practice. With a soft boot to the flanks, their horses were off at a steady pace. Shelby thought she should kick Lenore, too, but the mare started without the slightest nudge. Not used to the rocking of being on horseback, she clutched the reins to keep from falling.

A quick motion caught her eye. Shelby glanced down at a bizarre, bright green squirrel scurrying by, and a shiver ran up her spine.

She was glad Mr. Dempsey was with her. This place was certainly not home.

CHAPTER 5

How terrifying, thought Riley as she fidgeted with the hem of her leather skirt. Campfires guttered nearby, and a canvas tent perched at her back. Mulch, dusty horses, metal, and burnt food scented the air while swords and axes clanged, sounding just like the instant message that had popped on her computer a few hours prior.

Three others huddled beside her, a girl and two boys. Riley managed to coerce the fellows to give their names—Stuart and Max—but the girl refused to speak. She was pale, with long sandy hair resting on her skinny frame—the type of person Riley tried to befriend back home, but never succeeded in doing.

"Where do you think we are?" asked Max.

Riley's gaze slid to him. With a bold jaw and short brown hair, he reminded her of a boy she had a crush on at school.

Stuart lifted and lowered one shoulder. "England. Or a Renaissance Fair, maybe."

Riley shook her head. "No, we're not on Earth, I'm sure of it. Look at how we changed."

The noises and odors, though familiar, unnerved her, almost like something she experienced in a dream once. At the age of five, Riley had suffered a nightmare about a man, pale with wiry red hair, which still haunted her. He'd smelled just like this place.

Max opened his mouth to speak, but clamped it shut as a figure, garbed in silver armor and navy enamel, approached with an air of gazing sympathy. He stood tall with a calm face, his long dark hair peppered with gray. A blue cape fluttered from his shoulders, secured by enormous medallions with lion heads on them, and a sword hung belted at his hip. Despite her uneasiness, Riley spied kindness in his green eyes.

"Hello, I am Presage, a mentor here in the country of Meridia."

Riley examined him, her brow puckering, while Stuart gazed off to the side, distracted by another discussion a campfire away.

All around them, the clamor of the camp persisted as warriors used whetstones to sharpen their weapons, horses whickered and neighed, pots clanged, and the aroma of cooking food roamed the air.

Presage set his gaze on one of the boys in the group. "Max Tuttle, correct?"

Max's athletic build tensed and he locked eyes with Presage, fire blazing in his pupils.

Riley bit her lip and tucked a strand of her hair behind her ear. *I hope he doesn't try to hurt this Presage guy. He seems pleasant enough.*

Presage continued, "Riley Upchurch?"

She jumped. "Yes," she said, her voice even and guarded as her bright blonde mane tussled around her face. The band she used to tie her locks back had broken on her ride to the camp.

"Emily Lawson?"

"Yes," Emily replied, shyly staring down at her tea, her lengthy caramel hair concealing her features. She refused to meet Presage's gaze, and had her knees pulled to her chest.

Emily Lawson. The name sounded familiar, but Riley couldn't place it. The edges of her lips tugged into a frown.

Presage grimaced before continuing. "Stuart Lesser?"

"Depends on what you want," said Stuart at once, as he maintained his stare. His transformed clothing and long dark hair whipped in the breeze.

Riley flinched at the attempted slight. The boy seemed less friendly by the moment and his attitude nagged at her. No one talked that way around her—she didn't allow them. Not because she forced people to be nice, but rather because she tended to bring out others' good nature.

I'll have to get these guys in order. We might be stranded somewhere new, but I refuse to let them mope!

Presage bobbed his head. "Thank you all for answering our plea for help. I understand this may be a bit overwhelming, considering you were taken from your home through a portal to Azimuth. The interceptors, I'm sure, explained a little about what has transpired."

Another man, named Cumber, one of the pair who had found Riley, placed a stool close to the campfire. He had the look of a large, thick dwarf with a crimson and grey beard that grew down to his scabbard. Presage eased down and accepted a cup of steaming brew from him. The sweet, tangy aroma drifted into the air, while Riley glanced at her own empty teacup. Judging by his smile, Presage enjoyed a satisfying gulp before continuing.

"You are on the planet Azimuth in the country of Meridia, and we've called for your assistance. Recently, Meridia's governing body, the Aulic Assembly, disappeared. Each of you was born with a psychic link to one of the six members on the Assembly. As you passed through the mobile portal, you inherited the abilities of your links on the Assembly." Presage sipped his tea as he eyed each of the Kin.

When his warm stare landed on her, Riley smoothed her skirt.

Max rubbed his knees. "I don't understand how we can help."

"Forgive my candid explanations, but there is little time. An ancient evil, Biskara, has returned to our world. We believe he is responsible for the Assembly's disappearance. Biskara wages war through his mortal sons, and we believe an individual named Malefic Cacoethes has emerged and raised a powerful army with Biskara's aid. On your planet, some of the larger wars and catastrophes had Biskara's support as well. You would know him on Earth as Satan."

Biskara. Malefic. The face from her nightmare resurfaced, and then vanished. Riley shifted and her stomach churned. Their names sounded awful.

"How do you know about Earth?" She brushed a strand of loose hair from her brow and repressed a shiver. A gust whipped through and the chill worsened; even the crackle of campfires couldn't stay the thickening fog.

Presage gazed at her with deadpan green eyes, and sipped his tea while holding the cup with both hands. "My dear, we all originated from Earth."

They peered up at him, squirming as they sat. Even Stuart, who had stopped observing other soldiers and seemed focused on the conversation, fussed.

Presage's answer hadn't satisfied Riley, but she didn't press.

Cumber plodded over to the old officer, crouched down, and whispered into his ear. He was a soldier of middle age, garbed in wool garments instead of armor. A sword hung from his boiled leather belt.

"Alas, we must saddle-up and move from this location. Sitting in one place too long is not safe. We are off to the capital of Meridia: Meracuse."

Presage rose as several soldiers hurried around the camp and packed their belongings. Tents were broken down and stored, food wrapped tidy, fires stamped out, and horses loaded. Everyone rushed about, save the Kin.

Riley clustered with the others, trying to stay out of the way as warriors scurried around them.

Cumber walked up to them with satchel in hand. "You must be hungry. This here is chud, which lasts a long time when traveling and offers many

nutrients. It's made from the roots of druids, and it tastes pretty good to boot." He offered the chud.

Max accepted a piece and twirled it in his hand before taking a bite. "Mmm. Reminds me of beef jerky."

Nervous, yet intrigued, Riley nibbled. It was peppery like jerky, but stringy too, and held an aftertaste similar to oats and cashews.

Presage barked orders, directing traffic around the camp as wagons piled up with barrels of fresh water and supplies.

Soon, the Kin were on horseback around Presage, surrounded by several soldiers. A long train of warriors rode before and behind them, and the sound of hooves on hard earth thundered.

Riley glided closer to their guide. "Mr. Presage, even though we know a bit about your planet, what could we possibly do to help?" At school, she had the best grades. Math never stumped her, but this equation begged a different answer. It seemed like the old man was keeping a secret from them.

"We need the six active Kin to utilize their psychic links with their alter egos here on Azimuth, the members of the Aulic Assembly. They disappeared last week, all on the same day. Their rescue is of the utmost importance—besides the concern for their lives, of course—because the Aulic Assembly is made up of the only individuals able to operate the armillary sphere, or the 'Silver Sphere,' as it is called. Before I continue, have any of you heard of an armillary sphere before?"

They shook their heads, and Stuart murmured something. Riley glanced at Emily, but the quiet girl had her focus locked on the horn of her saddle.

"Well, an armillary sphere is an old astronomical model with solid rings. All circles of one single sphere, in this case Azimuth, are used to display relationships among the principal celestial circles. This particular sphere is special. The Silver Sphere gives the exact celestial coordinates of Biskara. It was created a long time ago when Biskara transformed from fable to reality. This ability to monitor Biskara kept him at bay, as his plans could be better followed and foiled. Without constraints, he can devise and carry out his evil plots—Azimuth, and by proxy, Earth, would be no more."

"Is it possible to monitor one of his sons through the Sphere and find out if Malefic is one?" Max asked.

Riley eased her mare around a sapling sprouting in the middle of the path. The horse whickered and tossed its massive head. She knew Malefic embodied evil—she just wasn't sure if he was really the son of this Biskara creature.

"The Sphere is a celestial tool," Presage said, "which cannot detect mortals. Biskara is able to direct the war through his offspring's corporeal existences and, when unimpeded, keep them one step ahead of their opponents. This is the Sphere's vital importance. Hence, the disappearance of the Assembly and

Malefic's increasing power leads us to believe he's not a typical terrorizing dictator. Otherwise, we could easily overrun him with our armies."

Each of the other Kin looked confused as Riley shuffled her feet, her forehead pinched. Though they spoke the same language, she did not understand everything Presage tried to tell them. It sounded like a lot of fantasy to her.

Still, she wanted to get home. "What happens if we make contact with our links?"

Presage turned to her. "Once we locate your links and are able to operate the Sphere, we can bring the war to Biskara and then handle Malefic."

"We are g-going to fight Biskara?" Emily stammered. Her eyes widened with fright, and she clutched the reins of her palfrey to her chest.

"No. The combat with Biskara is on a celestial battlefield. The truth seekers, some from Earth even, will pursue him. The truth seekers are defenders of this celestial universe. We'll encounter our own problems on the corporeal plane, though, I can assure you."

"Truth seekers?" Emily's voice quivered.

"Another time, my dear. Our war is with Malefic and the Nightlanders, here on Azimuth. We had Biskara's coordinates until the Assembly vanished, but we haven't been able to defeat him."

Presage coughed, pulled out his canteen, and took a sip. "If it is indeed true that Malefic is Biskara's son, he would be easier to oppose if his father were preoccupied on the celestial battlefield. Now rest. You will find comfort and familiarity with your new surroundings. Almost like you're home."

Max and Riley exchanged glances.

She hunched over and whispered, "We aren't anywhere near home."

CHAPTER 6

Zach curled against a log and held his knees, his heart pulsing in his chest as he stared straight ahead in a bewildered state. Dried tears stained his cheeks.

Somehow, he had lost track of the people he overheard. Vilaborg and Casselton were their names. They sought him, and that was a relief—at least someone was looking for him.

He rose from his position and worked his way toward the direction he'd last picked up voices. Leaves and twigs crunched underfoot, and odd noises permeated from the dark woods, followed by an ominous silence. Zach froze and listened, his head cocked, checking for more sounds. Convinced no one tracked him, he advanced alongside the log.

A clamor from the bushes to his left made him pause.

In a puff of dirt and dust, an odd creature burst out of the flora. The small, hairy figure stopped abruptly when he spotted Zach. The strange man only came up to Zach's knees, but seemed brutish. He studied Zach with wide, startled eyes.

"Okay, little fella, don't be scared," said Zach. The last thing he wanted was to terrify someone who might help him get home.

A wild expression exploded on its painted countenance as he bared his yellowed teeth beneath a wiry, whitewashed beard. "Kin! Alert—I have a Kin!" the little man screamed.

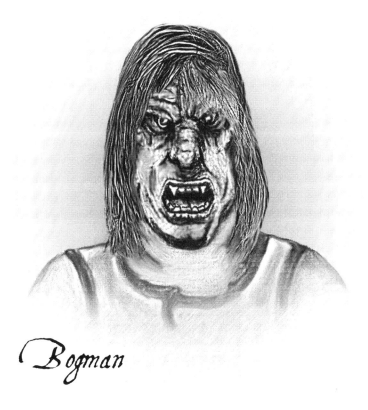

Bogman

The furry character brandished a large horn. He jerked the small opening to his lips and blew so hard, his cheeks inflated like two balloons. The blast echoed across the woods.

The blare jolted Zach's heart and he raced off down the side of the log. He veered into the first opening he spied in the trees, and thundered through shrubs and bushes, imagining a tribe of little hairy, painted men with spears giving chase.

Without warning, the right side of the forest vanished. The ground crumbled as the ledge gave way, sending him crashing down a steep hill and smacking into a sturdy oak tree.

He lay dazed and motionless for a few moments, praying he hadn't broken anything. A couple of parts throbbed, but nothing needed immediate attention, as far as he could tell.

Several horns from above trumpeted, and he sprouted and scurried through the thicket ahead. Leaves slapped his arms and face, and branches tried to hold him back, but he kept running. He moved adroitly in his newfound physique, aided by an adrenaline spike.

The lush and colorful woods slowed him to a jog as he marveled at his surroundings. Royal blue and lime green bushes, chocolate-colored roses, and trees full of violet apples sprawled everywhere. The farther he traveled, the more dazzling the forest became.

The echo of horns ebbed, and Zach stopped to rest against a boulder. He placed his hands on his knees while he panted, sweat dripping down his nose and forehead. Muscles he'd never used before screamed from the exertion of running hard for so long. At least he was alive.

He wiped his muddy hands on the brown leather pants that had replaced his jeans, sinking against the tree to contemplate his next move.

Out of nowhere, entrancing sounds reverberated around him. The volume increased, a chorus of several voices chanting a melody. His body grew rubbery as sparkles encompassed the area and choruses of female voices sang an unfamiliar language. The beauty of their song intoxicated him.

He had to find them.

The ground and tree vibrated and something flashed beside him. He glimpsed a pair of glistening blue eyes, but no other features appeared—only bright blue irises, the eyes of a comely woman. He rubbed his face and squinted, the cerulean eyes dancing all around. Dozens of them darted in and out of the foliage as the sweet, magnificent music continued. The symphony of choristers spoke to him.

The voices became more distinct when his eyes drifted shut. They directed him where to go. "*Follow the Eridanus River downstream a few miles to a man on a boat. The man's name is Throg. He'll bring you to safety. Leave now. It will not be safe here much longer,*" the voices chimed in unison. Behind the words, an unclear melody floated, one that made his entire being ache from its elegance.

The Fugues

"Wh-who are you?" He yawned.

"The Fugues. Tell Throg the Fugues have sent you, and he will take you to safety."

His body was steered—in fact *willed*—to travel the direction the Fugues wanted him to go. Walking was surreal—rubbery and foggy—as if he couldn't quite touch the ground. His legs moved of their own volition, wobbling beneath him. Trees and bushes almost seemed to stand aside for him to pass, like a dream.

Then his mind cleared and everything became real again. The rumbling of a river echoed, and the sudden return of reality bothered him. Before, the trees had been strange colors. Now only a few plants—mainly flowers—were different from those on Earth. Tree trunks were brown, leaves were green, and the forest floor was covered in pine needles and mulch.

He reached the riverfront by stumbling down a hill, and knelt down. He cupped his hands and doused his face with the freezing cold liquid. The trip hadn't been terrifying, being led by those voices, though it had shaken him a bit. Chilly water dripped along his neck and cheeks. Wet hair plastered to his forehead.

He squinted out across the stream, turned, and looked back the way he had come. "What in the blazes happened?"

A single memory burned bright: the Fugues had sent him to find Throg.

He rose from his knees and followed the river downstream.

CHAPTER 7

At Captain Jack's, Nick Casey's favorite restaurant, he ate a bowl of French onion soup and a Captain Jack's burger next to his friend Cliff. The next morning was going to be an early one for class at Densmore College, so he said goodbye to Cliff after eating and walked out to the parking lot.

The sounds of shouting and yelling erupted, and a van screeched by as the cries of a woman slashed the air.

Nick raced over to her. "What's wrong?"

"My baby!" she shrieked, tears welling in her eyes. "They've got my baby!"

"Call the police," he yelled.

Without another word, Nick launched down the street. The van stood only a few blocks ahead, forced to stop at a light behind ten other cars. He picked up the pace, his shoes slapping against the hard concrete, his heart smashed and his lungs already ragged.

He reached the van just as the light turned green, and jumped onto the back and latched himself to the door. A girl wailed inside, so he grappled the handle on the double door and wrenched it open.

The girl wasn't alone. A burly man shouted, "What the hell? Get out!"

Nick stumbled inside as the van lurched to life. He curled his hand into a fist and slammed it into the man's stomach, winding him. Just as Nick stretched for the girl, the man growled and knocked him into the side of the van.

A muffled voice came from up front. "Keep the kid quiet, Jordy!"

"Some nutcase got in! But he's not leaving," Jordy growled, glaring at Nick as he held him against the metal wall.

Nick glanced over at the teenage girl, who couldn't have been much older than fourteen. Long honey hair framed her terrified expression, and snot ran down her chin from her nose. She squatted while crying, her face scrunched.

"Run!" Nick gasped.

She was tied down, and rage filled him. What sort of *monsters* would kidnap a little girl? A sudden well of power hit him and Nick threw Jordy from him. The kidnapper's head smacked into the other side of the van and he dropped to the floor, hard.

Nick whirled around and pulled at the knot in the girl's ropes until it loosened. "I'm here to help," he whispered.

Jordy groaned off to the side, writhing with his head in his hands.

"My name's Nick Casey. Please, trust me."

She wiped her eyes and sniffled. Not once did she look away from the felled man. Her voice came out in a choked whisper. "Okay, I'm E-Emily L-Lawson."

Nick pulled her into his arms. "On the count of three, I'm gonna jump, all right?"

Emily nodded, her body shaking as she rose. Though she was in at least her early teens, she weighed less than he'd expected.

"Hang on tight!"

As the van sped along, Nick launched from the back, and a sharp pain jabbed in his side. He looked down and... an ice pick was stuck in his gut. Jordy snarled from behind as Nick dropped from the exit.

The first thought in Nick's mind was, *Roll over. Protect her.*

He landed so hard the wind rushed out of him. He wheezed and his fingertips ran cold. Emily crawled toward him as cars honked. Someone had their high beams trained on him and yelled for traffic to stop.

"Mister, you okay?" Emily's voice cracked as she took his hand in hers.

"I'm... fine." Even as he gasped it, he knew it was a lie. "Are you... okay?"

She nodded as tears dripped from her chin onto his neck. "Please don't die."

"Someone call an ambulance!" a man cried somewhere nearby.

Another voice shouted directions to the police dispatcher.

He vaguely heard the girl's mother yell out, "Emily! Emily, are you all right?"

As his vision faded, Nick spied the girl being pulled into her mother's arms, the mother weeping and repeating, "Thank you," over and over.

Emily darted to him and cradled his head.

Emily, he thought, and closed his eyes.

Nick gazed at the radiant stars of the clear night, his head light as a cotton ball. Ascending, he rotated and viewed the bright, spinning lights

below. Two ambulances and a few police cars formed a circle around his body. Its open eyes stared up at him from the stretcher while a paramedic tried desperately to revive it.

Cold panic rushed through him.

I must be dreaming, or my mind is slipping. He continued to glide higher, the image of the emergency technician over his figure fading away. Thick and murky blackness engulfed him with an arctic embrace as the shadows twisted and turned around him. Darkness ensued for a time, and he fell asleep.

Nick stirred and wiped away the chunky crust that had formed in the corners of his eyes. A haze of images prevented him from organizing his thoughts. *What happened?* His head ached.

Once more on solid ground, he brushed his hand through the grass. He stood and inhaled the chilly, crisp air, which invigorated him. A pair of hills emerged to his right, and beyond it swirled the remainder of an orange and red sunset. He lumbered toward the dwindling sundown, rustling his hair with both hands. The pain from the ice pick to his stomach grew dim, as if he'd only dreamt it.

Had he fallen asleep? Had the kidnapping been a dream?

He trekked a while, sticking to the flat parts of the countryside. The twilight made it too dark to view his surroundings for anything familiar. Grass and sticks crunched underfoot and echoed around him, but didn't offer any clues. Light emanated from over a hill, and he quickened his pace.

As he drew closer, crackling sounds and voices rose ahead. He crawled through the mossy, wet grass, and stayed as low to the ground as possible as he scaled the embankment. When he reached the top, he peeked over the hill.

Several shapes hovered around a campfire, holding out long sticks over the cozy flames. The scent of roasting meat filled the air. His eyes adjusted to the light, and.... *Am I going insane?* The figures below were wearing armor like Arthurian knights.

One man, draped in a cape, darted over to a horse tied to a nearby tree. He was dressed in a rich violet and red, and a large sword hung from a sheath at his side. On his cloak was a lavender bird of some sort.

Nick considered approaching the fire, hoping they might be a traveling circus. *What else could they be?* He circled the encampment and tried to maneuver closer to better survey the strange men. Bobbing up from nowhere, in the middle of the night, probably wouldn't be a good surprise for the warriors. Their weapons dangled as though real, and testing them would be foolhardy. After all, if someone came after *him* from the dark, he'd want to defend himself.

A sharp object poked into the small of his back. Nick stifled a yelp, thinking for an instant of the ice pick slamming into him.

"Where do you think you're slithering off to, little spy?" said a raspy-voiced man behind him.

Nick jumped up. "Uh, w-who are you?" The words stumbled out of his mouth.

"Who am I?" the man mimicked. "Well then, that is quite a question to come from someone lurking around our encampment like Malefic's spy, now isn't it? If you weren't unarmed and so frail looking, I would have slit your throat eons ago. To your feet, snoop, and be glad I don't stick you through."

The surly-sounding figure shoved Nick ahead. As the glow of the campfire cast on them, the man behind him moved around and into view. The stranger was tall, slender, and fair-haired. His armor sparkled, and several weapons hung from his waist and shoulder. He, too, wore red and violet. The sharp object that he poked into Nick's back was a long, thin blade.

"Speak quickly, outlander. I won't waste time on meddlesome spies. What is your business and who sent you?"

Numb with shock, Nick didn't respond. He searched for words to explain everything, and found none. An honest answer was best, he decided at last.

"My name is Nick Casey. I woke up on the ground nearby, and I've been having trouble remembering how I got here. I'm definitely not a spy, and I mean you no harm."

"Harm? My, my, now Mr. Casey," the warrior said, as he studied him up and down in the better lighting. "You're certainly not from Azimuth, and you're a bit too old to be one of the six Kin. And you're absolutely not in a position to harm any reconnoiters of the First Brigade of Meridia. Of that I can assure you. I'm Captain Spiro. You're fortunate I was walking in your direction to relieve myself. If I had not stumbled upon you, one of my sentries assuredly would have cut you in two without asking any questions. Walk now." Captain Spiro held his blade out and motioned toward the fire.

They reached the bonfire, and the men sitting around stirred, muttering under their breath. Each and every one wore uniforms similar to Captain Spiro's, and all struck Nick as fierce and unforgiving. He swallowed a lump rising in his throat. Unlike Captain Spiro's thin, young face, many of them had weathered skin and were unshaven.

"Clayborn," Spiro boomed, "fetch me some handcuffs for this intruder."

"Well, what have we here?" Clayborn rose, a massive man, and towered over Captain Spiro and the rest. A full beard and long, braided hair made him look more like a Viking than a knight.

"One more traitor from Malefic's legion to carve up?" another soldier seethed and drew his sword. A mole sprouting black hairs hovered above his eye, and when he smiled, Nick saw his teeth were yellow.

"Simmer down now" Spiro retorted. "We do not harm free independents, and I need to determine what side this oaf is on."

Clayborn hissed as he turned and stormed off. "Aye, methinks he reeks of Malefic's soldiers. Malefic has cost me my ship and crew, stranger. The gods be with you if you are associated with that lowdown."

A few of the men sitting around the campfire stood and walked toward Nick. They examined him and appeared only mildly interested in him. By their glares, he noted they had already decided which side he was on. It seemed not to be theirs.

"Tolbert, Molson, keep an eye on him till Clayborn returns," Spiro ordered.

Nick shifted from foot-to-foot and wrung his hands until Clayborn arrived with rusty handcuffs. The hulking figure passed them off to Tolbert and Molson, whispered something, and headed back to the fire to talk to Spiro.

Tolbert, the man with the mole, fastened the ice cold shackles to Nick's wrists.

"We're doin' ye a favor, spy" said Molson. "Ye will be less sore with the cuffs in front."

They forced him down near the warmth of the flames, not far from Spiro and Clayborn, who engaged in a heated conversation. The captain seemed to be explaining something when a small troop of men trotting down the hill interrupted him.

Spiro shouted to them, "Where is Canter's patrol? They are a fortnight late."

"Sorry, Cap'n, things look bad. Zumbaki have turned up out there," one of the men reported.

Spiro hissed and spat on the ground. "Zumbaki? Painted tribesmen. They shouldn't even be on this side of the forest!" He sighed and rubbed the bridge of his crooked nose, which looked as if it had been broken in the past. "I intend to retire for forty winks. Be sure to alert Clayborn of anything suspicious. Be wary in the field. Malefic and his troops could be close," he cautioned as he marched to a small tent.

Nick stared at the fire, licking his dry lips as his stomach rumbled. His back ached and his feet throbbed.

After some time passed, two men came running down the hill, glistening with sweat. They wore lightweight armor and carried fewer weapons than the others.

"Canter, you should signal us with flares," Clayborn declared as he rushed to meet them.

Canter panted, barely able to speak. "The f-flares... I-lost. W-we're lucky to make it back. We ran into a pack of Zumbaki. We lost Landon and Maniker."

"Bloody savages," Clayborn muttered.

Nick's head spun as he struggled to follow their dialogue. He didn't know how he'd arrived in this nightmarish land, but he would have to adapt quickly if he wanted to survive.

CHAPTER 8

Shelby decided Sculptor wasn't so bad after all. On the journey back to their division, Sculptor briefed her and Mr. Dempsey on their predicament, while Barrick rode ahead of them to scout for trouble.

The shrubbery around them burst in odd colors. Bushes blazed bright blue and teal next to flowers flaring yellow blossoms with violet leaves.

"Shouldn't be too bad," Barrick proclaimed from ahead. "We're on the southern side of the forest. No Zumbaki around here, and Malefic's patrols haven't been sighted. Over the eastern fringe, near the Cark Woods, I wouldn't be caught without an entire division."

"Um, what are Zumbaki?" Shelby asked.

He called back, "Savage tribesmen, cannibals who roam the Cark."

Sculptor sighed. "Ah, poor Vilaborg and Casselton. They had a Kin to fetch in the Cark Woods. I do hope they're all right."

"No better pair than that one to be in the Cark," Barrick said. "Borgy grew up there, and don't forget, both have intercepted before. I spoke to some Tuskarians who told me the Cark is infested with evil souls and vile monsters."

"You can't control where that portal of yours opens up, can you?" asked Mr. Dempsey.

Sculptor nodded. "Alas, although the device is efficient and transports our subjects safely, we cannot harness the powers needed to provide a specific location. The mentors bestow the coordinates where we can open the mobile portal. If an area doesn't consist of the proper nutrients and energies in the air, this may harm our passengers. We'd love the ability to utilize the portal with an entire brigade present, but the entry cannot operate with more than one or two living beings in the area. Hence our duty as interceptors. Do not fear. We aren't far from camp. We'll meet with our division in less than an hour."

"Let us ride now in silence while I find a safe spot to take a break," said Barrick.

Shelby stretched one of her legs. Both of her knees were growing stiff and sore from sitting so long in the hard leather saddle. Riding was new to her. She had imagined as a little girl how one day she might own a horse, but she'd never ridden one.

Barrick slowed down and dismounted. He waved a glowing compass along the perimeter, and then sniffed at the air for some time.

"The Tuskarian race is part ogre," Sculptor whispered. "They can smell a cigar a few miles away."

"We're close to the others now. We'll be safer when we join them," Barrick said as he returned to his mount. He grabbed something from his satchel and passed it back. "You must be hungry."

Shelby accepted the offering from Barrick and examined a hard strip. She sniffed it and debated taking a bite, as a growl from her stomach reminded her how famished she was.

"Very nourishing—chud. They're the roots of a druid." Barrick shoved a large hunk in his mouth.

Shelby took this as welcome news. "Oh, a root. I don't eat too much meat, so that's good."

"Aye, and I knew the druid we're eating—taught me to read the trails up in Tuska. Close friend for most of my life, he was. Name was Janor."

She glared at Barrick, unsettled. They were devouring a man? "I thought you said this was a root!"

"Aye, the root of a druid," he yammered, puzzled.

"Barrick, you ape," Sculptor shouted. "She has no idea what a druid is. Why, our own youth barely met live ones." He turned to her. "My dear, druids are tree people. They are mostly plant life, but with the soul of a person. They have become rare of late."

Mr. Dempsey said, "Tree people?"

Sculptor nodded. "Why, yes, they are part tree. Nearly all tree, in fact. The wood south of the Eridanus River had a village of druids at one point. The forest there is moist and lush, quite a salubrious setting for druids."

"We're eating tree people?" Shelby scrunched up her face and stared at the chud.

"The roots, my dear Shelby. Druids' stems can be found deep in the ground after they die. They last forever and are in abundance. Takes a while

to dig them up, though. Old Floater Clancy is a rich man, since his family began excavating druid roots for a living. They are excellent for long road trips and the sort, because they don't rot and are full of nutrients."

Mr. Dempsey inspected the chud, turning the slice over a few times. "Druids, you say. In our history, druids are ancient sorcerers who appeared in Welsh and Irish lore. I believe I remember reading that the druids were renowned for their power to transform trees into warriors and send them out to battle. Dryads were considered tree spirits. I wonder if that legend has any connection to your druids, the tree people."

Sculptor and Barrick shrugged, each of them chewing on the chud.

Mr. Dempsey took a bite. "Hmm, not bad. Actually very tasty."

Shelby took a small nip. She didn't relish the thought of eating something that had been alive at one point, even if it wasn't meat. Mr. Dempsey was right, though. The roots were flavorful. The chud was tough, like beef jerky, but it didn't taste bland or stringy. Instead, it yielded a salty-sweet effect.

After a few minutes of eating chud and swilling some water, Barrick remounted his horse, and they proceeded.

Shelby rode with Mr. Dempsey, if one could call it riding. Lenore needed no guidance from her. She smirked. Rather than trying to make the mare follow Barrick and Sculptor, she thought of their experience so far. This world was similar to Earth, with plants, animals, and society, but everything was skewed—strange underbrush, people who were part ogre, and food made from sentient trees.

"Whoa," Barrick called as he halted his steed ahead of them. "Presage and the rest of the Kin should be camped just down this path."

They trotted along and soon entered a large campsite. Several soldiers resembling Sculptor and Barrick stood as sentries.

Shelby shrank a little in the saddle. Hopefully these men were as kind as her new companions.

"Barrick, Sculptor... rookies no longer," bellowed one of the guards.

Another said with a snicker, "Well, well, broken in now, are we?"

"Aye, Sol, you're just jealous Achernar didn't send a grizzled veteran like you out, aren't you?" Barrick chided.

Sol cackled. "You can bet a hundred coogles I'd rather be with division, my dear Barrick."

"Coogles are hard to come by these days, Sol. Or haven't you heard we're in an economic contraction?"

"Oh, contraction, extension—balderdash! I'm just a soldier for division. I wouldn't know how to invest a coogle in the Companies Square if you gave it to me for free. Though I might spend some in Vixen."

A fellow with a stethoscope around his neck said, "The Square sank another five percent today, boys, so perhaps you should get on after Malefic before we lose our solitude savings, eh?"

"I made quite a bunch of coogles off of Floater Clancy's place last quarter," Sculptor boasted as his horse cantered forward. "They dug sixty acres of chud right outside Prickly Peak."

An older man wearing a well-tailored leather suit lurched up. "You speak of coogles and the Square, fooling around and bragging. Do you understand Malefic is gaining power, and that we'll be fighting for our lives? The time for gibberish and joking is gone. Peace has made you soldiers soft. I pray you'll soon grasp the circumstances. Lord Achernar has called the Kin to Azimuth, and if Biskara is involved, many lives will be lost."

The old soldier bowed before Shelby, then gave a scowl to the officers and trudged away. The troopers stood in silence for a few seconds, their expressions sobered by shame.

Barrick turned to Shelby and Mr. Dempsey. "He's Rufus Morder, a colonel in the Meridian Army. The last time Biskara gained power he lost one of his sons. Forgive me for my rudeness." He motioned Sol closer. "This is Shelby, and this here is Mr. Dempsey."

"I am honored to meet you. Name is Sol." He nodded his head once. Sol, taller than Barrick, was not as muscular and appeared more human than most. "Isn't he a bit on the gray side to be a Kin, Barrick?"

When he spoke, Shelby saw he had a gap between his teeth.

"Aye, he entered the portal with 'er," Barrick said.

"Such a thing ever happened before?"

"Pal o' mine, I sure hope so. I don't want to be the headmost interceptor in history to bring in a free independent from the mobile portal."

"Uh, no, no, Barrick," Sculptor said. "I believe I remember a reconnoiter telling me something about a whole bunch of independents, animals, vehicles, and the like advancing through the portal before. I'm certain we aren't the first ones." He peered over to Sol for reassurance.

"Oh, yes, fellas," Sol said. "I'm sure something similar to this has happened before. I do pray so for your sake, because you would never live this down. Bards will be singing rhymes and stories about your blunder for eternity."

Sol broke into a hearty laugh and then caught himself, as if recalling Rufus's comments just moments earlier. He looked off into the distance where the veteran had disappeared.

Shelby followed his gaze and gaped. She had not anticipated such a large camp. White canvas tents sprouted from the muddy ground. The pungent air smelled unusual—a mixture of horses, campfires, food, and people—but it felt almost familiar, as if she'd been in a place like this before.

Several soldiers jogged by. A few stopped and bowed to her. A couple even took their helmets off. Each had dirt on his face and armor, mud on his boots, and many of them were unshaven. Time out in the field had not been kind.

Apparently, few hot baths could be had. She felt a little sad, having hoped for a rinse after riding for so long.

Something nagged at her. "Sculptor, where are the cities?"

"Meracuse, Meridia's capital, is several hours from here. We may pass through a few villages, but we plan to avoid most in order to avert any detection of the Kin."

She frowned.

Mr. Dempsey swept his hands across the vista. "This camp is something else, don't you think, Shelby?"

"Sure is. Aren't people going to be worried, Mr. Dempsey? I mean, didn't we leave the library wide open? And it must have been hours since we left."

"Alas, dear Shelby, we can do nothing. When we return, I'm sure I'll have a fair amount of explaining to do. No sense worrying about things out of our hands. Who even knows how time passes between here and Earth."

While she and Mr. Dempsey spoke, Barrick and Sol also exchanged a few words. Barrick, though short, still towered over Sol atop his charger. The two comrades conversed in low tones, and Sol pointed across the camp to a small hill.

Banners fluttered above some of the tents, their colorful fields igniting a sudden passion within her. Mr. Dempsey was right; she couldn't control getting home. Lord Achernar had brought her here for a reason, and no one had treated her unjustly so far. While she missed her father, she knew these people needed her and the other Kin more.

"How nice to meet you, Miss Shelby, Mr. Dempsey." Sol gave a nod to them and then scurried away.

Barrick turned to them. "That there is Salty Sol Saunders. Good soldier to have on yer side when things go awry. He told me Cumber and old Presage got a group of Kin right over the hill here. What say we head on over?" He dismounted and handed the reins of his steed to another soldier.

"The prospect would be reassuring, Barrick," Mr. Dempsey said.

Shelby and Mr. Dempsey slid off the back of Lenore.

They trudged up the small hill, and every soldier they passed said hello to Barrick and Sculptor or shot them nods of encouragement. A few smiled at Shelby and Mr. Dempsey.

When they reached the top of the slope, excitement gripped her, and Shelby twirled her ponytail around her finger. She viewed a group of others her age sitting by a fire, with an older man in blue. He spoke while they listened.

As she and Mr. Dempsey approached behind Sculptor and Barrick, everyone rose to their feet.

"Ah, my dear Shelby has arrived," said the man in blue. "Now five Kin are present. Excellent. I see an adult independent is along for the ride?"

Barrick said, more than a little embarrassed, "Oh, yes, Presage, he is Miss Pardow's friend and accompanied her through the mobile portal."

"That's quite all right. An adult independent may be useful. Welcome to our campsite. Let us make ourselves acquainted now, shall we? I am Presage." He turned to the kids around the campfire. "Kin, this here is Shelby Pardow, from Ohio. You are?" Presage nodded to Mr. Dempsey.

"Walter Dempsey. Pleased to meet you all."

"Hi," said Shelby. She scanned the other Kin. *How refreshing to see human faces.*

Presage proceeded to introduce them. "Max Tuttle, from Virginia."

Max nodded as he raised his hand up and fixed his hazel eyes on her. Handsome and athletic, he resembled the quarterback from her high school. His brown suede top was even shaped like a football jersey.

"Riley Upchurch, from Washington State."

Riley stood and flashed a pirate's smile. Her blonde hair glowed in the fiery light. She plopped to the ground and held the front of her khaki-colored leather skirt down.

Shelby grinned back. No doubt about it. She and Riley would be quick friends.

"Emily Lawson, from Connecticut."

She waved as her flaxen hair danced past her waist, her green eyes flickering. Unlike Riley, Emily looked terrified. Shelby hoped she could talk with her soon. She knew how it felt to be insecure and abandoned. Now more than ever, they needed to reassure one another that they were among friends.

"And here we have Stuart Lesser, from New York."

He lifted his head with a taut expression and gave only a half-wave. His baggy, leather attire flapped around him as he reached for a cup of tea.

After Presage finished his introductions, the man with the stethoscope ambled up to him and whispered in his ear.

Shelby ran her fingers through her hair and began playing with her ponytail again. She gazed at Max and caught him in mid-stare. He blushed and flashed away at once. For a brief few seconds, her heart stopped. A shy smile graced her lips and she averted her eyes.

"I'll be right back, Mr. Dempsey," Shelby said. She strode over to Riley and Emily. "Do you mind if I join you?"

"Sure," answered Riley. "This tea is delicious. Can I pour you a cup?"

"Sounds good. I'm getting cold," Shelby admitted.

"Well, friends," Presage said, "please make yourselves comfortable around the campfire. I must attend to something. If there is anything that you desire, Cumber and Sol are more than willing to oblige. I shall return shortly." He walked off with the man who appeared to be a doctor.

Cumber explained, "He's Healer Beekman. Someone is a bit ill, so Presage will help old Beekman out."

Barrick waved and offered a kind smile. "Sculptor and I are off for a little while to freshen up. Don't worry, we'll be back to check on you soon."

Mr. Dempsey joined the circle, sat down, and pressed his hands up to the flames.

Shelby eyed a handgun Cumber had in his holster. "What shoots out of it? Bullets?"

Cumber pulled out the gun. "What? Boo-letts? This is a hand-cannon. It fires a concentrated form of air and molecules taken from the atmosphere, though most of the power comes from the person operating it. Each person shoots at different levels. Not many have the ability. Only the registered owner can fire the hand-cannon, as it's linked to their handprints. Mine can knock you back twenty feet on medium, and flatten you for days on high... if you aren't wearing armor."

Admiring the weapon, Stuart said, "Cool."

Mr. Dempsey said, "So how did everyone else arrive here? Shelby and I entered the portal from the library where I work."

"In my school computer room, doing some homework before practice," said Max.

Emily said, "On my laptop at the local park, across the street from my house."

Riley raised her head. "At my neighbor's place, feeding their dogs."

Mr. Dempsey gave Stuart a questioning stare when he didn't say anything.

"In my father's office playing a video game on his computer," Stuart muttered, though grudgingly, as if it pained him to talk.

Collectively, they sought Mr. Dempsey for guidance. As the lone human adult, he seemed the only person they could turn to. Shelby felt the same way as the others, but knew better. Mr. Dempsey comprehended about as much or as little as the rest of them.

Riley asked the question they were all wondering. "What do we do now, Mr. Dempsey?"

"This is extraordinary. It opens up a remarkable number of possibilities concerning the mysteries of the universe. As far as our next actions, I believe we simply have to do what's right."

Presage returned with a pair of soldiers. Cumber rushed over with two cups and a kettle. "Casselton, Borgy, come and sip some hot tea. Is the sixth Kin with you?"

Both lumbered forward, exhausted, their armor covered in mud. Casselton stared at the ground, long strands of wooly black and white hair and beard masking most of his face. Vilaborg carried a tense expression, his mahogany hair plastered backward from the temples.

"Unfortunately, they do not have the final Kin," said Presage in a low tone.

Vilaborg looked sheepish. "The readings on the portal say he came through. We searched and then a horde of Bogmen showed. We needed to retreat, but we must go out and find him with reinforcements." Dread was heavy in his voice.

Sol said, "Wasn't that Kin supposed to materialize near the Cark Woods?"

"Aye, we were in the Cark." Casselton's eyes fixed on the ground.

"I already sent out reconnoiters to scour the Cark," Presage said. "I pray he finds his way to safe hands."

Shelby watched Presage as he walked off. She absorbed his fear and insecurity as he stared out into the darkness with a troubled look.

CHAPTER 9

Zach thought about the magnificent creatures that set him on his course. Wondering if he was dreaming no longer came to mind; the world as he knew it had been left behind.

He followed the river, searching for a boat and a man named Throg. As he walked, he considered a few different things to explain his sudden arrival. Had he stumbled into a time machine or teleportation device in his backyard? Not likely, but then again, neither was a world with singing eyes and fresh brown roses.

The forest seemed normal now, and he longed for the earlier colorful environment. The grassy patches were green instead of light blue. Trees were typical heights, and the bushes were no longer purple. This place *looked* like Earth, but when a yellow squirrel scampered up a tree trunk, he reconsidered. *No, not quite Earth.*

Strange insects flew through the air. He flinched as an oversized bright azure dragonfly whizzed by his ear. The only time he'd ever seen such a huge dragonfly was in a museum display. Dragonflies the size of large rats hadn't existed on Earth since the Carboniferous era. He watched the blue bug flit away.

· *Blue.* He thought again of the Fugues who'd visited him a short time ago. They'd spoken to him telepathically, several soothing voices becoming one message. A feeling of safety and security had overcome him when they spoke. He still carried a lingering sense of trust toward them.

Walking along the riverside became challenging after a time. Rather than flat patches of grass and rock, he now scaled muddy walls with difficulty. His feet slipped under him, and more than once he almost fell into the river. The mud gave way to a rocky shore, which was flatter, but still cumbersome to cross. After an hour of hiking, he began to doubt what the Fugues had told him.

As he rounded a bend, he came upon a small, one-person campsite on the river's edge. Smoke billowed from a pile of sticks next to a hefty boat tied to a nearby tree. The smell of cooking meat made his stomach grumble. The encampment didn't appear vacant, so he approached cautiously, hoping Throg lived here.

"Easy, Hoss," came an earthy voice from behind him. "This isn't a public campfire."

Zach spun to face the camp's owner.

A tall man with short, wavy chestnut hair stood in front of him. The brown leather- and suede-clad figure held a walking stick. Lean and rugged, he tilted his sun-baked head and stared down at Zach with cobalt eyes. Dark stubble peppered the stranger's face.

"Are you Throg?" Zach kept his tone even, though his heart raced.

The foreigner examined him. "I don't believe we have met before, have we?"

"N-no, sir. My n-name is Zach Ryder. The F-Fugues sent me."

"The Fugues? Did you just say the Fugues?" His eyes widened and he stroked his bristles.

"Y-yes, they sent me to f-find you."

"Glory be the Fugues," Throg whispered. He peered up the river and tapped his stick on the ground. "Well then, I haven't heard or thought of the Fugues in quite some time. What did they tell you?"

"They told me to follow the river downstream until I found you. They said I'd be safe with you and that you would be able to help me."

"They said all this now, did they? Only certain Kin can communicate with the Fugues. You must be a Kin... haven't seen one in some time. So Biskara could be on the move again, eh?" Throg gazed across the river.

"Who?"

"Oh, yes, I forgot. Biskara is a pure evil entity. He's what you grew up calling Satan, Lucifer, the devil. He has many names, but on Azimuth he is known as Biskara. Uh, Zach, where are your interceptors?"

"Who?"

"You'd make a perfect full-bred Earth owl."

"Um, interceptors? I think I ran away from them. Two people were looking for me, but I was confused. I was on my computer and then in the backyard, and, and...," he sputtered.

The woodsman grunted. "Same basic story when someone goes through the mobile portal. So the interceptors let one slip by the goalie,

did they? The Fugues come whenever trouble's brewing. Was anyone following or chasing you?"

"Yes, yes, there was a little man, very hairy, with paint on his face and beard. He had a loud horn. I raced out of there and fell down a hill."

"A hairy little fellow with a horn? And looking for Kin? Sounds like the Bogmen have been contracted by someone to find you. It makes sense. Offer a Bogman a piece of chud, and he'll dance on hot coals for you." Throg spit on the ground.

"Uh, sorry, but that's a lot of information. I'm a Kin? Satan placed a hit on me?" Perplexed, Zach knelt down on one knee, nauseous as he imagined a red devil with horns hunting him.

Throg chuckled. "Yup, pretty much the gist of things. Before Biskara decides to strike, though, he has to do something about the Aulic Assembly. I do hope I'm wrong. If Biskara has returned...."

Throg twirled his stick. "This is a bad situation if Biskara's gotten rid of the Assembly. Those on the Aulic Assembly are the only ones preordained to operate the Silver Sphere."

Zach frowned, confused.

Throg continued. "It's an armillary sphere and can locate the celestial whereabouts of Biskara."

Throg swigged from his canteen and then offered it to Zach, who accepted. Cold water sluiced down his throat; he hadn't realized how thirsty the trip made him.

"Biskara is monitored by the Assembly. He's creative, though, attempting to set up clones of himself and similar strategies. My bet is he kidnapped them. You're kind of like a backup Assembly, just the way this is. Each Kin serves as a counterpart to a member of the Assembly."

The tall man took a deep breath and squinted at Zach. "Any questions?" He accepted his canteen back.

"Uh, Throg, who are you in all this? You seem to have an awful lot of info."

Throg gave Zach a warm grin. "Well, the Fugues must think I'm willing to help you reach the rest of the Kin, now don't they? At any rate, welcome to Azimuth."

The forester had a comforting way about him. Zach wondered why his stomach remained easy, considering he'd been whisked away to another world to help its residents battle their version of Satan. Perhaps he belonged here. Back home, he was never wanted.

He stood in front of Throg on the planet Azimuth, thinking about how life could change directions. At the same time, though, he missed Adrian. Still, Adrian would want him to be happy. Of anyone, Adrian knew what Zach went through every day. There was a lot to cover still. Zach pushed the thought of home aside.

In any case, it was better to be here than sitting on the back steps of his adopted home, depressed about where his life was headed. Even though he was bigger than the largest senior at Taft High now, he still felt like a scrawny fifteen-year-old nerd.

"Give me a second to pack up," Throg said. "We need to move out, and soon. The Bogmen may run with Nightlanders, particularly because you're here."

He proceeded to pick up his belongings around the small campsite, then took a bucket to the river and filled it. Zach offered to help close out the camp, and Throg thrust the full pail into his arms.

"Put out the fire, if you don't mind. I'll get my things from inside."

Zach doused the flames.

When Throg emerged from his tent, he carried a pack. "Food, blankets, all such stuff," he said with a wink. "Never know what you might need on a trip like this. Here, come give me a hand."

"I'm scared to ask what Nightlanders are," said Zach as he helped Throg.

"The Nightlanders are soldiers who operate under Biskara's sons. Every time an uprising occurs, the people banter about Biskara." Throg placed his gear onto the boat. "But the Nightlanders don't reveal who they are."

Zach wound a thick rope Throg had given him. "What do you mean?"

"Well, Biskara's sons never admit who they are until they're at maximum power. The Nightlanders have a dreadful reputation. The original Nightlander army, led by Biskara's first son, Hideux, was responsible for a reign of unspeakable horror. Back then, some mentors questioned the existence of Biskara."

Zach began to understand the dire situation into which he'd been thrust. He tucked the rope under a seat and helped pick up a few other things around camp. He shoved forks, spoons, bowls and the like into a satchel.

Throg placed some pots and pans into a sack. "Then Hideux took power. One of the mentors, the legendary General Rostand, had been sent to spy a military base on Andromeda. He witnessed Hideux speak to Biskara. General Rostand managed to escape and reported back to the Mentors' Academy. It was there that the Silver Sphere was created. It wasn't by coincidence that the truth seekers reached out at this time, and legend has it that they helped the Academy develop the Sphere."

Throg had finished packing and the two of them returned to the boat. The strong but slender woodsman adjusted his bags and motioned for Zach to hop aboard.

"Throg," Zach began.

"I know, I know, laddie.... Who are the truth seekers? Who are the mentors? Listen, we met not thirty minutes ago, and we need to travel downriver to be safe. Let's get going, and I'll fill you in, okay?"

"Sure."

This real, daring journey had heroes, and from what it sounded like, Zach was one of them. He was starved for knowledge about this world, and though he wanted to continue the conversation, a little more time wouldn't matter. Throg was right—they needed to get to safety, especially if Nightlanders were after him.

Zach boarded the boat, which swished and rocked beneath him. He managed to keep his balance as the enormous craft rested low in the water. A stove sat at the front, and a few rows of benches ran up close by the stern.

Throg used a pole to move them away from shore, then handed it to Zach. "Let's go, and keep it down 'til I say we can talk."

As they proceeded down the river, Zach held his tongue. He helped row out into the current, and once the vessel rode downstream, Throg motioned for him to pull the pole on board before he pushed a couple of levers near the prow, and two wheels on the rear of the boat began churning water.

Zach examined his surroundings to take his attention off all the data processing in his mind. Taking a break was easy, as the forest was more beautiful than any other he'd seen.

The plush foliage offered different shades of green and brown. Strange creatures darted around the bank. He spied a raccoon with bluish fur and an orange mask. A pack of ferret-like critters scurried alongside them, sprinting in and out of the bushes. A pleasant scent permeated the air and reminded him of a sweeter version of jasmine. He sucked in a deep breath, safe and at peace.

Throg broke his silence. "Are you hungry, laddie?" The sturdy man's gaze remained fixed on the shoreline.

Zach had been so preoccupied by his journey that he hadn't even thought of food. His gut rumbled. "Starved."

Throg turned toward the shore and slowed the boat down. Once they got close to a tangled bush, he dug his hand into a cluster of branches.

"Pegasi nest, excellent eggs." Throg fished out two of the largest eggs Zach had ever seen.

He eased the eggs into a basket and steered the schooner to the middle of the channel again. Each of the eggs, bright yellow with dark brown speckling, was the size of Throg's head.

"Pegasi are weird birds. Some animals you will encounter—as normal as cats and dogs in these parts—will astound you. The Pegasi, for instance, are rather large birds, common on the river, with heads that look like horses. Six eggs in there, so don't fret. Plenty left to be born for this Pegasi family."

He moved around the boat with ease, hit a few wooden levers, and then settled down to the middle of the deck. He stroked another lever and a hood popped open. From inside, he lifted out green onion-like plants, some mushrooms, and a bottle of yellow liquid that Zach figured was cooking oil.

He chopped the onion and mushrooms with a large knife and tossed them with the oil in a wooden bowl. Two long, thin sticks appeared from under a roaster, and Throg struck them on a piece of tar paper. The matches ignited, and he lit the oven, then pulled a black iron pan from his satchel and poured the mixture into the skillet.

Zach moved closer and spotted a Bunsen burner inside the compartment beneath the stove. "This is amazing!"

Throg pointed to the cooker as he stirred the ingredients. "I made the thing myself. The pilot underneath is encased in metal."

He cracked the eggs and beat them in the same wooden bowl as the onion mix, added some spices, and spilled the eggs into the hissing iron. The aroma of sizzling green onions, mushrooms, and eggs pervaded the air around them.

Zach's stomach rumbled like a blender chopping ice cubes.

Within a few minutes, Zach enjoyed some of the most succulent eggs he'd ever put on his tongue, and he wolfed them down. They were fluffy and salty. "This is delicious, Throg. Thank you."

"Aye, truffle oil is in season, and Pegasi eggs with radenook green onions and chipsami mushrooms is one of the best meals you can fix on the road." Throg devoured his eggs.

The bottomless skillet of cloud-like Pegasi eggs invited Zach to gorge until he almost burst. He was so stuffed upon finishing, he didn't care where they were or why. He gently put down the warm pan and rolled over to his side with a half-joking, half-serious moan.

"Aye, young Zach, happens frequently to first-timers." Zach's companion chuckled as he munched away on the delicious food.

Such a contrast. Zach lay bloated, yet he giggled at the sky. He couldn't remember the last time he'd been so happy.

CHAPTER 10

"Say now, did ye know the runes yer puttin' on that are for fertility?" Cumber pulled Stuart to the side and whispered into his ear, "Ye don't want the lassies to catch you with that on yer chest, do ya? It'd be devilishly embarrassin' for ya."

"Oh, no, no, Cumber, this is the Triforce. You know, from *The Legend of Zelda*? Trust me, this is really hip where we're from." Stuart sketched the sigil onto the middle of his leather shirt with a piece of charcoal.

"Come on now, laddie. Ye can't possibly be serious about tha' bein' stylish!"

"Whatever. I'm telling you, this is über rad where I'm from. If I'm going to be a warrior, I want the Triforce with me."

Stuart decided he was finished explaining his reasoning to someone he'd met not four hours ago. Cumber's garb was much nicer than any of his new clothes, but Stuart wasn't about to complain. Where Cumber had a cloak, Stuart now had the Triforce. He'd never felt cooler.

He stood up and sauntered away from a mumbling Cumber, displaying the three triangles over his chest. Stuart returned to the others, but stopped short and stared down at the charcoal drawing. Riley was one of the prettiest girls he'd ever seen, but he doubted she knew what the Triforce was. *Maybe I do look stupid.* He sighed and drifted away from the fire where they sat.

As he walked, Stuart considered his situation. He and the other kids had been brought here from their world—something every anime he was aware of had in common—and were now called 'Kin.' They had to save the world from an ancient evil, too, and were armored heroes. Heck, he'd even *changed*. Not only had he aged, but....

He gazed at his reflection in a water barrel, rubbed his neck and jaw, and smiled. The face in the water was tougher, meaner, and an overall improvement. When he'd passed through the portal, Stuart had gained a little weight. Before, he'd been stick-pole thin with pockmarks on his cheeks, but now everything fit and he boasted a smooth complexion.

He grinned and flexed one of his arms. Muscles bulged. He continued along and wondered if his new physique would help him achieve his dream of being like a ninja. Silently, he made a wager with himself: *I bet I could creep past those guards and out of sight without anyone noticing me.*

He slipped off to explore the rest of the camp. No one followed. Darting in and out of the shadows, he found the activities around the encampment much more interesting than the boring campfire and the monotonous old Presage. A bard strummed a stringed turtle shell as he sang to a small crowd. A handful of soldiers crouched and rolled dice. A few archers shot at targets. Not far off, another pair spoke as they whetted their axe blades.

He stopped at a busy group of boisterous troops and peered through the crowd to find out what kept their attention. Two soldiers stood in a circle across from each other, holding glowing joysticks in their hands. Closer to the middle of the ring were a pair of enormous, dazzling holograms. A muscle-bound warrior leered at an imposing Minotaur.

Stuart knew what a Minotaur was from the game, *God of War*. Kratos had run into them more than once. The Minotaur reared its bullish head as it swayed a huge axe in its hands, and the warrior across from it waved a large sword. The combatants rushed forward and met with a crash.

The soldiers wielding the joysticks jerked back and forth, shouting expletives as they twisted and turned. One wrong move could end the match.

The holographic warrior blocked an overhand swing with his buckler and then rolled under a blow from the Minotaur's fist. The crowd of battle-hardened soldiers surrounding the two players cheered.

Stuart grinned. The holograms seemed to be sweating and wheezing, as if the creatures fought in mortal combat. "I've never seen anything like this!" he murmured to no one.

The Minotaur caught the panting fighter with a swift kick to the ribcage. A wrenching sound, similar to a series of branches breaking, cracked through the air. The fighter grimaced and stumbled.

The Minotaur stalked the warrior in the circle as the man limped in retreat, trying to force the creature off by brandishing his sword whenever the Minotaur came too close. The feint of swinging his blade back and forth

worked for a time, but the holographic soldier grew weary and his poorly aimed thrusts slowed.

A knight cried out from the crowd, "Finish him!"

"Let's go now, Boozer. Get on with the stroke of grace," another man shouted from beside Stuart.

Finally, the menacing Minotaur swung its battleaxe with such fury that it shattered the warrior's blade of steel and drove right through to his chest. The warrior collapsed to the ground, and the soldier operating him groaned. The battle finished and both holograms faded away.

Boozer rambled inside the ring, his joystick raised to the sky amid a chorus of cheers and boos. He was a burly man with stringy red hair and a short, knotted beard. Crow's feet wrinkled around the corners of his eyes when he grinned.

Boozer goaded, "Ye cannot tangle with the Minotaur and live to tell about it, can ya, Kron?"

"Ah, double dung, Booz. Ya cheated after ye chose the old battleaxe anyway," pouted Kron in disgust.

"Oh, I did now, righty. And ya managed to sneak in the li'l' buckler w'out me knowin', but that's fine?" Boozer shrugged and chuckled.

Stuart stood mesmerized with delight. "Bravo, bravo," he shouted and clapped his hands.

"And so," Boozer said, "we have one of the fabled Kin here cheering on the ol' Minotaur, now do we? In awe of the skills of the Boozer, are ye?" His eyes befell the mark on Stuart's chest. "Wha' is tha'? The rune of fertility?"

"It's the Triforce," Stuart corrected. "Besides, I'm more impressed with the graphics. I'm a bit of a wiz at these games where I'm from. I bet I offer you a worthy challenge."

He just wanted a crack at playing. While he'd watched the other two play, he'd spied multiple ways the knight could have won. It was a matter of skill, of seeing the small things. He knew he was one of those irritating kids who were unnaturally good at all the new video games. *That's all I'm good at. That and my skateboard.*

A soldier standing next to Boozer said, "Now, young man, the resourcefulness of the Kin is well-known, but the Boozer here is undefeated in *Dire Conflict*."

"*Dire Conflict* is the game, huh? Well, Boozy, how would you like to take on a Kin and test what ya got?" Stuart walked toward him.

Boozer gaped at him with amazement. He smiled and then frowned. "Hmm, ye have never played *Dire Conflict*, and ye think you can whoop up on the Boozer, eh? Why, do ye realize if they included *Dire Conflict* at the games in Fornax, which they dang righ' should, I'd be grand champion, laddie?"

Stuart shrugged one shoulder. "Well, then this should be a global... er, universal... tournament. I happen to rule the roost back home. The Triforce doesn't lie." He grinned and put his hands on his hips.

The crowd came closer. A few troops muttered to one another. Stuart heard the word 'Kin' tossed around and he smiled. Maybe some of these men would chant his name when he outpaced Boozer. This would even top the arcades in his neighborhood.

"Let the Kin give the game a whirl agains' ya," yelled out one of the soldiers. Several soldiers cried, "Yeah!"

"Come on, Boozer," said his previous opponent, Kron.

"Alas, my dear Kin, ye will face the wrath of the Minotaur." Boozer winked and grinned. "Give the people wha' they wan' — tha's my motto."

"All right!" yelped Stuart. Not every day did he fight against someone on another planet with a video game. Now he really *could* boast he was the best when he returned home.

Energy burst throughout their vicinity as dozens of excited armored men came forward to watch the match. The chilly air warmed with the soldiers' proximity.

Someone shouted, "Bet you ten pints of Vixen blueberry ale the Kin wins!"

"I'll take tha' bet," said another.

Kron came to Stuart's side and whispered into his ear, "The buttons on the bottom are defensive blocks, and the ones on the top are offensive strikes. If ye hold the top lef' and bottom lef' buttons down together, this be your master strike. Use this sparingly, as it will sap yer energy. The stick itself pretty much controls the warrior's body. There's more, but ye will have to make do with tha'." He broke free of Stuart and disappeared into the crowd. His black-haired head bobbed away.

Another trooper came up to Stuart, gave him a pat on the back, and encouraged him. "Give this the old schoolboy try now, sonny."

Several other pats and nods followed, until one of the warriors thrust the joystick into his hand. Stuart smirked. The joystick was like a part of him, and no one could take that away now.

A wall of soldiers formed another large circle around them. A competitive Boozer replaced the jolly one as he shot a menacing glare at Stuart, who stared him down cold. Thick tension zapped between the two of them. Stuart refused to glance away from Boozer, even for a second. Everything got quiet.

"Now let's engage in *Dire Conflict,*" boomed a soldier. Somehow this event had become an official match.

Stuart's joystick began to vibrate and a blue glow emanated from the sides. He felt a rush of pure adrenaline course through him. A holographic console materialized in front of him.

"Pick the battleaxe," hollered out a voice from the crowd.

"The spear. Take the spear," declared another.

As he gazed down at the console, Stuart realized they were pointing out his choices. Caricatures of several armaments floated on top. Underneath each weapon was a colorful button. On the bottom of the console were the words: "Choose two weapons for your *Dire Conflict.*"

The double-edged sword looked too good to turn down. But he also knew Kron had just lost to the Minotaur bearing the same blade. He hit a button with an arrow pointing down, and another set of weapons appeared. One of the names caught his eye. "The Sword of Ariadne" was written under a long blade with a red handle.

Stuart smiled. Greek mythology was one of his favorite subjects. Kratos might have demolished the Minotaur in *God of War*, but real folklore was better than that. *The Minotaur* had been a recent reading of his, and the sword Theseus used to slay the Minotaur was given to him by Ariadne. He was sure of it.

He hit the button underneath, forgetting the image was holographic, and the sword vanished from the console when his finger passed through where the icon had been. He continued to scan the choices and settled on a large chain titled, "Battle Chain." The console dematerialized after his selection.

His warrior appeared, standing tall while twirling the battle chain and holding the saber high over its head. His muscles rippled with each twirl, and the rich, burgundy-colored armor he wore cast a regal aura. The sword of Ariadne glistened like a beacon in the dark night.

Across the way, Boozer completed his weapon check on the console and the Minotaur emerged straight from the ground. A mixed reaction of boos and cheers again riled the men.

"Now you're in fer death," Boozer shouted and chortled.

The bull-headed monster charged the warrior, battleaxe in tow. Stuart, operating on instinct, jerked his joystick to the right, and the Minotaur ran directly into the crowd, surprising a few of the soldiers even though it was a holograph.

"Harrumph," Boozer blurted.

Stuart was engrossed in the game now, armed with years of determined practice from his own video games back home. Adrenaline sped through him and his heart pounded.

The battle intensified.

The Minotaur once again leapt at the warrior, and Stuart pushed his joystick down while he flicked the left "up" button in a circular fashion. It worked to perfection.

The battle chain whipped cleanly through the air as the warrior ducked at the same time. The Minotaur missed with the swing of his axe, and the chain wrapped violently around its legs.

Stuart thrust the joystick forward while he leaned on the left button. The Minotaur was ripped right off its feet and came thundering down with a loud crack. The warrior cast the Minotaur a stony glare.

Wild cheers resonated from the crowd as Stuart continued to push the joystick forward, the warrior dragging the Minotaur around the circle amid the roaring soldiers. Then he made the warrior stop and raise the sword of Ariadne high over his head. The blade dropped, preparing to end the match.

Instead of striking true, however, the holographic blade passed right through the Minotaur. The bull-headed brute rose from the ground, its earthy tones now much darker. Rage overtook the Minotaur as the beast forged past the warrior hologram.

A stunned gasp emitted from the crowd as Boozer clicked at his joystick, bewildered. For an instant, no one moved.

"It's come alive. The dang Minotaur is alive!" one of the soldiers shouted.

The Minotaur marched toward Stuart. Shock kept him frozen to the spot. He gaped at the creature, his eyes wide.

It stopped a moment and let out a tremendous screech as it raised its ferocious head to the sky. Several of the soldiers scattered. Boozer charged at Stuart, grabbed him by the collar, and shoved him backward.

"Get runnin', Kin. He is looking for ya, laddie. Now go for it. Dash back to Presage!" he yelled.

The Minotaur leapt toward Boozer, who had turned his head just in time, lifting his sword up in front of the axe. The blade shattered on impact and the blow knocked Boozer to the mud. Other soldiers swarmed the Minotaur amidst yells and battle cries as Stuart charged back to the campfire.

CHAPTER 11

The Kin sat around the campfire, content with the warmth of the flames and tasty tea as they discussed their new world. Vilaborg returned with a pair of soldiers and a cook carrying a large black pot. Max watched as Stuart slipped away from the group. He frowned and caught the eye of Presage, who grinned and winked at him before resuming his conversation with Vilaborg.

A stomach-rumbling aroma filled the air as the cook lifted the lid off the pot. Max touched his gut as his mouth watered.

"I figured you would all be hungry for real food," Vilaborg said. "This is what I call summer stew. We rarely eat anything other than dry bread and chud when we're on the road. Anyhow, our reconnoiters found an overgrown, unkempt garden about a mile east from here, so good old Lars came up with enough to make stew."

Lars thrust the black pot down, his soiled chef's hat falling off in the process. Ladle in hand, he began filling large wooden bowls and handed them out. The Kin stood in an orderly line.

How nice to have something hot to eat, Max thought. The chud he'd devoured was wearing off.

Cumber returned with a basket covered with cloth. "Another treat. Some toasty bread for ye." He pulled the twill off the steaming carton.

No butter, but the heated bread and stew made up for its absence. They all plunged into their bowls. Max smacked his lips. Garlic and onion mixed with other flavors, like a strange melon or orange and creamy bits of rice-like grains.

Lars clapped his hands together. "Ye know the chow is good when no one is speaking."

Max dunked his bread into the dish. The mix of baby carrots, spinach, corn, and mushrooms in rich gravy grew addicting, and he scarfed the meal down. The heel was flavored like sourdough bread, but warm. Small chunks of dried chud had been baked into the loaf.

He finished the stew and wiped his bowl clean with a hunk of bread. When done, he strode over to a bin Lars had set up, deposited the saucer, and returned to the fire.

A sudden stabbing pain in his crown doubled him over. He placed his fingers on his temples as the head rush spun into a brain freeze.

Riley dashed to his side. "Max. Max!"

Presage glided over, patting his back. "It will pass. Hold on a little longer, Max, just a minute."

Max sensed satisfaction in Presage's tone. The pain forced him to close his eyes, and the image of a man materialized. The blurred countenance had a narrow jaw and large ears; his eyes were shut, and the lips emitted a groan as he attempted to speak. The face dissipated, taking the discomfort along. Max's eyes fluttered open. Everyone had gathered around him.

Presage smiled. "Are you all right now, son?"

"Yeah, yes. What was that?" Max held his groggy head.

"Did you see anything?" Presage's brow arched.

"Yes. I mean, I think so. I saw the face of a man, but only for a second. He tried to say something."

"Good news then. That is your fellow Kin. He's alive and attempting to establish his connection with you."

Max had recognized the man's face from somewhere. Down ten-nothing at the homecoming game a few weeks ago, he'd had a similar experience and hadn't been able to complete the scoring drive. Still a bit unsettled, he rose to his feet. Nausea turned his stomach for a moment. Though it passed, he remained agitated.

Riley massaged his neck. "Are you okay?"

"Yeah, I'm fine, a little light-headed. Is the experience like that every contact?" Max looked up at Presage.

"Oh, no, they will get much less painful over time—akin to working your physical body into shape. You're sore in the beginning, and eventually, you build up stamina."

"Uh, Presage, what is my link's name?"

"Ah, your link—a good man, well-liked by the people. His fellow Assembly members consider him quite the socialite." Presage grinned. "That is Macklin Morrow who is trying to contact you."

"Macklin Morrow," Max whispered.

"Who is my link?" asked Riley.

"Yes, Rowan Letty would be your Kin. You have a striking resemblance to her, Riley." Presage placed his gaze next on Emily. "Emily, your Kin is Elita Ezmer—quite the politician. In fact, she—"

A terrible screech wailed from over the hill. The men around the Kin all went for their weapons and dashed toward the sound. Max shivered as a gust of wind whipped through camp. One man came running at them. *Borgy,* Max recalled.

"Sir," Vilaborg said and then gasped for air.

Presage shut his eyes for a few seconds as a noisy surge of bedlam carried from over the ridge. He opened them and gazed out to the huddled group.

"It has commenced," he whispered, and scanned the hilltop in the direction of the inhuman wail.

A few moments later, a shadow appeared at the crest of the highland and scampered down.

"That's Stuart!" Max jumped to his feet. His head still ached, but letting his companion get hurt wouldn't be a good play.

Stuart slipped and fell, clutching something in his hand. He rolled down the slippery slope, coming to a stop only when he hit a canvas tent. In a flash, he sprang up and bolted toward them.

"Should we saddle up the Kin and get a move on, Presage?" Vilaborg said.

As he stared at the approaching Stuart, Presage paused a moment before responding. "No, we will be just fine." He winked at Vilaborg.

"*A min-oh-toor... Minotaur!*" Stuart yelled with a gasp as he ran up.

"A Minotaur in the camp, you say? Now, now, Stuart, that is simply a game the soldiers play—some high sorcology, *Dire Conflict.* You scared the stars out of us." Vilaborg exhaled as he patted the crouching Stuart on his back.

Stuart shook his head as his chest heaved, sweat dripping off his forehead. Max walked over to the two of them.

"No, no, I know *Dire Conflict* is a game. I played against Boozer." Stuart paused again to catch his breath.

"You were playing *Conflict* against Boozer? Well, Boozer is always the Minotaur. Darn near unbeatable, he is. He did tell you it was a game, Stuart?"

"You aren't listening. I know it's a game. I was playing the Minotaur when he came to life. The soldiers are fighting him now!" Stuart pointed in the direction from which he'd come.

Men's distinct shouts reverberated throughout the camp, and the scrape of metal rang out as a hundred swords were drawn.

Though he couldn't see it, the sounds alone made the thought of combat real. Several voices raised in a cry against the Minotaur. For an instant, he remembered being on the field with the crowd cheering for him. A battle was no different than trying to score a touchdown—except the penalty was your life.

Vilaborg struggled to say something and hesitated. The soldier looked down at the joystick in Stuart's right hand and frowned.

"Presage?" Vilaborg glanced at the older man, his forehead scrunched.

A horrific screech thundered down at them again. Someone shouted. Another soldier hollered so loudly that Max's shivers became goose pimples. Uneasiness filled the air as they all gazed up the slope in the direction of the wild shrieking, advancing ever closer.

Mr. Dempsey ended the taut silence. "Presage, what in the world is that? I've never heard anything like it."

"Why, Stuart has told us. A barbaric, rabid Minotaur is descending upon us. We need to be strong in the face of evil, my dear Kin. This will be the first of many horrors we must conquer."

Shelby yelped. "Well, what are we supposed to do when this Minotaur comes crashing down on us, Presage? We haven't been given any weapons."

"Ah, but we have a powerful weapon, have we not, Stuart?" Presage fixed upon the shuddering teen.

Max frowned and examined Stuart.

"Huh? What do you mean?" Baffled, Stuart peered at Presage.

Presage's eyes fell to Stuart's right hand, where he still clutched the joystick. His white knuckles shook around the object. Max had no idea what the thing in Stuart's palm was, but figured it had something to do with the game Vilaborg had mentioned.

Stuart turned the joystick over in his hand, shaking his head. Max wondered what Presage was talking about. Men were fighting for their lives just over the hill, yet no one moved. He contemplated grabbing something—anything—and sprinting to assist, when Presage shut his eyes. The joystick began vibrating and a bright light emanated beneath the base.

A few feet away, a flash like that of a camera blinded him, and in its stead appeared a huge, brilliantly clad warrior. The Kin gasped at the sight of the muscular soldier. With his gleaming sword and battle chain at the ready, the combatant nodded at Stuart.

Max frowned. He didn't understand how a holograph could hurt something physical.

Atop the hill, the Minotaur came forth. Covered in blood with arrows sticking from its flesh, the beast rampaged. Tossing its huge head, the creature screamed at the night sky.

The thing loomed bigger than any linebacker he'd seen. "Holy cow," Max wheezed.

"Stuart, your responsibility is to defend the Kin. Remember, you are not alone. We're all here. But you must take the point on this offense, since you are best equipped to handle things."

The monster, wild-eyed and coated in blood, charged down at them, howling its treacherous attack.

Max had never seen anything run so fast. His legs cemented to the ground; he couldn't believe he'd wanted to charge in and fight this thing only a few minutes before.

Stuart pulled his joystick up and positioned the warrior. His palms shook. It wasn't every day you fought a real monster.

The adversaries met with a bang. The fighter Stuart controlled viciously clanged his sword against the Minotaur's axe in a savage parry. The noise left Max's ears ringing.

"Fantastic," Mr. Dempsey mouthed in wide-eyed disbelief.

The Minotaur hefted its axe away from the blade. With a grunt, he swung the weapon downward, aiming for the warrior's vulnerable side. In a flash, the warrior barred the attack. The strike made the warrior slip. In an instant, the Minotaur fell upon him, preparing to behead the stumbling man.

Stuart held his own as he furiously jerked his regulator back and forth in an effort to keep the monster at bay. He forced the warrior to his feet with a grunt.

Max gaped in awe as the soldier swung its chain. The enormous chain slammed into the Minotaur's side and wound around the creature's torso. With a yank, it was pulled toward the warrior, who aimed his sword at the creature's heart.

The Minotaur parried the warrior's blade. Metal rasped. The Minotaur yanked the chain from the warrior's grasp and threw it aside. Now the battle was even. Stuart struggled to stay each blow of the heavy axe, operating the joystick as though he were actually fighting.

The movements were more realistic than a Wii-mote's in any video game Max had ever seen. He wanted to help, but found himself taking a step back, too terrified to say or do anything.

The Minotaur grew stronger as the battle carried on. It grabbed the warrior's arm after dodging his thrust and flipped him to the ground. A crack resounded. For a moment, Max thought the warrior's back had broken. The armored soldier swung his massive blade up just in time to keep the Minotaur from striking him in half. The axe shook as the Minotaur pressed downward. The beast seemed determined to shatter the saber.

Presage stepped behind the Minotaur and aimed a large pipe at its back. The pipe blasted out a broad metallic net and entangled the Minotaur. It roared as it struggled with its steely snare. The axe dropped from its clutches and hit the ground with a thud.

Max couldn't tear his gaze away. The creature frothed at the mouth as it fought for freedom.

Stuart pounced on the opportunity. He forced the warrior to his feet. In a flourish of metal, the soldier thrust his sword into the Minotaur once, then again. A shriek pierced the night air.

Max trembled. It was a horrific wail, a scream of death. At last, the monster emitted a defeated groan and lay still before it evaporated. Seconds later, Stuart's warrior vanished as well.

They stood in a stupor for a short period. Max glanced around and his eyes landed on Shelby. She was shaken, too, as were the others. Some small part of him was relieved he wasn't the only one scared to the core.

"Excellent, young Stuart. A gritty battle," said Presage, applauding.

The Kin followed suit and clapped languidly, still in awe. Max began to wonder if they had ever been in any true danger. He'd figured Presage would have tried to defend them, but he seemed to be mistaken. He realized rather suddenly that this was all too real.

They weren't here to be chaperoned. They were here to protect themselves, their Kin, and everyone else.

Max turned to his fellow Kin.

Stuart surveyed his surroundings, rubbing his hair with both hands. "This world is my world now."

Max nodded.

CHAPTER 12

The cordless phone rang, smothered somewhere in the sheets. Nick had been in a deep slumber, and now he patted the blankets for the moaning phone he had taken to bed. He groggily glanced at the caller ID, and read, "out of area."

His mind darted to his sister. Calls this late were usually grave. He hit the green button.

"Hello?" he grumbled, his throat dry.

"You have been chosen, Nick Casey," a robotic voice said.

Nick gurgled to clear his windpipe. "For... what?"

"You already know. And you will understand more when the time has come."

The dial tone blared before his sluggish mind computed a response.

As he lay looking at the phone, his bed shook and a thick fog materialized around him. He stepped off. The hardwood floors were as slick as ice. He advanced toward the door, but slipped and crashed down, immersed in the mist. His body shook, and the room dissolved.

Spiro stood over him, prodding Nick's chest. The pounding of hooves echoed close by.

He stared at his hands, which were bound by handcuffs. A trickle of blood and sore skin made his head spin. The manacles chafed his wrists. They didn't resemble the sort of cuffs he'd seen on television or that police officers carried. Thick, heavy rust covered the shackles.

"Wake up, outlander. A fog is upon us, and this is not natural. *Thieves' fog* and we must bolt," Spiro bellowed.

Nick recalled saving the young woman, Emily Lawson. The name rang loud and clear as memories flooded his mind. He'd awakened on the grass and stumbled over a strange campsite.

He rubbed his head. Chains clanked when he moved.

"Wha-what do you mean 'thieves' fog'?"

"What I mean is that this mist is manmade or, more precisely, Nightlander-made."

Something about the way he talked made it sound like Spiro himself didn't believe their plight. "Now, we need to hasten." Spiro grabbed Nick by the arms and hoisted him to his feet.

Nick stumbled forward, trying to follow the captain. Spiro stopped abruptly and stared into Nick's eyes. The glare made Nick's blood run cold.

"Outlander, I am going to unshackle you. I'm doing this because you may be easy prey if I do not." He leaned in and whispered in his ear, "Stay close behind now."

Nick wanted to ask where the rest of the soldiers were, but decided not to. The captain was already on edge, and Nick didn't want to risk upsetting him more. He was content to be rid of the heavy cuffs and chains.

He stumbled as if wearing two left shoes behind Spiro, in an effort to keep pace. Although he considered running, Nick had no intention of losing his former captor. The idea of being alone out in the mist—with Nightlanders, thieves, and the fog—didn't sound appealing.

Nick's heart beat hard in his chest, as he glimpsed a shape out of the corner of his eye. Sprinting and panting behind Spiro, the figures emerged with greater frequency. He wondered at first if they were Clayborn and the other soldiers.

Something was not right with the shadows. They darted in and out of the gloom around him.

Spiro turned to check if he kept up, but hunger and thirst made it hard to follow. Exhaustion clouded his mind as the awful shapes contorted at close range in the dark mist. His ribcage tightened and a head rush overcame him, and he fell.

He rolled a few feet and settled onto his back. Chest heaving, Nick tried in vain to stand. Spots danced in his vision and his head swam.

"Outlander, Outlander!" Spiro cried in his booming voice, lost somewhere in the woods.

Nick strived to respond, tried desperately to call out to Spiro, but his tongue was thick and dry.

A shadow moved toward him. His vision blurred and, even squinting, he couldn't focus on the murky shape.

"S-Spiro?" he murmured.

The figure drew closer—a foreboding man wearing charcoal armor with the emblem of a skull on his chest. The dark form stalked him, sizing him up. A gleaming blade raised high in preparation to smash upon him. A black cape fluttered behind the soldier.

Nick compressed to the fetal position. How many times could one person die in a day? Had he actually died after being stabbed with that ice pick? Was this some strange afterlife? Perhaps he'd go home now. He shut his eyes, expecting the painful deathblow.

The strike never came.

He heard a crash and a yelp. Someone moaned in pain. When Nick opened his eyes, the dark man-thing curled recumbent on the ground a few feet away. His sword lay nearby.

Another shape stood close by and peered down at him. The figure walked over, reached behind Nick, and hauled him up.

Nick exhaled, the tightness in his chest and the throbbing in his head both gone.

"Thank y-you." He doubled over, panting.

"Shh, Nick, be silent and travel this way. This way is safe. Now go," the man whispered, and then walked off.

Nick stared at the back of the mysterious figure as he disappeared into the thieves' fog. A strange shock of recognition struck him. The man who'd saved him was famous—Nick couldn't believe it—or had a striking resemblance to Lucas Denon, one of the greatest poets and rock musicians in American history. Nick shook his head, trying to clear it.

The man may have passed for Denon, but the world still mourned Denon's tragic death in a car accident almost fifteen years ago. Nick thought for a brief second; Denon saving his life from some bizarre knight showed how unhinged he'd become. This all had to be an insane delusion.

Denon, or whoever he was, had said Nick's name clear as a bell. Didn't that make what Nick saw a delusion? How else would Denon know Nick's name? His temples pounded again. Regardless of the man's identity, he'd saved Nick's life. Even if he weren't real, Denon had shown Nick the way to go.

Shaking his head once more, he stumbled after his Good Samaritan.

Nick shuffled along, but he lost his sense of direction. By this point, he didn't care. His exhaustion had doubled, and he welcomed death. The fog had an eerie odor and even a creepy flavor to it. The more he inhaled this thick air, the further he became disheartened.

A morbid depression subdued him. He trudged, contemplating why he didn't just ball up and allow whatever followed him to complete its task. He pushed on, despondent and spiritless.

Wait. Maybe I've already died. The ghost of Lucas Denon had appeared to him. Perhaps he should go back and find Denon's spirit—if Nick were dead, why couldn't Denon be here, too? He stopped and laughed hysterically, raising his arms to the sky. He dropped to his knees, rubbed his face, and then rustled his hair.

He always tapped an inner strength, which seemed to materialize when he needed it. Nick never reflected much on it. As dangerous as the action was, he hadn't thought twice back in the van about saving Emily.

Weary with confusion, his inner strength now rose, and the madcap laughter ended.

Whatever lay ahead, he would deal with it. He strode forward.

CHAPTER 13

Throg guided the boat downriver.

Zach, his stomach full, nodded off into a deep and much needed sleep. With the problems he faced at home, he rarely slept. A long while had passed since his eyes felt as heavy as they did the seconds before they shut.

Hours later, he awoke revitalized. He'd had no dreams or nightmares this time. The glow of the sun warmed the deck of the ship. He smiled and stood, but a piercing pain erupted in his head and he doubled over.

"Stay calm. Let the communication happen," Throg said.

A face took shape when he closed his eyes: a man, someone he thought looked familiar. Smooth skin, dark hair, and glimmering eyes were all Zach could make out. The image tried to speak to him, but like a car radio under a bridge, the message broke up.

"We... m-morning... v-valley," the man murmured. He disappeared as abruptly as turning a television off.

Zach's vision dissolved, and then focused as he captured the experience.

"Wha-what just happened? I saw s-someone."

"Your link to the Assembly contacted you. He is trying to send a message. Did he say anything?" Throg asked, as if such correspondence was commonplace.

Zach rubbed his temples because a slight throbbing remained. "I couldn't make out most of the words. He did say something about a valley."

70

Throg patted his back. "The irritation will pass, and the next connection will be easier. Valley, eh? I hope it's not Tomb Valley. We must hike through the Cark to get there—a death trap."

"You mean the Cark Forest with all those creepy little men?"

"Aye, the Bogmen. We can't go there alone, though; too dangerous. Besides, he may not have meant Tomb Valley. We need to trek down the river a bit more. I passed a large encampment of Meridian soldiers on the way upriver. With any luck, they're still camping there."

Zach decided to lie back down and gaze at the sky as the boat chugged along. The blue heavens offered occasional spurts of marshmallow clouds. He drew in a deep breath of clean air. The aroma was of the river, fishy, warm, and sweet from the gurgling flow of fresh water.

The throbbing in his skull subsided and he sat up.

Throg smiled. "Head better now, laddie? The transmissions will become easier as you get more of them. It's a good sign. Your link is attempting to reach you, and he must be strong to do so. Keep quiet a bit now. This particular part of the river sports some surly types."

They glided on for a couple miles. Throg slowed the boat and steered to the east bank. A few bugs swarmed nearby and Zach swatted at them. Gnats kept flying around his head.

Throg whispered, "This is the last place the Meridian Brigade encamped when I traveled this way the other day. I stopped in and had some chud and tea with them. The captain's name is Spiro."

Smoke billowed through the air, hugging the treetops. They drew nearer and viewed flames dancing along the shoreline. Burning tents mixed with the fishy river—Zach's brow creased.

"Heathens," grumbled Throg.

The boat pulled up to the rocky shore and Throg leapt over the side and tied the vessel down to a thick bush. The camp had been pillaged. Several bloody figures dressed in armor lay still.

Zach stood stunned, eyes wide; he'd only seen dead bodies on television or in video games. Those men in the mud had once been alive. Flies danced around the mouth of one soldier.

"Stay on the boat, Zach. Should I not return soon, don't come looking for me. Steer the boat straight down the river. Stop before the Invunche Lake and walk east to the Dorado Path. The course will lead you to Meracuse, Meridia's capital."

"No, I'm coming with you. I don't know w-where to go. I'd get lost in these w-woods without y-you."

"Laddie, take a quick peek. Someone slaughtered this brigade. Meridia is my home. I need to find out who did this, and I'm not bringing you. Understand?"

Zach nodded, but he hated being left alone. He hoped Throg wouldn't be gone long.

CHAPTER 14

Throg strode into the encampment. Several of the Meridian soldiers still had their swords holstered. Most of them had been butchered in their sleep. To the left, a Meridian lay with his throat slit—like a sick, red grin.

Throg forged on through the grim setting. Someone moaned to his right, and he dashed over to the downed soldier.

The warrior stirred.

Throg turned the man over and put his canteen to the wounded soldier's lips. The man guzzled, opened his eyes, and looked into Throg's. Death was in his blue gaze. He had a black mole under his chin and a thick blonde beard.

"Y-you are Throg. You w-were here the other d-day."

"Yes, I'm sorry, soldier. I was not present to fight by your side."

The fallen warrior gurgled, then grasped the canteen and poured water over his face. Otherwise, he did not move. His left arm was mangled. Slick blood wept from beneath the plated steel he wore.

"Many of your brigade's weapons were not drawn," Throg said in a clear, deliberate manner.

"Aye, Throg, it w-was... they w-wore the a-armor of N-Nightlanders. They were as s-silent as l-legend says. That m-means...." The trooper gasped for air.

"I understand, soldier. Biskara's son. It has begun again."

"Then G-God-speed, dear Th-Throg. Do not let our d-deaths be in vain. You must w-warn Lord Achernar."

The soldier coughed, a spray of blood coming up. His eyes closed, and Throg knew it would be for the last time. The body went limp in his arms.

Throg set some chud on the man's breastplate and said a prayer over the soldier, "May Horologium be your guide and your shield, the truth seekers your armor, and Eridanus give you wisdom." He unfastened the dead man's sword and walked back toward the boat.

Grim remorse settled over him. These soldiers were friends of his. Families would miss them, but he could not spare time to bury any of them. Nightlanders were in the area. He had to get Zach to safety, and fast. No telling when a Nightlander might strike.

He approached the craft and Zach's head popped up.

"Who did this?" Zach asked, sounding rattled.

"The Nightlanders. They've returned."

"W-what?"

"What we spoke about earlier—that you are a Kin and Biskara returning—is true. The Nightlanders are wearing armor, which means they are ready to battle. They would never do such a thing unless they were close to full power. The skills they possess, coming into a Meridian Brigade camp undetected, and your presence, can only mean they are back and will come again."

"What now?"

"Here is a good soldier's sword. He was about your size, and I possess few extra weapons."

He handed the sword to Zach, who paused before accepting the gift. Throg watched the Kin hold the hilt across his body with both hands and study it. The scabbard had been stained with blood, but the blade shimmered clean.

"I need to go through the area now to make sure I do not leave any survivors behind. Stay low and keep the sword ready. I will return in a short time." He turned and started back toward the camp.

"Throg?"

"Yes?"

"I've never held a sword before."

"Don't worry. We've all lived other lives."

Throg gazed at the scattered bodies and burning soil, and pursued the dreary business of confirming no one remained alive. He made his way through the camp, inspecting each body, and pulled a piece of chalk out of a pouch on his belt to mark the armored bodies as he moved along. After he was done, he counted fifty-three fallen.

Not one had a pulse.

Some are missing, he thought. At least sixty men had been in camp when he'd supped with them. Captain Spiro had not been among the dead, either, which heartened him a little. Perhaps his companion had escaped.

Another option loomed. Spiro may not have been with his men. The Nightlanders may have captured him and taken him for questioning. Such an outcome would not have surprised Throg. The thought made him sick with fear for his friend. He removed a piece of chud from his satchel for each of the fallen men, and rested it on their chests or in their hands. They would need it in the afterlife.

His work done, he returned to the boat.

Zach leapt over the side to meet him. The Kin didn't say anything as he helped Throg untie the vessel. Zach took the rope from him and wound it.

"Get on," said Throg.

Zach nodded and hopped inside.

Throg paused, giving one last look at the destroyed camp and dead bodies. Would that he had time to bury them, but with Nightlanders on the move, they couldn't afford to stop for long. With a heavy heart, he pushed the boat out to the river and hoisted himself aboard.

"I'm not quite sure what to say," Zach mumbled.

"Nothing to say. I was hoping we would have more time to organize, to get back to Lord Achernar, and reunite with your Kin. The Nightlanders have wiped out a Meridian Brigade. We are at war. I'm not certain who's in charge of this army of the Nightlanders, but I recall last year a fellow by the name of Malefic Cacoethes creating quite a stir up in the Canopus Hills. I heard his name a few times when I stopped to sup with Meridian soldiers, but I sensed no fear of a Nightlander uprising."

He paused. "We'll need to abandon the boat soon. This river is a main path and leads to the Invunche Lake. Both are too easy for an ambush. Time to go on foot."

"How dangerous are these woods?"

"Well, outside of the prowling Nightlanders, the woodland is as perilous as any on Earth. Instead of bears, the wealds offer some other creatures, monsters and such, which we need to avoid. Not like the Cark, of course, but we must be careful just the same."

They traveled without speaking for a while. Several Pegasi erupted from the brush to the right. They neighed, their bright white wings flapping as they soared into the woods. Half a dozen otter-like mammals emerged to the left, scrambled to land, and scampered away.

"Something's out there," Throg whispered, raising his brow.

They cruised a few more minutes. Disliking the silence, Throg shifted. He grabbed one of his weapons, a sturdy long-shafted pike, and scanned the thick brush on the east shore of the river.

"There's a good spot to cast," he said and pointed to a clearing ahead. He steered toward the place.

The boat jerked and knocked Zach to the floor.

"Dang it all. A wishpoosh," Throg called out in disgust.

"A... a w-wishpoosh?"

"A man-eater. We need to get to shore, now!"

"How can you tell? I can't see anything," Zach said as the craft continued to shake.

Throg couldn't reply. A loud crunch echoed as the vessel flipped over and they were hurled into the cold river.

CHAPTER 15

Zach struggled back up to the surface and spat out a mouthful of water, grateful the river was calm as he swam to land. He still held to the heavy sword Throg had given him, and considered dropping it since the blade weighed him down, but then he pictured a giant man-eating monster and decided otherwise. Besides, he didn't know what was waiting for him on shore.

Every stroke was more difficult than the last. Water sluiced into his mouth, making him cough. Finally, he squished into the muddy bottom beneath his shoes. He slipped and sank with each step. Out of breath and exhausted, he made it ashore.

He turned in the mud and spotted the capsized boat floating away. He scanned the murky water and found Throg paddling across the river. Zach stood and hurried over to where his friend would beach. He waded out and offered a hand to Throg.

The wishpoosh thrashed close behind, snapping its huge fangs and lifting claws the size of hunting knives as it surfaced just yards from the shore.

"Look out!" Zach backed away, watching as Throg fought the enormous creature, which looked like a giant beaver.

The man buried his pike into the monster's wet fur.

A vehement growl pealed to the side of Zach. Swimming toward him was another wishpoosh, its fangs forming a morbid sneer. Zach glanced at Throg, who had managed to pull himself back ashore.

Wishpoosh

"Take off for the woods," yelled his friend. "The wishpoosh won't follow for long."

Zach didn't hesitate to turn and run. Listening to Throg's advice was his best bet, though he hated to leave his companion even as the wishpoosh flared out of the channel.

Zach raced through the forest for several minutes before he paused. The woodland behind him was still. He panted a few moments and waited, hoping Throg's friendly figure would emerge from the thicket. Guilt consumed him; he had left Throg behind to battle at least two of those wishpoosh, if not more.

He decided to double back to the river. Perhaps Throg needed his help.

Zach jogged and passed a grand tree with numerous fruits hanging from its limbs. Apples, oranges, plums, and pears protruded from its many branches. Other strange trees marked the landscape.

For a while, he forged onward, though he hadn't thought he'd run so far. Soon he came upon a clearing, and as he drew closer, sounds emanated from behind a thick oak tree south of him. He poked his head around the trunk to identify the noise.

A shiver raced down his spine at the sight before him: a fence made out of bones.

Inside sat a small log cabin—a plain dwelling, except it rested on a pair of massive chicken legs. The building wobbled. The front resembled the face of a chicken, with two windows serving as its eyes, and a single door shaped like a beak. The cabin spun again, and repeated the process over and over. The chicken-house seemed to be looking for something.

Zach watched for a few moments, and decided to move away from the bizarre sight. As if wishpoosh weren't enough, he didn't want to get attacked by a ferocious bird-like house, too.

He backtracked and stopped at the large fruit tree he'd passed earlier. A heavy wind roared, whipping leaves and dust through the air. A terrible screeching grew around him. Timber creaked and groaned.

He spotted a whirling movement in the sky, and scanned overhead. Several figures circled above the trees, emitting horrible shrieks.

They had no legs and their tattered gray robes flowed from their bodies. Their gruesome faces contorted around their crooked chops and dark eye sockets. Boils, black as rot, circled their eyes and mouths. The sound of flies buzzing surged in Zach's ears.

The beautiful fruit tree began to putrefy. Fruit dropped around him and crashed with a ghastly odor. Oranges broke open on impact. Green gunk burst from them, and several black spiders scurried out. The lush grass below him crinkled and turned yellow. Zach stumbled away from the tree.

"You are doomed. You will suffer," the forms above screeched.

Without a second glance, Zach bolted from the rotting fruit tree. He shoved bushes aside as he ran. Branches slapped him, but he did not stop. The howling monsters and sound of creaking trees followed him.

A pair of floating hands blocked his path, forcing him to skid to a halt. One of the hands pulled a saber from the mist. It brandished the blade, ready to strike Zach down.

"You dare confront us?" a voice wailed from the direction of the hands.

He held up the sword given to him by Throg, hoping he could use it. The opposing blade descended upon him. Instinctively, he blocked the hand's first strike and then started a counterattack, forcing the hand back.

Throg had been right: sword fighting came naturally to him, as if he were fully trained. Rather than running forward, he advanced with one foot behind the other. His legs and body flowed beneath him. He blocked a second blow and lunged for another strike.

The haunting figures flew closer and whirled around the battle. When one dove at him, Zach swung the blade, ducked, and struck the trailing end of its cloak. The creature didn't seem to notice.

"You dare. You dare. You dare," the creatures chanted and moaned.

Zach pushed forward in a blazing attack and drove the hands backward. He feinted right and jabbed left. The hands tried to block his offense and failed. A screech came from where he stabbed the empty hand, and crimson liquid drooled from the cut.

"Take that," he cried. "Now back off! I'm only passing through."

The hands vanished along with their blade. Above, the treacherous creatures continued their shrieks. Zach turned to them and readied his sword.

"She is coming. All is lost. You are doomed," they crowed. Then, they dove as one.

Too many for him to fight alone, Zach ran again. Not ten yards later, he stopped dead in his tracks. Hovering in front of him was a mortar with a large pestle jutting out. Something crunched behind him. He spun, his weapon raised high.

A monstrous hag stared at him. She smirked, flashing teeth made of a bright metal, blood dripping from them. Her face was gnarled and wrinkled, and a gigantic wart close to bursting pulsed on the side of her nose. Hair like black wire crept from under the rotting rags on her head.

Baba Yaga

The repulsive witch strode forward. Her tall and stick-thin figure glided. From beneath a mound of cloaks, her hunched back protruded. She

glared at him, her leathery skin oozing yellow pus, her matted hair whipping in the gust, her sharp snout twisting as she drew closer.

She fixed her malevolent gaze on him and pointed her lengthy, clawed fingers forward."You have returned. Were you sent to me, or have you come of your own accord?"

Returned? Zach did not answer, sensing his response would be linked to his safety.

"Answer me!" she roared.

"I have come of my own accord."

"I see," she grumbled, her grotesque, crooked teeth dribbling gore. She strode forward, her bones creaking with each step. The howling monsters whirled by her.

"You come to death willingly." She studied him for a few seconds. "Your fate lies on the other side of the Shattered Woods... if you live." The witch then droned in an unrecognizable language.

A noose dropped around his neck and snapped him off the ground. The cackling figures circled his dangling body. He swiped at the invisible snare to no avail.

When he started to black out, the noose loosened its grip, and he crashed down. As he caught his breath, he looked at the soil. The dead grass was now a vibrant green with several colorful flowers spread out. Beautiful music had supplanted the screeching chorus of the whirling creatures. He gazed into the direction of the witch.

She was clawing at the blue eyes twirling around her. The familiar voices spoke to him again. Their presence lit the world—bark changed color, becoming spectacular hues of gold, orange, and green. *The Fugues.*

"Leave now," said the comforting voices. "She will not follow. Throg is safe and searching for you east of here. She has cast the nightmare charm on you. You must go to Baku, the dream-eater, to be healed. Quickly now."

He walked off in a daze, leaving the screaming hag behind.

"Biskara is coming," the witch wailed. "He will eat you whole, young Kin. He will tear the flesh from your bones."

Sweet, reassuring music replaced the angry cries. Zach hummed along as a wonderful foggy tingling in his head made everything seem so far away. He paused to smell a bushel of strange sunset-colored flowers.

"Keep going. You must go to the dream-eater."

He lumbered forward, his sword out in front of him for some time, the blade weightless. Trees sang and moved about him in the lovely wind. Zach was so at peace, he wondered why he was walking at all when he could just lie down and sleep. Yet he kept trudging forth. Nothing hurt. No one bothered him. It was pure bliss, until a crashing in the underbrush snapped him out of his tranquil state.

"Zach, thank the druids I found you," Throg shouted as he ran over. "Are you okay?"

"Yes, I am fine. I encountered a witch." He touched his head, a little dazed. The sword hung heavy again.

"Witch? Here in these parts? They prefer the Cark Woods."

"The Fugues appeared and rescued me." Sadness crept over Zach as the dream evaporated. He realized he had been saved, again, by someone else. Part of him wished he'd been able to fend off the hag himself.

"It's a good thing they showed up. Most witches are powerful here."

"The Fugues told me I had a nightmare charm put on me by the witch and that I needed to find Baku."

"The nightmare charm? She must have slapped it on you when the Fugues appeared and realized you would escape. I'll summon the dream-eater next time you sleep. We need to travel farther east now. I don't know if the Nightlanders are still around."

His brow furrowed. "She also said my fate lies beyond the Shattered Woods."

Throg froze for a minute, seeming to ponder this comment. "The Shattered Woods is an ancient name for the Cark. Most witches on Azimuth are evil, but if you answer their questions correctly, they're forced to be honest. Then they'll try to kill you."

"Does that mean we have to go through the Cark?" Dread knotted Zach's stomach. The way Throg had described it, the Cark was not somewhere he wanted to be.

"Aye, perhaps pass Tomb Valley to get to the Canopus Hills."

"How did you escape from the wishpoosh?"

"Dang wishpoosh. They usually live closer to the Invunche Lake. They surprised me. Just as some witches moved from the Cark, the wishpoosh probably migrated upriver. The evil creatures of Azimuth tend to act strange when Biskara comes into power. I fled the wishpoosh the same way you did. I ran off in a different direction to lead them away. They do not stray far from the water."

"The witch screamed that Biskara would tear the flesh off my Kin body and that I had 'returned.'" A tremor wracked him. This was nothing like outsmarting bullies at school. This was *real*. The swordfight, the monsters, even his physical changes all pointed to the same thing—if Zach died here, he *died*.

"She said that? How odd."

A thought occurred to him. "Hey, Throg, do you think Biskara might have contacted the witch for an alliance?"

"Could be. Wouldn't be the first time. We'll need to keep a sharp eye out for anyone else, especially Nightlanders. Their magic is dangerous. Legend says they come in thieves' fog."

Zach nodded. He sheathed his blade and they scampered into the forest. A few birds screeched overhead.

CHAPTER 16

Shelby approached Stuart and patted him on the back. She glanced at the charcoal drawing on his leather jerkin. It looked vaguely familiar, but she couldn't place it.

"Way to go, Stuart. A tremendous battle," Shelby said.

Riley jumped closer. "Yeah, awesome!"

"Thanks. I'm a video game nut back home. My mom is always on my case about playing too much. Who'd have thought how handy that skill would be?" Stuart grinned.

"This is just the beginning, I'm afraid," Presage said as he walked away from another soldier. The two had been talking for almost ten minutes. "We must head to Meracuse now. Lord Achernar awaits us. The uprising has begun, and Nightlanders have circled the city of Degei, the main port of trade for Meridia."

The camp began packing for the journey to Meracuse. Several soldiers wounded by the Minotaur were being placed on wagons. Tents were broken down and rolled up, food was stored, barrels of water hefted onto carts, and men suited up.

Smiling, Boozer approached Stuart. "So the Minotaur lost his firs' conflict. Way to go, kiddo. Ya weren't fooling when ya said ye could play the game. Now I've got to find me a different warrior to be undefeated with." He laughed.

"Anytime, anywhere," Stuart said, smirking.

Shelby smiled. Everyone seemed in high spirits.

As soldiers took down the camp, Vilaborg strode over. Even with everyone's help, breaking camp and moving out would take a while.

"So, my dear Kin," Vilaborg said, "your interceptors, along with Boozer and Sol here, will be traveling with you at all times. Of course, soon you'll be surrounded by a brigade for the sojourn to the capital. Lord Achernar wished us to be your personal guard. I have chosen two other soldiers, two of the best here, to join us—Dukas Rendle and Crater Mathers. The march will be short, about three hours. When we arrive at the headquarters, Lord Achernar will greet you and explain his strategy. Mr. Dempsey, you are welcome to join the Kin."

Mr. Dempsey nodded. "Anything I can do to help, Vilaborg."

Barrick handed out leather backpacks. "Each contains a bunch of useful goodies. Don't lose these."

Now that Shelby was accustomed to him, Barrick didn't seem as terrifying as before. In fact, he was quite a nice guy.

He clasped her on the shoulder and murmured low enough for only her to hear. "Shelby, while we ride, keep Miss Emily company. I fear she may be scared. No Kin should return home and be terrified."

"Return?" Shelby asked, but Barrick had turned away to help deconstruct Presage's tent.

She inspected the contents of her bag: chud, canteens, blankets, a teakettle with cups, knives, and a compass were the featured items. The pack weighed heavier than most she'd carried before, but now that she was stronger, she slung it over her shoulder with ease, amazed at how effortless it was.

The two new soldiers, Dukas and Crater, arrived. Dukas was slender and fair-skinned, and would have been a handsome individual had his nose not been broken and a pair of his teeth knocked out. Across his back, he shouldered a claymore, and a short sword was strapped to his hip.

Crater was also tall and fair, but his hair was darker than Dukas', and he carried a crossbow and knife. Both bore several other weapons. Vilaborg helped set them on the ground.

"Kin, gather around. These here are your weapons. You'll find you are skilled in certain areas, which mirror your Aulic Assembly link. As Presage explained earlier, you inherited specific abilities when you came through the mobile portal, though you all will carry a primary blade."

He motioned them closer and resumed. "For instance, Emily, your counterpart is Elita Ezmer. She is quite the archer, one of the best in Meridia. Your skills will be similar to hers at your age. You may need to shoot a few to sharpen up, but you'll tap your link's expertise to a certain extent."

Vilaborg fixed his gaze on Max. "Macklin Morrow is an excellent all-around soldier and adept with a long sword." He hefted an elegant blade up and placed it in Max's hands. "Take some time to get used to its weight."

He motioned to Stuart, who approached. "Stuart, Satchel Spool is your link and has never misfired a hand-cannon. He also can handle a scimitar rather well." Stuart lifted the two weapons from the pile. "Take care when you aim with the cannon. The backlash is pretty harsh."

He turned to Shelby. "Yours was difficult to narrow down. Let's just say Bianca Saddler is good at almost everything. You will carry a rapier and a crossbow."

The rapier was heavier than Shelby expected, and the sheath was of white leather embroidered with leaves and vines. The hilt of the blade shone in silver, with gold and bronze leaves interwoven, creating a hard shell to protect her hand. She gathered the two weapons and belted the saber to her side. If the beast approached her now, he'd tremble and cower in fear.

Presage smiled at Riley. "Rowan Letty is an excellent rider and also a fierce adversary with many weapons, in particular a slingshot she has patented."

Riley accepted the slingshot and a bag of metal bullets, as well as a rapier.

Shelby spied her friend examining the specialized weapon, carved from bone with steel inlaid for extra strength. The bed of the slingshot was soft leather and fitted each bullet snugly.

Vilaborg finished handing out the weapons, and they all packed up their newfound belongings. Some, like Max and Shelby, took time feeling their armaments and getting to know them.

Shelby glanced at Stuart as he studied the hand-cannon. When he put his fingers around the handle, the weapon started humming, and a small red light switched on at the nozzle.

"Be careful with that now, laddie," Cumber said. "As I told ya earlier, it can be very powerful. The nozzle will control the pressure of the blas'. The more ya turn the mechanism clockwise, the more po'ent the blas'. On low, ye can blow a candle ou' from across the room." He winked.

Stuart smiled. "Thanks, Cumber. Why don't we all have hand-cannons?"

"Ah, good question. Because of sorcology, it will shoot on low for anyone, but to be po'ent, the wielder mus' bear the proper inner-energy component. Turns ou' mos' folks don' possess it. Satchel Spool is the only member of the Assembly tha' can operate a hand-cannon on full power. I'm one o' a few in this company tha' can, along with Sculptor."

Stuart moved in closer. "You mentioned sorcology. What exactly do you mean by that?"

Shelby paused to listen.

Cumber said, "Sorcology is technology enhanced by the grea' arts, more commonly known as magic on Earth. They are a strong combination."

"I also noticed the skies are clear," Stuart pointed out, "and that we're riding instead of being picked up by a helicopter or a truck or something. I don't see any advanced technology outside of some weapons and games."

"Well, we do share a fleet of star darts, opera'ed by the United Forces, but they're called into action only as a las' measure if our planet is being attacked. Ya need to be aware, the First Grea' War with Biskara and his son, Hideux, was one of the bloodies' in this universe. When Hideux was defea'ed, the Aulic Assembly and the mentors, along with the other grea' leaders on Azimuth, agreed tha' a better way to live needed to be found. Since then, we abide by a code. The United Forces is supplied by the world to protect it from outsiders, and they run the star darts. If the battle sways in the Nightlanders' favor, the United Forces will respond. But they are mos'ly an aerial assault, with a few smaller groups of highly trained ground soldiers."

Cumber stretched his back.

"So, although we enjoy many o' the pleasures and some weapons of technology and sorcology, cer'ain things — all voted on by the people o' Azimuth — we live withou'."

He paused, took a swig out of his canteen, and continued. "Millions o' lives were lost against Hideux. As the mos' powerful son, he did no' simply attemp' to take over Meridia or Azimuth. He wan'ed the whole southern hemisphere of the universe, and he wouldn' have stopped there. Lord Achernar the First defea'ed him after a long war. We were losing because Biskara was involved. Then the truth seekers showed up and the Silver Sphere was crea'ed. Tha' was when the tide turned. I'll tell ya more later on, though we need ta ge' on the road."

It was all very interesting, but as Cumber walked away, Shelby wondered what was so bad about technology. On Earth, people got along just fine in general. *Then again, we don't have evil beings trying to take over.*

Max unsheathed his sword and swung the long blade effortlessly through the air a few times.

Shelby unleashed her rapier and did the same thing. She looked over at Max and smiled. Mr. Dempsey approached her.

Max strolled over to them after she caught his eye. "Hi, you look like you're pretty good with the blade."

"Almost as talented as you." Shelby offered a shy smirk.

Barrick trotted over. "Mr. Dempsey, can I have a word with you?"

"Sure."

Barrick steered Mr. Dempsey a little way from where the Kin prepared for the journey ahead. Meanwhile, other soldiers in the camp finished taking down tents, dousing fires, and packing carts, horses, and wagons. They were nearly ready.

Shelby motioned to Max and the two sidled closer to Barrick and Mr. Dempsey to listen in.

"Well, sir," Barrick said, "I wanted to check how you were doing. To the Kin, part of them is at home here. You came through the portal and are not a

Kin. We have been blessed with your presence, but Presage wanted me to make sure you weren't having any anxiety or irregular feelings."

Mr. Dempsey placed his hand on Barrick's shoulder. "No, although this is a bit of a shock, I am fine. But thank you for asking. I'm comfortable around kids. I know Shelby, and I want to look after her."

"Well, Mr. Dempsey, Shelby and her Kin may be the ones looking after you. You see, since you have no link to connect with here, no skills have transferred over, though you probably sense greater strength than you did on Earth."

"I'll be fine. Presage mentioned these Nightlanders have surfaced and have attacked a main port?"

Barrick *tisk*ed and shook his head. "Yes, horrible news. I think we all held out hope it was a false alarm, but Malefic raised an army, mostly of Lampurians, and reports are this group is of considerable size. The army will pick up steam as evil beings come out of the woodwork to join them. With Biskara's involvement, war is inevitable. We need to return to Meracuse as quickly as possible, locate the Assembly, and operate the Silver Sphere to find Biskara and summon the truth seekers. If Malefic reaches Meracuse before us and takes control of the Sphere, legend has it he'd have the power to unleash Biskara on the mortal plane."

The sound of pounding hooves emanated from the forest ahead of them. Shelby and Max scampered over to Barrick. Both left their blades unsheathed, ready in case of an attack.

"Sounds like a lot of horses," said Shelby.

A horde of glorious warriors burst from the thicket, the early morning sun glaring on their polished armor. Several of the Meridian soldiers froze and gazed up at the newcomers in awe. The man leading the swarm pulled his imposing steed right up to Barrick.

He leapt off the charger, his long golden locks swished. He stood in full confidence, peering down into Barrick's face with piercing blue eyes based with a chiseled jaw. He extended his herculean arm.

Barrick shook his hand.

"Milo Morgante, now yer a pleasure for my weary eyes. At least I hope so."

"Biskara has arrived, Barrick. The Stonecoats and I are prepared for battle," Milo boomed.

"So, you're here to serve Lord Achernar?" Barrick shifted his feet, his eyebrow twitching.

"No need to ask a stupid question. I will aid no politician or self-proclaimed royal family. I always said I'll fight alongside Bianca and the Aulic Assembly if Azimuth is in danger. The time has come."

"The Assembly is missing. The Kin have been summoned," Barrick said.

Milo nodded and fixed his authoritative gaze on Shelby and Max. "Then we'll fight with the Kin. Where is Presage? I need to speak to him."

"He is at the head of the camp about fifty yards down the road."

Milo motioned a few hand signals to the Stonecoats. He mounted his pearly steed and spun the reins in the direction Barrick had indicated. The horse snorted and tossed its mane as it started through the muddy camp.

"Milo?" Barrick called out.

The Stonecoat stopped and turned.

Barrick thumped his chest once. "I'm as proud as a Tuskarian can be to ride with you and the Stonecoats."

Milo dipped his head down and galloped off, leaving the other Stonecoats behind.

Barrick turned to the Kin and beamed. "Milo is the greatest warrior of our generation. And these men here are the Stonecoats, the best soldiers assembled today."

"They are not Meridian soldiers?" Shelby asked.

"In his younger days, Milo was a Meridian. He does not see eye-to-eye with Lord Achernar. He signed up with the United Forces, and then went on his own for adventure as the leader of the Stonecoats. The Stonecoats, a brotherhood that has been around for hundreds of years, have always been loyal to the Aulic Assembly. But make no mistake, Milo and the Stonecoats serve no one." Barrick pumped his fist in the air.

Sculptor joined the conversation. "Renegade heathens is what they are, shunning responsibility for adventure."

Mr. Dempsey waved his hand toward some Stonecoats that unpacked. "Well, they certainly don't resemble heathens. They look in tremendous shape, and their armor sparkles."

"Sure, sure," Sculptor said. "They come thundering into a Meridian camp, barking orders after having their armor polished by the Bogmen or some other poor souls for a bit of chud. They live life in careless abandon like a big men's club, and then they expect Lord Achernar, whom they despise, to open the red curtain for them."

"Aye," Barrick said. "They march to a different tune, Sculptor, but the Stonecoats could wipe out an entire Nightlander regiment. Do you remember your history? The Battle at Canopus Hills against the Nightlanders was legendary. Blindsided and ambushed, the Meridian Army faced defeat, until the Stonecoats stormed in and beat back the Nightlander troop within an hour, allowing our soldiers to retreat and then launch a counterattack." Barrick shook his fist in the air again.

"They may cost us allies, friend. They're feuding with the Battleswine, but Lord Achernar is negotiating with the Battleswine in hopes they'll join us. When they find out Milo and the Stonecoats are marching with us...."

"They will still join us. The Battleswine are well aware the Stonecoats are in good relations with the Aulic Assembly. We are talking about the

Nightlanders here, Sculptor. Azimuth will unite. Adversaries will coexist, if only to battle the minions of Biskara."

Max beamed at the Stonecoats, his eyes wide. "Wow, these guys look awesome."

Shelby and Max met the Stonecoats' stares. Their armor glistened in the sunlight, a blend of gold and silver mixed with rich, dark brown leather. Shelby had dreamed of such armor as a little girl, and this exceeded her images. A white knight from Arthurian legend couldn't hold a candle to these guys. Their helms shone brilliantly, each forged with the Stonecoat eagle sigil atop the brow.

"All right." Sculptor patted Max and Shelby on their backs. "We need to get you packed up now. We will be leaving in a moment."

They returned to the rest of the Kin. Riley twirled her slingshot, and Stuart and Emily engaged in conversation while packing their bags. Shelby was glad Emily opened up to someone. She decided to give them space while they rode.

"You guys won't believe this, but I slung this pellet thirty yards and hit the tree I aimed for," Riley exclaimed, pointing in the direction she had thrown. She tilted her head back a bit and smirked.

"I believe you," Max said. "I can handle this sword with as much ease as the lacrosse stick I grew up with."

Stuart walked over with his backpack fastened. "Well, let's get going. I'm anxious to learn what Lord Achernar has to say and how we can help."

"I'm with you," agreed Shelby.

The rest of them scurried to retrieve their new belongings. Shelby slung the crossbow across her back and sheathed her saber. Having the blade by her side seemed natural, almost as if she'd been missing half her arm her entire life and hadn't known it until now. She smiled at Max, who had strapped the long sword scabbard to his back. He wore his pack over the saber and was still able to unsheathe it in a flash.

Barrick called the Kin over.

"Okay, now, not only will you be riding with us, but Presage has asked Milo and the Stonecoats to accompany our group to Meracuse along the Dorado Path. Let's saddle up and head out."

The five Kin and Mr. Dempsey mounted their horses, joined by Vilaborg, Casselton, Sculptor, Cumber, Boozer, Sol, and the two new Meridian soldiers, Dukas and Crater. Within a few minutes, Milo and the Stonecoats swarmed through and enveloped the Kin, Milo taking the lead at the forefront with Barrick.

"Let's march," Milo cried out.

They traveled at a good pace and in unison like a well-disciplined army. Previously, Shelby had been uneasy in a saddle, but now she was at home riding the dappled charger they'd given her. The group fell in line with the rest of the soldiers, and together, they created an enormous column of riders, wagons, carts, and mounts.

Tall oaks lined the muddy path on both sides. The vegetation alongside the road was thick, and several odd-looking birds rested on branches. One in particular had an owl's body with a hawk's head.

Sculptor caught her observing and said, "Those are called howls, my favorite birds. They're the easiest to train as messengers... very smart. Earth creatures interbred with ours, and the results are amazing."

Shelby also spotted a pack of checkered ferrets scurrying along, trying their best to keep up. They chattered and squeaked. About a mile down the path, they vanished into the underbrush.

The pace of the army quickened from a canter to a gallop. The course was wide enough for the horses and wagons to move along at more than a lumbering clip.

Shelby glanced at Mr. Dempsey, who rode next to Emily. His head tilted in close to Emily, focused on her word. *Good. Emily seems to be having the hardest time with our summoning. Mr. Dempsey is a great person for her to talk to.*

After an hour of riding, Milo halted and waved his arm back. The Stonecoats followed his signal and moved into action, forming a wall around the Kin. Barrick appeared confused, looking to Milo for an explanation. The Meridian Army ahead continued riding, and after a short pause, Barrick called out to them.

Milo said to Barrick, "I heard the cracking of branches and what sounded like a sword being drawn."

Barrick raised an eyebrow. "Milo, no disrespect, but with all of us riding at a gallop, you heard a sword unsheathe in the foliage?"

At that moment, a distinct snap erupted from the right side of the forest. The Stonecoats all drew their swords in unison with one large swish. Barrick and the Meridian soldiers followed suit. Up ahead, one of the soldiers shouted.

A wind swirled in, succeeded by a fog that seeped from the forest on both sides. The smoke cloistered the Kin, separating them from the rest of the group. It smelled awful, not at all like the mist around the lake near Shelby's home.

"Thieves' fog. On your guard, Stonecoats," Milo hollered.

Dark soldiers, with black leather masks and a skull emblazoned on their chests, stormed from the thicket. Each brandished steel. Axes were held high, swords pointed forth, and maces swung to the ready.

Alongside Shelby, Dukas was snapped down off his horse by a net thrown from a handful of the dark warriors. Without hesitation, she pulled out her crossbow and fired at the Nightlanders that converged on the struggling Dukas.

Behind them, several more bodies emerged from the shadows and the thickening mist. Savage tribesmen charged forward, a sea of war-painted faces bouncing up and down, feathers of every color tied into their matted hair and beards. White paint covered their tan chests. Most had spears, and some had hatchets and bows.

Sculptor hissed, "The Zumbaki have joined the Nightlanders. Unbelievable."

As several of the Zumbaki lunged at Shelby, they were cut off by members of the Stonecoats, whose skill thwarted their efforts. She was dazzled by how well the specialized knights battled. The one beside her parried an attack as if swatting a fly. He stabbed men through their leather armor as they came, felling them as fast as they closed in. Milo galloped across the ambush, shouting orders and fending off Nightlanders and Zumbaki in droves.

Riley, surrounded by Stonecoats herself, placed silver pellets in her slingshot and started picking off the attacking horde. Many of the bullets she used were covered in points, which broke skin and bone alike.

Shelby joined Riley and aimed her crossbow into the crowd of marauding Nightlanders. She loaded a bolt and launched it, hitting a Nightlander square in the heart. From atop her mount, no one could stop her.

Emily cantered up from behind and shot arrows with deadeye accuracy. The three girls dropped men faster and faster as they got used to their new weapons. Emily's wooden missiles whistled through the air, smashing into each target she aimed at.

Stuart set his hand-cannon on high and blasted away at the Nightlander and Zumbaki armies. Every blast sent men scurrying for shelter. Beside him, Max used his sword and hacked at the men who attempted to pull him from his saddle.

The main army with Presage was coming back now, and Shelby's resolve fortified when the first armored soldier slammed into the wall of Nightlanders. The armored soldiers came in a wave of yells, curses, and battle cries.

The soldiers knocked the assailants back in droves, repelling their ambush. A maniacal cry roared from the foliage, causing Barrick and Max to pause. For a second, the Nightlanders gained an upper hand. The moment they did, Barrick began striking at them again.

"By the Trifids, it can't be." Barrick exhaled heavily.

Max yelled as he fought off a Zumbaki, "What? What is it?"

"Disembowelers." Dread laced Barrick's voice.

"Disembowelers? That doesn't sound good," Mr. Dempsey said. He was trying to fight with a broken lance, clubbing those who came near Shelby.

"But, tha' can' be," Cumber said. "They're extinct. They haven' been seen in years." He swung his blade, cleaving through a Nightlander's neck. Yanking it back, he and his maple mount were sprayed in blood. The Nightlander collapsed and another took its place.

"I know what they sound like," Barrick said. "Glimpsed one at the animal grounds as a youth. It was an old one, but that was how it sounded. I will never forget it."

Even Milo appeared concerned as howling blared from the forest.

Max had one sword out in his right hand and a long dirk in his left. From atop his horse, he was death to anyone who came close.

Several Disembowelers ran out of the brush with collars around their necks. They were monstrous, with rabid hyena heads foaming at the jaw, while their multiple arms spun on each side like windmills with knifelike claws, cutting through the smoky air. Branches broke in their wake as they surged close to the ground on large goat-like hooves.

Milo leapt off his steed, lifted his shield higher, and charged the Disembowelers, meeting a few head on. Several of the Stonecoats rushed to their leader's side. At once, Stuart, Emily, Riley, and Shelby fired their long-range weapons in support. The hideous beasts were lethal, lashing at the Stonecoats with a steady downpour of six arms and sets of claws.

As the focus of the battle shifted to the Disembowelers, several Nightlanders poured in behind the Kin. Men screamed as they charged.

Shelby whirled and aimed her crossbow. Sharp pain flowered on the back of her head. Her vision swam as she was dragged down from her horse. Stunned, she could move no more than a hair's breadth as a Nightlander carried her from the fray.

She looked on helplessly as Max fought against the Nightlander ambush. He struggled to advance his steed past the raging swarm, then dismounted and leapt, soaring over the crowd of fallen Nightlanders. Soon she could only make out snippets of the battle. Trees were in her way, and she was too dazed to fight back.

Shelby spied Max as he rolled athletically behind the Nightlanders and ran into the forest after her. She caught sight of him as he burst through the trees. Part of her felt relieved, but most of her was terrified.

She snagged glimpses of Milo, fighting the Disembowelers with ferocity. Suddenly, the Stonecoat leader turned his head, and Shelby met his eyes in an attempt to call for help. He broke away from the Disembowelers at once.

"Barrick," Milo yelled. "I'm off after the captured Kin. The Stonecoats will defend the rest of you to the death."

That was the last she saw of him before the forest closed around her.

CHAPTER 17

Zach shuffled along, tired and in a haze. Ghosts wailed overhead. Demons sneered at him from the shadows. Nauseous, he vomited as insidious shapes laughed in fits of haunting tease from the darkness. Gray, rat-like creatures darted in and converged on his puke, fighting over the scraps. Zach wiped his mouth and stumbled forward.

In the path ahead, the hag's hideous features and bony fingers pointed at him.

"You are mine now, Kin. No Fugues to save you this time," she screeched.

He buried his face into his hands and dropped to his knees. When he opened his eyes again, the gloom around him was silent. Movement ahead in the murkiness prompted him to reach for his sword, but the sheath was empty. He rose to his feet.

A deep voice rumbled, "You have traveled a long distance, young man."

Moonlight peered through clouds above, creating an eerie glow while illuminating the trees and woods. The demons and witch had vanished, no more rats scurried on the ground, and he didn't feel as sick as he had moments ago.

A magnificent animal walked toward Zach. The creature cocked its huge, white lion's head as it approached; its stallion's body was sure and strong. Its broad tiger paws treaded with a delicate touch to the soil. The hybrid paused before him and examined him with brilliant golden eyes, circling Zach little by little. The beast's coat glistened with shades of black, tan, and cream.

Zach was too mesmerized to move.

Baku

"Yes, a tremendously long way you have traveled to return. You are a Kin?"

"Yes, I'm Zach. Return?"

"I sense Meridian blood in your veins. I am Baku. You are in trouble, dear Kin. This is a powerful nightmare, a curse thrown upon you. I know this witch. She is strong and experienced. Eating this nightmare for you may be risky."

"You are the dream-eater the Fugues spoke of?"

Baku studied him. "I am." The dream-eater continued to circle Zach with regal grace. "I will need you to concentrate on the witch who placed this spell upon you. Think only of her. Push everything else away. Do you understand me?"

Zach nodded and closed his eyes. He thought of the repulsive hag, the yellow pus oozing down her face, and her blood-drenched, twisted metal teeth. He opened his eyes.

Baku was gone now and she stood before him again.

"You think you can reverse my spells, poor Kin? You are doomed, and I'll eat your soul as a sacrifice to Biskara." She wailed a monstrous laugh.

He dropped to his knees again, weak and powerless. Pressure pressed on his head, all movements suspended, and his vision clouded. She was using some sort of sorcery to force him down, he was sure of it.

She pulled an axe out from her tattered robes.

What odd grace for such an ugly creature.

She stalked him and lifted the hatchet high.

"The soul of a Kin... mine to eat."

Behind her, a large shadow loomed. She whirled around and stared into the glowing golden eyes of the dream-eater. Baku was even more massive than before. The witch wailed in fear as he opened his grand jaws and let out a deafening roar.

"Please, please, Baku," she begged in a small child's voice.

Baku closed his gaping maw with no hesitation and swallowed her whole. He tilted his head to the sky, his stallion legs lifted high, and he roared into the night. He landed, towering over Zach, emitted a loud belch, and licked his lips.

"The nightmare spell is eaten now, Kin. You will sleep soundly."

"Thank you. How can I repay you?"

Baku let out a vigorous laugh. "One of the finest meals I have had in ages. No further payment required." The dream-eater examined him as if pondering something. "Some of your Kin are in danger, not far from here. The Aulic Assembly is held near an ancient battleground. You must find them and regroup with the rest of the Kin. I must go."

"An ancient battleground? Where are my fellow Kin?"

"I am only the dream-eater, and I must leave you now. Good luck, dear Kin. You will need all the well-wishes I offer and many more." Baku turned and disappeared into the forest before Zach could speak.

A flash of bright light burst from the woods. Zach closed his eyes.

His body jerked. When he opened his eyes, Throg was kneeling over him, poking him gently.

"Wake up, Zach. Baku has feasted, and we are not safe here."

"Baku informed me some of the other Kin are in danger and are nearby."

"Interesting that he told you. Baku liked you, or perhaps he was happy with his meal."

"He also said the Aulic Assembly is being held at an ancient battlefield. He said I must regroup with the Kin and find them. He sensed Meridian blood in me."

Throg nodded. "Hmm, your link on the Assembly mentioned the word 'valley.' Tomb Valley opens up into Canopus Hills. A legendary fight occurred there, the Battle in Canopus Hills, with Hideux's Nightlanders. The

Meridian Army was being overrun and was rescued by the Stonecoats. Other ancient battlefields exist, but this one makes the most sense."

His earthy hair was matted from days of travel, and his stubble grew rough around the edges. "I still think the prudent path to take is back to Meracuse and Lord Achernar. The main road to the city is not far from here, and we can follow the course straight in. We'll report our findings to Lord Achernar, and he will know where your fellow Kin are."

Zach's guts ached but he knew he must push on. In a steady, deliberate motion, he got to his feet and balanced himself. Throg handed him some chud to chew on as they walked.

The faster they traveled, the more his strength returned. A question burned at him, one he'd been meaning to ask. "Throg, who are the truth seekers?"

"Ah, the inquiry of the century. The truth seekers appeared during the war against Hideux."

CHAPTER 18

Nick trudged into the fog, continuing in the direction of the Denon clone. The mist dissipated and the Denon twin appeared ahead. Several others stood with Denon, and Nick recognized Captain Spiro among the group.

"Welcome, Nick. I hope the walk cleared your head." Denon said.

"Yes, thanks. You look like Lucas Denon. He was an unbelievable musician."

"I am Lucas Denon."

"H-how can that be? You were in a car wreck. Your body was f-found." Nick took a step back, his eyes wide.

"My time on Earth came to a close. I was chosen for a higher calling."

"You... you're dead?"

"On Earth, yes. I am no ghost, Nick. I'm a celestial being now, a truth seeker. We are the protectors of the celestial universe. The southern hemisphere may be under siege, and we must protect it as best we can. Even though we are no longer mortal, we can die on the celestial battlefield and reach an elevated plane. Yet we're here for a reason, chosen because of special qualities we exhibited in our corporeal forms."

Stepping closer to him, Nick asked, "Spiro, you are one of the truth seekers?"

"Aye. Just found out myself. I'm well aware of who the truth seekers are. In my culture, it is an honor to be one."

"What? Wait.... Do you mean I'm a truth seeker, a celestial being?" Nick waffled on his feet.

Denon said, "Yes, Kinsaver. If you allow your instincts to control your emotions, you'll find you're comfortable here. You always possessed an inner goodness. You are a truth seeker now, though you will need to be educated. The truth seekers promoted from Earth usually do."

"A truth seeker is a protector of the celestial universe?" Nick arched his brow.

"Yes. A long time ago, the hemisphere we're in, between the Fornax and Eridanus systems, stood in grave danger. A powerful and evil being, Biskara, conducted a war against the benevolent cultures of this sector through his first son. Hideux, in mortal form, led an army called the Nightlanders. Due to Biskara's celestial involvement and his tremendous resources, Hideux prevailed during the conflict.

"At that point, a celestial adversary to Biskara named Atum created the truth seekers and assisted the Meridian forces against Hideux. The truth seekers fought Biskara on the celestial battlefield, which left Hideux on his own. They developed a device to identify the coordinates of Biskara in the future, and to summon the truth seekers when Biskara attacked. The truth seekers can only communicate with the mortals through this tool. It is called the Silver Sphere."

Nick paused as he registered this new information. "But what's my role in this?"

"We suspect renewed danger with Biskara. The Silver Sphere is currently inoperable, and search recons are being sent out to find Biskara. My calling is to greet you, a task which I have done many times in the past when a chosen one from Earth is involved. And... you are the Kinsaver."

"What does that even mean?" Nick ran his hands through his shaggy locks.

"You're a good person. We've had our eye on you for quite some time," admitted Denon. "But it takes more than a strong heart to become a truth seeker. Nick, you've done the one greatest thing anyone could—you rescued a Kin, and died so she could live."

"What's a Kin?"

"All in time, Nick."

"Well, shoot, you're really Lucas Denon."

Denon smiled and nodded.

Nick gazed out into the distance. "Okay then, what's expected of me now?"

"We'll travel back to Horologium, the truth seekers' home base. There you will be further briefed on our cause and prepared for battle, as I was."

"Have you ever fought against Biskara?"

"No, I have had other more minor celestial confrontations, but this will be a war, Kinsaver. One we cannot lose. We are off to Horologium to regroup. Welcome aboard. We're proud you're joining us."

CHAPTER 19

Throg said, "So the truth seekers created the Silver Sphere and attacked Biskara on the celestial plane. The United Forces helped to defeat Hideux and the first army of Nightlanders on Azimuth."

"An amazing story." Zach rubbed his head. "I think Atum was a big Egyptian god or something. I read about him in a book on the old pyramids."

"Sure, Atum moves around. Who can guess where he is today? Even though he is the founder of the truth seekers, they elect a new leader every so often."

"Okay, Throg, now who are *you*?"

Throg hesitated a moment as if making a decision. "My name is Axel Throg. I was a member of the Meridian army, specifically the captain of the Aulic Assembly's personal guard."

"I could tell you weren't just a woodsman. Why did you leave?"

"Perhaps a broken heart had much to do with it. I found it more comfortable in the wild." His eyes carried a sad tinge.

Zach twirled his blade a few times, not wanting to push Throg too hard about his past. "Wow."

"What?"

"You have a heart."

Throg grinned and released a branch he held, swatting Zach in the face. "Ow!"

"My *sincerest* apologies."

Zach glared at Throg, who grinned and motioned for them to continue.

"You're a powerful adversary now, as you have inherited the abilities and strengths of your link on the Aulic Assembly. You'll need a little practice to sharpen your skills, and won't be as polished as your link. Members of the Assembly are among the most dominant soldiers on Azimuth, along with Milo Morgante and the Stonecoats. The war ahead, however, will be dangerous for all."

"You mentioned the Stonecoats," Zach said.

"Yes, Milo is their current leader, and a good man. The Stonecoats are an elite outfit of warriors. They are adventurers, a freelance club with a long history. It's fortunate their allegiances are usually with the Aulic Assembly, although Milo disagrees on some issues with Lord Achernar."

"What kind of issues?"

"Well, he says they are political in nature. I think the problem is more personal—tension over a woman. Lord Achernar spends a fair amount of time with Bianca Saddler, a member of the Assembly. She happens also to be the representative who's served longest on the Assembly. Milo is fond of her from their youth."

Throg knelt to the ground and ran his fingers through the dirt. "We are close to the Dorado Path. We should keep quiet from here on in."

They paced silently for several minutes. Had Throg not insisted on their hush, Zach would have burst out with more questions. An oversized butterfly with spectacular shades of green, yellow, and red lines on its wings fluttered nearby, hovering gracefully alongside them while they trekked. Zach spied it, but froze the instant his eyes fell upon the being in their path.

"Throg," he began.

"It's okay. He's a Leshy. They're forest spirits, guardians of the animals and trees. I happened to befriend this one, whose name is Drake."

The Leshy gazed at them with large emerald eyes, and stroked his green beard with blue hands. As they drew closer, Zach noticed the Leshy wore his jacket and pants backward. His face was as pale blue as his hands.

"Good day, Drake. How have you been?"

"Been better, Throg. Huge disturbances in my sector."

"I'll bet."

"Is that a Kin with you?"

"Yes, this is Zach Ryder. We're looking to reunite him with his fellow Kin."

"Oh, yes, the sooner the better. The disturbance started with the nasty hag Baba Yaga coming down from the Cark." Drake shook his head. "Now the Nightlanders are ravaging the Dorado Path. His Kin are in danger. Quite a battle they're having at the moment."

Throg jumped forward a step. "The Kin are on the Dorado... in battle? With Nightlanders?"

"Yes, they are. The Zumbaki, of all beings, joined Biskara. They also brought back those dreadful Disembowelers."

"Zumbaki and the Disembowelers?" Throg gasped.

"What are they?" Zach tensed at his companion's unease.

"The Zumbaki are a savage tribe—cannibals," Throg said. "They believe they gain strength by eating their enemies, and most of the time they are too wild to have any allies. The Disembowelers are terrible beasts. The Nightlanders trained them in past wars, but they were thought to be extinct. Malefic must have bred them and kept them in hiding."

"Well, they're making a mess out of the forest," said Drake. "I don't like how the Disembowelers are hurting some of the horses in the battle. These Nightlanders never respect the woods and its animals as you do, Throg. So, I'm happy to assist."

Leshy

"Thank you, Drake. How far up the Dorado is this happening?"

"Maybe a couple of hours northeast from the river here, a little less perhaps. I always forget how slow mortals travel. I spied the wishpoosh pillaging your belongings. Their behavior has been unusual. I warded them off and managed to grab a few of your things, some weapons and such I thought you might need. The bag is up ahead behind the third tree to the right." Drake motioned forward.

"Thank you. I will do my best to preserve your forest. You have my word," Throg said.

The Leshy nodded. "Nightlanders captured two of the Kin, and took them to a small camp near the battle. The leader of the Stonecoats is attempting to rescue them on his own."

"Milo? I'm glad the Stonecoats are with the rest of the Kin. *We* are too far to help them, but... *you* can get to the battle quickly." Throg looked at him.

"You understand my kind doesn't like to get involved, but you have done much for me in the past. I will go to assist the two Kin to return your kindness."

Throg smiled, his eyes crinkling, and then Drake disappeared into the woods.

"The Leshy are shape-shifters. They can shrink to the size of a small rock or plant. On a rare day, you might view them in their natural state. They can be formidable allies... if they like you. They can also be a royal pain in the arse if they don't—double for the younger Leshy, the mischievous critters. I befriended Drake some time ago.

"If what he says is true, then we're near your fellow Kin and close to battle. The Disembowelers are rabid and dangerous. We'll need shields if we encounter them. The Zumbaki are more threatening when they travel in packs."

The two of them jogged along the path Drake had pointed out to them. Throg stopped at the third tree and found his knapsack, a canteen of water, and several knives. A chipped sword leaned against the bag. Throg lifted the blade once he pulled the pack on.

"We need to move without delay. We will run into the Dorado Path in a short time. Stay close to me, and remember, if anything happens to me, the Dorado Path leads straight to Meracuse."

He glared back at Zach, and the Kin saw determination in Throg's eyes.

They accelerated their pace, and a surge of adrenaline rushed through Zach. A war, other Kin, and to top it off, blue men with green hair, seemed to be the norm around here. He wondered what Adrian would think of all of this.

CHAPTER 20

Crisp morning air made Morgana's heart swell. She smiled as she tied her light chestnut hair back. A soft whine came from the floor and she looked down. Otis, her Meridian Sheppard, barked and lolled his tongue. He gazed with big, brown eyes, begging attention.

"Just a minute, Otis," she said, rubbing his side with her bare foot.

She sluiced cold water over her face and neck. The dry air promised a hot day. As she left her bedroom, she overheard her father speaking in hushed tones with another villager right outside the door.

"I got wind of rumors Malefic's soldiers are moving west now," said the old man. Borgen was a priest and a healer. Last summer, he'd bound Morgana's sprained ankle. Borgen's healing went unsurpassed in Chapton. "That merchant from Vixen said so."

"West?" her father murmured. "Well, good, I suppose. He'll pass near us, but I think we should be safe."

Morgana rapped on the open window. "Father, did you want breakfast?"

"I broke my fast early today, dear. Why don't you have a bite before you go to the temple?"

"I'm planning to do some chores, first," she said. "Not that hungry yet."

At her heels, Otis whined and wagged his tail.

"Borgen, how soon do you need Morgana?"

"She can take her time. Been a slow morning." Borgen smiled at her.

"Thank you, Borgen," she said, returning his smile. "I'll be along in about an hour. I just have a few things to do around the house before breakfast."

"Good, good. I'll see you then. Take care, El." Borgen clapped Morgana's father on the shoulder, his frail fingers looking bony and weak. He walked with not so much of a limp as a wobble. Morgana feared at times that a hale wind would knock him clean over.

"Morgana," her father said after Borgen had gone, "if you're doing some chores, don't forget to tidy up the hutch in the back. You know how the rabbits get this time of year."

"Sure. Otis, to me."

She really hadn't needed to say anything. Otis followed eagerly as she took some stew from the gigantic cauldron over the fire pit, and spooned the meat into a large bowl. He nuzzled past her and began to eat, licking his chops as he downed the cold beef.

Morgana patted him, then slipped her shoes on and hurried out back to tend to the rabbits. She paused at the feel of something in her father's coat pocket. She reached in and pulled out a weapon.

"Father?" She approached him with the gun. "What are you doing with this?"

Her father snatched it from her. "It's a hand-cannon."

"They're banned!"

"No, they're not. Blasters are illegal. Hand-cannons aren't. Not anymore. Now, go take care of the rabbits. I'll handle this."

Morgana shifted from one foot to the other and bit her lip. In the end, she had no choice, and hurried around back. The hay needed cleaning and their water replacing.

She eased the three rabbits into a small wooden crate and covered the top with chicken wire. "Don't fret. Just a little bit."

She pulled out the dirty hay, tossing a bushel into the yard for the chickens to pick over. A few hens clucked and fluttered aside as she bustled back and forth between a bale of fresh straw and the rabbit hutch. Once she'd laid the new straw, she pulled out the bowls and cleaned them, refilling one with cold water from the rain barrel, and the other with chopped carrots and lettuce.

"There we go." She set a white rabbit back in with the others and latched the chicken wire door. "All neat and fresh."

She hurried inside. "What else needs straightening, Father?"

Elund shook his head, his pitchfork in hand. "The cattle are already to pasture, and there's no sweeping to do. You could go and fetch water for Borgen. I imagine he'll want some at the temple to wash the paintings. But you should eat soon. Getting late."

Cleaning the hutch hadn't taken too long, though Morgana's gut growled at the thought of food. "I'll take a biscuit with me to the well. Is that all right?"

"Sure. Stop by the temple first, and find out if anyone wants breakfast."

"Okay. Otis, come." She patted the meat of her thigh.

The dog, lying beside the empty fire pit, wagged his tail, jumped to his feet, and hurried after her.

She took a biscuit from the tray on the counter and was halfway out the door when her father called, "Just a moment, Morgana."

"Yes?"

"Don't forget your knife. That rope gets stuck too often." He handed her the short blade. "I can't tell you how many times Ms. Lantern's had me replace it!"

"Thanks, Father." She tucked the knife into her work belt.

He pulled her into a tight hug. "Have a good day."

She wrapped her arms around her father and smiled. "I love you, Father."

"Love you, too."

Morgana flashed a grin and hurried outdoors, Otis trotting along behind her. She wolfed down her biscuit in a few bites. Taking a pail from outside of the house, she began a brisk walk to the temple, just down the street from where she lived.

Most of the humble building had been covered in canvas sheets to keep the dirt out. A few women talked outside as they refurbished a painting under the warm forenoon sun.

"Good morning, Morgana," said one with a kind smile. Her cheeks crinkled.

"Morning, ma'am," Morgana clucked with a curtsy. The sound of hammers and saws reverberated from within the temple. "They're already to work?"

"Oh, my, yes. They started early this sunrise. Why, Kal was up before the sun!"

"My father sent me to check if anyone wanted some breakfast. I was headed to the well and can stop by the baker's on the way back."

The woman stood and hurried inside to ask. The others working on different paintings chatted amiably with Morgana while she waited. Only a moment later, the elderly lady returned.

"Kal said they're fine for now, but they could use your help when you get back. The new wall's giving them a hard time, bless the Father."

"Didn't they paint yesterday?"

"Oh, my, yes. Took almost the entire day, too! But they want a mural done, and you're the only one with an artist's hand, Morgana."

A hot flush rose into her cheeks. "That's kind of you. I'll start when I return."

The old woman knelt again beside the image, and dipped her brush back into the bowl of red paint. Morgana's mother had painted many of the others inside. The walls showed somber-faced saints and glorious, smiling gods. The years had dulled their colors and cracked the clay floors.

When Borgen had suggested restoring the temple to her father, he'd readily agreed. The whole town had gone in on the project. Rather than pay workers, though, everyone took turns volunteering. The women painted and cleaned while the men repaired the floors, ceiling, and walls. Near the back, they were building a nursery.

Morgana turned to Otis. "Wanna race to the well?"

He barked and hopped.

"Good! Ready?" She stood in place, leaning forth, and Otis crouched. "Set...."

Otis nearly jumped forward, but she laughed and *tisk*ed him.

"Wait a minute. No cheating!"

Otis's long tail flapped excitedly.

"Go!" Morgana took off at a run.

Otis easily outdistanced her. Her heart slammed against her ribs as she darted forward. Chapton harbored a fair sized village, with the well stationed at the other end, past the main square and the gurgling fountain. Chapton's outskirts contained mainly farmhouses. Cattle and sheep dotted the green fields beyond the main square.

"Good morning, Morgana," called Ms. Lantern as Morgana and Otis sprinted by. Old Ms. Lantern had her knees in the dirt as she tended the garden.

"Good morning!" Morgana's chest heaved.

Racing Otis took a lot out of her. By the time they reached the well, her lungs ached. She laughed and knelt to ruffle the dog's ears. "Good boy!"

Otis licked her cheek, then sniffed around the well, his nose to the ground.

Morgana lifted the pail and set it on the wall of the well, then lowered the bucket attached to the rope, and hummed. A few moments later, the bucket plopped into the water below, and she let it fill before hoisting it up.

After she'd poured the fresh water into the container, she asked, "Are you ready to head back?"

Otis froze, his pointed ears perking.

A chill wind came on, and Morgana tucked a stray strand of mousey hair behind her ear.

Otis growled, the pitch rumbling deep in his throat. He crouched, his hackles prickling.

"What is it, Otis?" She turned the direction he was looking. At first, she heard nothing. Then, the sound of distant thunder rolled across the terrain. She frowned. The sky was clear and blue—if there was a storm, it wasn't anywhere nearby.

The noise grew louder, though, and she recognized it. The pail she had been holding dropped from her hands and cold water splashed onto the ground. A banner, black with a gold sigil, was the first to cap the hill outside of Chapton. Atop the crest, only a few forms in dark armor appeared.

Then they came. The entire hilltop was crowned with soldiers garbed in black. The army roared.

"No," she whispered. She simply couldn't believe it, yet there they stood. Fear shook her very core. Twirling, she stumbled back toward the village. Her legs turned to jelly, but she ran on, screaming and waving her arms as she darted from the well.

Ms. Lantern stood up from her garden, facing opposite the hill. Morgana dashed to her, crying, "Run!"

"What? Morgana!"

Otis yowled and bounded into the yard, trying to pull Ms. Lantern away from her plants.

"Otis, stop!"

"*Nightlanders!*" shrieked Morgana. "Run!"

Only then did Ms. Lantern look toward the highland. Smoke rose behind the Nightlander battalion. Morgana gasped and stepped backward, tripping over a rock. She landed hard. The soot came from poor old Mr. Ender's farmhouse.

At first, she wondered what the army was doing. Perhaps they were hoping the villagers would leave without a fight. Then a loud cry rose from the black warriors. They were almost five hundred strong, a small battalion, but one that could easily overthrow the village. They swarmed down the slope, hundreds of them rushing toward Chapton, and at the head towered a cloaked rider in obsidian armor atop a gigantic war horse.

Morgana launched to her feet and ran, with Ms. Lantern now in tow. Otis howled as they sprinted, his pink tongue lolling from between black lips. His powerful legs carried him ahead of Morgana, but he never once left her sight.

"Everyone!" she shouted. "Run!"

Villagers who'd crowded around the central water fountain stopped what they were doing. Workers at their small stalls and shops turned toward her. When they gaped at the black army coming for them, they screamed. Women dropped baskets of goods and men hustled to get weapons.

Chapton was by no means a small village, but most of the citizens were women and children. Dogs growled and barked in the cobblestone street. Ahead, a little boy stood frozen in the middle of the square, his blue eyes wide as skipping stones, crying.

Morgana raced up and grabbed him. She lifted him and continued running. Ms. Lantern was huddled between an overturned cart and a house, and Morgana pushed the boy into her arms.

"Morgana!"

"Run!" she said. "Take him with you and go! *Now!*"

Ms. Lantern hoisted the boy and rushed down the road toward the tree line. Halfway there, a Nightlander arrow struck her down.

Morgana bolted to the shrieking boy.

The army stormed the village with fervor, ruthlessly cutting down men where they stood. They seized the women and children and herded them into large cages on wagons. Nightlanders infested the village, searching houses for anyone who tried to hide.

They must be looking for someone.

Otis remained at her heels, zipping to the Nightlanders trying to capture the little boy. Morgana pulled the knife from her belt and prepared to stab a horse, hoping to spook it. One of the Nightlanders swung about and thumped her with the blunt end of his spear.

Dizzy, she stumbled and fell to the cobblestones. Blood oozed from a gash on her forehead and her lip swelled. She tasted iron.

"A fighter, eh? Don't want you causing no trouble," said the Nightlander, his voice echoing within his metal helm. He spun the spear around and aimed to strike.

Otis sprang from the street and bit the Nightlander's wrist. The man yelped as plate mail crunched and ground against his flesh. His partner whirled, but Otis was too quick. He dropped from the first warrior's arm to the soil and nipped the second's horse. The mare reared, throwing her rider.

Otis backed off, growling. His teeth were wet, dripping with saliva, and his hackles bristled. He barked ferociously at the two Nightlanders.

The little boy wailed nearby.

"Run!" Morgana shouted at him and tried to get to her feet.

A spear came from nowhere and hit the soil where her hands had been, between her and the boy. The youngster hollered and scampered off into an alley. She floundered along the dirt.

An explosion rocked the temple right down the street from her. A torch must have struck the vat of oil the priests used for anointing. In an instant, all of their work was ablaze and smoldering. The love for their village meant nothing to these men. They looted and pillaged, taking what they pleased from the stack of icons outside the temple door.

Borgen ran from the building, his robes on fire. Morgana bellowed his name, but he did not hear.

Her eyes were drawn from Borgen to a figure galloping down the main road of the city, straight toward her. He raised a black crossbow and pulled the trigger. The bolt flew even and true, and Borgen collapsed to the ground, where he lay unmoving.

Morgana shrieked in horror. The imposing figure reined in beside the Nightlanders. His destrier whinnied, showing pink gums and gnashing white teeth.

"Malefic," she murmured. It could be no one else.

His black helm sported a pair of enormous, demonic antlers rising from the temples. Ebony armor shone in the sunlight. Firelight from the village reflected off the plate mail, and his billowing raven cape whipped out behind him in the icy breeze.

Malefic

Tendrils of charcoal gray smoke carried across the path. Houses, stained with gunk, crumbled as tongues of fire licked at the windows and doorways. The wails of children and crying women reverberated through the town.

She glanced around, terror wrapping its icy fingers around her heart.

"You could have lived, little pest. Kill her." The words, spoken with such coldness, stunned her.

"Otis, run!" she begged, hoping at least to save him.

The Sheppard ignored her and launched at Malefic with a bark. The Nightlander leader smacked Otis aside, and a pained whine broke the air.

Morgana sprang to her feet in an instant, running to his side. "Otis!"

Malefic stormed forward with steely resolve on his devilish steed, and hissed, "I will burn you alive."

Morgana whirled on him, tears streaming down her cheeks, and raised her knife, ready to plow it through his armor and into his foul heart. She froze.

Her father burst out from the alley, the hand-cannon held high, forcing the nightmarish horse and its hellish rider back.

"Run, Morgana!" he shouted.

"Father!" Morgana backed away. She glanced around, searching for the boy, but he was nowhere in sight. She knelt, trying to lift Otis as he whimpered.

Elund cried, "Leave him! I'll get him! *Go!*"

Hot tears dripped from her chin. "I'm not leaving you!"

"Run, now!" He shoved her away and she stumbled.

Before Elund could fire his weapon, Malefic lifted a broadsword and brought it down on her father's hand-cannon, shattering it. He crumpled to the ground.

Morgana gasped and backed off, choking on her sobs.

"Get help!" he yelled to her from the dirt.

Malefic turned his wintry gaze onto her.

The only thought in her mind was '*run.*' Though she fought to stay, her legs wouldn't listen. Her feet flew beneath her as if with an intellect of their own, as she instinctively sped down the cobblestone street.

No! She thought, forcing herself to stop. She needed to get Otis.

When she turned back, a handful of Nightlanders were chasing after her. Behind them, a light blue figure with green hair glided in from the woods. Morgana rubbed her eyes and squinted. The odd man knelt over Otis's shivering body and stared up at Malefic. Nightlanders backed away from him, though their weapons were drawn.

All at once, her father's form dropped beneath Malefic's sword. Too shocked to scream, she merely stood, frozen, as Nightlanders rushed toward her. The soldiers drew closer and an arrow whizzed by her ear.

She couldn't save anyone if she died. She needed to escape and find help. Tears streamed down her face as she vaulted toward the trees.

CHAPTER 21

Milo raced through the woods on his steed, Shara, to no avail. He had lost the Kin. At last, he slowed and cursed under his breath as he strained in all directions for a clue. Nothing but foliage surrounded him in every direction. None of the plants appeared mussed or torn, and no obvious tracks had been left. The Nightlanders had been smart enough to take their time.

From behind a tree, a Leshy emerged and stood before Milo, smirking.

Milo tensed with his sword raised. Shara, in contrast, remained at peace. She even lowered her head toward the Leshy.

The Leshy reached forward and patted Shara on the nose. "I am Drake, a Leshy. Throg asked me to assist you in rescuing the two captured Kin."

"Throg, you say? Well, it's about time he joined the fray. You are my first Leshy," he said warily, still holding his blade at the ready. "I've heard your people pillage camps and run soldiers out of the forest for simply making a campfire."

"My dear Milo, great warrior that you are, you will need to dismount Shara if you wish to track, unless you would like to announce to the entire quadrant your presence." Drake ignored his comment.

Milo focused on his mare as his cheeks flushed red. "I thought I could catch them quicker, but not a hair of them has been spotted." He dismounted. "Shara, back to the Stonecoats." He clapped his hands twice and she raced away.

He twirled to Drake and sized him up. "I'll follow my instincts, Leshy, and trust you."

"Throg is a few hours south. You will be pleased to know that the sixth Kin is with him. The two captured Kin are being held just over this hill. They ambushed the one named Max. You'll need my assistance if you wish to rescue them unharmed."

"Your help is welcome, Leshy, as is the news of the missing Kin."

"Sneak over the hill. When you are within sight of the camp, you'll await the Kin," Drake said, and disappeared behind the tree. "When they are free, you will take them back to the army. Then, leave my forest in peace."

Milo stood a moment and gaped in the direction the Leshy had gone. After shaking his head, he turned, crouched a bit, and sidled toward the highland, quiet as a leaf on the wind.

CHAPTER 22

Shelby stirred next to Max, and groaned.

"Shelby, you okay?" he asked.

"I think so. My head smarts. Where are we?"

"Caught by these Nightlanders is where. We aren't far from the ambush site, but they seem to be regrouping and waiting for reinforcements. This rope is tight."

Shelby could tell he was struggling to breathe. "Did anyone see us get carried off?"

"Well, I spotted you being taken. I followed, and a bunch of these guys jumped me." He jerked his head at the Nightlanders.

"You followed after me? Alone?" She vaguely remembered seeing him rush after her, but the memory was muddled.

"Well, I had to. Those Disembowelers ran everywhere—a crazy battle scene."

"You followed to rescue me? Max, thank you." She felt herself blush.

A rather large blade of grass sprouted up between them, and Shelby gasped. Though she felt at home here, she was not yet used to the abnormalities of this world. Magic was as common as the wind in this place.

"*Psst.* I am Drake, sent to assist you." The voice came from the grass.

Max and Shelby exchanged perplexed glances and returned their gaze back to the green speaker. About to reply, Shelby paused when she glimpsed someone coming.

One of the Nightlanders walked over, his eyes boring down at them through his leather mask. He hunched over them a few moments, then grunted and rambled off.

After a short pause, the voice returned. "I will cut your ropes. Remain as if you are bound until I distract these wretched soldiers. A friend awaits you at the bottom of the hill."

Max strained his head forward. "Uh, who and what are y-you?"

"I am Drake the Leshy, and I want my woods clean. Keep still and await my distractions."

The blade of grass shrank into the ground. A sharp object materialized between Shelby's ankles. It moved up and down as it cut through the coarse rope. Before long, the loops loosened under her ankles and the tool slid behind her, again rubbing against the cord. Within a few moments, the bonds eased. The wooden shiv appeared between Max's ankles and repeated the process until both his ropes drooped.

Max and Shelby held their position as if bound, waiting for the diversion Drake had promised. Two of the Nightlanders stood just a couple of yards in front of them. Another pair was stationed behind their tree. Farther off in the center of the makeshift camp, a handful of Nightlanders engaged in an animated discussion. From above them, the sounds of a baby's wailing drifted down.

The Nightlanders stopped their conversation and looked skyward, bewildered. A few of them muttered and pointed. The soldiers behind the tree joined the two in front, and they walked over to the group that had been huddled.

As they all continued to search up in the trees to locate the bawling baby, several wolves emerged from the far side of the camp. The Nightlanders drew their swords sluggishly, as if drugged. Snarling, the pack raced at full speed, not attacking but running in circles around the disoriented soldiers.

"Now," Max whispered.

They sprang to their feet, the ropes falling to the ground. Max grabbed Shelby's arm as she wavered from the earlier blow to her head. He pulled her forward, and they dashed off to the bottom of the hill.

When they arrived closer to their destination, Milo stepped out from behind a tree—a welcome sight. Shelby smiled in relief.

"This way, Kin," Milo said, ushering them onward. "How good to take you back well."

"Same here. What of the battle?" Max asked.

"I had to leave in order to follow you, so I do not know the status. The Stonecoats will not lose. At worst, they'll beat back the ambush and regroup not far from here."

He nodded in the direction of the besieged troopers. "We won't need to worry about these Nightlanders. From what I read, the Leshy is closest with the wolves in the forest. Drake appears to have placed a type of mind spell on the soldiers, which I heard is similar to being drunk."

They traveled at a speedy pace through the weald. Shelby and Max jumped felled trees and bushes as they ran. Milo dodged trunks and roots. The forest ended and they burst onto the Dorado Path.

"Who sent Drake to help us?" Shelby asked. She was panting hard, and sweat dripped down her brow.

"Throg is his name, and he found the last Kin. Presage will be relieved. I feared for his life." Milo looked over his shoulder.

Shelby sighed. "It must suck to be lost and alone. At least we have each other and some information. So will they be joining us?"

"They are a few hours away. It is crucial that you are all together. I'm sure Presage will rethink his plans and send out reconnoiters to find them. Such patrols will be risky, as the woods are full of Nightlanders and their allies."

After a short time, they heard the galloping of horses ahead. Milo turned and smiled. "I know my Shara's gallop. She is leading the Stonecoats to us."

Max's forehead scrunched. "Are you sure she isn't leading back a Nightlander patrol?"

"She would lead the enemy over a cliff before sending them to me."

Shara rounded the corner and neighed when she viewed Milo. A squad of Stonecoats followed close behind, their armor glinting in the sunlight. Crimson blood smattered their plate mail, and one man had deep gashes and dents around his side and chest.

"Milo, have you the Kin?" asked one of the Stonecoats. He sounded shocked, as if he'd thought Milo dead. The warrior smiled and blood gushed from his nose, where something had smashed into his face and broken the bridge.

"Yes, Cetus. What of the battle?"

"We managed. After you rode off to rescue the Kin, only the Disembowelers and a few Zumbaki remained. We regrouped with the main Meridian Army up the path. Lucky for us, some came back and helped us. We worried when Shara returned without you."

"How many casualties?"

"Considering the possibilities, not too bad. We lost Barton. Romden and Pratus are injured, and two of the Meridians died. Aside from my nose and a couple of scrapes, that's about it."

"Which Meridians?" Max blurted out.

"Alas, dear Kin," Cetus said, "I did not get their names. We are close to where we have regrouped. Let's move in haste, as the woods are not safe."

Milo heaved himself back on Shara and gave his arm out to Shelby. She accepted his help, and he hoisted her up behind him. Cetus followed suit with Max. With Shelby and Max situated, they raced along the path.

When they arrived, Healer Beekman and his helpers were attending to the many wounded. A glum Barrick sat while his arm was bandaged. He appeared better than most, though an enormous flap of flesh had been torn from his triceps. Shelby shuddered at the sight of muscle underneath.

Vilaborg immediately straightened. "Milo, you have returned with the Kin."

"Actually," Milo said, "Throg had the two Kin saved by a Leshy. He has also found the missing Kin, and they're traveling to us. Just a few hours away according to the Leshy."

"We have been unable to locate Throg. Presage could not link with him, and the messengers sent out have not returned. You couldn't pick a better guide than Throg, though."

Several Stonecoats approached, patting Milo on the back, congratulating him and expressing gladness at his safe return.

"Thank the druids. We feared the wors'," Cumber said, relieved.

Shelby walked over to Barrick. His spirits seemed lifted but he still carried a defeated face. She refused to look at his mangled arm as she sank down beside him. "Barrick, are you okay?"

"Aye, I am fine, dear Shelby. I cannot say the same for Sol and Dukas." He sounded despondent, and winced as the healer sewed his wound closed.

Max and Shelby bowed their heads in sorrow. They'd lost men already. Shelby bit her lip. This wasn't a dream. She'd known it from the moment Stuart battled the Minotaur, but the reality stung. People had died today.

Presage, who had been speaking with another soldier a second before, disengaged and approached them. "They fought valiantly, and they will be remembered. We are at war. Focus on the positives. We must unite the six Kin and transport them to Meracuse, where they can strike up communication with the Assembly in safety, and find some way to connect with the Sphere. I'll send out reconnoiters to bring them in, and attempt to establish a link with Throg again, although that will be difficult—his mental shields are up."

Mr. Dempsey joined the conversation. "Presage, I was curious, as morbid as this may sound, why Malefic would risk keeping the Assembly alive in the first place?"

"A very simple reason, Mr. Dempsey: when an Aulic Assembly member is killed, their power to operate the Sphere is passed to their link. And since we have all six Kin, Malefic will hold the Assembly alive, if only to keep us from using the Sphere."

Mr. Dempsey nodded. "From what I understand, the Aulic Assembly must be together to operate the Sphere. Is it in Meracuse?"

"Yes, the Sphere is in a secret chamber there."

Milo walked over to Presage and motioned him aside. Shelby could hear them speaking, though. "Presage, I suspect a spy in our midst. This ambush was too well planned to be random."

"This possibility I must consider." Presage turned his head.

Shelby caught his gaze wandering to Casselton, who stood grieving over the covered bodies of Sol and Dukas.

Presage called Vilaborg over to him. "Vilaborg, I am curious. Who operated the mobile portal when you were in the Cark to retrieve Zach?"

"Why, Casselton did. He is very experienced with the portal."

"Correct."

For a moment, Vilaborg looked confused. Then his eyes widened and he frowned. "No, Presage, Casselton is a seasoned interceptor. He is loyal to Meridia. I grew up with him. Such a thing is not possible."

"I question not his loyalty to Meridia."

Presage walked over to the grieving Casselton and placed his hand on his shoulder.

"I've known them since the third level of education, when I transferred in to Pictor Academy."

"It is terrible to die without warning in an ambush, dear Casselton."

Casselton shifted his gaze to Presage, tears drizzling down his face. Gore and grime covered him head to foot, but he appeared unharmed. The blood was not his.

"I am to blame. In my selfishness, I caused this." Casselton clenched his fists to his chest, shaking.

Presage kept silent. Even Shelby saw the fear and hopelessness deep inside the officer. Casselton turned away, and at first, it seemed he would not speak.

At last, he flared, his jowls shaking. "My boy, Presage. They took Simon. He is but a child."

Milo interrupted. "You risked the fate of a country for your son, Casselton. That is a choice punishable by death." His words were hot with anger.

"Calm down, Milo," said Presage. "This is no normal act of treason. He will be judged, but no need to damn a loyal citizen of Meridia when his only son is held hostage."

"One of my Stonecoats is dead, Presage. He is lucky I do not judge him now with my sword."

Presage shook his head at the Stonecoat to signal that he must not act here, then returned his attention to the traitor. "How did they contact you, Casselton?"

"In Meracuse. They placed a letter in my chambers. It instructed me to tell a staff member of the Assembly, one with his sister held captive, of our plans of travel. I was also instructed to botch up the mobile portal. If not, they would behead my boy," Casselton whimpered.

"The staff member's name?"

"Mapleton."

Presage raised an eyebrow. "Previous to this, Mapleton was a loyal man. That may explain how the Assembly was captured. Mapleton discovered where they held their weekly meeting, and they were likely ambushed."

Vilaborg stood behind Presage, his eyes welling with tears. Sculptor crept up.

Casselton looked up at them and dipped his head in shame. "My Simon means the world to me. I was confused and disoriented. I figured if I reported the abduction, he'd be killed. I thought maybe a different way out would emerge, where we could all survive, that I could strategize as time passed." His chest heaved.

"We are fortunate. Zach has found Throg and is safe. You will be judged in forum, Casselton. As disappointed as I am with you, I do promise we'll do everything we can to rescue your son."

As two Meridian soldiers were ushering Casselton off, Shelby darted over. "Where are you taking him?"

Presage explained the circumstances to her.

"You're going to hold him? They took his *son*."

Milo said, "I have studied your country's laws in school, damsel. Treason is punishable by death."

Shelby cast him a stern look. Casselton continued to weep, and she scurried over to him and rested a hand on his arm.

"Please, dear Kin, whatever happens to me, please try to help my little boy," he pleaded.

"I promise," she said and hugged him.

The Meridian soldiers escorted him away. Disheartened, Shelby stared at them a few seconds and then whirled around to Milo. His hair was mussed, his armor dented, and his expression somber.

"I'd like you to tell me what you would do if your only son were abducted, you brute," she snapped and dashed off.

Shelby returned to the Kin, who had been sitting and trading stories. She explained what had happened to Casselton, and they fell silent for a while, staring at nothing and brooding. Casselton betraying the entire country seemed too unreal. Even if they'd kidnapped his son, what he did just wasn't right. Shelby knew it, though she didn't want to believe it.

Max said, "Shelby, I know this is horrible, but you'd feel the same way as Milo if one of us had been killed due to Casselton's actions."

"It still doesn't make things better. They have his little boy. He was thinking with his heart."

"I shudder to think of where a man must decide between what is right and his son," said Mr. Dempsey.

They chewed chud and drank water. Shelby tried to enjoy the sounds and sights of the forest. The sentinels and oaks spread onward forever, but she only felt sad.

Before long, Presage strode over to the Kin. "Reconnoiters will assist in locating Throg and Zach and escorting them back to us. I can't tell you how relieved I am that he found his way to Throg. We cannot stay in one place for long, so we'll be moving again shortly. Milo and Barrick are discussing an alternate route back to Meracuse, as the Dorado Path appears too perilous for us to travel. We will let you know as soon as we make a decision."

The Kin reclined for some time. Shelby played with the dirt, tracing her fingers through it in random patterns.

"That poor boy," said Riley with a shake of her head. "I remember when I was little. I got lost in the supermarket, and was I ever scared. The whole experience freaked me out for a long time!"

"I can't imagine getting lost here," agreed Stuart. "Above all, without anyone to explain things to you."

"I hope this Throg guy was able to tell him what's going on," said Riley.

"I'm sure he was," said Max. "And if not, we can bring him up to speed."

Shelby noticed that Emily pulled her knees to her chest and refused to look at anyone. *Such a quiet girl.* Shelby was about to ask Emily if she wanted some chud, when Mr. Dempsey strolled over to Emily, handed her a steaming mug of tea, and sat down beside her.

"The evening approaches." The Kin turned to behold Milo. He didn't meet Shelby's gaze, but he did motion for them to get up. "We should move on."

They packed their belongings and prepared for the coming journey. Shelby paused and peered into the darkening wood. The twilight air carried an arctic hush.

CHAPTER 23

Throg and Zach continued at a light jog, slowing every few minutes to examine their surroundings. Zach recollected his experiences so far, as they traveled. He'd barely had a chance to let them soak in. He thought of the Bogmen and the Fugues. Had the Fugues not intervened, he might have been killed twice already. The encounter with the witch still made him nervous.

They stopped for a respite. Zach's shirt clung to him, as sweat streamed down his back, neck, face, and chest. They had been sprinting for nearly an hour. Without his new body, he could never have run quite so long.

Throg said, "I wish it was possible to put my mental shield down to contact Presage. He's a trusted advisor to the Assembly and a mentor. I fear, however, this would alert others to our location."

"Is it also dangerous when my link tries to contact me?"

"No, it's a different type of transmission. That message would go directly to you, so do not fear."

"I was wondering about the witch I ran into and Baku. Are these creatures back on Earth as well?"

"In different forms, absolutely. Some originated on this planet. Beings having access to certain magic—such as the case with the witch or a celestial being, like Baku— can travel to wherever they want. Azimuth is a more comfortable setting for witches. You might remember in Earth's history when they were burned at the stake. Some pure dwarves still live on Earth in

underground cities far from man and Biskara. Biskara attacked the Meridians' home on Earth, Atlaseria, through a tremendous wave. The mentors managed to establish contact with Azimuth and decided to travel here."

Zach nodded and the two were off once more. Constant racing was mundane, and he was thirsty, licking his dry lips. Sometime ago, he had stopped looking at the trees and shrubbery. For now, he just avoided running into anything while gasping for air. They had a cask of water thanks to Drake, but no food except for some berries Throg had picked from a bush.

In a short time, they came upon an older man working a campfire. Throg slowed and Zach was grateful for the relief. He inhaled a few deep breaths, glad to fill his lungs and take a drink. Cold water slaked the worst of his thirst.

They approached the campfire as the old man shot them a suspicious look. He poked a stick into the fire with leathery mitts, his long grey hair expertly missing the flames by an inch.

"We are simply passing through," said Throg, holding his hands out at hip level.

"My, that's been said before," declared the man in an accent that reminded Zach of British English. "This part of the woods, nobody is passing through. You are either on the run, looking for someone, or a bandit."

"Where do you fall?" Throg asked.

"Me? I'm a bandit."

Throg smirked and rested his hand on the hilt of his sword. "We're looking for someone. Friends of Meridia."

"You're not the only ones. A troop of dark soldiers passed through a few hours back. Never seen their type before. They left me alone. I pretended I was deaf."

"You're luckier than the last group we ran into. They encountered that same troop, but didn't live."

"No kidding? Well, my share of bad luck is full, so a little good luck is due. My name is Brodeur. If you're hungry, I can offer some smoked lattice with salt, and plenty of tea leaves as well."

"We are flying light, and although we are rushed, it won't do us any good to walk with an empty belly. We accept. Few bandits offer lattice. Dang hard fish to snag." Throg grinned and sauntered toward the campfire, and Zach followed warily.

"They're plentiful in the Invunche Lake," said Brodeur. "I had a good run on them last week, so much that I had to smoke most of my catch to keep the meat from spoiling."

They sat around the flames, enjoying the warmth. Brodeur unfolded a soft leather rag and pulled out a generous hunk of the smoked fish for each of them.

The lattice was delicious. Zach likened it to trout, except much better. The taste wasn't quite as salty as he'd expected, and it was buttery.

Brodeur boiled tea and gave them both a large clay mug laced with rope. He shuffled in his bag. After unfolding another tan rag, he pulled out a sticky honeycomb and poured a spot of honey into their cups.

They cradled their warm mugs and ate their fish. The crackling of the flames reminded Zach of a camping trip he'd been on with his foster parents when he was younger—one of the best times of his life, right before they'd started yelling.

"They were looking for you, this troop," said Brodeur, sipping his tea.

"Did I mention we're also on the run?" Throg smiled.

Brodeur coughed, nodding his head. "Usually, men run for more than one reason. I guess you can say a bandit is always on the run."

"May I ask which way they were headed?"

"Sure. The same way you're going. They're Nightlanders, aren't they?"

"They are."

"Well, then I am lucky, because these woods will be turned inside out. I may need to head to Vixen for a spell."

Throg grinned again and looked at Zach. "Vixen is a village about a day's walk from here, off the Dorado Path. It's an entertainment town, a bit like Earth's Amsterdam mixed with Las Vegas, but smaller. You can travel with us part of the way, Brodeur, if you can keep up and don't mind that the Nightlanders are looking for us."

Brodeur didn't answer for a few moments. He then gathered his belongings and placed them in his bag, and strapped a crossbow to the side.

"I guess I can take a chance. Maybe my luck will still be good for a little while, and I have missed the comfort of companionship for some time. I did hear some Zumbaki are on this side of the wood, so company is a trade-off. Much safer to travel in numbers. By the way, I'm not so ancient that I can't keep up a brisk pace yet... long as you don't turn it into a marathon." Brodeur winked.

They walked for about an hour before the woods began to stir. A pack of ferrets scampered by, accompanied by a gang of gophers. The animals started getting bigger. A trio of oversized boar raced to the south of them, followed by a score of terrified bearcats to the north.

"Something spooked them, for sure," Brodeur observed.

A throng of deer and cheetahs bolted past them, thrashing through the brush.

Throg stopped. "Okay, now, when cheetahs are running with deer instead of hunting them, something bad is going on."

Ahead of them, Drake emerged from the woods. His hands were on his temples, and he appeared distressed. The Leshy sighed when he spotted them.

"What in the world...." Brodeur fished out a knife.

"It's okay," said Throg. "I know him. Leshy do not like speaking to strangers. Stay here." He walked up to Drake with Zach.

"Dimshootz! I knew these dang Nightlanders would be a problem for the forest," said Drake.

"What got the wildlife all roused up?"

"The Nightlanders' stupidity. They caught a chimera up in the Evern Mountains. They brought the thing down here with its jaws wrapped in a muzzle, but one of the Disembowelers tussled with it and knocked the gag off. The chimera panicked and shot flame. Half of my woods are ablaze. I'm calling out to my brethren for assistance, but it'll take us some time to extinguish this conflagration."

Throg shook his head. "I'm sorry, Drake. What of the battle on the path, and the Kin?"

"The skirmish subsided. I assisted the two Kin in escaping, and Milo brought them back to safety. I told him you rescued this Kin and asked for aid. Then the fire started, and I got my hands full. You will not be able to travel through it. You need to travel westward if you wish to go to Meracuse."

"Blast. Going west is completely out of the way," Throg muttered.

"Aren't the Canopus Hills west?" Zach asked.

"Yes, they are. Don't get any ideas, though." Throg gave him a stern look. "If the Assembly is held there, you're not the one who will rescue them. That job will fall to a Meridian division, or to the Stonecoats."

Zach shrugged. "I wonder if the rest of the Kin had contact with their links. If they're also headed to the Canopus Hills, maybe this Presage will be going there, too. Do you think they'd wait for us?"

"A good point, but we must assume Presage will send out reconnoiters to bring us in. Until then, we'll go around the fire and hopefully meet up at the Dorado in a day or so."

"Well, I have work to do," Drake said. "Nightlander patrols are scattered west. Keep a lookout." He disappeared into the brush.

Brodeur strode forward.

"A large fire in the forest means we can only travel west," Throg said. "It's far out of the way to reach Meracuse."

"Not much we can do about those things. West we go," Brodeur said.

The distinct smell of burning wood, and the sight of billowing smoke in the sky, accompanied them on their detour. Animals of all kinds continued their steady escape from the fire.

As they hiked around the blaze, Brodeur entertained them with tales of his past. One of his stories was especially interesting—how he had impersonated a Lord Falconer in a king's court near a city named Tobor. He'd enjoyed a fabulous meal, sat only four seats from the king, and snuck away with several gold chalices.

Although Brodeur was a thief, Zach sensed Throg trusted him, and his own intuition agreed.

After a few hours of traveling, they stopped for a rest. A rustling clatter erupted from the bushes, and Throg and Brodeur crept toward the noise, their swords drawn.

"Monganese turtles. We're in luck." Brodeur rubbed his hands together.

"In more ways than one. Their shells are excellent shields," Throg said.

They caught and skinned the two large turtles as Zach watched. Brodeur lit a fire, and before long, Zach enjoyed the first turtle meat he'd ever eaten. The tangy meat reminded him of a cross between pork and chicken.

As Brodeur and Zach continued to devour the grilled turtle, Throg started working on the shells. He'd asked Brodeur for some extra leather hides, and pulled out a few smaller tools and nails from his knapsack.

After an hour's work, Throg packed up the husks and insisted they move on. "I'll finish these on our next stop. They'll come in handy if we run into a Nightlander patrol."

The farther they traveled west, the more the woods returned to normal. After taking another break, Throg finished constructing the Monganese turtle shields. He laced the shields with soft goatskin on the inside, and fastened a tough leather sling to cradle the defensive unit between the forearm and the elbow.

"These shells are hard as any metal," Throg said.

The front of the turtle shields was winter green with light jade edges, and one fit snugly on Zach's wrist. His body felt like he knew exactly how to defend himself with the shield, even though he'd never seen one.

They'd marched for an hour when high-pitched shrieks rose from the south of the forest, over a knoll. They studied each other at a standstill, until reaching an unspoken agreement and dashing up the mound. When they reached the top of the slope, they crawled on their bellies to catch a glimpse of where the cries had originated.

At the bottom of the hill, a girl no older than fifteen sprinted. A second later, a quintuplet of Nightlanders emerged, running and howling with their weapons raised.

"I count only five soldiers with none following. They shouldn't give me a problem," Throg said, eyeing Brodeur. "How are you with that crossbow?"

"I last tested my aim a while ago, but I should be able to even the odds." Brodeur unwrapped and loaded his bow.

"What about me?" Zach snapped.

"I can take these few on my own. I'm not risking you in this." Throg bounded down the hill.

Brodeur aimed and fired his crossbow. The bolt whistled through the air and sliced into a Nightlander's back.

The soldiers spun around.

Throg thrust his sword into one, pulled it out, and parried a blow from a different nightlander, slashing him on the side while a bolt whizzed by him and struck down another.

Battle cries echoed from down the path, and several more Nightlanders burst onto the scene.

Brodeur fiddled with his crossbow. "It's jammed. He won't last long alone."

Zach stood and stared at Throg as he struggled against the throng of soldiers. *I need to help him.*

He sucked a deep breath and charged down the hill.

Zach rolled under a soldier to the middle of the pack, then jumped up, knees to his chest as an axe swished underneath. His leg extended in mid air, right into the head of a warrior. He deflected two swords aimed at him, pushing the soldiers back, and then jabbed a pair of warriors to his left with lightning speed.

A large trooper bear-hugged him from behind. Zach launched his legs forward into an oncoming Nightlander, and then propelled his head back into the mouth of his assailant. Next, he twirled forward, blocking swords and hacking with each turn. Not a thought entered his mind, his body moving with pure instinct.

He turned to Throg, who was heaving on one knee. The last one remained before them, standing his ground, which was almost admirable, considering that his group lay slaughtered at Zach's feet and he could have fled.

"Hah. Doesn't matter to me," rasped the soldier. "Biskara promised us a rich afterlife. Meridia is doomed already, and the United Forces are crippled thanks to our lord. No hope for you now."

A crossbow flew between them, sticking the Nightlander in the chest and knocking him backward so far, it pinned him to a tree.

"He can chew on that in his afterlife," mocked Brodeur as he strode forward. The thief gazed at Zach. "And you told him to stay behind?" he blurted, switching his eyes to Throg.

Zach scanned the pile of men around him. *How did I do this?*

Throg stepped closer and patted him on the back.

"The girl," Zach said.

They looked up in the direction the girl had been running. Zach could see nothing but trees. A flock of birds fluttered across the sky followed by smoke.

"Damsel, we wish you no harm. Are you well?" Brodeur called out to the woods as he motioned to a large fir tree on the right of the path.

The girl sidled out from behind the trunk, her light brown hair tussled, her face with the look of a tense cat. She was damp with sweat despite the cool breeze, and her oversized tunic was shredded. In her right hand, she gripped a small but sharp dagger.

"Thank you, dear sirs," she said. "I assure you they would not have taken me alive."

"My name is Throg. These here are Zach and Brodeur. We were happy to help."

The young woman gaped at Zach, and then sauntered over to them.

"I am Morgana, from the village Chapton. They hit us this morning, burning and pillaging our homes. My father ordered me to run. These soldiers spotted me, and chased me as if possessed. My father was not so fortunate." Her eyes welled with tears.

"Well, my dear, we may not be the safest crew to journey with, but it would be better if you came with us. We're headed to Meracuse, and can provide you with shelter when we arrive. I am sorry for the loss of your village. If your father survived, he would travel this way looking for you, and then probably on to Meracuse."

"I do not think he persevered." She winced, holding back whatever image she had glimpsed.

"I insist you come with us. Brodeur, are some warmer garments for her possibly stuffed in that bag of yours?"

"Yes, of course," said Brodeur. He placed his sack down, rummaged through the contents, and pulled out a piece of cord and a hooded cape. "This rope can be used for a belt to wrap the tunic around you a bit more snugly, and this cloak will keep you warm."

"I'll repay you when I can," said Morgana, coming forward and accepting them. She wiped her eyes. Tears had made them puffy and red, and her lips trembled.

Despite the redness of her cheeks, Zach thought she was a lovely young woman.

"No need," said Brodeur. "A girl your age isn't legal to barter. Consider them gifts."

Throg interrupted. "Well, we should walk to a safer spot and allow Morgana to rest before we move on. I am sorry we cannot camp long, considering what you have been through, but we are stressed for time. However, we will boil some water for tea before heading out."

Morgana nodded, her expression strained.

In silence, they covered ground to a more secure location. Brodeur deftly set up a fire while Morgana hunched with her arms wrapped around her bent knees. Her brow recoiled with anger as tears rippled down her pearly cheeks. The mood ripened with dismal emotion, and Zach could sense Throg was deep in thought.

"That Nightlander said they crippled the United Forces," Throg said. "And they're scouring and pilfering villages in Meridia with abandon. We may need to consider other options." He took a long swig of hot tea.

CHAPTER 24

With Sculptor on his left flank, Barrick approached the Kin. "We've decided the best way to journey is to separate into two contingents. The main Meridian Army will continue on the Dorado Path as a decoy, and you'll travel with the Stonecoats and your personal guard on a less visible route. We will travel west and around the Invunche Lake. It's a bit off course, but east is the Evern Mountains, which is too rough a go."

"Is it wise to split up?" Mr. Dempsey asked.

"We would not even contemplate it if Milo were not here. We have ultimate confidence you will be safer traveling on a less direct course with a more nimble platoon than on a main path with the battalion. We cannot journey with such a large force on the smaller roads or through the dense forest. We've sent a squad of reconnoiters ahead to scout, and we will be traveling by foot."

As the group prepared to leave, Shelby noticed a distinct shift in the moods of Barrick and Sculptor. No longer the bickering duo poking fun at each other, they were now clutched and uneasy. Casselton's betrayal and the death of their companions had left them raw and angry. Shelby couldn't blame them.

"This... seems so hopeless," she whispered next to Mr. Dempsey. "My life is so... hopeless."

Mr. Dempsey arched his brow. "Put your fears aside, young Shelby. Forget the past. You need to learn that your life is worth fighting for. You are needed. The fate of this world and ours depends on it."

She stared at the ground and folded her arms across her chest.

Milo walked up with Cetus and several of the Stonecoats. They had switched to lighter chainmail with earthier tones. Shelby was impressed. It reassured her knowing they had the ability to diversify when needed.

"We move out immediately," said Milo.

They trekked through the thicket for almost a mile before coming to a clearing with a large, rocky slope leading down to the bottom. Trees and brush surrounded the gap, and from her post, Shelby could see for miles in all directions. Meridia was enormous. At first, she'd thought the world was smaller than Earth, but as she gazed across the countryside, she felt overwhelmed by its size. A flock of howls launched from the treetops. In the distance, a roar echoed. Mist settled amongst the hills, fading as the day warmed.

Milo sent a handful of Stonecoats ahead to scout. After inspecting the area, they marched down and beyond the glade. At that point, strained yelling rang from over a hilltop.

Shelby whipped toward the noise.

Milo stared up the mound, his expression tight. At the top of the hill was a man racing downward. He fell and spiraled down the slope, but regained his footing and continued his descent.

"He's Marty, one of the reconnoiters we sent ahead," said Sculptor.

Marty rolled down a few more feet as Sculptor and Milo rushed up to meet him. Blood seeped from his several small wounds amidst mud and sweat. His hair was matted and his eyes wide. A rough, heavy black beard covered most of his jaw.

"Nightlanders. Close b-behind me," he gasped. "They h-had us surrounded, almost as if they were expecting us. I'm the l-last one. They wiped out the rest."

"Right behind you? How many?" Shara shifted from one hoof to the other under Milo's weight.

"At least a thousand. They have a c-cavalry leading and s-some Disembowelers."

Pounding hooves echoed in the near distance. Shelby raised her crossbow and loaded it. *The mist must have sheltered them,* she thought. She exchanged glances with Max, and they both nodded. If it came to a battle, they'd fight to the death.

"Barrick, your guard and Cetus take the Kin straight north to the outskirts of Bevenia Creek," ordered Milo. "We'll divert their attention, but you must leave now, before they glimpse you and give chase."

"Milo, should you not come with us to protect the Kin?" said Barrick.

"Nay, dear friend. With these odds, the Stonecoats will need their leadership. Cetus is my best. We will lead them away. Go now!"

The Kin followed their guard into the woods, accelerating like runaway wagons. Shelby turned to glance up the embankment as she drove into the foliage. At the top of the hill emerged a score of dark horsemen. Milo bellowed out orders from behind her. Mr. Dempsey grabbed her arm and pulled her forward.

Cumber raced up behind and whispered, "Hurry. Don' look back."

They sprinted through the shrubs and branches with fervor, their leather garments shielding them from most of the sharper thorns and brush. The woods thickened and trunks blocked her way. Shelby could view little ahead of Mr. Dempsey, except for a glimpse of Stuart. Fog crawled along the forest floor, splitting in their wake.

Then she caught the sound of war cries, followed by shouting and the clanging of metal. Mr. Dempsey stopped in front of her.

Stuart turned to them and pointed behind. "They're everywhere—Nightlanders. Cetus and Barrick are fighting a score of them. What do we do?"

Sculptor circled back with Riley and Emily and shouted, "We can't risk you getting captured. You are ordered to head east for now and hide until someone fetches you. If no one comes, go straight for Meracuse. You have maps in your backpacks."

Max burst out of the tangled brush, his sword drawn and bloody. "We need to move." Blood spatter dotted his chest.

Shelby's heart skipped a beat. She hoped it was not his.

Sculptor nodded. "Go now. I'll find the rest and bring them as soon as I can."

"Don't wait for me," said Mr. Dempsey. "You are all too important, and faster. I will catch up."

As they ran, intense pain shot through Shelby's skull. She fell on one knee and held her head. Around her, she sensed mayhem and confusion. The world spun. Smells vanished. Sunlight faded.

And then there was nothing.

CHAPTER 25

Shelby lay tranquilly. After a brief hush, a face materialized through the shadows. The woman bore a striking resemblance to her, and Shelby perceived this to be her link, Bianca. No sounds were uttered when Shelby tried calling to her. Bianca's features became clearer, and she wore the crunched expression of pain.

Bianca attempted to speak, but the words came out slurred. Then a clear sentence emerged: "*Go to the Canaveral Caves. You will find....*" Her voice trailed off and she drifted away.

Shelby slipped back into consciousness, and found herself staring down at the moving ground. Someone had slung her over his shoulder.

She stirred. "Hold on now. What's going on?"

They stopped abruptly. Max was carrying her.

"You blacked out and a horde of Nightlanders attacked us. We fought a few moments, and then Sculptor had us run east. We... lost Mr. Dempsey. Sculptor may be behind us, but I haven't seen or heard him. The rest of the Kin are right ahead of us."

"We lost Mr. Dempsey? Oh, no, we have to go back. We cannot leave him." She jerked back.

He shifted. "Shelby...." He looked as though he had something to say, but couldn't quite spit out the words. "We have to keep going."

"But... Mr. Dempsey. Sculptor. We can't just leave them behind."

"Sculptor might be nearby for all we know. It's too dangerous to search for him right now."

Shelby looked at the ground as tears welled in her eyes. Max wasn't telling her everything, she knew, but she drew in a deep breath and collected herself. Mr. Dempsey would be behind them, right? After all, they had made it this far, hadn't they?

She peered behind and hoped Mr. Dempsey and Sculptor were nearby. Sculptor would protect Mr. Dempsey. She decided they couldn't afford to backtrack.

She looked up at Max. "You're making a habit of saving me. I hope I can return the favor." She smiled weakly. "I received a contact from my link. I have some information."

"Tell us later. We need to keep moving. The woods aren't safe yet. Run ahead, and I'll bring up the rear."

She sped forward and within a few moments, outlines of her fellow Kin appeared. Stuart ran next in line and stopped several times to glance back. The resolute concern of a professional soldier adorned his features. She wondered how much her own countenance had changed.

Shelby tried to keep an eye out for Nightlanders as she ran, but the thick, foggy air kept her from detecting anything beyond the lush, green trees around her. A few birds squawked, but other than that, the forest grew hushed. Her booted feet crunched against a blanket of pine needles and pinecones. After several minutes of running, they stopped at a small clearing and knelt down for a short respite, wheezing and catching their breath as quietly as possible.

She stared back in the direction from which they'd come. The only sound was their controlled panting. "When was the last time anyone saw Mr. Dempsey?"

Everyone remained silent for a long minute.

Finally, Stuart shook his head. "We started to run and you fell to your knees. A second later, a score of Nightlanders came through the bushes. We fought a few seconds. Max picked you up and Sculptor sent us packing. He had his hand-cannon to bring up our rear, with Mr. Dempsey ahead of him." He paused, refusing to meet her eyes. "I... checked and Max was doing okay with you, but... Mr. Dempsey...."

Shelby's heart stopped. Her knees trembled and grew weak. She scanned each of the Kin's faces. None of them would look at her.

Voice shaking, she whispered, "What happened?"

Max emerged from the shrubbery. Dark bags hung under his eyes. He was exhausted, same as the rest of them.

He finally spoke, breaking the stretch of quiet. "Shelby, I'm sorry. There was nothing w-we...." He shifted uneasily from one foot to the other. "Mr. Dempsey... a Nightlander cut him down. I saw him jump out in front of one on horseback to slow him down after you fell unconscious. I grabbed you and didn't have time to help him."

At first, Shelby thought she'd heard him wrong. *I... I must have. There's no way. Absolutely no way....* She couldn't bring herself to ask Max to repeat what he'd said. Without warning, her knees buckled and she collapsed. Emily and Riley ran to her side. Wet tears dripped down her chin.

"Mr. Dempsey... he's dead?" The words rang thick and hollow in her mouth.

"I'm so sorry, Shelby," whispered Riley as she wrapped a comforting arm around her shoulders. Even then, Shelby didn't sense her touch.

Emily crouched beside her, silent as ever. The other girl's long, auburn hair hid her eyes from sight.

Shelby tried to reason with what Max had said, what they were all saying. She held her skull and trembled.

She raised her glare and scowled at Max, her voice guttural and angry. "*You....* You let him die! You could've saved him—you *all* should've done something! But you just let him *die!*"

"Shelby, please," Max tried to reason, looking hurt. "Please don't say that. You were unconscious—it was either save you or him. He *told* me to take you and run... his dying words, Shel—"

"*No!*" She jumped to her feet and curled her hands into fists. Nearby, a rock skidded across the ground, smashing into a boulder. "*No!* It's not true!" Anger vanished, replaced by an empty fear. A nagging pain wrenched at her heart. "Please, Max, tell me it's not true."

He shook his head slowly.

She'd hurt him; she grasped it in the way he turned from her.

"We should rest," he said. "All of us."

Before Shelby mustered an apology, Max stalked away. The other Kin were mute for a time.

Riley stood at last and said, "He was a brave man, Shelby. I... I don't know what we could have done. He...."

Shelby pushed Riley's arms from her. "Leave me alone." Without another word, she stormed over to the boulder, crouched, and closed her eyes, letting the tears fall.

He's dead. That was the only thing repeating in her mind. *He's gone, dead, dead, dead. All because he followed me through the portal. Why?*

No matter how hard she tried, she couldn't think of a reason. Max had left him. They all had. *I... did.... And for what? So I could live? It should've been me, not him. He never did anything wrong. He never hurt anyone.*

It sank in, slow but sure. Yes, Mr. Dempsey was gone, the hole he left behind, bottomless. She squeezed her eyes shut, trying to make the pain go away. He'd died saving her; he was gone, but she was here.

Malefic killed him. Malefic and his Nightlanders murdered Mr. Dempsey.

Emily sat next to her, placing a hand on her back.

"I'm going to miss him too, Shelby. I'm so lucky I got to know him a little while we traveled."

Shelby glanced at the other girl.

"He cared. He really cared about all of us."

"He did, and look what it got him. It's my fault he was even here."

"No. He liked it here. He kept saying it was the sort of adventure you could only read about in books."

Shelby nodded and wiped at her tears. "I know, but all he did was look after me. And help me. Comfort me. What did I do for him, or myself?"

"He helped me too—all of us. He listened to me." Tears welled in Emily's eyes.

"Listened to what?"

Emily shook her head.

"Please, I can be your friend, too," Shelby said.

"This is so hard—all of this."

"I know. I'm here."

Emily embraced her, and Shelby held her a few seconds.

"I just realized I haven't hugged anyone in so long," said Shelby.

"I know. Since home."

She reached across and brushed the tears from Emily's eyes.

"Shelby, I was kidnapped."

"Well, we all kinda followed the messages and—"

"I mean back home. A few days before the... portal."

"Oh my God. Emily—"

"The worst part is the guy who rescued me... he... died saving me. Right in my arms."

"Oh, Emily." She wrapped her arms around Emily again.

"It's okay. I'm working on it. Mr. Dempsey didn't treat me like I was weird. Like he sensed something—a lot of things."

"Yeah, I think he did."

"What do you think he would say right now?"

Shelby sighed. "Probably to trust each other. Pick each other up and focus on the problem."

"Malefic."

Resolved, they stood. Shelby's leather gauntlets squeaked as she clutched her hands into fists. Returning to the Kin, with Emily behind her, she said, "Where do we go from here?"

The others seemed depressed. They'd been munching and drinking, but quietly, as though they didn't have the heart to nourish themselves.

Shelby's guts roiled. The mere smell of food made her nauseous. *Mr. Dempsey will never eat again.*

Thrusting the thought aside, she turned to Max. He and the others looked to her.

"You said you had contact with your link?" inquired Max, his voice hollow.

She'd hurt him by yelling. Shelby sucked in a deep breath. When they headed out, she'd apologize, but right now, she wanted to decipher their next move.

She nodded. "She said we needed to go to the Canaveral Caves, and that we would find something there. I couldn't make out what."

Stuart pulled off his backpack and produced a map. They circled him and studied the topography. "We're somewhere around here. This is the clearing where the reconnoiter, Marty, warned us about the Nightlander army." He pointed down at the diagram. "The Canaveral Caves are only a couple miles north."

"Okay," Riley said, her forehead scrunched. "If you guys agree, I think we should camp out for a half-hour, and if nobody comes for us, we make for the caves. We can only hope Sculptor is working his way through the woods, looking for us. He might have been captured, and we can provide little help. I believe we have to move forward soon."

Though the Canaveral Caves could be dangerous, Shelby figured they had a better chance of success if they went where an Assembly member directed them. She hoped her understanding of the communication was right.

They all agreed with Riley's plan. One by one, they sat down, swilled water, and broke out some chud and hard biscuits. Even Shelby ate, though sparingly. Max cleaned his sword, the long strokes of his whetstone echoing around the clearing. Riley and Emily followed suit with their rapiers. Stuart fiddled with his hand-cannon. Too drained to talk, they did not wish to make any unnecessary noise and draw attention.

Shelby surveyed the area while keeping low. She didn't like the idea of not posting a lookout. The sky grew overcast and heavy, the tops of the trees electric against the gunmetal gray clouds. Nothing stirred, and soon the agreed upon time passed. Still, they waited a quarter-hour more. Shelby prayed Sculptor would appear from the brush. Even though Max had seen Mr. Dempsey fall, she hoped he might show up, too. Some part of her remained convinced Max was wrong.

Nothing happened. Shelby turned back to the group, and when she spoke, her voice cracked with grief. "All right, the clock is ticking. We need to go."

The map illustrated the Eridanus River along the way, northwest, to the Canaveral Caves. They decided to travel there to refill their canteens and refresh themselves. As they forged west, the woods grew less dense.

Shelby relaxed a bit, as improved visibility lessened the chance of an ambush. Her legs screamed as she climbed a rocky hillside. After running all morning, the pace was better than she'd thought. It distracted her, too. Rather than dwell on Mr. Dempsey's death, she could focus on searching for the caves.

They reached the stream well after midday. It was hard to believe that they'd only broken camp that morning, and had already been ambushed twice, on their way to Meracuse. The Kin washed in two groups. First, the girls went, the boys standing guard, and next the boys took their turn.

"I wonder what we're supposed to search for when we get to these caves," said Riley as she stood with Shelby and Emily.

The two girls gave Shelby space to mourn, but she knew they were right. All of them needed to be prepared for anything at the caves.

She told them as much as she remembered about what Bianca had said. "I couldn't make out the last part of the message. We'll find *something* there, though. Maybe we'll get a map or some clue to where the others are being held."

She felt clean and refreshed, glad to have washed the grime from her face and neck. The current had swept away her tears, and she felt strong once more, ready for vengeance. She shoved the pain of Mr. Dempsey's death aside; that, she'd deal with later.

"Or, if nothing shows up," said Emily, "we'll go straight to Meracuse. These caves are close to where we were, so thankfully it won't take us out of our way."

Shelby nodded. Presage had informed them that as Kin, they had an innate ability to adapt to Azimuth. Adapting, however, did not change the fact that they functioned as catalysts in assisting this world to defeat a supernatural, evil force. How overwhelming it sounded when she thought about their situation that way. Now they were fierce warriors, not students. Every one of them had killed men in battle, and they'd barely had a moment to reflect on it.

That lack of processing was a good thing.

After the boys finished washing, the group crossed the river and continued traveling toward the Canaveral Caves. They all smelled like fish and algae, but at least they were clean. The roaring water ebbed behind them. As they left the river, Shelby sidled up beside Max.

"Hey," she said softly.

"Hey." His reply wasn't warm.

"About before.... I'm sorry," she mumbled. "It... it shocked me. I'm sorry." She couldn't think of what else to say.

He shook his head. "It's okay, Shelby. It just stung, that's all. I know you cared about him a lot, but I had to save you. I didn't have time to do both, and the others were too far ahead to come back and help."

"I understand. If they had, we'd all have died."

He just nodded.

"Please forgive me," she begged. Her chest ached; the thought of Max being mad at her for the rest of their time together was almost too much to bear. Mr. Dempsey was already gone. Losing Max would destroy her.

"I do," he said, and when he looked at her, she knew he meant it. His hazel eyes were soft and comforting. "He was a good man, Shelby. We'll make it right. I promise."

Shelby gave a firm nod. "Yes, we will. Malefic won't ever hurt anyone we love again. I swear it."

"Me too."

They hiked for an hour through wild country, then stopped and brought out the map. Shelby figured they should have reached the caves by now. With a grimace, she scanned the area. The clouds had receded, moving south, and the sun blared upon them. It wasn't a warm day, but the chill of winter had not ravaged the land yet, either.

"The caves are supposed to be right around here, two different entrances," said Stuart, stroking his chin with his hand as he examined the scroll. He'd tied his long hair back with a length of twine.

"I hope we're reading this map correctly. One wrong turn could put us off track," said Riley.

"No, no, we made it to the river without difficulty. The caves must be close," he said, jabbing the vellum right where they stood.

A rumbling noise surged through the woods east of them.

A Disemboweler burst through from the thicket. Stuart blasted it with his hand-cannon, and Emily whistled an arrow into it as the beast writhed on the ground.

A horde of Nightlanders swarmed in behind it.

"We tracked the escapee to this point," one of them bellowed.

"Ah, what have we here? Drop your weapons or die!" another ordered.

The Kin glanced at each other.

Rage boiled in Shelby's stomach. "I was just about to say the same thing to you."

Stuart fired into the last speaker, knocking him back several feet. Emily cocked her bow and let fly three arrows at once into the mob.

The dark warriors charged forward.

Max lunged and swished his sword with a clang into the closest one. He lifted the soldier up and hurled him into the others.

Shelby picked up a downed man's sword and leapt into the throng, spinning with both blades gashing through the air.

Pellets hissed from Riley's slingshot, smacking troopers in the face and knocking them off their feet. The hand-cannon echoed in Shelby's ears while she twirled in savage combat. She channeled her anger and exploded through the Nightlanders on a bloody rampage.

The last few soldiers scrambled into the forest.

"They can't get away. I'm going after them," Max yelled.

Stuart followed as they barreled into the woods.

Shelby scanned the area, now littered with dead Nightlanders. Her heart thumped and she inhaled a lungful of air. *Calm down now.*

Before long, Max and Stuart returned, sweat and blood dripping from their brows.

"We got them," Max said.

Emily wiped her blade with a rag. "They said they tracked an escapee to here, but I don't see the caves. What were they talking about?"

Shelby pointed to a dense part of foliage. "Hold on. What's over there?"

Her boots snagged a few brambles as she walked. A pair of holes gaped in the greenery, where thick, leafy vines and ivy covered the rock.

"The two openings," Max said. "I didn't think of this before, but these are Meridian Army maps. Perhaps only they know of this place. It's camouflaged to keep it secret. You'd go right past this if you weren't searching for it."

He looked around cautiously. At any moment, more Nightlanders might attack them. Everyone was on edge, listening and watching.

"Well, now what?" Emily folded her arms across her chest. "Do we go through one entrance, and try the other one if we don't find anything?"

They stood silent for a few seconds before Shelby spoke. "We aren't supposed to split up, but we should in this instance. A couple of us can go in each tunnel, not too deep, and we keep one stationed outside in case any trouble erupts." She walked closer to the caves and faced the others.

"Hmm, I'm not convinced splitting up is a good idea," said Stuart.

"Well, why not?"

"Okay, go on," said Riley.

"Bianca sent us this message, and something important is here. It has to be this escapee she wants us to find. The last thing she would want to do is put us in danger. The tunnels are narrow. We should be able to handle anything coming our way, or at least to turn and run. And then we will have one of us waiting out front to help, as well as listening for any strange sounds. In the event one of the caves is dangerous, at least we wouldn't all be together. We'll be finished quicker, too, and time is important."

Max chimed in. "I agree. And I have the same feeling. Time is essential."

"All right, let's do it," said Stuart.

Shelby noted the charcoal sigil on his chest had smeared.

"I'm game," Max said.

Emily and Riley bobbed their heads in agreement.

Riley said, "Emily, you're the best with a bow. You should stay out here and keep guard." She raked her hands through her knotted blonde hair.

"Done," Emily said.

They decided Shelby and Max would go up the cave on the left, Stuart and Riley to the right. Emily hid herself where she'd be able to guard, but not be seen.

Shelby strode to the cave with confidence, and Max sped after her. At the mouth of the cavity, she knelt and lifted a thick branch from the ground, broke it in half with a *crack*, and tore a strip of cloth from her cloak.

Max frowned. "What are you doing?"

"We need something to illuminate our paths. Caves are dark." She wrapped the material around the top of the stick, then took some twine from her backpack and used it to hold the cloth in place. After striking two pieces of flint, which she found in a pocket on the satchel, she lit the makeshift torch. "Come on."

They inched in as the cavern dimmed. Shelby's eyes adjusted to the darkness, illuminated by flickering light. Several torches protruded from the stony walls, and she lit them as they advanced. She glanced back at the access to the cave and spied Emily squinting after them, her bow cocked.

Rocks crunched underfoot as she moved through. Max crouched down and treaded behind her. They made little noise as they went, but each time a footfall echoed or a pebble skipped across the stone, her heart bounced into her throat.

Almost ten yards in, the cavern came to its first turn. The rocky walls made things difficult to take in, even with the aid of the torches. Beards of moss clung to the craggy walls.

They followed the curve deeper. After a few minutes, the tunnel widened and a wooden door emerged.

"All right, open it." Max's voice bounced off the rock as he raised his blade. "I will enter first."

Wood ground against stone as Shelby pulled the door forward. Max stepped past the entry, his sword leading the way, and she followed. More torches lined the sides, and she lit them.

A large wooden desk with a splintered chair sat in the center of the antechamber. The petrous walls surrounding them contained several file cabinets and hanging pictures.

"Looks like some kind of old office," said Shelby. She drew closer to the wall, where a map had caught her eye. The title of the print read *Earth*.

The diagram was mostly black and white, except one area. The spots she spied on the map were colored green, just off the coast from Morocco in the North Atlantic Ocean. The islands were named the *Atlaseria Islands*; in parentheses it read: *now known as the Canary Islands*.

Max gaped at the map. "Atlaseria. I've had dreams about a place called Atlaseria. My brothers teased me about them."

"Hmm." Shelby squinted as her mind raced. She recalled the sound of an ocean lapping the shore, the scent of fish and salt, and the warm sun. "I've had dreams of a place named Atlaseria, too. I never told anyone, either. I've read about the Canary Islands. I remember some mystery regarding its earlier inhabitants."

She picked up a dusty textbook underneath the map. The title read, *The History of Meridia.*

She turned the cover and a picture of a huge tidal wave about to hit a coastal city poked out. Under the image read, *The Great Deluge: Atlaseria Destroyed.*

"I recall Presage saying they were all originally from Earth," Max whispered.

Shelby turned another page, and a photo of a colossal ship hovering over the ground appeared with the caption: *The Atlaserians decide to leave Earth and travel to Azimuth to begin anew.*

"Do you think because we are Kin we've been having the same dreams about Atlaseria?" she asked.

One of the wardrobes shook to their right. Shelby and Max backed away, swords high. The doors crunched open and a boy plopped to the floor, his tattered clothing flowing as he fell.

"Kin? You are K-Kin?" He scrambled to his feet.

Shelby examined the boy. A mop of sandy hair covered his head, shaggy bangs falling before his blue eyes. He was pale, and the threadbare shirt he wore kept slipping off one of his shoulders. Ash and dirt smudged his cheeks and clothes.

Max asked, "Who are you and what are you doing in this cave?"

"I'm Simon. The Nightlanders kidnapped me until I escaped two nights ago. I hid here ever since." He shielded his eyes from the torchlight. A thin boy, he no doubt lost much of his weight during his time in the cave. He looked rather familiar.

Shelby and Max glanced at each other, nodding.

Simon shivered and stumbled forward a step. "I've only ventured out for berries and water."

"Come with us. We'll keep you safe," said Shelby, offering her hand.

He accepted and she led him back to the mouth of the corridor, tossing the expired torch aside. She and Max worked their way over to where Emily stood sentinel, and found the rest waiting for them.

"A dead end in our cave," said Stuart, "and an empty tunnel—just some hollow barrels and boxes. Any luck?"

Shelby raised her brow as she pulled the boy forward gently.

"We found Simon hiding," said Max.

They all glanced at each other. Shelby nodded behind Simon. Though the day had been long and tiring, she couldn't help but smile. "Simon, is your father Casselton?"

"Yes, yes! Do you know him?"

"Oh yes, he'll be so happy to find out you're fine. He's traveling with a Meridian battalion on the Dorado Path back to Meracuse."

Simon's face contorted with fear. "Oh, no, Malefic will attack Meracuse, if he hasn't already!"

"Where did you hear such news?" asked Max.

"They held me in a jail, underground, right at the brink of the Canopus Hills. I overheard the guards speaking. In fact, they celebrated the fall of Degei while I escaped. They became careless after drinking ale, and I managed to pick one of their pockets for the keys when he stumbled by my cell. I waited until they dozed and made my break." His stomach rumbled, and he held his hand over it, as though embarrassed.

"Here, let me get you some chud. We need you to answer a few questions, but I don't want you starving. Are you thirsty?"

Simon nodded and grabbed the food and canteen from Shelby.

She smiled. "Now, you said your prison was outside the Canopus Hills. Did you notice any other prisoners?"

Simon swallowed a chunk of the chud. "I did, I did. I meant to tell you first thing. Ms. Saddler, of course, was drugged and chained. I stopped at her cell, and she couldn't speak much. She told me I would be safe at the Canaveral Caves. The caves were easy for me to find because of my dad's maps in his office. I should have thought of this straight away, but I haven't had much to eat or drink in days, and I... I'm sluggish." He rubbed his temples as he spoke, and devoured the chud Shelby had given him.

"Do you think you would be able to lead us back to the prison?"

"Why, yes. Its underground location makes it difficult to find if you aren't looking for it. A large entrance is manned by hidden sentries, mostly archers in the treetops. I stole one of the knave's clothing and managed to walk away unobstructed. Distracting the guards is easy because the dungeon is not as heavily protected as you'd expect—about a hundred soldiers, maybe." He took a long swig of water. The torn, black clothing he wore had faded.

"Yes," Riley said, her expression unsure. "However, once they found out you escaped, it's likely Malefic sent a battalion to defend the place. No one knew of the location before, and now you're running around the countryside with valuable information."

"I'm sure of what *I* would do," said Stuart.

"What?" asked Max.

"I would usher them to a different location. Always works with the flag in *Halo*."

"We need to get a move on," Shelby said. "How far from here is the Canopus Hills on foot?"

Simon frowned. "I'm not sure. I ran until I almost passed out, but I'd guess several hours, at the least."

"We have to leave now," she said.

The Kin gathered their belongings and helped their new guide along the path to the Canopus Hills. With a full belly and some water, the youngster seemed to be doing much better.

Shelby gazed at the caves behind her. She wondered where in the woods Zach Ryder might be. Her gut twisted as she thought of Mr. Dempsey's fate, and Sculptor was still missing, too.

And time was running out.

CHAPTER 26

Throg rose from the campfire and plopped down closer to Zach. "I sense things are much worse than I feared. The United Forces are detained, and the countryside is likely overrun with Nightlander troops. We may need to take some risks."

He spoke in a hushed tone as he kept an eye on Brodeur, who was consoling Morgana. "I believe the Assembly is being held near the Canopus Hills. Your link mentioned the valley, and the witch specified the Shattered Woods. Plus Baku said they were close to an ancient battleground. It's possible your fellow Kin must have had contact, and you are right. With things being this dire, Presage may well be headed to the Canopus Hills." He rubbed his hands together.

Zach nodded. "So we should go to these hills as well?"

"Yes, Brodeur might want to continue onto Vixen, but maybe not. I don't think he is a thief, and if he is, he wasn't always. Although her time with us will be dangerous, we cannot allow Morgana to roam the woods alone, so she must accompany us." Throg stood.

Once they were agreed, Throg walked over to Brodeur and the girl. "Are you well enough to travel, Morgana?"

"Sure. I want to get as far away from this place as possible." She stared down into her cup.

Throg turned to the thief. "Brodeur, we may need to part ways. We altered our plans, and will not be heading to Meracuse."

Brodeur nodded, sipping tea. "Where are you going, then?"

"The Canopus Hills. We believe our friends may be traveling in that region." Throg poured the rest of his brew onto the ground.

"Well, I'm not sure if Vixen is even standing right now, and I realize it might not be safe to poke around these woods by myself with war breaking out. Let me finish my drink and think a bit. Am I welcome to join you?"

Throg nodded, though Zach sensed he wasn't sure about Brodeur's company. They both judged Brodeur as trustworthy, but sending him away with their plans in his head was risky. However, the larger their group, the more likely they would be spotted. Still, Brodeur had proved useful when they rescued Morgana.

They packed their belongings and put out the campfire. Smoke sizzled as Zach dumped dirt over the flames. The woods were quiet, as most of the animals that had tried to escape the earlier blaze were long gone. Zach sniffed the air. Thunderheads rolled over the sky, mixing with the black smoke rising from Drake's forest.

Brodeur approached Throg. "I got some friends I can visit up in the village at Canopus. Also, I know a secret spot to stop at along the way—a hidden cabin up near Aventail Point. The nickname is the Spangenhelm, and the place is well stocked with armor, weaponry, and dried goods. We will need to replace whatever we borrow when we can, and add some extra as a fee." He slung his bag over his shoulder.

"Who monitors the Spangenhelm, and what if we didn't reimburse the stuff?" asked Throg.

"Honor among thieves." Brodeur cast a wink.

They traveled on the sides of a path, out of sight of the road. The terrain grew rougher, yet they did not want to be open game on any of the direct roads. After an hour's journey, they caught a glimpse of a figure scurrying down the trail in their direction. The man carried a backpack with a bevy of arrows sticking out of the top.

"He's traveling alone," whispered Brodeur, "and our company is four. I think we should stop and ask him if he has come across anything peculiar up ahead."

Throg nodded. "I'll step in the path, and you will keep a finger on your string."

The figure bustled along closer to them. He resembled a beaver and wore a stolid expression. Throg moved onto the course and placed both his open hands at hip level.

"Good day, traveler. I am curious as to the road ahead. Strange things have been occurring in the woods."

The man stopped short and studied him. "You can say strange again. Bedlam replaces sanity. In a week's time, Meridia seems to have collapsed." He shook his head and shifted the sack to his other shoulder.

"What do you mean?"

"Dear sir, perhaps you have camped in the Cark the past week? Degei has fallen. Ardent's fallen. Lancer's fallen. Even Halcyon's been pillaged. I'm a Fletcher in the village Marbank, which the Nightlanders ransacked yesterday. They are in full force, and have overwhelmed the Meridian Army. All Meridians of good health are being called to defend the capitol, the last large city standing. An enormous Nightlander host is marching to Meracuse as we speak."

Throg cast his eyes at the ground and back at the Fletcher. "I suspected as much. The villages behind me endured the same fate. Did you encounter any Nightlanders from where you came today?"

"Nay, a few scattered patrols, but from what I gather, excess Nightlanders are ordered to storm the capitol."

"Well, be careful on your journey. It is not safe to travel alone, and I suggest you stay off the main path."

"Some friends of mine are not far from here. Godspeed to you," he said, and then with a nod, he scampered past Throg up the road.

"Unbelievable," exclaimed Throg, stroking his goatee. He worked his way back into the brush on the side of the trail, where Brodeur, Morgana and Zach waited.

Brodeur stepped from behind the tree, his arrow still nocked on his bow. "I've never heard of this swift an offensive by the Nightlanders. It's obvious the Aulic Assembly has been disabled, and the Silver Sphere inoperable. The Nightlanders wouldn't be able to overwhelm an army as efficient as Meridia's without Biskara's assistance, and the truth seekers would never allow such a thing to happen unless no one had summoned them. Lord Achernar must have called the Kin, so some hope should remain." He sighed deeply.

Throg frowned. He was watching the way the Fletcher had gone. After a moment of silence, he spoke. "All is not lost, Brodeur, I can assure you. I need to know your history if you are to travel with us. I suspect banditry is not your entire life."

"Ah, yes. I hailed from Candelaria, to the west. I came to Meridia in my youth and joined the Auxilia for some time, then settled down for a bit, actually in Meracuse. I ran with the Blunderbuss centurions. I have traveled alone a few years, thieving mostly, but I lifted from those with abundance, and only the nasty ones." He took his arrow off the string and placed it in his quiver. "And now, if you'll return the favor, why are the Nightlanders looking for you?"

"For the time being, let's just say we are friends of Lord Achernar and are on a mission to assist him." Throg placed his arm on Zach's shoulder.

Sounding aghast, Morgana cried, "How? By what means did this happen so quickly? One of the strongest countries in the world fell to chaos in such a short time."

"This well-orchestrated attack is under Biskara's care," Throg said. "Left unchecked, Biskara can send his son information on where the Meridian forces are advancing, they're weakest points, and when to strike. They would literally be one step ahead of us at all times."

Brodeur nodded. "We need to keep going and get to the Spangenhelm. No sense anguishing on things we cannot control."

Throg walked over to Morgana and placed his hands on her shoulders. "I promise you all is not lost. Shocking, a setback—I agree. You have suffered greatly, but you are not alone, and this revolt is not over."

Zach soaked in the situation, continuing his osmosis of Azimuth. Again, he felt relieved to have found Throg, and he was comfortable with Brodeur. Morgana's plight saddened him, however. She had seen her father slain and her home destroyed. The anger in that alone gave him motivation to persevere in the battle against the Nightlanders.

They trudged on for a few hours. On their walk, Brodeur informed Zach about the Blunderbuss clan, a freewheeling band of soldiers living in the woods. They sounded like an honorable gang, Zach thought, as he pushed past a low-lying tree. He held the branches aside for Morgana and Brodeur. Still holding a branch, he peered around. The forest was quiet, save the sound of birds and small animals scurrying about. He refocused and followed the others as they approached the crest of a grassy knoll.

Brodeur smiled. "Ah, right past the hilltop here." He pointed as he picked up his pace.

They hurried up the mound. Zach slid a bit on the pine needles littering the ground, and righted himself. When he reached the top, Brodeur and Throg were already in place. He offered a hand to Morgana, who shook her head.

"Spot the entrance?" Brodeur asked with his hands on his hips.

They all stared down the knoll and spotted nothing except four large oaks towering in a circle. The ground was soft and grassy, but otherwise unchanged from the woodlands floor. Beyond the four oaks, the forest continued, a massive ocean of pine and oak trees. Hills rose further yet, and in the distance, a few jagged peaks rose.

"I don't see anything," said Throg, squinting.

"Well, the place wouldn't be hidden if the door was out in plain sight, now would it?"

They followed Brodeur down the slope and up to the front of one of the large oaks. He pulled down on a small but thick branch protruding out of the right side of the tree. A crunching, creaky sound reverberated from the wide trunk as the center pushed forward. Brodeur placed his fingers into the creases of the jutting wood and swung the core open. Inside, a staircase descended into the darkness. They all looked at Brodeur, impressed.

"The tree is actually bogus, made by a mentor many years ago. I'm not sure who originally obtained access to it, but the thing is old. I learned about this hideout when I was running with Blunderbuss."

He lifted a dormant torch out of the inside wall and lit it with a flint. After motioning them forward, he descended the stairs.

Zach discerned the orange glow of the torch bobbling over Brodeur's head, but noticed several carvings in the wood on the walls as he passed them. He read one and smiled. "Gurny was here." It was the same as the stalls in his school's bathroom. Thinking about home made him wonder if Adrian was doing all right. He hoped his friend was safe. *Safer than me, ha!*

They reached the bottom and Brodeur lit several other torches to illuminate the room. The antechamber resembled a medieval armory. Wooden panels made up the walls, nailed together with thick, metal spikes. Weapons of all kinds hung from hooks, and several chests and trunks were neatly tucked to the sides. Although a bit dusty, the room was surprisingly clean.

Zach took in a breath of air, tasting a mixture of dust and aged wood. He breathed deeply again, and smiled.

"Okay, now," Brodeur said, "everything we'd want is here. From bardiches to morning stars. I already spy an arbalest I plan on taking. Its steel bow can pierce most armor. In the chests should be tunics, breeches, cloaks, garnaches, and gloves in almost every size. We may also be able to find chud and water, perhaps some wine. Out of respect, we need to clean the room, and pledge an oath we will replace what we use plus bring additional useful items as payment, when we can."

They all nodded in agreement and began going through the trunks. Morgana found a pair of brown leather pants and a chestnut-colored tunic. She changed behind a large chest, and emerged with the first smile Zach had observed that day. Her new apparel fit as if tailored for her.

Zach had less initial success hunting for a change of garb. He eventually came upon olive-colored suede trousers and a brown tunic, which fit nicely, and a leather breastplate that he placed over his tunic—comfortable, yet tough and well suited to travel the rough terrain.

Throg approached them with a pair of oxhide knapsacks. "Here, fill this with extra clothes. We might need them. Also grab some food and water. Whatever you like that may come in useful—and isn't too heavy—go ahead and take it." He plopped the knapsacks down on a chest.

Zach pulled down a sword mounted on the wall, and marveled at how comfortably its handle fit in his hands. Its silver blade shone in the flickering torchlight. The iron pommel contained a single, inlaid, fist-sized ruby. The scabbard was black suede with a sheepskin interior.

In its place, he left the short saber Throg had given him.

Brodeur strode by and placed some items in his bag. "That's a bastard sword. Good choice for a primary blade. You can wield it with one hand or two."

Morgana picked out a rapier and a bow. Zach walked over to her as she conversed with Brodeur. The bow was a finely carved weapon, with vines of ivory inlaid in the dark red wood along its front. A leather grip, the right size for Morgana's smaller hand, had been secured around the bow.

"This bow is similar to the ones from this region," Brodeur said. "I am happy to hear about your skill with a bow. It will come in handy, I assure you. Did all the girls in your village learn to use one?"

"No, my father taught me. He said archery would be a good trait to have for hunting and self-defense in case...." She sighed. "In case something happened to him."

"It sounds like your father was a wise man. He will be avenged."

"I won't rest until he is," she hissed. Her tears were gone now, fiery doggedness replacing the grief of the girl they had rescued.

After a few more minutes of jostling around and looking for items of interest, Brodeur insisted they all clean the space. They finished, and the chamber was organized and free of dust.

Zach wondered about the last time anyone had used this armory. He watched as Morgana wiped down a carved etching in the middle of the room that read, "The Spangenhelm."

"We will rest now for a couple of winks, make some tea, and be off," said Throg as he pulled out the teapot from Brodeur's bag.

Zach withdrew a small dagger he had fancied and walked over to the end of the stairwell. Underneath one of the torches, he tidily carved, "Zach was here." He stepped back when done and grinned. Morgana approached, stood next to him a moment, and inspected his carving. She accepted the dagger from him and etched, "So was Morgana." She smiled again, a warm and pleasant simper, and handed the knife back. Zach wished she would smile more. It fit her naturally.

"I didn't tell the others, but my father taught me to use a bow because of a seer. She came into town and gave my father a reading for a meal. She told him a battle was coming and training me was important. My uncle grunted at the notion, and I thought my father agreed. But the next morning, he took me down by the river and began teaching me. Every sunrise for the last several months, I learned both archery and fencing. Spooky, huh?" She shot him a saddened glance.

"No, I don't think so. This seer had the ability to foresee trouble. With your country at war, those skills are indispensable." He placed his arm on her shoulder.

Suddenly, she hugged him. It was a surprising embrace, which he returned, though his face reddened. They had been through the wringer, and it felt good. When she released her grip, she gazed at him, her cheeks flush.

"I'm sorry. I don't know what came over me. I'm comfortable in your company, and I don't even know y-you. I, I...."

"No need to apologize. I needed a squeeze as much as you. I could always use a good hug these days." He grinned.

Brodeur walked over with a wide smile, holding a large ham in his right hand. "This ham is cured with salt. It can hold for a long time. Be careful not to eat too much though. It will make you thirsty."

He pulled out a blade and sliced several layers off. He gave them a few slices each and wrapped the rest up and placed it into his bag.

The Spangenhelm sparkled. The chamber still had an earthy yet pleasant scent; they had wiped down all the chests and weapons, and Morgana even swept the floor with a diamond-handled broom and a golden dustpan she had found. Those, it seemed, were permanent residents to the Spangenhelm. Some gift from a thief, no doubt, who wanted to repay his dues.

"All right," Throg said. "We picked up supplies, weapons, fresh clothes, and we rested. Now, comfortable as the Spangenhelm is, we must leave. Our breaks should be frequent but short." He slung his knapsack over his shoulder.

They agreed and headed back up the stairs through the throat of the phony tree. Brodeur doused the torches with a wet rag as he followed, and they came out of the opening one by one. Brodeur swung the hinged trunk closed, as they all marveled at how authentic the tree appeared. Even knocking on the trunk, Zach couldn't tell it wasn't real. The wood was so thick it didn't sound hollow.

Afternoon light flooded the knoll as they continued their sojourn. Morgana sidled over to walk beside Zach. Her elbow brushed against his arm.

CHAPTER 27

Stuart and Max pulled out the extra clothes they carried to replace Simon's tattered rags. The garments were a little baggy, but Simon seemed to appreciate their dryness and comfort. After a few pieces of chud and some water, his pasty green complexion turned rosy and stronger.

They allowed Simon to lead the way as they traveled. After two hours of silence, he stopped.

"I need to rest a bit," he said. "I am weak, and my throat is getting scratchy. Do you mind if I make a fire and boil water for broth?"

"Sure," Riley said. "We don't want you passing out on us. I carry a small teakettle in my knapsack." She fished around for it.

They all grabbed some dry wood and shrubs. Shelby took out her flint and struck the two rocks together, which produced sparks and the pleasant sight of flames.

Simon stepped back from the warmth and scanned the area. "Usually, the woods are abundant with castor leaves and sander roots, both good for broth and a sore throat. I should be able to find some here."

Shelby stepped toward him. "Okay, I'll go with you, but stay within a few yards of the campfire. We need to remain close."

He nodded, and they walked in the vicinity counterclockwise as Simon checked the leaves of small trees and knelt in front of some plants, inspecting them.

"Do you know if they demanded my father to provide information for ransom or anything?"

The straightforward question surprised Shelby, and she thought through her words carefully. Simon was mature for his age and should be aware about his father, but she hesitated and wondered if the others would care if she decided to brief him on her own. She determined that lying to this boy would not be right.

"Simon, I do want to tell you some things. We held back at first because of your condition. You're stronger now, and I'd want to know if I were you. The Nightlanders held you as ransom and told your father to botch up his duty on the mobile portal for his assigned Kin, and to report the whereabouts of the current Kin, or they would behead you. He did what they asked and admitted his fault after an ambush. He is in custody, and will be taken to Meracuse to be tried fairly. We all feared greatly for your safety. I think Presage will put a good word in. He seemed sympathetic."

"I wondered why only five Kin showed up. I figured they held me to blackmail for information, and that my father gave whatever they asked of him, since I was still alive. He has been loyal for many years, and considering I am his only son, I believe he may receive a reasonable punishment. Presage will make sure he isn't sentenced to death... if we emerge victorious in this war. Any word from the missing Kin?" Simon knelt down beside a dry-looking plant and began to dig out the root, which went fairly deep.

"Yes, we received information from a Leshy. He found a man named Throg, who was with a Kin. They were sent for when we were separated. Since then, I haven't heard a thing. The Meridian soldiers knew of this Throg, and it sounds like the final Kin will be all right."

"Throg. Yes, I am acquainted with him. He is a good man, private, but fiercely loyal to the Assembly. The Kin is in excellent company, then." He dug out the root with his hands.

"Okay, I found sander roots, and I see castor leaves up ahead, so we are done." He motioned to some low-hanging leaves in front of them, plucked a few and turned them over in his hand, and nodded.

They walked back into the campsite, and he dropped the mix into the boiling liquid.

Simon sat quietly with his legs crossed, watching the kettle. The rest of the Kin hunched around the fire. Most of them ate something or sipped water. The journey had not been easy, physically or emotionally.

Shelby motioned Max and Stuart over. While she'd hoped they would make the decision as a group, she had to tell the others. "I told him about his father. He asked, and I didn't want to lie. He assumed the Nightlanders kidnapped him for ransom."

"I don't blame you," said Max. "He may as well be informed now, and if we waited, he might have held it against us."

Stuart asked as he stretched one of his ankles, "How did he take the news?"

"Like I said, he suspected they captured him for a reason, so he had an idea about it. He also thinks Presage will watch out for his father, considering the situation. He took the news okay."

"Well, no harm done. He should be aware. We'll need to discuss some plans while we rest." Max rubbed the back of his neck. "Simon mentioned a manhole-type entrance, with archers guarding the access. Security has likely strengthened since his escape. Depending on how Malefic judges the scenario, as Stuart pointed out, they easily might have moved the Assembly in order to reduce risks. We can't give in now. This is the final push—it sounds hard, but I know we can do it."

"I think moving them to another location is likely," said Stuart.

The sun sank low and the air turned chilly. Though they needed rest, it wasn't practical to stay for long. They had maybe an hour of daylight left, as a hint of yellow laced the blue horizon.

Night was the beast's time. Shelby shivered and pushed the thought from her mind.

Max cracked his knuckles. "Well, Simon said he escaped a couple of days ago. It's possible they moved the Assembly, but probably not quickly. Simon is nowhere near a Meridian Army, and time would be needed for such information to get out, especially with Meracuse surrounded. There's no Internet here. If they transport the Assembly out of their cells, and we're nearby monitoring the situation, then things may work in our favor."

"Sure," said Shelby. "Unless they're being moved with an entire battalion. Not much the six of us can do on that front."

Max nodded. "True, but Malefic sounds arrogant and might be reckless. He may call every able Nightlander to Meracuse, seeking a quick, decisive victory. His haste and overconfidence could give us a good target. I don't think Biskara can predict everyone's movements, especially ours. I overheard some things about how Biskara seems to be able to channel certain information to Malefic regarding military activity, but probably those are in large numbers. Otherwise, he would've directed Malefic to where Simon was hiding. So the element of surprise should be in our favor."

Stuart shook his head. "Your analysis assumes a lot. One wrong move can kill us and doom these people... not to mention Earth. I think we continue to travel with care and piece the puzzle together. One of us might make contact with our link. Even a single message should shed light on what we need to do."

They shifted to Shelby.

"Okay," she said. "You're both right, and some elements don't really matter this second. I think we all concur to follow Simon back to the underground jail and hatch a plan as we go. Let's check with the others and keep going." She motioned them over to Riley and Emily, who had started looking toward them.

After they explained their plans to the two girls, they agreed to forge ahead and hope for the best. Discussion was fraught with anxiety. If they arrived too late, the Assembly already moved, all they could do was wait for a link to be established. Yet making the trip in such short time might be perilous, but necessary if they wanted to help. Everything hung on the size of the force Malefic had left behind to guard the Assembly.

Simon boiled a couple batches of broth, and they all poured some in their teacups. It tasted like chicken soup, and raised their spirits and warmed them. As the cold night closed in, Simon had two cups of broth and seemed to regain more strength.

Shelby finished her last sip and Simon stood.

"I want you to understand what an honor it is for me to be with you," he told the Kin. "I also want to tell you that some months ago, an old seer passed through Meracuse. He declared I'd be part of an important mission, one that would determine the fate of Meridia. My friends laughed, and I did, too. But when you found me today, and after I regained some strength, I realized that this has to be the mission. I cannot think of anything more crucial. We must free the Assembly, summon the truth seekers, and get the Silver Sphere to locate Biskara's coordinates, or Meracuse and Meridia will fall."

Shelby walked over to him and placed her arm around his shoulders. "We'll do the best we can, Simon. We decided to follow you, and to make plans when we have an idea about the number of men Malefic left to guard the Assembly. Remember to tell us anything that could be useful."

"I shall."

They doused the flames and continued toward the Canopus Hills. They decided to walk in pairs and throw some ideas out to each other, though they spoke in hushed tones. They traveled at a hearty pace, but a little less frantic than earlier, as arriving at the Canopus Hills exhausted would do no good.

Night had fallen, and they whispered through the forest. None dared ask for rest. All shared the unspoken hope that they would reach the Canopus Hills before dawn, and then hatch a plan.

Crunching through the leaves, Shelby considered their options. What could they do other than wait? After touching the hilt of her saber, she felt more at peace. She had proven herself in battle, and if it came down to it, she would again. Her breath rose in puffs before her.

The moon hung pregnant in the night sky, surrounded by glittering stars. A few clouds veiled the orb, throwing shadows across the dark landscape. Still, they walked. Simon seemed to be doing well. He didn't speak other than to point out markers along their path.

After some time passed, a chilling snarl peeled from the east. The growl came from a distance, deep and grating. Everyone froze.

"What the heck is that?" Max whispered.

"A Manticore," said Simon, sounding nervous. "We must stay closer together. They do not tend to attack groups of people."

Shelby swallowed hard. It was like hearing the beast. "Well, I'm all for tightening the group. That Manticore sounds pretty big. Simon, what exactly is a Manticore?"

"Picture the head of a man, the body of a lion, and a tail with a spiked ball at the end. Even though the head appears similar to a man's, its intelligence is more like a beast's. I read they are almost extinct, so it is rare to encounter one. But I heard one from a distance once, and my father told me it was a Manticore."

Manticore

"Well, we should be ready if this one decides to attack," Emily said. She pulled an arrow out and placed it on her bow.

They continued walking, trying to remain as quiet as possible. Shelby loaded her crossbow, and Stuart drew his hand-cannon. The roar grew fainter as they walked, and before long, they put their weapons away.

After a while, they rested to discuss their ideas. This round, they did not make a fire, despite the chill. No time to spare. Rather, they sat huddled together. Shelby drew her cloak tightly around herself.

The crunch of a snapping branch came from their right.

Shelby jerked to her feet. The Kin whirled to the direction of the noise, and a gangly man stepped from behind a tree in front of them. He moved forward a few paces, and Stuart aimed his hand-cannon at the intruder.

The figure froze.

"Not another step until you tell us what you seek," said Stuart.

"Well, your hand-cannon won't help you much here, son. You are surrounded by twenty crossbows. One move on your part, and they will release," he said coolly. "Nice fertility sign, by the way." The man smirked at the smeared sigil on Stuart's chest.

CHAPTER 28

They all peered around uneasily, seeing no one but the gangly man.

Shelby frowned at him and moved her hand to rest on her crossbow. An arrow was loaded up and it was ready to be fired. Should the trespasser make any sudden movements, she would shoot him. "What do you want?"

He folded his stick-thin arms across his chest and strained his blade-shaped face. "I think I'll be asking the questions. What are you doing here, and where are you going?"

Simon blurted, "Our town was burned and plundered, and we are simply trying to find someplace safe to go."

"From which village do you hail, child?"

"Gaston."

"Nightlanders, I assume."

Raising his arms, Simon snorted, "Who else?"

"Some pillaging has been done by bands of thieves and the like, taking advantage of the confusion."

"Are you a band of thieves?" asked Simon.

"I am Blunderbuss." He moved forward a few paces again.

Simon didn't respond immediately. He stood motionless a second before he spoke. "I recognize your name and have heard many things about you—some good... some bad."

"Of course you have. All you need to know right now is that we hate Nightlanders." Blunderbuss whistled.

Several men, expertly hidden in bushes and trees, came forward. Every one of them dressed in earthy tones, with mud on their faces and matted hair. In the dark, they were impossible to see until they moved.

"The woods around here aren't secure," Blunderbuss said. "A Manticore is roaming, and we fought and killed a Nightlander patrol and, of all things, a Zumbaki pack. Nightlander activity just picked up in the last day. They are looking for something around here. Offer us payment, and we'll honorably assist you through."

Riley glared at him. Shelby nodded and motioned for her friend to relax.

She then stepped forward. "We only carry the clothes on our backs and the weapons you see, plus a little food. We cannot spare any provisions."

Blunderbuss studied them and smiled. "Well then, we'll give you safe passage, and you will owe us a debt." He pointed his spindly arms to the woods behind him.

"And if we can't ever repay you?" said Riley.

"I'm good at reading people. If you can't, I will assume you're dead. Then the tab won't really matter. I'd rather hold a bad debt than a guilty conscience, letting a group of youngsters be killed in my territory."

Blunderbuss placed his right hand down as if petting a dog, and his men all lowered their weapons. Some slung their crossbows around their backs. A few grunted and muttered to one another.

"You mentioned you're looking for someplace safe. Any idea where you're headed?" Blunderbuss strolled over to them with a warm grin plastered to his face.

"Some friends up in the Canopus Hills are waiting to meet with us," said Simon.

Blunderbuss gave him a wary glance, and shot a look at Max, who stood closest.

Shelby had forgotten that they appeared much older and formidable now. She hoped Max had caught on.

"Yes," said Max, "we visited Gaston when it was attacked, and are not familiar with these parts. Simon is guiding us."

Shelby relaxed a hair.

"So, from where do you hail?"

"Meracuse," she blurted, wondering if she supplied the right answer.

He rubbed his pointy chin. "Ah, city kids looking for adventure?"

"Visiting Simon and his family," said Stuart. "Figured a little country air would do us well. We're all from the same school, Pictor Academy."

"Not safe in these woods right now, laddie. We are heading to Vixen. We aim to restock and find out more information about Nightlander

movement. Vixen isn't far from here. I insist you join us, and you can make your plans from there. I assure you that no Nightlanders are in the city."

"Safe in Vixen?" said Simon, wringing his hands.

"If you are with me. I own a private section at the Scuttlebutt."

Shelby motioned everyone closer and they huddled. "Vixen is a city?"

Simon looked horrified at the thought of going to the town. "Yes, but different than the others. Vixen is loaded with taverns, gambling, black markets, and the sort. Local villagers go for entertainment, though my father told me it was dangerous."

"Plenty of us together to protect each other," said Riley. "We'd probably find out some things, and a couple hours of rest shouldn't hurt. With all the Nightlanders tracking Simon around here, Vixen sounds safe for a stop. We've been through a lot."

Shelby's brow creased. "Can we trust Blunderbuss? What if he is leading us into a trap?"

"Vixen is populated by armed gangs," said Simon, "and Blunderbuss and his kind would never want the Nightlanders to take over. He is right: they would not allow entry to Nightlanders. The tales of Blunderbuss I've heard did not include him harming children and youngsters."

"Okay then," Max said. "We go, eat real food, and pick up intel and goods for the journey. I noticed a pouch of coogles in my knapsack. I think you have the same too, guys."

They bobbed their heads in agreement.

Shelby turned to Blunderbuss. "Thank you. We accept your offer. We wish not to stay long in Vixen, though."

"Fine by me. We planned on having a drink or two and grub, gathering some supplies, and then heading back to our base. When we leave, we will take you as far as our camp. Happens to be along the way to Canopus. After that, you're on your own."

They hiked with Blunderbuss and his men for a half-hour. The soldiers seemed a playful, merry group, snatching hats off one another's heads and pick-pocketing each other's belongings. Their loud behavior shocked Shelby; had they any fear of the Nightlander patrols, none of them showed it.

They waded through an area thick with brush, and Vixen came into view as the group emerged from the thicket. The walls sprawled high, built with massive lacquered logs lodged into a broad and polished concrete base. Shelby didn't spot a gate or entrance, but she could hear the city. The muffled noise carried through the air — the sound of civilization.

Blunderbuss and a few of his men led them to a space on the ground, where a rusted, brown clamp protruded from the soil.

He grasped the hook and yanked the large hatch up. "There are several entrances scattered around Vixen, all underground tunnels that lead into the city. No horses or carriages allowed. They operate a stable for those near the main hatch on the far side. I know the guards at this post."

They followed him down the shaft. The corridor at the bottom of the stone steps was well lit with torches, and wide enough to bring in cattle and other livestock. The tunnel smelled of earth and salt. There was another odor, too—richer, sweeter, and it made Shelby's mouth water. A handful of blue-clad sentries nodded to Blunderbuss as they drew closer.

"Been a while, Blunderbuss. I was worried with all that's happening," the sentry said.

"Yep, troubled times, Torf."

Torf adjusted his pike and buckler. "Vixen is on high alert. Main tunnel is closed. We spied a squad of Nightlanders passing by last night. Go on in."

He was as wide as a wall and tall to boot. Shelby wouldn't want to fight him in a scrap. Unlike most of the soldiers she'd seen, he was clean-shaven and had short brown hair.

"Much obliged." Blunderbuss waved them into a foyer past the guards.

They climbed a set of earth and stone steps. Torf hit a lever and metal doors in the antechamber grated open. Bit by bit, the city came into view. The Kin stepped forward.

"Wow," murmured Shelby.

Vixen teemed with activity. Rows of huts selling merchandise spread out across the middle of the cobblestone square. Jugglers stood a few feet away, garbed in brilliant motley. A jongleur strumming a banjo sprang up to them, singing.

> "VIXEN HAS WHAT YOU DESIRE,
> COME FORTH I SAY AND SIMPLY ADMIRE,
> GO AHEAD NOW ENJOY ALL YOU REQUIRE,
> FOR THIS TOWN WILL NEVER TIRE,
> BY THE WAY I'M FOR HIRE."

A florist in a tight-cinched tan bodice and a trail of calico skirts carrying a bevy of roses approached Max. "Just one coogle a blossom for your pretty lady," purred the florist, arching up to him.

Max's cheeks reddened. "Uh, sure," and he fished out a coogle. He accepted the rose and turned to Shelby. "Milady," he chirped with a flourish and a bow, handing her the flower.

Shelby felt herself blush, probably as crimson as the petals. She twirled the stem in her fingers.

"Okay, now, follow me to the Scuttlebutt and stay close," Blunderbuss said as he strode forward.

They advanced through the bustling crowd. Smells and sounds assaulted Shelby. Salts and dried meats were rich, and the odor of smoke hovered around their stalls. Fruits and vegetables stormed her with ripe, citrus-like scents.

"Fresh eel from the Invunche here," cried out a fishmonger.

A fruiterer shouted, "Tasty Landorian apples, name your price."

A scantily clad ecdysiast sidled up to Max, ruffling his hair while swirling her curvy figure. Her violet and copper robes dipped low on her bare, white back. The front of her shirt was covered with a shawl that glittered like cloth of gold. Black hair fell in neat ringlets around her narrow face.

"A few coogles to dance with me, my prince," she crooned.

Shelby cut between them. "I think he'll pass!"

The dancer giggled and moved to one of Blunderbuss's men. As she passed, the scents of myrrh and cinnamon wafted from her.

A stilt walker sauntered among their parties, clothed in violet furs. His face was painted with a joker's mug. Swinging one leg over the Kin, he yelled, "Free blueberry ale at the Whistler for the next hour!"

To their right, two dwarves on ponies galloped at each other in a game of joust, their blunted lances high in the air. The crowd behind the ropes placed bets and urged them on.

"For the throat! The throat!"

"Are ye mad? The knee! He'll lose 'is grip and fall!"

"Thirty coogles to the Slayer!"

Rainbow-colored confetti fell around them; boys with bucketsful tossed the paper about. Kids younger than Simon and garbed in rags picked up handfuls and ran down the lanes, screeching with laughter.

On the outskirts of the marketplace sprawled stony specialty shops, inns, boutiques, casinos, and saloons. Balconies perched atop the humming stores, each one offering a different tale. Red Bucket Inn, one said. Game o' the Ace, exclaimed another.

A new kind of smell hit Shelby. Outside of the market, the inns and taverns left the scent of cooking meat and stew thick in the air. She breathed deep, her mouth watering.

Mummers and bards hovered by the square, darting in and out of the conflux. Numerous bands played, their songs muddling together to create one fantastic noise. Shelby thought she spied a thief snatch someone's purse, but before she could check if she was right, the bandit vanished into the throng.

"Almost there," said Blunderbuss.

The Scuttlebutt sat beyond a festive band of musicians dressed in black leather tuxedos. The name crouched over the entrance in bright green letters, with grey statues of one man whispering into another's ear at the door. A brutish bouncer stood at his beat.

He stared down at Shelby over a snubbed nose. "Greetings, Blunderbuss. You are recruiting youngsters these days?"

"Friends of mine. Had their village plundered by Nightlanders."

"If I spot any Nightlanders, I'll rip them in two," the bouncer snarled. "Come on in."

The tavern was dark with earthy tones, and the glow of the candles on tables flickered among shadowy faces. A pair of warriors played Nine Men's Morris nearby, contemplating their next moves amidst the ruckus of the bar. The star-shaped board had almost a hundred black and white pieces, all of them carved to look like goblins, dragons, knights, and horses. Shelby thought a maiden was at the center, but couldn't tell.

A man with a calvous dome sprinted up to Blunderbuss. His once purple doublet had lost most of its color and was lackluster, though it fit him well.

"Ahoy, Blunderbuss, I've had a bad day at knucklebones. Can you help out an old friend?"

Blunderbuss handed him a fistful of silver coogles. "If your luck is short forthwith, Mantor, stay away from the tables. You hear any news on Malefic today?"

"It's not good. Most of the towns and villages have been decimated. A large contingent is marching to Meracuse."

Blunderbuss turned to the Kin. "I'll take you to my section back of the tavern. No one will bother you there."

They clung to his shadow past the rowdy patrons of the Scuttlebutt. He led them to a roped-off area and pointed to a wooden booth. A merry fire crackled in a small pit beside the table.

"You kids sit. No ale for you, little one." He eyed Simon.

Shelby slid into the alcove as Max and the rest filtered in. The wood was shiny and worn, slick to the touch, except where a few patrons had carved their names. Across the back of the bench pressed against the wall, someone had written a list of Blunderbuss's men.

Shelby said, "Let's eat and try to pluck any info possible. Later we'll pick up some stuff we can use in the square, but we should go in an hour."

Stuart nodded. "I agree. Blunderbuss seems okay. I was worried a bit. At least everyone in Vixen appears to know Malefic is bad news."

Riley flattened out her leather skirt. "Yeah, I freaked out heading into the underground tunnel, but everything Blunderbuss has said so far is above board."

Shelby spied Emily, who stared down at the table. "Emily, what do you think?"

The shy girl glanced up from the wood. "I don't trust strangers. Vixen looks exciting, except a lot of creepy dudes are around. We should definitely leave soon." She folded her arms across her chest and leaned forward.

Several blue-clad soldiers burst in past the bouncer at the entrance. They wore garb similar to the sentries in the corridor. Their armor glistened in blue enamel chips, with a velvet shirt draped over, emblazoned with the image of a golden fox on the front.

They surrounded a table of men playing cards. One of the gamblers jumped up and they wrestled him to the ground. An officer pulled a black shiny gun from the man's pants.

"A blaster. The tip checks out, sir," said the sentry to his superior. "This is against the code of Azimuth."

"Fellas, it's my granddaddy's. I was nervous with the talk of the Nightlanders invading Meridia," the man said as they cuffed him.

"The law was created for a reason," the officer said. "And the fine is heavy. Under no circumstances is lethal technological weaponry allowed on Azimuth. The rules are clear. Take him away."

They dragged him out of the tavern amidst the grumbling crowd.

"He should know better," said Blunderbuss as he angled over their table. "The code is serious. Weapons of that sort have been abolished since the war against Hideux."

Stuart turned red. "Um, I have a hand-cannon."

"A different type of weapon under the statutes. Hand-cannons don't kill, and magic is involved in their creation. People who are born with abilities like that are a kind of sorcerer, and aren't against the law. They aren't supposed to use their talents to heist a carriage or anything, but they are okay to utilize them in self-defense. Ya can't tell a fast runner to slow down in a race. Don't you guys know this from Pictor Academy? Pretty high-end school." His forehead scrunched.

"Uh, yes," Max said. "We're a little frayed with the invasion and our first time in Vixen."

Servers arrived with plates of fried cheese, glazed ribs, steaming baskets of bread, sautéed spinach, and jugs of apple ale. The aromas were rich. Frizzled cheese smelled crisp, and the ribs wafted garlic, onion, and some other strange spices Shelby didn't recognize. A few glazed mushrooms circled the ribs. The bread was so warm that the butter melted as soon as it was spread.

"Enjoy. This one's on me. Let's just say I'm an investor in the Scuttlebutt," said Blunderbuss.

The Kin gorged on the platters. The apple ale tickled Shelby's nose, at once sweet and tart.

Simon chugged water and juice as he gnawed on some cheese.

"Awesome to chow on real food," Stuart said while riddling a rib.

Shelby swigged the apple ale. She had sipped beer before and never cared much for it, but she was quickly growing fond of this drink. The malt had the perfect sweetness, and it warmed her.

Wiping her mouth, Shelby turned to their benefactor, who sat a few places down the table. "Thank you, Blunderbuss. Why are you helping us, may I ask?"

Blunderbuss chugged a pint of brew clean, and placed it on the table. "You were in my territory. War is breaking out. Whatever is said of me, dang it if I'll allow a group of youthful refugees to be harmed under my watch. Ansel, another pitcher of ale!"

Shelby kept a wary eye on the room. Several of the patrons whispered and cast glances in their direction. A bunch of warriors played at darts, and seemed to take particular interest in Blunderbuss's section.

The group finished their meal and the platters lay empty. Shelby's stomach was sated for the moment. She wondered if she might find dried meats to carry with them, and perhaps some bread that would keep. It was nice having her belly full and a mug in hand.

She said, "Is it just me being paranoid or are we getting a lot of stares our way?"

Stuart rubbed his chin. "Maybe it's because we are the youngest here?"

"Yeah," said Max, "but I think we should get going. Hit the market, grab a few things, and go to Canopus."

"Agreed. Let's tell Blunderbuss and head on out." Shelby downed the rest of her ale, stepped out of the booth and strode to the Centurion leader. "Blunderbuss, thanks again for your hospitality. We really need to be going, though."

"Milady, you are much safer here than heading to Canopus at this hour. What's the rush?"

"We have family and friends at Canopus and are anxious to meet up with them, especially since the village we were visiting has fallen."

"All right, we will stock up on supplies at the market. Afterward, we'll lead you back to our camp and you can travel to Canopus from there." Blunderbuss gulped his ale.

"Perfect." She returned to the booth, but uneasiness quavered through her. She was still edgy about the group of men playing darts, who continued to chatter among themselves and spy on their area. "Blunderbuss said it was fine. He's ready to leave. I don't care for the looks we are getting, even if we're younger than most."

Max frowned, his brow furrowing. "Don't be paranoid, Shel. Blunderbuss has a big crew with him and seems to be pretty well-liked in Vixen. We'll head back to his camp and get on the road."

Despite his reassurance, Shelby's skin prickled whenever the men gazed in their direction. She tried to return their stare with a glower, but one man with a scar running around his neck and shoulder only laughed.

The beast is in him, she realized, horrified.

Once everyone had finished their drinks, they filed through the crowded tavern and out onto the bustling street. Shelby was glad to leave the men behind. Peddlers converged on them as they pushed their way to the market stands.

"Let's buy some apples," said Riley as she approached a cart bursting with them. Red and green looked familiar, but there were also purple, orange, and blue apples.

"Name your price," the fruiterer said.

Shelby squinted. "Um, three for a coogle?"

"Sold." He packed two reds and an orange.

They ambled down to a table of chud and bought a few pouches' worth as Blunderbuss haggled over the cost. The stall tender burgeoned from beneath his tight doublet. His chins wobbled as he spoke.

"Are you kidding me?" shouted Blunderbuss. "Fifty coogles for ten pouches? I say five coogles and be glad we're not mugging you!"

"Thirty coogles, and that's my final offer," snarled the salesman.

"Ten coogles and I'll come back and wreck your stall!"

"Who do ye think ye are? Blunderbuss or somethin'?"

Blunderbuss barked a laugh. "Oh, I wouldn't go so far as to say *that*. Now, fifteen coogles. Final offer. If you refuse, I'll go to that lovely lady down the street and get just as much for less."

"Fine, fine. Fifteen," he muttered, handing over the goods.

Shelby glanced over the crowd and recognized one of the men from the Scuttlebutt—the man with the ragged scar. When he locked eyes with her, he saluted and grinned, revealing brown teeth.

Shelby snatched Blunderbuss's arm. "That guy over there... he was staring at our section in the Scuttlebutt and now he's following us."

"Which one? Bane? He's a wily rat, but what would he want with a bunch of young'uns?"

The table of almonds and walnuts in front of them blasted in the air. Several men charged forward, and the square turned into a twister of activity. Shelby spotted Bane sprinting in with others from behind. The stilt walker wobbled back and forth amidst the rolling nuts before crashing down on a cart of fish and ice. People shouted, nagged, and wailed, but mostly, they fought.

Shelby drew her rapier, the other Kin following her lead. One of the pursuers grabbed her arm, and Max brought his long sword down. The ruffian screamed as blood spurted forth in a crimson spray.

"What in Fornax are you up to, Bane?" Blunderbuss hollered as he drew his blade.

"Your half-grown gang matches the description a Nightlander captain gave us. Kin. He offered us a rich bounty and amnesty when they are in power, if we spot 'em."

Blunderbuss stuttered, "Wha...? K-Kin?"

The sounds of clanging metal rang as Blunderbuss's men engaged Bane's gang. Bards, proprietors, and dancers shrieked and jumped out of the fray holding their heads. Salesmen tried to retrieve goods from the ground before they were soiled or lost. A few of the tougher men drew knives or short swords, and hacked at anyone who came too close.

"This way," yelled Max, motioning the Kin behind the huts.

They rushed through the pack and up the corridor. Shelby's heart slammed against her ribs as Bane's goons gave chase. Max led the Kin across the square to the other side. Stuart, bringing up the rear, sliced the posts of the apple cart as he passed, spraying multicolored orbs onto the cobblestones.

"Sorry!" he shouted to the distressed fruiterer.

They raced past the Scuttlebutt, the bouncer eyeing them. Shelby glanced over her shoulder to see him plow his huge frame in front of the thugs. They all smacked into each other in a pile, and the bouncer gave a hearty laugh.

The Kin barreled down the path; Shelby had no idea where. She tried to dodge anyone who got in her way. Riley was just behind her, and Shelby yanked her aside when she almost hit a cart.

A lady wrapped in a blue cloak stepped onto the street. "Kin, in here if you wish to escape," she said.

She pointed to the entrance of a store, over which hung a wooden sign: *Wintress the Channeller.*

Shelby stopped as Max glanced back at her. She nodded, and they darted into the shop. The lady closed and locked the door. Aromas of sage, chamomile, and patchouli hung in the air. A broad parchment lay on a desk with the words, *Kin return*, written at the top. Five figures were painted in the image. It was them running through a busy city.

"To the rear. They will check every store. Quickly now," the woman ushered, whipping back a curtain.

Shelby scurried past the channeller, the Kin in her wake. The woman's glittering golden eyes followed her.

More vellum hung on the walls. One showed a picture of six children holding hands. The caption read: *The Kin's identities breached; sent to Earth.*

Shelby gasped. The Kin were *sent* to Earth as children? Her jaw hung open.

"My name is Wintress. I have gifts as an augur, and am an ally of the Assembly." She pulled up a carpet, revealing a wooden hatch. Lifting the opening, she motioned them through.

"Th-those pictures...," said Shelby.

"No time, lass. These tunnels run underneath Vixen. Go now. Seek out Blunderbuss. Listen to your soul guides and instincts. They will lead you back to him."

Shelby wanted to ask more, but Riley pushed her through. Without speaking, they entered the shaft and dropped to the bottom.

Wintress peered down at them. "The Assembly will contact you soon. Godspeed," she whispered, and shut the lid.

They stood in the dim passageway, their foreheads glistening with sweat. Rats scurried past them to the side of the walls. Glowing stones lined the passage, lighting the halls. It smelled of moist earth and dust.

"Okay, which way? Because I'm not sensing anything," said Stuart.

Shelby turned north and then south, and pointed. "I think this is the direction to the gate we came in through. What was the guard's name?"

"Torf," said Riley. Her braided blonde hair had some loose strands. Dirt smudged her left cheek.

"Then let's make our way there. Wintress said these run under Vixen. I'm sure we'll spot another hatch as we go."

The dark labyrinth coiled several times along the course. They trudged forward for a few minutes, and noticed a hatch. Max reached for it, but Shelby touched his arm.

"Not the right one. I sense this isn't the proper exit."

"Me too," said Riley. "In my gut. Remember what Wintress told us."

Max nodded and continued down the tunnels. Stuart began to lag, and Shelby fell back beside him.

"We should hurry," she said.

"I know. Was just making sure no one was following us."

"Good idea."

Before long, another wooden hatch appeared. The rock around the edges had chipped and worn away.

"This one," Emily said.

Shelby glanced at her. She seemed stronger, bolder, as if she had begun to escape her shell.

They stared at the latch, and each dipped their heads in acknowledgement. A warm touch of reassurance spread through Shelby.

Max pulled on the lever and it popped open. "Boost me up."

Stuart clasped his hands, and Max placed his foot in them and inched his head above the opening.

"All clear. An alleyway."

Max hoisted himself up and held his hand down. Shelby grabbed it and he pulled her up, and the others followed suit. Trash was piled against a warped wooden fence at one end. The alley gave a slight turn, and they peeked around the corner. The square was ahead, the market still brimming with performers and bystanders. A few men shouted, but most were back to business.

Shelby said, "I see the florist. We are near the entrance we came through."

They stayed close to the wall and filed to the end. Shelby tried to ignore the grime and mud on the ground, sidestepping a bundle of cloth that reeked like sour food.

Max checked around. "Okay, left is the gate. Let's go."

The Kin turned and treaded to the exit. Shelby spotted one of the boys with a bucketful of confetti, and an idea sprang to mind.

"We love confetti. How about a gold coogle if you can toss some around us as we walk?"

"Sold," the boy stated, and rained confetti on them as they strode.

A balladeer burst out of the crowd playing an accordion. He pranced beside them, singing in a melodious tone.

> "THE KIN ARE SAID TO HAVE ARRIVED,
> BE JOYFUL NOW HOPE IS ALIVE,
> FOR ONCE THE SILVER SPHERE IS CALLED,
> BISKARA WILL THEN SURELY FALL!"

Shelby nodded and smiled as they marched ahead. Max clasped her hand amidst the falling paper, and a rush of heat filled her as her heart gave a little dance.

As they approached the outlet, Blunderbuss's gangly form emerged from a foyer. "I figured you'd be headed here."

"We have to leave," Shelby said, her eyes locked on Blunderbuss. She released Max's hand and laid her palm on the hilt of her sword. The cold metal felt almost alien after Max's tender fingers.

"Of course you do. We are all doomed if Biskara takes over. Whatever you need of me, it's yours. First, let's get back to my camp—the crowd here is buzzing about Kin. Bane won't be the only bounty hunter in Vixen." The sly Centurion pushed his way to the gate with the Kin trailing behind, and shouted, "Torf, time for me to leave."

Torf poked his head through the metal grate. "Sorry, boss. Vixen has been ordered to lockdown."

Yells rose up from the masses to their rear. Shelby spotted Bane and his heathens working around the herd. They looked like dogs sniffing for the scent of their prey. A shiver sped down her spine.

"Laddie, you must trust me. If I don't get the Kin out of here, Vixen won't last more than a few weeks once Malefic is in power."

Torf peeked over Blunderbuss's shoulder and to the Kin, fear and confusion in his gaze. Behind them, the goons cried out and catapulted forward. Torf nodded and pulled the lever. The iron grate lifted and they all ran under. After Blunderbuss's men passed, Torf dropped the gate.

"Run," Blunderbuss shouted.

They scurried down the shaft as Bane and his gang bellowed at Torf to open the door.

Shelby sucked in cold air. Her lungs burned from running. Even the beast had never chased her so much back home. At last, they arrived at the hatch and clambered up the wooden steps and out into the weald.

Once all were atop, Blunderbuss stared at them, kicking the dirt. "The Kin. Glory be. I hope you have a plan in Canopus. Let's go." He dashed off into the forest.

CHAPTER 29

They arrived at the campsite and found the place well organized. Several leather tents and fires formed three circles, and a few sets of transparent wires wrapped around the trees spanned the whole site.

Blunderbuss led them through a section where he unhooked the wire. "Welcome to our hideout."

After re-rigging the traps, Blunderbuss directed them to a small campfire and motioned them to sit down. One of his men brought over a cask of ale and mugs. Meat roasted over the flame. A crew of Blunderbuss's men had stayed behind to tend and watch the headquarters. They'd been cooking for some time.

"Isn't the hour a little late to cook?" Shelby glanced up at the full moon.

"With the hours we keep? Nah. We're always hungry." He winked. "Now, please excuse me. Pour a drink. I will be back in a few minutes." He placed his arm on the shoulders of one of his men and whispered as they strolled off.

Max's expression contorted and he rolled to his side, holding his crown. He gasped in agony.

Shelby rushed over while the rest of them formed a small circle around him. "Don't fight it, Max. Let the message come. Soon, the sharp pain will be over." She remembered Presage's words.

Blunderbuss returned and lurched into the circle, his eyebrows raised.

Shelby watched her friend for a long time. She held her breath.

Finally, Max sat up, rubbed the back of his head, and groaned. "They are being moved. Tomorrow... early evening."

Stuart poked his head closer. "What did he say?"

"Nothing. Different this time. I was looking through his eyes, and I overheard two soldiers discussing the orders to transfer them. Something about the Gida Path."

Blunderbuss moved forward, and they all stared at him. "Well you are definitely Kin. I can't believe earlier I thought you needed an escort through our territory."

"Did they say how they planned to move them?" said Shelby.

"Yes, in a large stagecoach. They are headed to an old house near the Canopus Hills village." Max rose to his feet with her assistance.

Blunderbuss walked directly up to him. "So your communication means the Assembly is alive, I take it?"

"We need to leave... *now*," said Max.

"Whatever you desire from me, I already told you, I will give it—on one condition."

"The condition is...?" Shelby cast a hardened glare.

"We get through this all right, and you need to put a good word in for us with Achernar and the Assembly. I'm not a pig, but a reward wouldn't hurt, either. That's if we deserve one. Mostly, I want the government off our backs."

Shelby glanced at the other Kin, and they all nodded. "I think the Assembly would be gracious to all those who assisted in the welfare of Meridia, but we will certainly put in a good word."

Blunderbuss rubbed his palms together. "Okay... much to do. You say the Assembly is being moved from one prison to another location, riding a stagecoach with a large contingent on the Gida Path?" He placed his tin mug down and glanced up at Max.

"That is correct."

Shelby remembered how drained she'd been after her last link.

"He's sharp as a shiv," Stuart whispered in her ear.

Blunderbuss clapped his hands together. "We're in luck. I have an idea. On the Gida Path is a tunnel that we've rigged. Let me meet with the boys and check on some things."

"How many are in your gang?" said Max.

"Fifty-five. I'll have to leave a portion behind to guard our camp and valuables." His gaze spanned the encampment.

Riley stepped forward. "This is a critical time for everyone. We'll need every resource."

"Listen here, I said I would help, but I must protect what we own. We will close up two circles of the camp and bury our valuables, and station ten men behind. We can't travel with all our haul, and I'll have a mutiny if I leave our things unprotected."

"Those valuables will be worth scrap metal if the Nightlanders win this war," said Stuart.

Blunderbuss peered off into the distance, contemplating. "I'll call a quick meeting and have a poll. I suppose if we hide our better pieces, I can get away with leaving five behind, but it has to go to a vote." He trudged off.

After Blunderbuss was out of earshot, Emily spoke. "We shouldn't push that much. I was worried they were going to lock us up and steal everything we owned when we first met him. We should be grateful he's helping us at all."

Shelby nodded. "Yes, but we owe it to the Assembly to gather as many resources as possible. The five of us can only get so much done against a battalion."

"Six of us," said Simon. "And don't underestimate your own prowess. The history books are rich with the Kin and their abilities."

As they awaited the results of Blunderbuss's meeting, a twitch tickled Shelby's head. Bianca was reaching out to her, and little pain came with this linkage. Presage was accurate in his assessment of the throbbing. The ache lessened with each contact. She heard Bianca's low voice and made out her words.

"*We leave at dusk tomorrow... Gida Path. You must travel... less than fifty if you possess no mentor to shield you. Biskara... senses the movements of fifty... more if... move... and... no shields....*" Bianca's voice tailed off.

"Shelby, are you okay?" Riley asked.

"Yes, I had a brief contact." She massaged her temples.

Riley tucked a stray strand of hair behind her ear. "The pain?"

"Not bad, and the communication has gotten easier. She said they leave at sundown tomorrow on the Gida Path, and for us to travel in groups less than fifty if we do not have a mentor with us, or Biskara may detect our movement. So that solves Blunderbuss's problem. Six of us and, to stay on the safe side, our group should be no larger than forty-five. He can leave seventeen behind."

"That doesn't make sense, if you think things through," said Riley, stroking her chin.

"What?"

"I was just thinking. If Biskara can discover certain movements and report them, then why did Presage not know this? It explains the second ambush... and, uh, well, he put us in danger, no?"

And Mr. Dempsey, Shelby thought. She tried to keep back the tears, wiping her eyes with the heel of her hands. Now that she had time to rest, he kept jumping to mind. "This must be new. Otherwise he would've known. I should believe what Bianca tells me, don't you think?"

Riley pulled at her blonde braid. "Yes, we should assume this ability of Biskara's is something new, and go with what our contacts say. So far, only you and Max have had success linking with your Kin. I feel an itch in my head sometimes, even an image, but nothing otherwise."

Simon gazed up at them. "I can tell you from my history texts that I do remember reading that Biskara can follow large military movements, much more than fifty, so this is different—his ability to monitor smaller groups. As far as your contacts go, from what I read, all Assembly members have certain talents in which they excel. Making contact can be one of them." He stood up straight.

Shelby nodded. "I'll be right back." She turned to seek out Blunderbuss.

He was nearby, huddled with a few men. She told him about her contact.

"That's good news. The boys will want to help. They all hate the Nightlanders. But votes keep the group harmonious, and I'm not exactly a ruthless dictator." He turned back to the men.

She returned to the Kin and Simon, and sat down. Glancing around at their faces, she saw they all were deep in thought. A tired bunch, they looked as dead as a group of students after pulling an all-nighter studying for exams.

Blunderbuss returned, his spindly shadow announcing his approach. "We are ready to go. We will need a little bit of time to pack up and get the camp situated. We also lifted Nightlander uniforms from their barracks a few days back. I knew they would come in handy." He picked up a mug, filling it to the brim from the jug of ale, and chugged the entire thing.

"So what is the plan?" asked Shelby.

"Ah, I'll be back in a few minutes. Be ready to go. Still checking on some things. Then I will give it to you." He wiped his mouth and sprinted off.

From a distance, the roar of the Manticore came once more, echoing through the desolate, foggy woods. Shelby shivered. Dawn would be coming soon. Hopefully, they'd have time to rest again before setting their plan in motion.

"Seems like the Manticore is following us. Do you get the same sense?" Simon flashed a nervous smirk.

"Sure do. From what you told us, we shouldn't fear it. We're traveling with a large group." Shelby hooked her thumbs in the straps of her knapsack.

"I know, except the thing still sounds scary."

They all looked off in the direction of the roar, and patiently waited for Blunderbuss. Shelby scanned the dark trees. Her eyes felt heavy, but there was too much at stake. If what she'd seen at Wintress's place was correct, if Azimuth fell, Earth would be next.

Both her homes would be gone.

CHAPTER 30

Zach was tired. Anxiety swept over him. He stumbled a few steps, and Morgana placed her hand around his arm.

"You okay?" she asked, the intensity of her green eyes heightened as she arched her brow and fixed her gaze on him. Brown hair spilled over her shoulders. She had tied most of her locks up in a ponytail, but some strands had come loose.

"I'm okay. A little spent, I guess." He felt foolish saying that after what she'd been through.

She tucked a strand of hair behind her ear. "Spent?" She shook her head.

"Uh, mentally tired. I'll be fine." He smiled, and tugged her hand.

Ahead, Throg and Brodeur were engaged in conversation.

They walked for a couple hours, and Zach felt much stronger. Night had fallen, but moving around was safer. Staying in one place so late might be more than a little dangerous.

A deep roar emanated from the west of them, and they all stopped to stare in the direction of the sound.

"Manticore. Not a good omen," Brodeur said, his expression stolid. "They say they appear only when unnatural events occur. Rare to come this close to a Manticore."

Morgana edged closer to Zach, gripping his hand through the moonlight.

Brodeur raised an eyebrow. "At least we aren't in the heart of the Cark Woods. Battalions of men have disappeared searching for treasure. We will be passing the edge of the Cark heading into the Canopus Hills. Not too dangerous on the outskirts, yet more of a possibility to run into something. I've gone through this part on numerous occasions and have never seen anything."

An hour passed as they hiked the woods. Often they were forced to take a slower pace around the steeper areas. The darkness made the terrain hard to read, but when the clouds drifted away from the moon, a chalky glow illuminated the forest. They traveled for some time before reaching the edge of the Cark, which they needed to pass.

Throg motioned to Zach and Morgana. "Better pause for a breather now. Don't want to stop often until we are past, and rest will give us strength to hustle."

They went through the familiar routine of gathering dry wood to make some brew for their respite.

They sat once again sipping tea, and a large multicolored owl hooted next to them. The fire blazed, casting orange and red shadows across the faces of the trees around them. Warmth flooded Zach as he sipped the hot liquid.

Brodeur eyed the nocturnal bird. "Another omen, although I couldn't say good or bad. Owls are magical birds, the messengers of dead souls. This one is trying to tell us something." He peered up into the dark trees.

The tea was soon finished, and the fire nearly burned out. Zach helped to extinguish the last small flames, and he and Morgana fixed their packs to their shoulders.

Once more, the four of them headed out. They continued for a half-hour's length without any further roars or disturbances. Near midnight, they stopped for a brief rest, as Morgana asked for a few minutes.

"Nature calls," she said, smiling coyly.

Throg dropped his gear. "Okay, but stay in shouting distance, and bring your rapier."

Throg and Zach sat and listened to one of Brodeur's stories. This one started with a dog, a wheel of cheese, and a harp.

Brodeur laughed and said, "You wouldn't believe what the wench told me next. I thought for certain I was going to sleep in the barn, but no! After the cheese mess, I ended up staying in the worst possible place."

"Where was the worst place?" Zach asked.

He was about to reply, but was cut off by a deep, guttural roar. The three of them sprang to their feet.

"That sounded way too close," said Throg. He scowled out into the dark forest. His breath came in puffs of steam as they listened.

Morgana's screams followed a second roar. "Help!"

Without a word, they picked up their weapons and bolted.

Fleet as a gazelle, Zach arrived to the scene first. "Man alive!"

Morgana was pinned against a tree, her rapier in front of her. The Manticore circled her and gave a low growl. The moon's glow offered enough light for Zach to make out the details. The beast's head was human, except larger and with a red face. The creature reared toward Zach, its blue eyes fixed on him and its vast mouth opened, revealing a triple row of teeth. An eerie cacophony of trumpets and flutes emerged from the Manticore's gaping maw. The beast abandoned its pursuit of Morgana and strode a few feet closer to Zach.

Throg arrived and stood still, his broad sword raised. "Don't move, laddie."

The Manticore stared deep into Zach's eyes and held his gaze. It roared into the sky with the distorted sound of fanfare. Seconds later, the monster bounded off into the woods with exceptional speed, leaving them behind.

Throg looked at Zach and sighed. "Whatever made it leave, let's be thankful. That beast was twice the size of a lion and quicker than I care to fight."

Zach turned to Morgana, who stood petrified against the tree, her rapier still raised.

"Are you okay?" He jogged up to her, his empty hand out. The sword weighed a ton, but he refused to put it away until he knew they were out of danger.

She snapped out of her paralyzed state and slid away from the trunk. "The Manticore could've swallowed me whole. I thought I was done for."

Brodeur ran up, huffing, his arbalest loaded. "What happened?"

"The Manticore sized up Zach, and then took off," said Throg.

"Good guy to travel with, eh? Next time something like this happens, you need to grab my arbalest since you are quicker. Would be your only chance against a Manticore, or any beast its size."

They walked back to their belongings and collected themselves.

Still shaking, Morgana sank to the ground. Zach offered her some water from the canteen, but she refused. "I'll be okay. I need a minute to get my wits back is all."

A tickle in Zach's brain announced a familiar voice: "*We... transported from... the Canopus Hills at sundown tomorrow on... Gida Path. We will be... large stagecoach and....*" The voice of his link cut out. He whirled around to Throg and relayed the message.

"So they are in the Canopus Hills as we suspected, and they are being moved. Something must have happened for the Nightlanders to take such a risk."

"No doubt the Assembly members will be heavily guarded, but it may be the only opportunity we have to act," said Zach.

Throg nodded. "Well, we should be out of the Cark in a half-hour. We'll stop then and figure out a plan. Canopus is a few miles from here, and Gida runs directly through it."

"Well, whatever you need, I'm game," Brodeur said at once. "No reason to pretend. I suspected Zach was a Kin for a while now. Should the Nightlanders take over, none of us will last, so count me in."

"You got the situation right about our chances," said Throg.

Brodeur placed his arbalest on the side of his sack.

"Let's pick up the pace," Throg said. "No telling what might migrate from the belly of the Cark to the outskirts. Things much worse than the Manticore, I understand."

They drew closer to the edge of the Cark, and the temperature dropped. Their thick and misty breaths floated up from their lips. The trees loomed larger, warts grew on their gnarled branches, and some had enormous knots that appeared as eyes.

Morgana wrapped her tunic tighter. "Brr. The temperature has dropped twenty degrees in the last few minutes."

Throg stopped and stared straight ahead.

In the distance, three figures stood wearing gray cloaks. They were tall and thin, their faces sitting in the darkness of their cowls. Each of them had a walking stick, and black gloves covered their hands. They stood in place as if statues.

"Demons of some sort, but a different type than I know," whispered Throg.

Brodeur walked forward a step. "I've heard about them—Gray Cloaks. They reside deep in the Cark in all the stories. The tips of the sticks got blades on them, and they reach a long way. Should we keep walking or try to go wide?"

"No sense. Those who want trouble always follow. I'm surprised they didn't ambush us. Makes me think they might leave us alone. Zach is with us. They may simply crave a closer look at him."

They continued walking in the direction of the Gray Cloaks, and several more emerged on the sides of them. They made no movement.

Morgana stared up at Throg. "There must be at least a dozen now." She effortlessly strung an arrow on her bow.

"I see them. Morgana, you and Zach keep eyes on our rear. Brodeur, watch the left flank. I will take the right."

Around them, the sound of whispers emanated from the woods, several voices speaking in an unidentifiable language. The voices called out their names simultaneously. Hair on Zach's neck prickled. The leaves on the ground began swirling, and the temperature continued to drop. Throg was up front, and he and the others grew closer to the three Gray Cloaks ahead. Behind them, snapping pierced the incessant whispers. Morgana raised her bow as she whirled around.

Drake strolled toward them. He appeared exhausted. Moonlight illuminated his blue skin and made his green hair seem dark as pitch.

Throg placed his hand on her arm. "You can put your bow down, Morgana. This is Drake, a friend."

"Drake?" Her voice shook. She looked as if she wanted to say something, but before she could, the Leshy spoke.

"Well, seems most of the fire is under control. I sensed trouble among you, and brought a few friends."

"We seem to be in a pickle," said Throg, nodding his head.

Three Leshy walked in the distance to their left, and likewise to their right. They sauntered between the Gray Cloaks and their party, and stared up at the demons.

"I told them the woods would be destroyed by Biskara if we did not assist the Kin. We'll be able to walk you to the end of the Shattered Woods. My fellow Leshy will want to return to their own forests to protect them, once you're safe. A Leshy rarely leaves his domain. The Gray Cloaks will not follow past the boundaries. They don't like it on the edges of these woods, much less past them." Drake motioned them to keep walking.

"Thank you, Drake," said Throg. "We would never have overcome these demons by ourselves. We ran into a Manticore. He bolted when Zach appeared."

"Yes, the Manticore, a magical beast, which wouldn't harm a Kin. I do sense the Assembly is in the Canopus, if you didn't know. I cannot tell you more than that. The channels are distorted ahead."

"Zach's link managed to contact him, so our suspicions were confirmed, but thank you again."

The Leshy's eyes glittered. As they spoke, the Gray Cloaks eased closer. "Brock Fergus is his name," Drake said.

"My link is Brock? The name seems familiar," Zach said. He tried to stay calm; after all, if Drake was relaxed, he needed to be as well.

"Knowing his name may help when he attempts to contact you."

"New visitors," Brodeur warned.

Several ragged shapes darted in and out of the woods around them. They came closer, and Zach caught a glimpse of their latest stalkers—hideous creatures with the appearance of rotting corpses. Their eyes were bloodshot, and in some cases, missing entirely. Fungus grew from their mouths, and Zach swore he noticed one with a worm wriggling in its ear.

"Green-teeth," Drake said. "Now we got problems. They will follow past the boundaries. They do not possess supernatural abilities, however, and you'll be able to fight them."

Brodeur said, "I suggest we pick up the pace to a run. The Cloaks won't pass the edge of the Cark. I would rather face one adversary than two."

"As long as you can keep up." Throg shot a wink.

"Let's go."

They sprinted ahead, Brodeur bringing up the rear, but keeping up.

Zach's legs pumped hard, and his chest ached. After walking and running intermittently all day, he was growing weary. Every muscle

strained, and he wanted nothing more than to lie down and sleep for a week. Still, he pressed on, fueled by fear.

"Almost at the edge. Keep going. You mortals move so slowly." Drake glided along.

The surrounding weald abounded with frightening shapes. The Cloaks cruised forth, and the Green-teeth moved a bit closer, running as fast as they were. The Leshy were on the inner parts, moving as a shield against the creatures of the Cark.

Trees flashed by. Plants and roots tried to snare Zach's feet, but he nimbly escaped their clutches. The sky was open.

"We are past," said Drake.

Warmth slammed into them with sweet relief. Drake accompanied them as they continued to run. Zach glanced over his shoulder, and the Gray Cloaks stood motionless. The other Leshy were also still, staring them down.

The Green-teeth ran after the group, white foam emanating from the corners of their mouths. Watery snarls and grunts blared through their nostrils. Without the Leshy shielding them, the Green-teeth charged from the trees.

Drake chanted a few unrecognizable words.

Two of the Green-teeth appeared from behind a hulking bush and barreled at Zach. He raised his sword, and a trio of large wolves tackled the assailants straight on.

Several Green-teeth blocked the path ahead.

Morgana and Brodeur halted and aimed their weapons. Morgana's arrows flew first. She had three strung and let them go. Two hit their targets, and the demonic creatures howled in pain and scampered off. Brodeur's arbalest reached its target a second later with more devastating results. The projectile struck the creature in the chest, lifting it high off its feet and sending the thing into the brush. It writhed a few seconds before lying still and dissolving into a slimy green moss.

Behind Morgana and Brodeur, Zach and Throg stood with their backs to each other, hacking away at the greenish marauders. Drake's wolves ran in and out of the bushes and viciously tackled the Green-teeth. In the distance, several wolves chased Green-teeth through the woods. Drake hovered between them and continued his incantations.

One of the Green-teeth stopped in front of Zach, out of the range of his sword. The fiend stared at him. "He'll die, you know, and you will never return to Earth again. The vision is clear right now."

"What are you saying?" Zach cried out.

"Don't listen to such nonsense," said Throg, sliding toward Zach. "The thing is a demon, a liar."

It cackled and ran at them. As they prepared their strikes, two of the wolves hit it from the side and smashed the horror straight through the bushes. They chased after him. Some snarls and shrieks emanated from a distance, slowly petering out.

The forest became quiet. Zach and his friends stood, panting.

"You should be safe now. I sense no demons ahead," said Drake.

Throg walked toward him. "How can we thank you? I am so glad we even came to know each other. We are certainly blessed. It would have been impossible to have traveled this long without your continued assistance."

"I am a Leshy. I can sense what is right for my woods. You're the only humans I've ever befriended. You are also with the Kin. I help you to keep my land safe. I am weakened this far from my territory, so I must return. Good luck to you now. I'm afraid my assistance will be scarce as you go farther away." He tipped his hat to them.

"Wait!" Morgana gasped. "Please, Drake, Chapton was attacked, my dad and my dog, Otis. I saw someone just like you standing over him and my father. Are they all right? Was that you?"

Drake frowned. "'Twas not me, child, but I can speak with other Leshy and learn what I can."

"Thank you."

Drake nodded and turned, his tie and button-down shirt beaming back at them. He looked tired and sick, as if he had caught the flu in the last few minutes. They watched him for a bit.

Once he was out of sight, Throg sheathed his sword. "We should go."

They continued on the path, following Throg's lead.

He called back, "We will distance ourselves from the Cark some more and stop for a break, then figure out our plans."

Zach realized the mood had become cheerier—like the feeling one got right after acing a big test. They were tired, yet content. Morgana seemed thoughtful, but less distraught. Still, running so much was draining him. A comfortable, warm bed sounded wonderful. He wished he could sink into his pillows at home and sleep. He stifled a yawn and shook his head to keep himself awake. They had to continue moving.

After twenty minutes of hiking, Throg motioned to a small clearing off the side of the path, and they set their knapsacks down and began their habitual activity. Soon, Brodeur had a kettle of tea brewing, and they passed out to each other slivers of the cured ham with some dried bread.

Brodeur pulled out a jar of jam. "An indulgence. Quince jam from a plant, already cooked. 'Tis the only way you can eat this. Delicious with smoked and cured hams. I was saving it for a special occasion, as it is hard to come by, but there is enough to have some left if we are careful."

The quince moistened the dry bun and the sweet jam countered the salty ham. The combination tasted as if someone had created it just for ham

and bread. They sat and enjoyed the treat in silence. Brodeur's sack had endless delicacies and tools.

Brodeur stood up and poked the fire with a long stick. "The Gida Path is a few hours' walk from here. Two parts on the course might be suitable for ambush. The first is a tunnel, a short one. They'll most likely post sentries on the sides, but they can't put too many, because the shaft is tight. With more manpower, that would be a good place to set a trap. The second spot is a sharp turn, about a mile past the tunnel. They will have to slow down, and the woods are thick with brush and trees there. The rest of the Gida Path is straight and not dense. If we make our move, it'll have to be at one of these two spots. What do you think?"

Throg chewed on a piece of ham and swallowed it. "The turn sounds like our best bet. They're long odds, but we have no other options available. We have to get to the path quickly. We should hack up a route at the turn without bringing attention to it. Brodeur and Morgana will take out the drivers of the coach, and Zach and I will replace them and steer the carriage off the path. I'm not sure what happens after that. I need to see the landscape."

Zach rubbed his temples. "We will have an entire battalion on our heels, with six drugged bodies to hide."

"I keep a canister of oil," said Brodeur. "If we get the coach, we can pour it on the route behind us and shoot flame-tipped arrows down at it as we go. The fire will buy us some breathing space."

"Sounds like you've done this before," said Zach.

"More than once has this saved my skin. We should scout out a hiding spot close to the path. A cave would be best. We can unload the Assembly members, and then send the stagecoach off on its own, leading them away from us." Brodeur sat back down scratching his head.

"What next? They will scour the woods for us," said Morgana.

Throg sipped his tea. "Well, we need some time for the Assembly to recover. Once they sober up, they'll know what to do."

Brodeur nodded. "Not to mention they're powerful adversaries when the drugs wear off. Depending on what they are doped with, I can mix certain elixirs to hasten their recovery. Malefic needs to keep them alive, yet limp. I believe he may be injecting them with Gaston greens, and we are in luck if so."

They finished their tea and cleaned the campsite of any evidence suggesting they'd been there.

After an hour of walking, Throg stopped and took a slug of water from his leather canteen.

Though the chill of night ran deep, Zach was covered in sweat. He wiped his brow. "Throg, where do you think the rest of the Kin are?"

"Well, they may be receiving transmissions, as you have, from the Assembly. But with the fires and the Nightlander patrols, Presage could have sent them back to Meracuse."

"So we might be Meridia's last chance?" Morgana said, stepping forward and pulling out her canteen.

"Yes."

After a few quick gulps of cold water, they headed off. They continued on for over an hour. The crunching of mulch underfoot became a steady, slow beat. The trees gradually grew sparser, and the ground harder with more rocks.

Brodeur stopped and squinted off to the west. "The path is a little less than a mile away. I see something that could help us." He pointed.

They followed him off their trail and through the brush. Rockier terrain emerged ahead. The stony area they arrived at was covered with greenery. Moss clung to the rocks alongside lichen. A few enormous boulders littered the ground. Between them, scraggly trees grew.

"Okay, might be a cave somewhere in here. Should we find one, it could be a place to transport the Assembly and bide our time."

They spread out and canvassed the immediate vicinity. Throg pulled Morgana with him north. Zach and Brodeur searched south. As far as Zach could tell, no caves were present, only rocks and boulders. He wiped aside some pine needles near a bush in hopes of finding a secret entrance to a cave. No such luck.

Throg called out. Zach exchanged a glance with Brodeur, and the two of them jogged up to Throg and Morgana. Both were smiling. Morgana motioned to a hole in the rock.

"Perfect location," said Throg. "This cave was built for our plan. We need to disguise the entrance a bit. Take a look inside."

Zach and Brodeur walked in the direction he was pointing. The opening was between two boulders, a chasm of sorts, large enough to slip one person through, and well hidden, too.

"A good thing, that they can only inspect one at a time. Gives us the ability to react," said Brodeur as he ran his fingers along the exterior.

Zach entered first, and followed the outlines of the cavern when he detected running water ahead. In the back of the cave, water streamed via one large crack down what appeared to be a small cliff. This was much too tight to crawl into. The rear of the cavity had a couple inches of water spread out, but it was mostly leaking through various cracks and crevices.

"Excellent," said Brodeur. "This cave gives us access to fresh water. We could stay hidden here for days if need be."

They returned outside one at a time, giddiness in their steps. The interior of the cave was easily large enough to house the six Assembly members and the four of them.

"Great find!" said Throg. "I think I spy a good hiding spot at the top of the chasm. I can sentry in that space if any patrols come by. Let's uproot some large plants and relocate them at the entryway." He motioned to the brush.

Zach and Morgana sought out a few bushes and small trees. Within a half-hour, the entrance was completely concealed. Zach stepped back to admire their handiwork. He dusted his dirty hands on his pants and nodded to himself.

"Works well," Throg said.

Brodeur grinned, his hands on his hips. "Okay, now we must pray enough time remains to cut and conceal a trail to take us straight here from the turn of the Gida Path. I think the bend is this way, with a slight twist about thirty yards in front of it."

He and Morgana raced to the Gida to monitor any activity, while Throg and Zach began the tedious chore of hacking a track to the path. It was hard work. Zach's already sore muscles screamed as he knocked aside brush and heather. Throg encouraged him as they slashed their way back to the road. Sweat dribbled down Zach's temples and into his eyes.

"Good so far, and we are almost done. Only a little more," panted Throg.

Soon, they made it to the path. Zach wiped his forehead and drew in cool breaths of air. He just hoped they'd be able to rest before the Nightlanders brought along the Assembly.

By the time they'd finished carving the route, midmorning sun rested on their heads. Brodeur glanced over his shoulder.

"Anything?" asked Zach.

"Not a soul. The trail?"

Throg sheathed his blade. "Luck is on our side. We cut a pretty nice path right to the cave."

"Well, you fellas done a great job," said Brodeur.

They examined each other. Soot and shrubs covered them, and sweat dripped down their temples. A twig poked from Zach's hair and he tugged it out, then took a long draft from his canteen. The cold water slaked his thirst.

Brodeur strode forward and inspected their handiwork. "Good, good. Let's throw some fluffy shrubs and the sort on the scene."

Throg squinted down the path. "They may be sending sentries ahead of the wagon soon. We need to finish before they arrive."

"Well, let's get to the final tasks," said Brodeur, and turned down the makeshift trail.

CHAPTER 31

After Blunderbuss and his men finished burying their valuables, he disappeared to the other side of the camp. The Kin remained where they were, ready and waiting, until he returned as quickly as a spider scurrying down a web, carrying a bundle of dark clothing.

"This here is the Nightlander garb I was telling you about. We got enough for thirty of us. We painted a thin brown line on the right shoulder of every one of them. This'll look like dirt to them, but should things go awry, these lines will be a sign to the rest of us. I got a basic and simple plan. You Kin are the best suited for the main part of the job, and this could be a pivotal point in history. Blast it if I'm going to screw things up so bards sing songs belittling me for eternity, understand?" Blunderbuss's lanky arms extended, and he dropped the garb down before them.

"We wouldn't expect anything less," said Shelby as she stared into his eyes.

He stood rooted for a moment as she gazed at him.

"Go on," she said.

Blunderbuss shook his head, as if to empty water from his ears. "Okay now, should the whole thing blow up, my crew won't be able to stick around *too* long. We're probably outnumbered a hundred to one. If that happens, you are better off with us out here trying to figure out how to spring you. We are as good as gone if Malefic takes over, so you can trust us on that." He sifted through the clothes.

"What is your plan?" Max asked.

"Easy. This tunnel I was telling you about is roughly forty yards long and in the middle of the path. We dug a chamber underneath it last year to ambush a snobby carriage or two, and we scooped out some hiding spots on the walls inside. Even got a trapdoor at the entrance. We were waiting for a real score, since we could probably only use it once before word spread. This here is our best shot. What we need is a distraction that will slow the stagecoach long enough to take it over."

He swigged his canteen. "Now a member of my group, Briscane, is knowledgeable regarding Manticores. He seems to think he can lure the one we been hearing over to the path at the proper time, and then irritate the beast enough where it will cause a big to-do. I'm checking on him now, seeing if I think it's an honest shot. I know a lot of things have to go right here, but if we pull it off, we will be running the coach in disguise and can figure a good time to make a move." Blunderbuss cracked his knuckles, looking at them for a response.

"Which part are we involved in?" Max asked.

"I'm thinking you Kin go in the chamber underneath. My boys will be in the hidden slots on the sides. The Manticore's distraction comes, and they'll ambush the soldiers behind, freeing you up to hijack the stagecoach. Anything happens, things are probably best you be with them, with your links and whatnot."

They peered back at him as he rubbed his nose with a handkerchief. "All right, then. Pick out your size, and I'm going to check on how Briscane figures he can lure in the Manticore to our favor." He trudged off.

The Kin began probing the pile of Nightlander uniforms. Shelby found one close to her size. The suit looked like it would fit easily over her garb.

Emily paced over to Shelby and Riley, carrying a bundle of the dark clothing. "Let's go change in the tent. The fellow standing in front said no one was using that one, and he would keep a lookout for us." She motioned to one of Blunderbuss's men, a husky man with a toothy grin.

"Actually, gals, we'll stand watch," said Max as he walked toward them.

"No reason to have one of these goons leering instead of us protecting you," said Stuart.

"Great. We'll do the same for you," Shelby said as she sorted a stack from the pile.

"Ah, we will be done by the time you get out," blurted Stuart with a grin.

The girls entered the tent, leaving the boys to change into the Nightlander uniforms directly in front. Shelby assisted Emily with the back of her shirt, fastening a stubborn button while Emily looked at the ground.

"I know how important this all is," Emily said softly. "But when I think of the odds, I have this paralyzing sense of helplessness. I'm scared I may die in this place and never see my family again." She wiped a tear from under her eye.

Riley pulled a boot on. "We all get that feeling, Emily."

"I don't," said Shelby.

"What do you mean?" Riley gazed up from her boot.

"We're needed here. This is why we were born, to defend Azimuth. Did you read the parchments on Wintress's wall? We were *born* on Azimuth, and moved to Earth to protect our identities. I would rather be doing everything I can to fight this evil, save lives from death and slavery, than sitting at home, watching television with my drunk father." She snapped a button through and strode to the entrance.

Riley and Emily stood motionless, gaping at her.

"We are responsible. Now is our time to grow up and understand we could be all that's left to defend *our* people, the children of Azimuth. We need to put our selfish fears aside and forget the past. We must learn our lives are worth fighting for. So much is at stake." She nodded once and turned out the opening.

The maturity in her voice surprised even Shelby. She was still adjusting to her growth since passing through the mobile portal with Mr. Dempsey. She thought of him and winced, wishing he were with them.

"Hey," Max said as he and Stuart joined her. "Everything okay?"

"Sure." She adjusted one of the gauntlets around her wrist. "Why? What's up?" She tried not to stare at him. Max and Stuart looked really good in their armor. The dark suits fit them well.

"Dawn is almost upon us," said Stuart, eyeing the lightening sky. He had sketched a copy of the three triangles on his outfit again in charcoal. It was nearly invisible. "We don't have much time to get this plan in gear. The link said tonight, right?"

"Prior to sundown," said Shelby. "And we have a lot of ground to cover."

Blunderbuss strode over, his gangly figure moving with purpose. "Good news. Briscane's father and grandfather worked at the animal grounds. They gave him a bukkehorn that hunters used to lure the Manticore. He's been looking for the dang thing the last half-hour and finally found the horn. The Manti we been hearing isn't far, and my best trackers are out with Briscane to lead it into the tunnel. This'll be dangerous, but will cause mayhem." He chewed on a toothpick.

Shelby nodded.

"Okay now. Our valuables are buried, and we are ready to trek to the Gida Path."

Riley and Emily emerged from the tent. "We look pretty scary, huh?" Riley asked as they studied each other in their new gear. "Reminds me of being on a Goth cheerleading squad!"

A short, stout man approached them with well-groomed steeds. "Sappy is my name. I tend to the horses here. You will be riding these to the tunnel." He handed one of the reins to Shelby.

They mounted the chargers. Shelby was glad to be back in a saddle. Reaching the Gida Path on horseback would take far less time than on foot.

Blunderbuss trotted up with a detachment of his centurions, complete with Nightlander garb. "My fifteen best swordsmen will station in the walls inside the tunnel. Garrick is my second in command here. He will lead you in. The rest of us will ride ahead of the shaft. A turn is a mile or so past it. When all goes well, we will meet you there. Simon will stay behind. Let's move out."

Simon sprinted up to the Kin. "I want to come, but Blunderbuss won't allow me," he said sheepishly.

"A child's blood will not be on my hands," said Blunderbuss, and his steed ambled forward.

"Good luck to you," the boy said.

"Stay safe, Simon. We'll see you soon," Shelby said.

Max's horse cantered over and the Kin muffed Simon's hair. "Take care, little man. We'll be back."

When they left the camp, the sun was well above the horizon. They galloped to the Gida Path in time to catch the bukkehorn's echo, which sounded much like the Manticore's cries. Soon, the louder sound of the Manticore itself resonated. It was close.

Shelby's horse twisted its ears in the direction of the Manticore and nickered, but Shelby pressed the mare onward.

The ground flashed by as they rode. Trees whizzed past. When they arrived at the entrance of the tunnel, the sun stood above the treetops. Ten of Blunderbuss's scouts were waiting, sweaty and breathing heavily.

One of them said, "We took care of a Nightlander patrol that was sent ahead of the stagecoach. All is clear."

The Kin and fifteen soldiers dismounted.

Blunderbuss nodded. "Okay now, Garrick will take you into the shaft. Godspeed to you." He took their horses and raced through the passage with his men.

"Let's head in and station ourselves," Garrick said. He lit up a torch as they filed in.

Garrick was a stout man with a moustache and beady black eyes. He wore a pointed hat, but a friendly smile. They walked for a few minutes before he stopped and inspected the walls.

"Here." He motioned toward the wooden panels.

The Centurions began pulling out planks from the wall. Garrick knelt down in the middle of the shaft, brandished a blade, and wedged it into an area of the ground. He lifted a board and popped up two more.

"Okay now, judging from the sounds of the bukkehorn, we estimate less than a half-hour before the stagecoach arrives. I suggest we relieve ourselves before getting in, in case it takes a little longer."

The men did so against the sides of the corridor as the girls exited the tunnel. After a few minutes, they returned.

"If all goes to plan," Garrick said, "Briscane will lead the Manticore in first. He is doing his best to keep ahead of the coach so he can lure it in at the right time. When the carriage enters the tunnel, the men above will drop the trapdoor. That'll block out the rest of the troop from the shaft. We have archers posted in the trees to keep them busy, but they'll race up the sides to get to the exit. We will also set some traps outside to slow them down. You've got only a few minutes to take over the stagecoach and race down the path to meet Blunderbuss."

Garrick wiped his brow and continued. "The Manti should be inside, blocking the coach's way. The troop in front of the coach will be preoccupied by the Manti. We'll exit the walls and engage the ones in back. That's your cue to come out and capture the coach. Briscane will forge ahead and lure the Manticore out, which will clear your way. Hopefully, the Manti will attack the Nightlanders that arrive from the sides as well, but it may just take off into the woods."

"Good luck," said Max.

"We'll need every ounce of luck, laddie."

The Kin descended into the ground, and Garrick placed the planks over them as they nestled in.

Shelby rested with bundles of hay beneath her. She admired Blunderbuss's preparation.

"They are loose and will pop right up," Garrick said to them from over the covering.

The Kin lay in two groups. Max settled next to Shelby, their swords positioned at their sides. His hand found hers and gave her fingers a light tug.

She gripped his in return, her heart hammering against her chest. Despite her earlier cool, nerves kept her tingly now.

"Everything will be okay," he whispered.

"You are present once again to save me, right?"

"Always. We've got this. It's just like a game back home. We were down, ten-nothing, and rallied to win in the fourth quarter. This is our comeback."

They lay in silence for some time, their controlled breathing the only sounds. Soon, the eerie cries of the Manticore hurt their ears. A few minutes passed, and the bukkehorn and Briscane's voice from above added more noise.

"Come on now, Manti. This way," Briscane shouted from atop, followed by a bukkehorn blast.

The frantic sound of pounding footsteps echoed overhead, accompanied by the blare of the bukkehorn again. Then it came. The tunnel reverberated with a cacophony of fanfare, succeeded by a deafening roar.

"Here now, Manti. Come in a bit more," Briscane said from directly over them, with a blow of the bukkehorn right after. The trumpets blared again in response. The Manticore was almost on top of them.

Shelby tensed without realizing she had stopped her breathing.

The floorboards groaned and pushed down. At one point, they touched the tip of Shelby's nose, and she gasped. A heavy, hoarse panting followed each creak of the floorboards. The Manticore was right above them.

In the distance, the sound of hooves pounding the path emerged. Shelby took a deep breath as she readied herself for the ambush. Her grip on Max's hand tightened.

The whips of the stagecoach's driver snapped through the tunnel, the hooves smacking down. From beneath, the clamor was thunderous. Shelby resisted the urge to cover her ears. They were coming.

"Hah! Hah!" the driver shouted.

She heard a loud swooshing grate and then a crash. Several voices hollered. The trapdoor had been dropped.

Her pulsing blood thundered in her ears. She was terrified, yet her resolve wouldn't let her do anything but wait.

"Whoa," yelled the driver, the coach screeching to a halt above them.

The Manticore's roars doubled in volume as voices screamed atop. The stagecoach rumbled to a stop. Nightlanders pounced from the carriage and engaged the Manticore. The beast bugled again, and bit by bit, the Nightlanders fought it back. At some point, the black-garbed warriors would be between the Kin and the Manticore.

Shelby tensed, waiting for the signal.

"Now!" shouted Max.

They all pushed the floorboards up and sprang into the shaft. Garrick and his men popped out from the sides and engaged the Nightlanders from behind. The sound of swords clanging echoed in the tunnel.

Riley picked off the driver with her slingshot and gave a rallied *whoop* when he came crashing down off the coach. Shelby charged to the front with Max, and Emily strung her bow and fired off two arrows with uncanny speed. The bolts knocked a pair of Nightlanders off the top of the carriage. Shelby swung her blade, catching a Nightlander under the throat. A wide, red mouth split across his neck, and he dropped.

Stuart forced the stagecoach door open. A Nightlander emerged and took a swipe at him. He ducked, and then blasted the Nightlander with his hand-cannon. Stuart entered the cabin as Shelby and Max leapt to the head of the carriage. Max grabbed the reins.

Up ahead, the Manticore thrashed wildly and threw Nightlanders ferociously into the wall.

At the exit of the tunnel, the bukkehorn erupted, and the Manticore raised its bloody maw and bounded down the shaft. The sound of trumpeting roars followed.

Shelby's heart pounded so hard she noticed little else. At one point, she remembered a Nightlander trying to stab her. She cut him down, sticking her blade clean through his chest.

She glanced behind, where Riley and Emily hopped on the back of the coach. Emily gave her a thumbs-up.

"Now," she said to Max.

"Hah!" Max snapped the reins.

The stagecoach propelled forth and raced down toward the Manticore. The wheels rumbled against the planks beneath them. Horses brayed and swung their heads. Shelby leaned forward, her rapier at the ready. Once they exited, Nightlanders might be waiting for them.

They burst from the tunnel, but the Manticore had stopped in front. Max pulled in the reins and the coach halted. The Manticore turned and placed its fiery gaze on Shelby and Max. Soft rumbles came from the beast as he growled. The creature stood and held its glare.

From the right side of the shaft, several Nightlanders bounded in on horseback. They halted at the sight of the Manticore. It grumbled and then lunged at the Nightlanders, clearing their path.

Cold sweat rolled down the nape of Shelby's neck.

"Hah!" Max shouted again, and the coach thundered forward. "Here we go!" He smirked and glanced over at her. "Told ya we'd do it."

They sped down the Gida Path, Shelby's heart racing with the carriage.

CHAPTER 32

Zach sat on a thick branch and stared down the Gida Path. Morgana was stationed across the way, perched on a tree, her arrow nocked and at the ready.

Before long, the sound of hooves rumbled down the trail. He motioned to Morgana, who nodded. His body tensed, and his heart pounded as he aimed the arbalest at the path.

A score of Nightlanders came into view, with several un-mounted horses trailing them.

Brodeur slid up next to Zach. "Blazes!"

"What do we do now?" said Zach. "We expected a smaller group of scouts and archers. I count at least thirty of them."

"Hold tight. Maybe they're passing through. We can't battle this many, so let's see what they are up to." Brodeur pulled out his bow.

Zach motioned to Morgana to stand down, and she nodded.

The troop arrived at the turn and halted. Horses neighed and tossed their heads, tramping the ground. One of the soldiers dismounted and shouted out some orders.

Beside Zach, Brodeur drew in a deep breath. "Wait a minute. I know that spidery build anywhere. Stay here."

Before Zach reacted, Brodeur hurried down the tree and scampered over to the troop. Zach raised his arbalest. Morgana set her aim on the crowd of Nightlanders.

"Blunderbuss!" Brodeur shouted.

The lanky soldier squinted and walked closer to him. "Brodeur? What the blazes are you doing here?"

"I can't believe the Centurions have joined Malefic, you long-limbed traitor." Brodeur spat on the ground.

"Traitor? We are working with the Kin to ambush a stagecoach carrying the Assembly, you fool. We can use all hands on deck!"

"The Kin? Well then now, we had plans of our own to take the coach at the turn. Four of us are here."

"Four of you to take out the coach and scores of Nightlanders? You are as brave as I remember, Brodeur." Blunderbuss chuckled and clapped him on the shoulder.

"Desperate times call for desperate measures."

They embraced one another heartily.

"Come, we must be quick," said Blunderbuss.

Throg crept up next to Zach with a concerned expression, panting. "I picked up voices. What's happening?"

"That is Blunderbuss."

Throg smiled as he watched the two men break their embrace.

"Looks like the Centurions have chosen sides."

The two men spoke a few moments as several Centurions approached Brodeur and slapped him on the back. Brodeur then motioned to where Throg and Zach were stationed.

Zach frowned.

Brodeur shouted up to them, "Throg, it's Blunderbuss. He is working with the other Kin. They have a plan in action to overtake the coach."

Zach glanced at Throg, who shrugged. "Better go check things out."

Throg began to work his way down from the tree.

Zach gave the scene one last glance before following him. He landed hard on the ground, then trotted over to the others, warily looking around. After the things he'd seen, he wondered if these people really were trustworthy.

Blunderbuss said, "If they pulled this off, the Kin should be coming down the path in the stagecoach soon. A regiment of Nightlanders will be in hot pursuit, though."

Throg nodded. "We cleared a trail leading back to a hidden cave. If the Nightlanders aren't too close, we can steer the coach to the area without them knowing for some time. We may be able to pull this off." He turned to where their fourth was hiding. "Morgana, come on down. You're safe!"

She slipped down the tree and ran over, relief in her eyes. "Brodeur, you scared me half to death, walking over to a horde of Nightlanders like that."

Brodeur grinned.

Throg showed Blunderbuss the trail, and they made their plans.

"I will position some archers in the treetops to provide cover," said Blunderbuss. "Now we have to wait and pray the plan comes to fruition."

They stood on the sides of the path and stared at the road as a handful of Centurions ascended the trees. Zach took the reins of one of the horses, again eyeing Blunderbuss warily. Everything was contingent on whether or not the other Kin succeeded. He only hoped they had.

Brodeur stared down the Gida path. "Godspeed to the Kin."

CHAPTER 33

The stagecoach rumbled down the path. Max snapped the reins with fervor and urged the horses on. The road underfoot grew rough and uneven.

Shelby gulped hard, hoping Blunderbuss waited ahead.

Riley slid over the top and joined them. She gave a peppy wink. "Emily is in back with her bow drawn. We spotted a band of Nightlanders breaking away from the Manticore, and they aren't far behind. More poured out from the sides of the tunnel."

"I'm pushing these poor horses as fast as they can go," said Max.

"I'm going in the cabin to check on Stuart," said Shelby. Max nodded, his green-eyed glare fixed on the road.

She deftly scaled the side of the jiggling coach, as though she had done it before a hundred times, and pounded on the door. "It's me, Shelby."

Stuart popped open the hatch. "What's the password?" He smirked.

"Raging Minotaur." She darted inside.

Stuart tried to keep balance as he pointed across the cabin. "Here they are."

The Assembly sat snugly in a row, hunched over and bound with shackles. They wore tattered silken robes that no doubt had been white as cream once, but they now lay smudged and dirtied. Their time in captivity had left the Assembly weak and exhausted.

"I tried to take the shackles off but... too dang thick. I checked the Nightlander I blasted for keys, but couldn't find any."

Shelby crawled over and inspected the Assembly. She stopped at a female whose long, dark hair framed a pale, gaunt face. Age lines creased around the now familiar woman's thin lips.

"Bianca," she whispered, and caressed her hair.

Bianca discharged a dazed moan, and opened her eyes to gaze at Shelby. She forced a faint simper and then nodded off.

"Don't worry, you're safe now," Shelby said, and turned to Stuart. "The Nightlanders are right behind us. I think we have to abandon the coach first chance we can and get off the Gida."

Stuart crouched down next to her. "Blunderbuss said the bend was a little over a mile ahead. We should reach it shortly. Hopefully, he has a plan."

"Okay, I'm going back outside. Let Emily know we have them."

"Will do." Stuart exited the cabin.

Shelby followed and closed the door behind her. She climbed back to the front of the rattling carriage and, once seated, exhaled her pent-up tension.

"All six are there, shackled and unconscious."

Max and Riley nodded.

"Here we are," said Max.

Up ahead, Blunderbuss waited in the middle of the road. Next to him stood three men she didn't recognize, most likely Centurions. Last night, they had been hard to spot.

Max pulled back the reins and the carriage came to a halt. "Hordes of Nightlanders right behind us."

"Okay, we're in luck." Blunderbuss motioned to his companions. "This here is Throg, and this is your fellow Kin, Zach."

"Ahoy, Kin, you are a sight for sore eyes," Throg said as he waved.

They returned the gesture, Shelby fixing her gaze on Zach. He had a wide grin and his shaggy brown hair flopped as he rushed the coach. He stared up at her with piercing blue eyes. He was dressed in warrior's clothing, though he looked like he'd been hiking for days.

"I've been trying to find you guys for ages," said Zach.

"And we, you," Shelby said at once. "We must be quick. Nightlanders are coming fast."

"I'll drive the coach," said Throg. "Zach and Morgana will also come. We've cut a path to the right that leads to a hiding spot we staked out."

The thunder of hooves rang behind them.

"Morgana, hop on the back with your bow. I will get in front. Zach, head into the cabin. Let's move," Throg shouted.

The Nightlanders came into view, charging with their swords drawn. The wave of black-garbed men sent a thrill of fear through Shelby.

"Dang it all," Throg cursed. "Now they will watch us go off the path."

"Get going. We'll cover you best we can," Blunderbuss yelled.

Throg took the reins from Max. "Heeyah!" he hollered, and led the carriage down the makeshift route.

The coach shook and bounced as they advanced. Max held onto the railing with a tight grip as Shelby locked arms with him. Riley, who was sitting on the other side of Throg, yelped as she jolted forward.

Throg pulled her in. "Hang on!"

The coach traveled slower and rougher on the bumpy terrain.

Emily called out.

Shelby stood up and looked back, hanging onto the roof of the carriage, and gasped. Hundreds of Nightlanders were in pursuit. Emily and Morgana fired their arrows one after another at the oncoming swarm, which was closing with great haste. Some came up along the sides, trying to reach out and pull Emily from the back.

A flock of soldiers enveloped the carriage. Riley jumped over to their side. "Hold me," she said.

They grabbed her legs, and she whipped out her slingshot and launched pellets at the Nightlanders. She knocked several of them off their horses, only to have them replaced by others. For each one she shot down, another two joined the fray.

A Nightlander burst through with a large mallet and blasted away at the coach door. He ripped the hatch off with a crunch. More Nightlanders poured in, and one jumped into the cabin. Shelby heard the blast of Stuart's hand-cannon, and the Nightlander blew out and smacked into a tree.

Two more Nightlanders leapt into the cabin, and the sounds of struggle reverberated inside.

"I'm jumping in to help." Max pulled out a dagger and placed it in his teeth. He scaled back toward the cabin and punched a Nightlander in the face before entering.

A clearing emerged ahead, and Throg took in the reins at the base of a large rock covered with ivy.

"Go!" he screamed.

Shelby and Riley hopped off as the two Nightlanders flew from the cabin. One had a dagger in his chest. The other's face was twisted and distorted from a blow right to the mug. Shelby grinned. That hand-cannon-gun thing could do some real damage.

Throg circled to the back of the wagon, his sword drawn. Shelby and Riley followed.

Shelby drew her rapier and held the blade at the ready, her ears pounding with the sounds of trampling hooves and the ferocious beating of her heart.

Emily and Morgana stood beside them. Their bloody fingers had arrows cocked and set.

Hundreds of Nightlanders spilled into the clearing. One of them held his hand up to the rest. With a smirk, he dismounted.

Max and Stuart popped out and joined them, bloodied and bruised. Max's blade dripped bright red, slick with the blood of a Nightlander. His cheek was cut and one of his eyes was swelling shut.

Max struggled to catch his breath. "Zach is staying in the cabin. One of the Assembly men was stabbed during the attack, and Zach is trying to stop the bleeding."

The Nightlanders all dismounted, surrounding them. The sound of a hundred blades being drawn swished through the air. Those with their weapons unsheathed already aimed at the Kin and Throg. Their leader stepped forward.

"This lucky little ambush is over," he snarled.

"We'll fight to the death and take you with us," said Throg.

"Come now. Throg, correct? Meracuse will be stormed soon. If you surrender, Lord Malefic might spare you."

"How about I cut your head off, you rat?" Throg raised his sword high.

"Have it your way then. Take them!"

The Nightlanders rushed in. Stuart blasted the leader with his cannon and knocked him back. Throg charged forth and engaged the onslaught. Emily and Morgana hopped on top of the wagon, strung three arrows at a time, and propelled them into the charging Nightlanders. Max drew his sword and raced forward.

"Fight back-to-back," Throg yelled to Max.

Shelby grabbed Stuart.

"Go to the opening of the cabin and protect the entrance. Shoot the cannon from there," she ordered.

He nodded and scampered off. Seconds later, she heard the gun fire.

One of the Nightlanders tackled Riley. As he lifted an axe over her, an arrow whipped into his throat. Morgana fired two more into him, and he dropped hard, blood gushing from his neck.

Shelby ran over to Riley and pulled her to her feet. Nightlanders descended on them and knocked them both to the dirt. Stuart fired the hand-cannon from the side of the carriage and flattened them. Several scaled the vehicle and attacked Emily and Morgana. Shelby spat blood to the ground and wiped her mouth with her wrist.

"Help us," she murmured to herself, tears welling in her eyes as she heard Morgana and Emily scream.

A loud horn pierced through the sounds of clanging steel as Shelby was hoisted off the grass. She turned, her sword raised, her brow bent angrily.

"We are allies here to help," a man said.

Standing before her was an enormous armor-clad warrior wearing a golden helmet. The figure pulled his helm off and revealed the head of a boar.

She jerked back, a little shocked. Brown fur coated his head, split across his face with a shock of white, and he gazed down at her with black, watery eyes.

Battleswine

The boar-man nodded once and raced into the crowd. At that moment, hundreds of the boar-headed soldiers poured in from the forest, assaulting the Nightlanders with vigor. Axes cleaved through the heads of the Nightlanders. One of the boar-men used a war hammer to drive his enemy straight into the ground. A row of archers on the rocks picked off Nightlanders with a rain of arrows.

Throg dragged Max past her. She ran over and assisted him.

"The Battleswine have come," he said, his face covered in blood and sweat.

"Battleswine?"

"They are friendly neighbors to Meridia, to the south. Thank the stars!"

Shelby slung Max's arm over her shoulder. "Oh, Max."

"I'm fine, just bruised my ribs." Max gritted his teeth.

Blunderbuss and Brodeur sprinted up to them.

"You okay?" Brodeur asked.

Throg and Shelby nodded.

The sounds of battle echoed around them. Men screamed and died, metal clashed on metal, leather ripped, and bones broke. The iron stench of blood filled the air.

Blunderbuss caught his breath. "The Nightlanders left a squad behind and kept us at bay. They sent a few hundred men after you. As we fought, the Battleswine showed up, an incredible stroke of fortune. They were marching to Meracuse on the Gida Path."

The Battleswine had an entire battalion and were easily wiping out the Nightlanders, driving the enemy back. Soon a moat of gore surrounded Shelby and the other Kin. The Battleswine had saved them.

Emily and Morgana sped over. Emily's long hair was knotted and her fingers were bright red from pulling so many arrows.

"Anyone else hurt?" Shelby asked, concerned.

They all sprawled out on the ground, their chests heaving. Emily and Morgana were both bloody, and one of Emily's arms was scraped up pretty badly. Blood oozed from the wound onto the rock. Otherwise, she seemed fine.

"I'll live," Max said, wiping gore off his forehead. His black eye had swelled shut.

"S-same," Emily said with a strained stutter. She accepted a bandage from Throg and wrapped it around the scrape.

"Where is Zach?" said Morgana.

Max looked back at the stagecoach. "He must still be in the cabin."

They sped over to the coach. Stuart stood guard with a handful of Nightlanders lying at his feet. He leaned against the carriage, his brow dripping, with a knife stuck under his armor. When Max pulled the shank out, the blade was clean of blood.

"Just missed me," Stuart said, panting and grinning sheepishly. He tapped the Triforce on his chest. It was smeared and almost unrecognizable, but he smiled nonetheless.

Shelby and Throg darted into the cabin. Zach sat curled on the floor, the brown-haired head of one of the Assembly men in his lap. He held a canteen to the man's lips, his other hand pressing a bloody cloth down on his ribcage. The man was too young to die, but older than the Kin. He opened his blue eyes and fixated on Zach a few seconds before they shut, his thick body trembling.

"Brock," Throg said as he knelt down next to Zach.

Zach nodded. "He's been stabbed in the chest. He doesn't look well."

Brock's face had turned white as fresh snow.

Shelby crouched down and placed her arm around him.

Brodeur entered and examined the Assembly member. "Let's get him out into the air." He pulled a medical kit from his bag.

Throg and Zach carefully lifted Brock and carried him outside, and laid him down on the stone. Brodeur tore Brock's shirt open and inspected the wound.

"Blunderbuss," he shouted. "The Battleswine have healers. Send for one."

Blunderbuss nodded and sprinted off.

They carried the remaining members of the Assembly out of the carriage. Max used his great sword to break off their shackles. Since the Assembly still couldn't move, the team placed them against the rocks, where the Kin and Battleswine could better protect them.

Blunderbuss returned soon with a healer, who plopped down next to Brock and proceeded to work on his wound. Shelby eyed the Battleswine. It was an enormous creature that, like humans, stood on two legs. However, they had hooves rather than feet. Their fingers ended in thick, hoof-like nails.

One of the Battleswine came up to them, his armor dented and bloody. A bit of gore dripped from his chest plate and plopped to the ground. His left eye was missing, but it had been gone for some time. Three fierce scars raked his face, looking to have been the cause of his scarred cavity.

He nodded. "I am General Krupp. We have another battalion on the Dorado Path, on its way to Meracuse to assist Lord Achernar."

"Thank you, General," said Throg. "If you had come any later, we would not be standing here." He thumped his chest twice.

"Fate is with ye. We nearly traveled over the countryside on our march, but decided to take the more direct path of Gida."

Shelby smiled at him. "Either way, thanks. Your warriors are amazing."

The general nodded and snorted, but with a grin.

Brodeur was examining the Assembly members. "Just as I thought. They are drugged with Gaston greens. I have something that can hasten their recovery." He rummaged through his bag and pulled out several vials. "Ah! Help me give this to them."

Shelby and the rest grabbed the vials. She sprinted to Bianca's side, held the woman's head up, placed the small tube to her mouth, and gently parted her lips. After the vial was empty, Shelby cast it aside and caressed the woman's hair. Bianca could pass for an older version of herself.

Brodeur said, "Okay, leave them be for a spell. We need to get them conscious."

Shelby eased Bianca's head down and walked over to the healer. Zach knelt anxiously by his side as he tended to Brock. The Battleswine healer looked concerned.

"My name is Lito. A bad wound here—deep and into his lung. I will do my best."

"Thank you. He is my Kin," said Zach.

Lito nodded.

"Everyone, regroup here," Throg cried out.

They huddled in a circle beside the coach. More of the Battleswine's healers arrived and tended to their wounds. Each Swine was different from the last. Some were lighter, some darker, and one, a great female warrior,

had fur the color of snow with a black spot over her right eye. Her tusks were smaller than the men's, and they were capped with gold.

Shelby sat next to Max as a healer bandaged his ribs. Despite his pale complexion, bruised eye, and battered armor, he was handsome as ever. She rested a hand over his, glad he was safe.

"Take this for the pain," the Swine said, handing him a vial. Max swilled it down at once.

Shelby watched as General Krupp clustered with Throg, Blunderbuss, and Brodeur for some time. The four of them discussed their next move, no doubt. A few other Battleswine joined the meeting. An enormous Swine, two heads taller than Krupp and twice as thick, lifted his war hammer over his shoulder. Shelby recognized him—the first Swine she'd seen. Unlike the others, he had a bright, white stripe of fur arched across his snout and eyes.

"I thought we were done for," Shelby said, sipping out of a canteen.

"I had them right where I wanted them," Max chirped, winking at her with his good eye. His bloody sword lay beside him in the dirt. When he caught Shelby looking at it, he took a rag and wiped it clean.

Zach sat quietly next to Shelby, deep in thought, his fingers on his temples.

Lito walked over, his countenance strained. "I am sorry. He has passed."

"I know," said Zach softly, a tear sliding down his face.

They sat in subdued silence, gulping water from their canteens. The new girl, Morgana, slid over to Zach and placed her arm around him. The forest grew silent, save the blast of horns a few miles off. The Nightlanders who had survived were long gone.

Shelby kept looking over at Throg and the others, hoping there was some way to end the battle for good.

The Assembly members began to stir. The Kin rose and circled them.

Bianca propped up first, on her elbows, and gazed out to the Kin. She smiled. "Oh, my dears. My dear, wonderful children."

Shelby strolled over to her and knelt down.

Bianca pulled her forward. "Beautiful Shelby, I am so proud of you." Tears welled up in her green eyes as she drew closer still and hugged Shelby.

For a moment, Shelby thought Bianca smelled like her mother. It had been so long since Shelby had seen her mom. She held Bianca tightly for several moments, wishing that this woman could have been her mother.

CHAPTER 34

The Assembly members all came to. They rose groggily and set eyes on the Kin. Each of Shelby's friends strode forward and hugged their Kin counterparts instinctively.

Throg watched in silence, wearing a pleased grin.

Rowan Letty walked off with Riley, her arm around Riley's shoulders. Max discussed his battles with Macklin Morrow, who beamed like a proud father and fussed over Max's black eye. Stuart showed Satchel Spool his hand-cannon as he twirled it. Elita Ezmer caressed Emily's hair as they spoke over tea. Shelby looked over to Zach as he huddled on the ground nearby, his knees in his chest.

"Don't worry, laddie. You have me," Throg said as he sat down next to Zach and handed him some smoked ham.

Morgana moved closer too... gingerly. "And you are stuck with me." She ran her fingers through his hair. She bore scrapes and bruises from the battle, and a small gash bled at her shoulder.

"I love you both," Zach said. "I knew when Brock died. He came to me, told me he was proud of me, honored to be my Kin. He said he had to leave to join the truth seekers. 'Godspeed,' he said, and then he was gone." Zach chewed on the ham as Morgana continued stroking his hair.

General Krupp walked over to Bianca and Shelby, and bowed. "Madame Bianca, we are happy you are safe. Meracuse is under siege. We need to act quickly before the city falls."

"Thank you, General. We must ride to Meracuse immediately, and recruit along the way."

"The Battleswine are proud to be with you, madam. We have another battalion en route to Meracuse already."

Bianca nodded.

General Krupp bowed again and then returned to his soldiers to inform them of the plan.

Shelby watched Bianca's gaze shift toward Zach, who still sat hunched between Throg and Morgana.

"Come with me, Shelby. I need to speak to Zach."

They sauntered over to them, and Bianca said, "Hello, Captain Throg, great to see you. Thank you for coming through once again. You were always our best."

He rose, and they hugged. "Don't mention it. This is Zach, Brock's Kin."

"I know." Bianca knelt beside Zach. "My dear, you have been so brave. Brock would have been thrilled." She held her hand out, her caring eyes fixed on him. "Come with me. I have much to tell you."

Zach accepted, and the pair walked off, continuing to hold hands.

Shelby drew closer to Throg and Morgana, and sat down. "Is he okay?"

"Yes. An emotional experience when a Kin loses their link."

She nodded. "Presage told us if our Kin passes, we inherit the ability to operate the Sphere."

"Yes, Brock's power has passed to Zach. Bianca is explaining everything to him now."

"He's been through a lot. The rest of us were together. We worried about him. I feel like I already know him. I just wish we'd been able to meet him sooner."

"The link is powerful among Kin," Throg said.

Shelby smiled. "Presage was thrilled when the Leshy informed us he was with you. He thinks highly of you."

Morgana put her arm on his shoulder. "We all think highly of Throg. He saved my life."

"I don't think much of the oaf." Brodeur came up behind Throg with Blunderbuss. They both let out a snicker.

"We brought you a spot of ale," said Brodeur. He handed Throg a small jug and sat down.

Blunderbuss lit up a pipe as he spied the Kin interacting. "Like a family reunion, isn't it?"

"A soul family reunion," Throg said, and swigged the ale.

They settled for a time, enjoying the happy faces of the Kin and the Assembly as they socialized among each other. Shelby smiled at how well Emily and her Kin got along. It was good to catch her so chatty. Shelby's gaze slipped over to Max, and her heart clenched. What would happen once Meracuse was saved? Would they all have to go home? Where was home anyway? Would she ever see Max again?

The thought made her despondent. She pushed it aside and accepted a cup of tea from Lito. As she sipped, she considered everything that had happened. The beast would cower in fear of her here. He'd run wailing from the woman she had become.

Suddenly, through the forest, the thumping sound of hooves rang in the air. Shelby and the others sprang to their feet.

"General Krupp, we need some arms," Macklin cried out as he bounded forth. "They're coming!"

The general glared back, nodded, and sent one of his soldiers off. The enormous Swine Shelby had met earlier stalked forward, but didn't stray far from Krupp. The Battleswine hurried around the glade and prepared to defend. A soldier rushed over to Macklin, cradling a bag of swords. The Assembly armed themselves as the sound of thundering hooves grew closer.

"More Nightlanders?" asked Blunderbuss with disdain.

"If they are, let them prepare to be slaughtered," said Rowan with a hiss.

Through the clearing, Milo and the Stonecoats cantered in. The Battleswine surrounded them, several of them jeering. Milo and his men still wore their darker colors, blending well with the forest from a distance.

Shelby relaxed and gave a sigh.

"Drop your weapons, Milo," General Krupp commanded.

Milo retorted, "Drop yours, pig-head."

"Milo!" Shelby yelled, running out to him.

Max ambled forward. "Its okay, General. He's with us."

"Milo and the Stonecoats? We will not ride with these dissident heathens," General Krupp snapped.

Shara pranced in place. "That's okay, Krupp, because we don't ride with pigs." Milo spit on the dirt.

The mountainous Swine with the white fur streaked across his snout, roared and bared his tusks. "Pigs, are we? What does that make *you*?"

"Gunther!" yelled Elita, but her voice was drowned out as the Battleswine and Stonecoats bickered and shouted.

"Rock-brains!"

"Ham-butt!"

"Renegade traitors!"

"*Enough!*"

They stopped abruptly.

Bianca strode forward and cast a look of rage at the two sects. "You are both allies to Meridia, and we are under siege by Biskara. Put your differences aside. We need every sword in the coming battle, or we're all doomed."

The two parties grumbled as Milo and the Stonecoats dismounted. They maintained their glares, though, refusing to say a word to any of the Battleswine. Milo handed Shara's reins to another of the Stonecoats, then hurried to Bianca and bowed his head.

"Milady, you are free." He embraced her.

"Yes, thanks to our Kin... and the Battleswine. Please be kind to them, Milo. They came when we were in utmost need."

He seethed, but nodded.

"Where is everyone else?" Shelby asked with urgency.

"We retreated to lead the Nightlander army away from you, and then regrouped. We have been scouring the woods for you since. We came upon Blunderbuss's camp, and they led us this way."

"Sculptor and the others?" Secretly, she wondered if Mr. Dempsey had just been wounded. She closed her eyes and, mustering all her courage, asked, "What of Mr. Dempsey?"

"Sculptor, Barrick, and the rest are on their way to Meracuse." He paused. "I'm sorry. Mr. Dempsey is... dead. We gave him a proper burial. It is an honor, milady, to perish saving Kin."

Dumbfounded, Shelby's lips squeezed shut. When Max had said it, there had still been a chance. Max mentioned that Mr. Dempsey had been knocked down by a horse. The way Milo spoke, though... there was no mistaking it. Mr. Dempsey was truly gone and buried. She held her tongue, unwilling to meet Milo's eyes.

Simon peeked around the Stonecoats. When he viewed her, he raced to Shelby and hugged her. Shelby wiped away her tears and hugged him back.

"You did it. You did it!" he chirped.

"Not without your help," said Shelby, her voice cracking.

Throg jogged up. "They will not be well for long. Meracuse is under siege. We have to mobilize."

Bianca said, "We should be strong enough to attempt utilizing the Sphere by the time we reach Meracuse. There is a small hidden tunnel for the Assembly to enter the secret chamber and operate the Silver Sphere."

"Yes, Bianca, it is time to ride," said Throg.

CHAPTER 35

Throg stood with the six Kin. Brodeur, Morgana, and Simon joined them. Simon gathered brush and built a fire, and they all sat in a circle as he and Brodeur brewed some tea, the mood upbeat.

Shelby poured herself a cup, and sank back in the loop beside Max, with Stuart on her other side.

"Are you all right?" asked Max, his brow pinched.

"Yeah," she whispered. "Just a little beat up, inside and out. I thought... I know it's silly, but I was so sure that he didn't die...." Tears brimmed, making her vision murky. She rubbed them away.

"He was a strong man, Shelby. He did it to save you."

"Thanks. Just hard."

She sat in silence.

The Battleswine dashed around the camp and packed. General Krupp ordered them to bring armor and fresh clothes. Gunther, his second-in-command, the gigantic Swine, hollered orders to the archers above.

Shelby and the girls quickly slipped into the cave, and used the running water inside to bathe. The rest of them did the same when they were finished. Everyone relaxed a little after washing the blood from their bodies.

Max moaned a bit, and Lito came over and fortified Max's ribcage with a wrap before he put his armor on.

"Take these for the pain," Lito said. "One every couple of hours."

Shelby thought she could use some as well.

They mounted their steeds and rode back to the Gida Path. Despite Mr. Dempsey's death, Azimuth felt like home. Shelby tightened her grip on the reins, trying not to worry about what would happen when everything was over.

CHAPTER 36

The battalion galloped on the Gida Path, over a thousand strong. The Kin rode behind the Assembly, who marched along with General Krupp, Gunther, Milo, and Throg. Behind them cantered Blunderbuss, Brodeur, Morgana, the Stonecoats, and the rest of the Battleswine.

"How many archers do you have, General?" asked Macklin.

Krupp grunted. "Our battalion has three hundred. The one we have on its way has the same."

"Good. We'll place them on higher ground before we attack. They will fire as we approach, and if we need to retreat and regroup, they can cover our escape."

Shelby listened to Blunderbuss's discussion with Brodeur.

"My men are nervous they will be arrested by Lord Achernar," said Blunderbuss.

Brodeur laughed, "I believe some warrants are out for me as well. Bianca has told me Lord Achenar will pardon us if we join the battle, and welcome us to stay in Meracuse."

"City life is not for me. We will continue to live the way we always have," said the Centurion leader.

"Well, keep that to yourself. We are welcome for now, and if Malefic triumphs, none of us will be able to live the way we did."

"I know. That's why I'm here."

They passed several villages and gatherings along the course. Every village mirrored the one before. Stone houses with thatch or shingled roofs lined dirt or cobbled streets. Many had wells and inns where Shelby wished they had time to rest on their weary march. Forests gave way to farmland.

Innumerous men from the villages joined their ranks and the battalion swelled.

In front of Shelby, Bianca held her temple for a time. "I have made contact with Presage. Nightlanders have surrounded Meracuse and begun storming its walls. Their weakest flank is on the east side of the wall."

"How many Nightlanders?" Throg asked.

She tensed and rubbed her temples. "Twenty thousand."

Everyone gazed at one another, silent.

Bianca sucked in a lungful of air. "Okay then, we will have General Krupp's other battalion meet us on the eastward flank. You need to get to the central gate, which is the weakest point of Meracuse. You must protect it until we can summon the Sphere and have the Truth Seekers engage Biskara. Something is holding the United Forces back from launching the star darts, and my guess is Biskara is holding them at bay. If the gate falls, then the star darts will not be able to offer much help. They can't fire into the city. General, who is leading the other battalion? I'll contact him and confirm our plan."

"Colonel Demetrius Maza."

Gunther blew air through his nose. "Good Swine, but be wary. He may be foolhardy and try to take down the Nightlanders without our aid."

She concentrated again and held her temples. After some time, she looked up. "It is done."

"How much longer?" Max asked.

"A few hours," said Rowan. Though she and Riley were both blonde, and had the same pirate-like smile, Rowan carried stern and cold features.

Shelby noted that those on the Assembly were more than political figures. They were *warriors*.

They ambled forward, their ranks continuing to surge. As they grew closer, the battalion had doubled in size. The citizens of Meridia that joined the cause brought up the rear.

The march was long, and Shelby was growing tired. She nibbled on a piece of chud to keep her energy up.

"We will arrive soon," said Macklin. "We need to ride east now. Nearby the tunnel we will use to get inside Meracuse, there is a clearing. You can set up camp and plan your offensive there."

They broke off the Gida Path at Macklin's direction and hastened their pace.

"Scouts! I need scouts!" Krupp roared. A group of Battleswine rode forward atop their massive chargers.

"Yes, General?"

"Ride forth over the hill. Observe what's up ahead and report back to me. Do not go farther than two miles."

"Yes, General!"

The scouts buried their hooves into the enormous horses' flanks. Their mounts turned and lunged in the direction of the rolling hill ahead. Where green, lush grass once covered the ground, now only churned mud and soil lay on the slope.

"Halt!" boomed Krupp, his voice carrying across the field.

Banner men and other soldiers repeated his order, and the battalion stopped as they awaited the scouts. Flags and banners fluttered in the wind like snakes churning. Nervous whispers arose from the masses.

Shelby glanced behind her at the men who had come to fight alongside the Kin for the freedom of Meridia. A swell of pride rose within her, and she smiled.

Before long, the scouts returned. They rode hard down the hillside, racing toward the main battalion. Both reined in beside Krupp.

"There are several Nightlander sentries posted in the trees around the clearing, General Krupp."

"We will dispose of the sentries," said Milo. "Stonecoats, with me!"

He brandished his naked blade and charged forth. The Stonecoats raced after him, their camouflaged armor glittering under the late afternoon sun. While they were gone, the soldiers in the battalion shifted uneasily.

After some time, Milo returned. "All is clear."

"That was fast," said Shelby.

"'Tis but a warm-up for the Stonecoats, lass."

Macklin reared his steed to the front of the army, and cried, "March!"

"Move out!" thundered Gunther.

The battalion galloped up the hill, the men on foot marching behind. Captains and other leaders organized and motivated the soldiers, shouting encouraging words to those who came to fight.

Shelby followed the rest of the Kin up the slope, leaning into her steed as the mare raced.

Shortly, the army reached a grassy clearing. The Battleswine poured onto the field and dismounted, then scurried across and set up camp as Gunther and others called out directions. Krupp barked orders, commanding his men to arrange the tents first and get their weapons taken care of.

Milo said, "Meracuse is down the hill ahead. Let us scout out the terrain and make our plans." He removed his helm, and a red mark covered his cheek where the helmet had been too tight.

The Kin accompanied Macklin, Milo, Gunther, and a score of Stonecoats as they snuck their way to the top of the highland. When they arrived, Shelby looked down at Meracuse.

The city beamed. Bright lights of many colors emanated from inside the imposing walls. Enormous buildings of pristine white spiraled toward the heavens. The center of the city rose high on a hill, surrounded by a bailey, the better for defending against an army breaking through the gates.

Stone walls were the only things keeping out the Nightlanders, now a sea of black encircling Meracuse. The sounds of battle pierced the air.

Milo pointed to a large precipice. "We will position the archers on that bluff. They'll further weaken the eastern flank as we charge down. They will remain there, protecting the camp and providing cover as we carry the injured back or need to regroup."

"There will be no need to retreat," said Gunther, pumping his huge fist in the air.

The Nightlanders' numbers were massive. Disheartened at the size of the army before them, Shelby was sure the city would fall. Her gut twisted in fear as she stared down. The Nightlander legion was winning, and obviously so. Raging Disembowelers ripped Meridian soldiers clean in half. Their army slaughtered on sight anyone who opposed them. She wondered if they were marching to their doom.

At last, she and the others tore their gaze from the city and returned to camp.

Milo approached General Krupp upon their return. "We need to send scouts to a cliff we spotted. That will be the best position for the archers."

The general nodded. "Excellent. Colonel Maza is only minutes away."

Shelby sat alongside her fellow Kin, joined by Morgana and Simon, around a campfire as they awaited instructions. It was cold, even sitting in the middle of camp. The flames sizzled and crackled as cooks prepared food and men prepared for battle.

Colonel Maza's battalion soon arrived and reinforced the camp.

At last, Macklin cantered by on his steed. "Zach, you will accompany the Assembly into Meracuse through the tunnel in a few moments."

Zach nodded, wringing his hands.

Milo trotted up to the Kin. "And the rest of you will ride into battle with the Stonecoats. Remain here until I return." He galloped off, shouting orders as he rode.

"Stay close to me when we get down there," Max whispered to Shelby.

She nodded.

Zach said, "Morgana, I insist you remain in the camp with Simon."

"Nay, Zach, I will join the archers. My father trained me for this, and I will be safe while providing assistance. I do this in his memory, and I vowed vengeance."

Zach stared at her a moment. "Okay then. I forgot for a second what a good shot you are."

The fervent pace of the camp around them filled the air with electricity. Archers raced by, circling Macklin and Elita.

Morgana packed up her bow. "I'm off now. Godspeed to you all."

Zach walked her to her steed, and they clasped each other a long moment before she mounted and raced off.

Macklin returned, spotting Zach's gaze upon Morgana as she rode. "She will be fine, laddie. We must go now."

Zach turned his eyes upon his fellow Kin. "Godspeed." They all nodded, and he climbed on his horse and trotted away with Macklin.

The Kin fidgeted among themselves and inspected their weapons as they awaited Milo's return. There was little else to do.

Shelby was too nervous to eat anything. She kept tapping her foot, digging the heel into the soft earth below.

Max stood and tore the bandage from his eye. "I know things look grim," he said, his voice stern.

Shelby caught his good eye as he looked at each of them squarely. She shook her head. "This is different from anything we've ever faced. But we are Kin. Azimuth is our home. I know in my heart we will not fail. When we go down there, we're going to fight back. Malefic and Biskara can't hurt anyone anymore—we're here to make sure of that."

Max smiled, and a rush of warmth surged through her limbs. She stood, unsheathed her saber, pointed it into the air, and cried, "For Meridia!"

Riley jumped to her feet and met Shelby's blade with her own. "For Meridia!"

One by one, the other Kin stood and clanged their weapons against Shelby's. Shouts of, "For Meridia!" resonated in the chill air. Soon several men began chanting, and Battleswine screamed the words. Shelby's pride swelled and she nodded with great resolve.

Milo galloped up on Shara, with the Stonecoats right behind. "Let us ride. For Meridia!"

CHAPTER 37

They mounted their horses and followed Milo. Throg and Brodeur stood waiting with the Battleswine army. Blunderbuss rode up with the Centurions.

Shelby looked into each face they passed. Some she knew, some she did not. Her gut churned as most of these men, she realized, would probably die today. A number of the soldiers were on horseback. They would be the safest, she hoped. Those on foot carried pitchforks and sickles. She feared for those men most of all.

Milo turned in his saddle. "We will lead the attack and cut our way west to the main gate. Onward!" He turned and bolted toward the highland with the Stonecoats.

Shelby drew in a deep breath. She and the Kin raced after them with the Battleswine in tow. A scream sounded behind them, and all of a sudden, her fear subsided. The battle cry invigorated her and made her skin crawl with excitement.

The army advanced over the hill with zeal. Swooshing sounds rang overhead and hundreds of arrows cast down on the startled soldiers ahead. Scores of Nightlanders whipped to the soil in agony. Milo and the Stonecoats broke their ranks like a sledgehammer, pushing the throngs of dark warriors back. Swords clanged and axes smashed as hundreds of hooves pounded across the earth.

Shelby stiffened and tightened her grip on her sword.

Stuart blasted his hand-cannon as they engaged. Max hacked furiously away as he launched forward. In an instant, Blunderbuss was snapped off his horse, and he crashed to the ground. Riley provided cover for him from behind as she whipped her pellets at the black horde that converged on him. Throg hauled him up to his steed, and they ambled forward.

Shelby unsheathed her saber with a hiss of metal, and cut down every foe that came her way. One man she stabbed clear through the chest. Another lost his arm and then his head. Whacking and hacking, she pushed forward.

Max fought by her side, wielding his imposing great sword. Together, they downed two dozen men. More flooded in to take their places, followed by Disembowelers. Strike after strike left her bloody and covered in gore. One man's ear flung off into the fray. She cut his throat next.

The action blurred in a maddening whirlwind of sounds. At one point, a Nightlander hurled a war axe at Riley's head. The Kin elegantly slid from her saddle and latched herself to the side of her horse. The axe missed her and she swung back atop her mount.

Shelby engaged a swarm of soldiers. From the corner of her eye, she spied General Krupp cleaving Nightlander necks with his powerful axe. A dagger bounced off her shield as two Disembowelers bowled over a Battleswine and swiped their claws at her. She ducked and smashed one in the face with her shield, and then drove her blade into the other.

Milo stood ahead of her embroiled in a mob of black.

The fight raged on, and an hour passed before they reached the walls of Meracuse.

They battled west toward the main gate from there. The Nightlanders swarmed in, pinning the Kin to the wall as they struggled to gain ground, separating them from Throg and the Stonecoats. Several Battleswine fought beyond the ebony scourge that surrounded them.

Gunther's mammoth form reared up from the mass of black warriors. Three clung to his back and another tried to take him down. The gigantic Battleswine swung two war hammers, knocking his foes to the mud with thunderous impacts.

Max doubled over in pain after receiving a crack to his ribs, and slipped from his steed. Shelby and Emily dismounted and dragged him back as Riley and Stuart stepped in their wake, thwarting their dark pursuers. The sound of the hand-cannon firing was deafening.

They fought with their backs to the wall as the throng of Nightlanders grew and held them in place. The dark soldiers railed them against the stone, and the Kin struggled to hold their ground.

CHAPTER 38

Zach breathed heavily as the Assembly rode to the outskirts of camp. Battle cries and clanging steel erupted from over the trees.

"They have begun," said Bianca.

The Assembly dismounted their horses and Zach followed. Macklin and Satchel knelt down and lifted a large, well-hidden lid from the ground.

Bianca lit a torch and descended into the dark burrow.

Macklin waved Zach forward. "In you go."

Zach nodded and followed Bianca. The shaft stood encased in old wood and mud, and the only light that illuminated the passage was lodged in Bianca's grip. The ceiling hung so low that Zach had to crouch as he strode.

Sweat dripped of his brow as he walked behind Bianca. He lost track of time while trudging forward. A sharp pang hit his belly, and his head throbbed.

My Kin are in trouble.

"You all right, laddie?" Macklin asked from his rear.

Bianca stopped in front and turned the torch toward him.

"Th-the Kin are in danger. I can *feel* it." Zach placed his forefingers at his temples.

"Then help them," Bianca said.

"How? I... I am nowhere near them. They —"

"I sense you have a strong connection to the Fugues now — the strongest I have ever felt. They are the guardians of the Silver Sphere. Use that bond."

"But I don't know h-how to... to...."

"Concentrate, Zach. Call to them. They will respond to you."

Zach shut his eyes against the glare of the torch.

I need you, Fugues. Please answer me.

Chimes and bells rang inside his head.

"We hear you, dear Kin," the voices spoke.

The rest of the Kin are in peril. I beg you, please help them.

"We cannot last long on the mortal plane without your presence. But we will go to them," they answered.

A ringing melody swished in his ears, and they were gone.

Zach opened his eyes. "Okay, they said they would go to the others."

"Believe in yourself, Zach. You are needed." Bianca turned back down the mucky corridor. "We must continue."

Torchlight bounced off the walls of the cavern in time to the steady dripping of water from the ceiling to the floor.

CHAPTER 39

The Kin stood pinned against the wall. Nightlanders came in dizzying waves as the Kin battled for their lives. Shelby held her shield high, repelling blow after blow while stabbing back at anything in front.

Suddenly, and quite unexpectedly, angelic voices filled the air, blocking out the violent sounds of clanging steel. The walls of Meracuse turned bright red, the soil, golden. The ceiling of the world shifted, no longer azure, but now a deep indigo. Several pairs of shimmering blue eyes surrounded the Kin.

Shelby whipped out her blade, preparing to fight this new foe.

"We are the Fugues, summoned by Zach to protect you."

The dark warriors milled in confusion.

Shelby lowered her weapon as the Fugues created a bubble encompassing the Kin.

"Go now," the voices chimed. "Follow the wall to the main gate. Throg and Milo are right ahead of you. Quickly, as we cannot insulate you long without Zach present."

The Fugues followed the Kin as they bolted around the massive wall. Max's face contorted as he gritted his teeth. They ran into Throg, who battled furiously. As they joined him, the Fugues ensued and clustered closer to the Kin.

"The Fugues! Thank the stars," said Throg. He was drenched with blood and sweat, his chestnut hair frazzled.

They moved onward to the main gate, the Fugues protecting them and changing the landscape as they raced. The Nightlanders could not penetrate their ranks. The Fugues soon came upon Milo and approached him with their ethereal shield.

Then, one by one, the beings shimmered and began to vanish, the shield slowly growing weaker.

We must hurry, Shelby thought.

"Excellent! The gate is right around this bend," said Milo.

They stormed forward unimpeded, and arrived at the main gate to the sound of wood splintering and men shouting, heaving, and groaning.

The Nightlanders smacked the doors with a massive stone and wood battering ram.

The Fugues flickered faster, and a shrill cry pierced the air as a few of the blue eyes faded out.

"We c-cannot s-stay any l-longer or w-we w-will perish," the voices said, and then they disappeared.

Milo and the Stonecoats turned and leapt upon the top of the battering ram, and attacked the operators on the sides. Behind them, hundreds of Battleswine spilled forward. Screeches and feral roars filled the air, deafening the clang of steel and rock.

General Krupp swung his battleaxe. Shelby turned just as a javelin the size of a small tree flew from nowhere and plunged into the general's throat. A squeal, unearthly and devastating, echoed, and then was drowned in the hollering of battle. A Disemboweler latched onto the fighting Swine leader, who tried in vain to force the creature away, four feet of the javelin still sticking from his thick neck. The Disemboweler yanked him to the earth.

Shelby froze, but turned again as Gunther raised both war hammers. He catapulted over his fallen general and slammed the first hammer into a Nightlander's skull. He then gave a cry, "For Krupp!" and slung across the field the Disemboweler that had taken the general down.

Gunther bared his tusks and stood his ground against Nightlander soldiers that hardly came to his chest. All who faced the Battleswine second-in-command suffered the devastation of his iron hammers.

Shelby scanned the scene as man after man fell, almost all of them fighting for Meracuse. Desperate, she fought back, trying to stay the flow of black warriors. She gasped in horror as a villager collapsed into the churned mud.

"Please," she whispered as she battled closer to the gate. The enormous doors creaked and groaned. If they collapsed, Meracuse would fall.

"Please, someone... help us."

CHAPTER 40

The shaft came upon a sharp turn, and Bianca waved Zach forward. She picked up the pace, and then halted.

"Here," she said.

"Huh?"

She lifted her torch to the wall. A handprint stood etched in the stone. She placed her palm in the handprint, and a hidden door grumbled open.

"The Silver Sphere is located *under* Meracuse. That way, Biskara cannot find it, and his sons would search for decades before even learning of these underground passages."

Zach followed her through the doorway, and the cavern opened, revealing a wide space. Within, the scents of water, rock, and earth permeated. A few old pine trees had been melded to the clay walls of the cavern, their white trunks and branches holding the mud at bay.

Several guards came forth, bowing in the presence of the Assembly.

"The chamber is right ahead," said Bianca, her voice bouncing off the walls.

They came to another door, and she whispered an incantation.

The Fugues flickered and sputtered around the door, the eyes pale blue now. Fewer of them appeared, and Zach sensed their pain.

"W-Welcome, As-ssemb-bly members," the voices whispered.

It slid open and they entered. The dank cavity smelled of pine and mulch, the sprawling floor covered in ancient sentinel needles.

Satchel and Rowen gathered sticks and shrubs and tossed them into a pile. Macklin sparked some flint and orange fire licked at the air, illuminating the chamber. The walls of the cave were rough, and stalactites glinted above. Somewhere farther down, deep beyond a narrow crevasse in the wall, the sound of dripping water echoed.

In the middle of the stony room stood a shiny black armillary sphere. Zach walked up to it. The object came up to his chest, and he ran his fingers across the rings.

"Let us sit around the Sphere," said Bianca.

She led Zach to a spot next to her. The others took seats assigned to them — Elita to his left, and Rowan beside her. Macklin sank down adjacent to Bianca, Satchel at the end.

"Now clear your mind. First, we must meditate. Breathe normally and focus on inhaling and exhaling. Eliminate any stray thoughts. Picture light all around you. Accept the light and be one with it."

Zach crisscrossed his legs and tried to think of nothing. After a while, he was at peace, drifting off. Time lost all meaning — he could not have said if hours or minutes had gone by, but he recalled his hands clasping something. He opened his eyes and the cave dissolved. He floated in space, clutching Bianca's palm in his right hand and Elita's in his left. Beaming stars reflected on their faces in a dazzling radiance.

"Concentrate on the Silver Sphere. Think of a bright silver orb."

Zach focused on the object. Electricity crackled around them, then stopped.

"Continue," whispered Bianca. Her voice sounded far away, but clear, like an echo of an echo.

Zach tried harder. Currents fizzled and something struggled to appear. He started to panic; was he holding it back? His chest tightened as the stars spun, and his vision blackened in the center.

Elita tugged his fingers. "Relax, Zach. Take a deep breath. It will come naturally."

Breathe. He inhaled in rhythm with the repeated word.

Flashes of light refracted in front of them as sweat spilled off Zack's brow. Curls of lightning snapped, followed by thunder. Fire bolts shot through the backsplash of space. Energy swirled, spinning around and condensing into the shape of a silvery orb. Luminous flakes sparked out of the globe, forming rings amidst a bluish hue.

The Sphere remained a bright sterling while the halos glowed in red, gold, and white. A humming noise pierced the vacuum of space like some massive machine revving up. Numbers materialized one at a time along the colored bands. The Silver Sphere blossomed — the most beautiful object Zach had ever witnessed. A green skull appeared on one of the ringlets. Zach knew who it was. *Biskara.* The shape of a spacecraft emerged closer to the Sphere.

"I summon the truth seekers," Bianca said. Her lips pursed and her forehead pinched.

Across from them a blinding glare rose. When Zach's vision cleared, a man floated before them in white robes, tendrils of long ebony hair wandering around his face. The figure looked human, but Zach felt an innate bond with him. It was different than the link he shared with the other Kin; this man seemed almost part of him. Zach channeled the truth seeker's thoughts as they whispered across time and space.

"Welcome, Lord Sturge," Bianca said.

"Welcome, Assembly. We sensed upheaval on Azimuth. It is good to see you are safe."

Bianca nodded. "Biskara resides between the Eridanus and Dorado planes. The United Forces' *Fomalhaut* is near Fornax."

Lord Sturge examined the Sphere. He drifted closer, running his fingers across the circles. Luminous lines seared in the wake of his long digits.

"I sense confusion on the *Fomalhaut*. Something is keeping the Star Darts at bay." He hovered around the orb, silent as he worked. Before long, his deep voice resounded. "I have the coordinates. Time is crucial now. You must return to the mortal plane and defend Meracuse. The city is under great duress. Thank you, Assembly members. Godspeed to you."

A blaze of white whipped around him and he vanished. The Sphere spun in a slow, deliberate orbit, emitting a faint glow.

Zach's gaze locked on the starship.

"Shut your eyes again," said Bianca. "Meditate. Think of the fire in the cave." Droplets of sweat fluttered off her forehead and floated. They sparkled as they passed before the armillary sphere.

Zach focused on the campfire, and dreamlike fuzziness engulfed him, similar to when the Fugues first arrived. For a time, he existed neither on Azimuth nor in the presence of the Silver Sphere. The world became discolored; rock was blue, mulch was orange, and pine needles were purple.

Someone prodded his body. Zach opened his eyes and spied Bianca kneeling by his side. He was supine on the cavern floor, drenched in sweat. The warmth of the flames burned close and sleep clotted his mind. He rubbed his face, groggy, as if he had awakened from a deep slumber.

"Excellent, Zach. Brock would be so proud of you," said Rowan, rubbing his neck from behind.

"Th-that was amazing. Like a... trance." He slid to his knees. His boots scraped against the earth, the sound unusual after being away from the planet.

Bianca smiled and nodded.

"We must head back to the battle now," said Elita.

Macklin strode over and assisted Zach to his feet.

Satchel stamped out the blaze, and smoke smoldered from the ashes.

Bianca handed Zach the torch and grinned. "Lead us out."

Zach turned and ambled to the exit of the chamber. Though his boots touched rock and soil, he thought he still glided. His heart lightened, his head swam, and the image of the Sphere bedazzled him, even now.

CHAPTER 41

Nick sat on a deck overlooking the truth seeker's headquarters, Horologium. A glistening bubble encased the immense city, and a beautiful backdrop of space and dazzling stars surrounded the dome. Across from him was Corvan, who had been sent to brief him on his transformation.

"I am no different. My legs are sore from walking so much," said Nick, waving his hands.

Corvan nodded. "You are flesh and blood out here on the celestial stratum. You may be killed in battle and reach a higher plane. We eat, drink, and sleep as we used to." He had flaxen hair and dark skin, and claimed to be from a southern country on Azimuth.

"The desert is made of glass," Corvan had said when Nick first met him. "And our city, Mehabal, is of milky stone near an oasis. Perhaps one day, you will see it."

Nick returned to the moment. "Does a higher plane exist? Heaven?"

"We're not in touch with the higher plane, though our studies and customs suggest so." Corvan's shaved head shined in the starlight, as did his black leather jacket.

"Can I visit Earth?"

"We are unable to enter the mortal atmosphere. Albeit as a Kinsaver, the rules are skewed for you. I'm not sure what your abilities are."

Nick nodded, a little dejected, as he yearned to go home to visit his family once more. He gazed off into Horologium with its several high towers. In the center stood the tallest, a large silver clock adorning the top. The emblem of a sphere rested below it.

A knock drummed from the chamber's door behind them. Denon entered the room and approached the deck. Spiro strode in behind him.

Denon said, "The Aulic Assembly has contacted us. Biskara resides on a plane between Eridanus and Dorado. The star darts are having problems launching. We must go."

Nick wrung his hands. "Am I to participate?"

"Yes, we need every able soldier." Denon turned to Corvan. "You are to join the others in distracting Biskara."

Nick and Corvan rose.

"Come with me," said Denon.

They exited the chamber and walked down bright hallways flooded with brilliant moonlight. Nick met Spiro's gaze. He wondered what a star dart was.

CHAPTER 42

Denon said, "It seems Biskara has captured the *Fomalhaut*. She's being raided by celestial monsters, and we have to get rid of them. They are grounding the star dart fleet, which is needed to help repel the offensive on Meridia's capital, Meracuse."

Nick scratched his crown. He wondered what the *Fomalhaut* was, but figured he would find out soon enough. "I'm new. Aren't you going to train me more first?"

"No time. These are dire circumstances, and a Kinsaver may come in useful." Denon shook his head and sighed. "Besides, we need as many soldiers as we can rally, as most of the truth seekers are at the main battle."

"You said monster*s*. Plural," said Spiro.

Denon nodded, appearing grim. "You'll see what I mean. Come with me." He pressed a sword into each of their hands.

Looking back, Nick could not say how they traversed time and space in order to reach the *Fomalhaut*. All he knew was that one minute he was walking away from the brilliance of Horologium, and the next he floated just outside an enormous starship.

Even the city of the truth seekers paled in comparison to the ship, the most glorious thing he'd ever seen—sleek and beautiful, the color of a comet in the night sky. Windows glinted in the tempered steel hull, a thousand strong, each a portal into the small world within. Turrets and massive guns lay mounted across the bow of the ship, and a few hung from the underbelly. The gigantic bay protruded into the cosmos, akin to a shark lurking near the shoreline.

Inside rested a hundred smaller ships, each streamlined and elegant. Nick gaped at them. A red light flashed within the hangar, and he spied men scurrying over the deck. The hangar doors were only a quarter opened, providing not nearly enough room to launch any of the star darts safely. A force field must have been in place to keep the vacuum of space at bay.

Behind the *Fomalhaut*, Azimuth swelled like some behemoth, fertile moon. Azimuth's yellow sun rose, spreading its golden fingers along the eastern horizon. All around them, stars dotted the sky, and beyond, a shooting star streaked.

Nick's heart pummeled against his ribcage.

As they glided closer, Denon handed each of them a pair of metallic bifocals.

Nick handled his with care. "Sunglasses?"

"No." Denon put his on over his eyes. "The Sight. Nick, we cannot always behold both planes — mortal and celestial — and these spectacles allow us to switch from one plane to the other. Press the button here...." He touched just behind the hinge on the left arm of the glasses. "...and you can shift planes."

Nick slid the goggles on, and the vision of the *Fomalhaut* instantly changed. While he still observed the gleaming ship, he no longer glimpsed the troopers rushing around inside.

"Everyone's gone."

"Click the button."

Nick did so, and the crew returned. Rather than being in color, though, only their infrared images appeared. He switched again, and this time a single, pale specter glided across the hangar bay.

"Come," said Denon, and they glided closer to the hull.

Nick glanced around. "We are the only other truth seekers on this mission?"

"I told you, the rest are battling Biskara," replied Denon somberly. "Once aboard, we'll not be able to view the humans without the Sight. Our world is a reflection of theirs, but ours will not have life. The demonic apparitions you recognize there are stalling the ship and keeping the star darts from launching."

"How?"

"I do not know."

Nick repressed a shiver. At last, they reached the *Fomalhaut* and boarded the hangar. A slight buzzing rang in Nick's ears as they passed through the force field. As Denon had said, the crewmen Nick had seen on the deck were no more. He hit the button on the Sight and spotted them rushing about. They shouted in the dark hangar, trying to operate the power of the ship.

Nick grimaced. He couldn't hear anything, as if he'd gone deaf.

Once or twice, he thought he caught movement out of the corner of his eye, but when he glanced, no one was there. Switching the Sight again, he found a few pale beasts fleeing the hangar.

Denon said, "First, we must find out what they're doing to stall the ship. Hurry—the ghosts will know we're here soon enough."

As Nick scurried along behind Denon and Spiro, he scanned around. This was nothing like the craft he'd seen outside. Though brilliant to behold the exterior, the halls inside were dark and devoid of life. Cables hung from panels in the ceiling. A few sparks of electricity zapped when a swinging wire touched another. Nick turned away, and thought he spied something beside the cord. It was white and pale, but disappeared after he blinked his eyes.

A shiver thrilled down his spine. The things he'd seen in the hangar were everywhere, slipping in and out of the shadows. He hurried after Denon and glanced back.

A swarm of them materialized and now followed them.

"Denon," whispered Nick. "They know we're here."

"Keep walking," said Spiro gruffly. "Sooner we find out what's happening, the better off we'll be."

Nick tried not to eye the sinister beings. One he viewed clearly, as they strode by the thing in the hall. Its head was positioned upside down, its mouth gaping in an eternal, silent scream. Black eyes followed him as they passed it by. The creature froze and faded, reappearing almost directly beside him. Their bodies shifted and snapped, crackling like lightning. Any humanoid form they took lasted only a few seconds before they became something else entirely. A moan filled the hallway.

"A hive mind," said Denon. "They're monitoring us. If we don't interact, we should be fine."

A light glimmered ahead and the bellow of voices screaming down the dark corridor echoed on the portside.

Nick halted. He recognized one of the cries. *Emily....*

"Hey," he whispered to Denon, but when he turned to look, both Denon and Spiro had vanished. Skin crawling, Nick glanced down to the left, then back where his companions had gone. The flickering light ceased, leaving him in complete darkness. He tried switching the Sight, but only a few dark shadows hurried down the hall: human soldiers. He clicked the button again and another electric ghost vanished around a corner ahead. An eerie cackling followed behind.

Remembering Emily shouting for help, he sucked in a deep breath and hooked a left. He stalked down the hallway toward the voices. The clamor became louder near a sliding door. He rested his hand against the entrance, his heart hammering in his chest. Ever so slowly, he eased the metal door aside, and another cry escaped the room beyond. He whirled around the corner, prepared to strike anything that approached him.

Nick gasped and stiffened, his eyes wide.

The chatter came from four ghost-like creatures that hovered. Small voices, some like children's, others similar to old women and men, rang in his skull, yet they did not have mouths with which to speak. The beings transformed into rotting corpses garbed in rags, and he could almost smell the sour stench of their decaying flesh.

"Help us," one whispered.

"Save me," begged another.

Nick stumbled back and gaped. Heat drained from his body as he balled his hands into fists. "Stop!"

"Stop?" hissed one, the pitch echoing in his head. A sudden eerie silence filled the room.

All four of the things turned their attention to Nick. He felt them watching him, though their black eyes had shifted away, replaced now by sparks of electricity. Chills ran through him and goose pimples prickled up his arms.

"You cannot stop us," whined another, the voice as faint as wind.

Nick groped in the dark for his saber to fend the demons off. They approached, reaching for him with four, six, eight, twenty arms made of thin bolts of lightning. Anything those arms touched crackled and smoked. They were alive with electricity.

The cold steel of the blade felt heavy in his hands when he tore it free of its scabbard. He raised the saber, ready to slash at the first creature.

"Back off!" he called, his voice shaking. "I... I'm warning you!"

"You...."

"...cannot stop us."

"You do not have the power."

The voices mingled in his mind. Their whispers scratched inside his brain like rats scrabbling across the floor. He struck the nearest one, but the glittering steel didn't harm the beast. He hit them repeatedly, and each time, nothing happened. As they grew closer, Nick spied a thin tendril of energy linking one to the other.

Then, it clicked.

Power.

Nick shook his head and forced himself to focus. He aimed and swung the sword. "Don't have the power, huh?"

With a single blow, he sliced through the bolt connecting the closest one to the others. A loud *crack* reverberated in the room as he severed the tendril of energy. The horrific figure shrieked, but as it vanished, the noise faded. The other three hesitated only a few seconds before launching at him. Nick

slung the weapon, breaking one more of the connections—another *crack* and another shrill cry.

The remaining two froze as their companion dissolved. They seemed to be thinking, calculating.

Nick raised his scimitar, aiming to strike again, but both backed away and fled into the darkness.

I have to tell them. Spiro and Denon were on the ship, somewhere. He needed to find them. *The power is what's feeding them!*

CHAPTER 43

Milo shoved his way to Shelby and the other Kin. Blood dribbled down his face and neck. "Okay, now spread out across the entry. We need to push them back from here."

Shelby danced around the gate, clanging her sword, deflecting blows with her shield, and jabbing at the dark enemies flooding in.

Max parried an axe aimed for her, forcing the warrior back. He dropkicked the soldier off his feet and rolled up off the ground in front of her, fending off a charging Nightlander.

Emily and Riley stood at the end of the battering ram, firing away into the black horde.

Stuart fought on the other side, blasting his hand-cannon.

Nightlanders poured in from all directions, many squirting through and hammering the gateway. The doors rocked and a large hinge fell to the dirt with a thud.

Shelby fought to protect the entrance, striking every opponent she could. The doors would not stand much longer, she feared. One side began to collapse and a lump formed in her throat.

They were about to fall.

CHAPTER 44

Nick ran down the empty hallways for a long period before he found Spiro and Denon.

Dozens of the creatures swarmed around them. Snaps and clicks filled the air as the beings linked in circles around them, jabbing and striking like vipers of energy.

Nick raised his weapon and hacked one, two, then three apart from their companions. *Crack, crack, crack!* The blade went through the electricity. At last, he was near enough to shout, "They're feeding from the energy! Cut *between* them!"

Spiro and Denon began to slice as Nick did, and soon vanquished a number of the creatures. Those who had not dissipated turned and ran.

Nick wiped the sweat from his brow and approached his friends.

"How did you know?" asked Denon. The singer dripped with perspiration, and sported several ugly gashes along his arms.

The rotten stench of burnt flesh pervaded the air.

Nick shook his head. "Maybe its instinct." He winked as sweat-drenched hair fell in front of his eyes. "They're draining the energy of the ship. That's how they exist, their power source. We have to get the humans to cut the power."

"They must have already tried," said Spiro.

Denon said, "If they did, they probably pulled the switch back on too soon. It wasn't off long enough to break the circuit."

Nick asked, "How do we tell them?"

"We can't. Truth seekers can't communicate with mortals, except through the Silver Sphere, and even that's only when *they* contact *us*."

"Blast it! We need to find some way to interface with the people on this ship. We have to explain to them to turn the power off and *leave* it off."

The three of them clunked down the dim hall, headed for the bridge.

Nick switched the Sight again. He scanned the empty, dark gangways for someone to try and talk with, but any soldiers he had seen before were long gone.

Something clattered to the floor. Nick jumped and whirled around. A box had fallen.

He frowned. "One of those things?"

"Yes," said Denon. "They're following us."

Nick didn't need to change the Sight to know. He shivered and continued after the others, quickening his pace. "How far until the bridge?"

"We're close." Spiro pointed up. "See those flashing red bulbs?"

Nick squinted and spotted them.

"They're emergency lights on the deck. We have to be careful, though."

"Why?"

"Cutting power, *if* we can even manage to, might kill everyone. The oxygen will shut off, and so will the force field on the hangar bay. All of the air on the ship will be sucked out."

"Can't we tell them to move people behind doors and close them?"

Denon shook his head. "No way to secure the hatchways. Anyone below will be vaulted out into orbit."

Nick chewed his lower lip, unnerved by the thought of all of those people vanishing into space to perish. There was no other way, though; somehow, they *had* to cut the power.

"I don't want anyone else to die," he murmured, the memory of an ice pick in his belly bursting to life. He winced and grabbed his side.

Denon stopped, silent for a moment.

"What?" said Spiro.

The singer raised his eyes and caught Nick's. "Legend tells of Kinsavers. They've been few and far between—the last to join the truth seekers died and went to the next level almost a hundred years ago."

Nick shifted impatiently from one foot to the other. He switched his Sight and spied a gang of the electric vermin moving toward them. Denon seemed impervious to their presence.

"Aye," whispered Spiro. "My mother used to tell me about them, but 'twas a short tale indeed."

"Kinsavers, people like you who are guided to watch over Kin on Earth, are reborn differently when you transform to a truth seeker. You don't

simply die and become one of us. You first have a second chance at life, on Azimuth. Because you've treaded our ground and breathed our air, you are linked to the Kin, and to the mortal plane."

Nick squinted. "I don't understand. I thought I couldn't go into Azimuth's atmosphere as a truth seeker."

"You can't, but you may be able to connect with the people on this ship."

"Like with a link?" asked Spiro, rubbing his chin.

"Perhaps," said Denon. "I'm honestly not sure. The legends are vague at best, and no records exist of what a Kinsaver can actually do. You do have different abilities than other truth seekers, though."

Nick nodded. "I'll try. And all of those people in the hangar? Won't they die?"

"Not if they get into the star darts," said Spiro. A spark lit his eye.

"We must hurry," said Denon. He eyed the electric creatures. "Come, we'll talk as we go."

"Listen." Spiro scurried alongside them, talking fast. "When we enter the bridge, try to link with someone. Tell 'em to get everyone in the bay to board the 'darts. *They* aren't connected to the main vessel, and should be able to protect the crewmen just long enough for the ship to reboot."

"Okay." Nick nodded. "Except... how do I even go about talking to these people?"

"That, I don't know," said Denon. "You're on your own. Try something — *anything*. It may come instinctively." He winked.

They came to the bridge at that moment. Dozens of the creatures sucked energy from panels and wires.

Nick clicked to the other Sight and frowned.

Men scrambled about the bridge in disarray, some frantically trying to order the door on the hangar to open all the way. Others shouted into microphones, attempting to contact Azimuth. Nothing worked.

A soldier raced by with a message, running right through Nick. A jolt of hot, tingling energy engulfed his body. For a split second, he'd felt the man's heartbeat and inflating lungs.

Nick eased past the crowd as Denon and Spiro went about separating the beings from their feed. Once or twice, Nick switched the Sight. Each time, fewer creatures appeared on the deck, until more materialized and took the place of the fallen seconds later. It was hopeless.

He tensed and concentrated. Still, Nick could not communicate with any of the men. He ran his hands over their arms in an attempt to touch them, and even forced himself to imagine a coin levitating. Nothing.

Growing desperate, Nick stepped into the man nearest him. Maybe he could possess someone.

A rush overcame him. The man's heartbeat hammered loud as a riveter in his ears. The soldier's pulse throbbed and every breath echoed.

Somewhere deep inside, Nick knew he'd not taken over the man, but a bond connected them, however weak.

Nick tried reaching the man wordlessly, urging him to send a runner to the hangar and command the crew to board the star darts. Nick's head weighed heavy, and a humming noise spilled through his eardrums. The soldier replied with a loud grunt. When Nick thought he'd failed again, the man turned and waved a runner over.

Words escaped the gruff ensign's mouth. The runner appeared bewildered, but did as he was bid.

Time ticked by and Nick changed his Sight. The bridge flooded with more of the things each second. Cold sweat ran down his neck, and he sensed the ensign's fear as well. Somehow the man knew that something was amiss. Of course, no one on the ship could see the three truth seekers — or the grotesque monsters eating the energy.

Then, the messenger returned, shiny-faced and panting. Nick attempted to read his lips, searching to find out if all was safe. When the ensign asked, the runner nodded, and relief flooded Nick in a cold swell.

Cut off the power, Nick urged, *and leave it off for a few minutes.*

The soldier resisted him at first. Horrified at the thought of so much work going for naught, Nick forced images of the ghost-like creatures into the man's head. The ensign gasped, his beefy hands clasping his skull. Others nearby stopped working and turned to him.

You're okay, Nick growled, *but those things are feeding off your ship. Do what I say, and the star darts will go to Azimuth safely.*

The fear emanating from the man was almost tangible. Just when Nick thought he had pushed the crewman as far as possible, the ensign resigned and lumbered over to the switch.

Fresh air struck Nick as the man stepped away from him. The connection was cut. It was as though he'd lost a dear friend, and he gasped at the sudden loneliness, but he didn't have time to dwell on it.

Someone yelled at the soldier, and others raced to stop him as he reached for the main power lever. Then, as if in slow motion, the ensign pulled down.

The ship's loud humming ceased and darkness ensued.

Nick pressed the button on the Sight and held his breath.

The ghosts gave cries of dismay and faded. *Cracks* echoed around him as their ties to the ship were severed one-by-one. Others swarmed from the room in a torrent of energy. Their screaming forms flickered a few moments before they began vanishing.

Nick silently prayed the crew would be safe. The air on the bridge grew thinner as it was slowly sucked out of the rest of the craft.

Denon stepped by his side, bloody and exhausted, and smiled. "Good job. Now he needs to turn it on."

"Not yet," whispered Nick, nodding toward a figure that churned outside the ship, forming and growing bigger.

Denon followed Nick's gaze.

The pale, electric shapes shifted into something larger, joining together. Insect-like arms of electrons reached for the ship, but they were dim. A lithe, nasty body shivered as currents of weak electricity raced through the form. When the creature found nothing to feed on, it gave a final, hellish trumpet. It whirled its antenna around its bulbous eyes and wagged its femur. Its wings chattered, and it was gone.

"The Maroccanus," said Denon.

"What?"

"I've never seen one, but have read about them. Legends speak of the Maroccanus wrecking many vessels by feeding on their energy. It's gone. Tell him to switch the power."

Nick raced over to the ensign. The soldier had been tackled to the deck. Men started hollering at each other, and the man Nick had spoken to was uttering something, confused and dazed. Nick slipped into his mind—easier this time—and he didn't resist when Nick told him to turn the power back on.

Another of the men rose and yanked the switch. The trooper on the floor wriggled free as lights flickered to life. Air rushed into the cabin and crewmen cheered as their instruments began working again.

Nick backed away and wiped a film of sweat from his face.

Spiro clapped him on the back. "Good man."

"I just hope we're not too late," said Denon.

CHAPTER 45

The gates screeched and rocked.

Shelby fought to the center closer to Riley and Emily and yelled, "They're about to fall!"

Overhead, gleaming figures approached from out of the sky. They rocketed by, cracking the air with a thunderous swish. Shelby gasped as they raced back toward the city. They looked like smooth, flawless airplanes, coated in silver metal and glinting in the light of the late afternoon sun.

Throg pointed up. "Star darts! The United Forces have joined the fray!"

The star darts swooped down on the sea of Nightlander men. Fiery red beams launched from their wings and bombarded the Nightlander troops with aplomb. Nightlanders exploded in balls of fire, and searing flames raced across the field where the lasers struck.

Raucous cheers boomed from inside the gates of Meracuse. Strike after strike left the Nightlanders frenzied, but it wasn't enough. The tide of battle had turned, but only for the moment. Hundreds of Battleswine began to rush in around them, slaughtering those who drew too near and buying more time.

"We must strike now. Onward!" Milo charged forward with the Stonecoats.

The Battleswine followed close behind. A Disemboweler came from nowhere, slamming into one of the Swine. One of Gunther's men roared and sliced the beast in half, then helped his companion—the white-furred female, now pink and red, gore-sprayed from the slaughter—back to her feet.

Shelby launched after Milo, determined to make sure the Stonecoat had cover. She turned to Max and called out for him, but he was lost in the fracas. The other Kin had also vanished.

Not ten yards from the main gates, a furious figure slaughtered Battleswine and Meridian soldiers left and right. The dark warrior struck with terrifying accuracy and a maniacal resolve, all the while shouting orders to the Nightlanders. He obliterated every man who came near.

Shelby ripped her saber from the gut of a Nightlander and turned to spy Milo shouting at the demonic figure.

"Fight me in single combat, Malefic, you coward!" The Stonecoat leader brandished his long sword, and the blade glimmered in the fading afternoon light. "Come and best me, if you dare!"

Cold dread filled Shelby; that man was no ordinary Nightlander. She ducked as a Nightlander swung his morning star at her, and with a quick twirl of her blade, put him down. She strode forward, her boots sinking into the soiled ground. When she pulled them free, they made a sucking noise against the mud and mire.

Malefic descended off his mount and slapped the charger on its rear, sending the hellish horse galloping into the tumult.

Shelby watched, mesmerized as the enormous man lifted his black sword and prepared to bring it down on Milo. She turned away when Stuart called her name, lifting her rapier just in time to parry a blow that would have cleaved her in two.

Stuart came up behind the Nightlander and shot him point blank in the back. The Nightlander crashed to the ground with a cry.

"Look out!" Stuart cried over the noise of clanging swords and neighing horses. "And be careful!"

"Where's Max?" hollered Shelby.

"There!" He pointed.

Shelby followed the motion beyond the fight between Malefic and Milo. Max was busy hacking at Nightlanders, trying to keep them away from Milo.

Shelby whirled around, preparing to help him, when she was confronted by a dozen more of the black-armored knights.

High above, the star darts rocketed by, sending another wave of their lasers into the fray. They shot hoards of Nightlanders, but still the dark soldiers did not yield.

Shelby swung until her arm ached, and continued to parry and riposte with grace and power. Her body grew weary, yet the battle raged on around her.

From the corner of her eye, she caught glimpses of Malefic battling Milo. Every blow Milo placed on the Nightlander leader was returned by several strikes of inhuman strength. Shelby forced her exhausted body on, refusing to give up. If it would help Milo somehow to land that single thrust that would end it all, she'd gladly kill a hundred Nightlanders.

Then, as if a ghost, one of the Disembowelers bounded over Emily and Stuart. Foam dribbled from its maw and thick sludge covered its legs. The snarling beast propelled at Milo, whipping its claws through his side.

Milo collapsed, writhing in pain.

Shelby cried out, and turned to race forward and take Milo's spot, but before she could take so much as a step, Max was there, standing beside Milo's crumpled form.

Max buried his long sword into the chest of the rabid creature as it turned to him. The Kin retracted his blade from the convulsing monster and, in one bound, landed in front of Milo, parrying the blow meant to finish the Stonecoat leader off.

Malefic cursed and glared at Max.

"Little Kin, I will hack you to pieces!" Malefic shouted as he lifted his sword high and swung it forward with both hands. The blow shattered Max's blade and struck the top of his helmet.

"No!" Shelby screeched.

Max dropped to his knees, dazed, as Malefic raised the obsidian blade again, preparing to behead him.

Shelby bolted for Max, tears rolling down her cheeks.

Everything seemed to slow down. She fell to the ground, screaming Max's name. Then her fear and sorrow gave way to cold rage; as she viewed Max, she thought of Mr. Dempsey. With another cry, her body pulsated and heat coursed through every limb. A buried reserve of power welled up inside her, and then surged.

Just as Malefic moved forward and brought the sword down toward Max's head, a bright light blazed between them, swallowing Malefic as his momentum carried him into the glare. As quickly as it had come, the glow vanished. Echoes of Malefic's shouts of rage broke from the area where he'd once been.

Shelby's body trembled. Ignoring the pain in her limbs, she threw her saber aside and raced toward Max. Only footprints in the mud remained where Malefic had stood. Shelby dropped to Max's side and pulled him close.

All around, Nightlanders lowered their weapons and whispers flew through the crowd. Some of the stunned men were hacked to the ground before anyone knew Malefic was gone. Then, those who survived began to run, fleeing as quickly as their feet could carry them.

The damaged doorways screeched as they started to open. Nightlanders had raced from the main gates in hopes of retreating to their camps or escaping, but the Battleswine at the flank of the field made sure none left alive.

Shelby protected a woozy Max as thousands of Meridian warriors discharged and sprinted out. The Nightlanders who had stayed close were cut down in seconds.

She heaved Max up higher. As they stumbled, he lifted his head and their lips brushed. She locked eyes with him.

"I had him right where I wanted him," he quipped. He drew closer again and kissed her.

Shelby's heart throbbed as their lips met. She pulled him close, glad to have him safe in her arms, and smiled as she gazed into his eyes.

"Inside... now," Bianca ordered the Kin.

She cast a motherly glance to Shelby and Max before racing forward and helping Shelby pull Max to his feet. Stuart pushed Shelby aside and took the majority of Max's weight onto his shoulder. They scurried in through the edges of the barreling soldiers and followed Bianca as she dashed forward. As they passed the warriors, Presage stood behind, his piercing green eyes gazing upon them.

"Well done," said Presage.

Barrick and Sculptor burst down a ladder and trotted over, bloodstained and bruised. Sculptor's nose was crooked, but not broken. The side of his face had an enormous scrape on it, and Barrick had a nasty gash that broke his armor along his back.

"We thought we'd never see ya again," said Barrick.

"Look what the bearcat dragged in," Sculptor chirped, grinning.

Cumber trotted over, brandishing a bloody battleaxe. "It's good to be with ye, but I'm off to trounce some Nigh'landers," he said as he charged toward the gate.

"Why don't you join him, Barrick? You could use the exercise," Sculptor jabbed, and they all laughed.

A few moments later, a number of Stonecoats rushed through the gates. Shara trotted easily with a listless Milo across her back. Shelby exhaled as medics raced to his side to help him.

Battleswine entered the city with Krupp's limp body slung between Gunther and another Swine.

She turned to Bianca, disheartened. "We won, but at what cost?"

"Milo will live, and Krupp's men see death every day. They are a warrior race. Even so, the loss of their general is a stinging blow." She laid a hand on Shelby's shoulder. "The Battleswine believe that when they die, they are reborn to fight celestial wars. Krupp has gone to the place of his forefathers. His death was not in vain, though. Today is a victory we cannot forget."

She smiled warmly and pulled Shelby close. Bianca's hair was mussed and she had a scratch along her neck. A hole gaped from her shoulder. "You must not feel that this day was a loss, my dear. Malefic is gone, though where, I cannot begin to guess. He must have seen the tide turn and fled."

"No, Malefic didn't flee. He'll be back." Somehow, Shelby knew for a fact Malefic hadn't run away. She had done something out there, but couldn't begin to guess what. The mere thought of the Nightlander leader made her blood boil with rage.

"What do you mean?" Bianca looked as though she already knew what Shelby was thinking.

"I...." Shelby swallowed. "Is it possible to feel so scared, so angry, at someone, that you transport them away without understanding how?"

Bianca flashed a knowing smile. "Your mother, Samantha, is a witch, Shelby. My sister was a good witch until it was decided to send you to Earth. You may be a powerful Kin if you inherited her talent." She squeezed Shelby's shoulder and smiled.

Shelby's eyes burst open wide. "You... a-are... my a-aunt?"

"Yes dear. My sister loves you. Biskara turned her love against us."

Shelby buried her head in Bianca's bosom as she wept.

"It's okay, my darling. It is over for now, and there is much to discuss." Bianca caressed Shelby's hair.

Shelby trembled in her aunt's arms, overwhelmed with emotions. Regardless, she was glad it was over. At last, she and the other Kin finally enjoyed their respite.

CHAPTER 46

Meracuse stirred with activity as heroic tales flowed from every corner.

The Kin exchanged stories of their adventures inside their private lodgings. Chambermaids brought over jugs of libations and confections, while healer Beekman personally attended to the various cuts and scrapes of the Kin.

Bianca joined them. "The truth seekers defeated Biskara. He has fled the southern hemisphere for now."

Shelby nodded with glee and joined the others devouring cake, which was blissfully sweet after chewing so much chud. Any sort of real food tasted good after days spent running, hiding, drinking nothing but tea, and being terrified of the war.

Morgana stepped into the chamber. As healer Beekman cleaned out a cut on Zach's forehead, she gently retrieved the cloth from the healer's hand and continued cleansing the wound. Zach smiled.

Healer Beekman grinned and strode over to work on Max's sore ribs.

Shelby looked back to Bianca. "What now?"

"Lord Achernar is on his way to greet you. He already ordered a celebratory feast tomorrow evening. Tonight, we rest."

They sat and chatted, glad for the respite.

Throg entered their chamber. He collapsed onto a bench, inhaled a piece of white chocolate pastry, and chased it with blueberry ale. He smacked his lips and sighed. "Good cake."

A burly man burst into the room. He towered over them, wrapped in rich robes of blue satin. With hands on his hips, he scanned the Kin and beamed with a hearty grin as his long blonde hair glistened. Shelby had never seen someone who emitted so much power and energy.

"Oh, impressive Kin, how proud we all are of you! Meridia thanks you from the bottom of its soul. I decided to order a wonderful feast to celebrate tomorrow, and you will be seated at my table with the Assembly."

Lord Achernar walked over to Throg and they exchanged a jovial hug. "Captain Throg, I would like you to join us as well. Your courage and loyalty once again shines through. I am off to be briefed on the state of the countryside. Meridia is in need of much repair, but please, rejoice and rest for now. I will revel with you on the morrow." He clapped his hands together with enthusiasm and exited the chamber.

For a moment, Shelby was baffled. Then she laughed and drank some blueberry ale. It was tart, thick, and wonderful. The others joined in.

Once their wounds had been tended to, the Kin explored their chambers. What they found made Shelby grin.

"Looky here. A steam room," Max called out. His hand was gingerly pressed to his side.

Riley bounded to another door, her hair whirling. "There's a huge mud bath, too!"

"These bathrooms are divine," Emily cooed. She brushed a strand of her long locks back.

The lavatories were riddled with gold and silver, the faucets adorned with diamonds. Trays of sweets were placed throughout the chambers along with glowing pitchers of ale, juice, and water. Clean clothing had been laid out for all of them, and each Kin had their own bedroom.

"I'm hitting the steam room," said Stuart.

Max rubbed his side "That should help my sore ribs out."

The girls decided on the mud bath. Shelby, Riley, Emily, and Morgana slipped into the rich, warm mire, and Zach joined them. Throg walked off for a shower, talking about how time in the wild had made him miss hot water and soft featherbeds.

Zach slid in deeper. "I've never had a mud bath before. Even back home. This is so relaxing."

Shelby hadn't thought of "home" in a while. She grew uneasy when she envisioned her father. She'd fought a war, saved a kingdom, and had grown almost five years in only a few days, yet the idea of returning to the beast still made her edgy.

"Are you okay, Shelby?" Zach asked.

She found herself speaking from her heart. "Yes, I'm just thinking of home. Since my mother left, my father has been a mess. He wakes up wailing

in the middle of the night, and he drinks all the time. Once... he was so cool before. He scared me the morning... before the portal."

Zach locked eyes with her; he seemed to be deep in thought.

Her words brought them to reality. She could sense them thinking of their families as well, wondering what had happened to their mothers and fathers, sisters, brothers, and pets while they'd been away. How long had they been gone? No one knew.

Bianca appeared in the chamber and sat down beside the mud bath. "How are you all doing?" She offered a warm smile.

"Great," Riley and Morgana chimed in.

Zach added, "Not bad. Glad to relax a little."

Shelby said, "Bianca, how long can we stay... like... here on Azimuth?"

Bianca hesitated a moment, then wiped a spot of mud off the edge of the bath with a cloth. "Your identities were breached when you were young, so we sent you to Earth to insulate you. You can stay a bit, but you'll have to return to Earth for your own protection. Your families there are genuine Meridians. Except for yours, Zach. A horrible accident took your true Meridian parents' lives, as you now know. You are the only Kin that has a choice to stay, due to Brock's passing."

"I feel like I am more loved here," said Zach.

Morgana shot him a simper and rustled mud in his hair. "I'm not letting you leave."

Emily twirled a strand of hair around her fingers. "I miss my mom and dad. And my dog."

"I have four younger sisters to look after," Riley said with a sad grin. "I wonder what kind of trouble they got into while I was away. Are they Meridians, too?"

Bianca nodded, her eyes glittering with a secret smile.

Shelby said, "My father needs me. I couldn't abandon him, anyway. He won't... he c-can't...."

Bianca cast a look of sympathy to her. "Well, let's not think of that now. You must rest. There's always tomorrow for everything else. There will be some beauticians and the like coming up to help you all prepare for the feast. I'll come by, too. The Assembly will escort you to the gala once you're ready tomorrow evening. For now, enjoy your respite. Dinner has been brought to the main chamber for you." She plopped a pile of towels next to the mud bath and departed.

After some time, they exited the bath and rinsed off in the mineral pool next to the tub of mud. The scent of sulfur filled the steamy room.

As the others left, Shelby forced the thought of home aside. Tonight was a night for relaxation, not lamentations. Her aunt was right: tomorrow, after the feast, she could decide what to do.

She and the rest of the Kin moved on to the showers and prepared for the evening.

CHAPTER 47

The night before had been restful, and now the Kins' chambers buzzed with life and excitement. Beauticians had arrived and swept the girls away. Meanwhile, the boys chose suits and dressed in their own spacious bathroom. Each young man selected a suit of a different color. The velvet jackets lay emblazoned with gems and embroidered in fine twine. The silk and satin undershirts sat folded, white and clean. For slacks, they chose ivory to match their shirts.

Zach took it all in and smiled, content for the first time in.... In fact, he'd never been this content.

"Like royalty," Max exulted, glancing in the mirror. The sheen of his black eye had gone down, but it remained swollen shut. He examined his green blazer. Around the arm strung a cord of sanguine and gold, signifying his place as a Kin. The other boys had similar markings.

"Well, you are royalty here," said Throg matter-of-factly, as he fixed his bow tie. He had slicked his hair back and trimmed his goatee. All in all, he resembled a dashing swashbuckler garbed like a prince.

Zach pulled on his jacket, deep maroon with gold embroidery. "Bianca said I can stay here."

"I think I'll remain as long as possible," said Stuart. He had chosen a blazer of navy blue, with silver and gold buttons that shone in the candlelight. "My family must be terribly worried, though...."

"I'm staying for good," said Zach.

The boys froze and gaped at him.

Max's hand stiffened on his tie. "Your family?"

"Not great. My parents passed in a car accident and I was adopted at six. They have me call them by their first names. They never truly felt like my family, and they're getting divorced. I never had a choice to pick my family. Now I do. I'm staying. Meridia is my true home."

They all nodded. While he knew he would miss Adrian, he just couldn't go back to that life. How could he live in a house with no love?

The boys finished dressing and entered the main chamber of their suite. There, they enjoyed some refreshing tea and ale. Zach sipped his ale, admiring the others and enjoying their company. When they returned home, he would miss them. Max and Stuart were like brothers to him; their links had accelerated that bond.

Throg patted him on the back. "You know, Zach, the Assembly will be thrilled with your decision. With Brock's passing, they need you to operate the Sphere, but they would never ask you to stay. Plus, I want a fishing partner, and Morgana requires someone to tend after her since her father is gone."

"No fishing at the Invunche Lake, though. I never want to encounter a wishpoosh again." They laughed, and Zach gazed at his friend, hesitating before asking one question that burned at him. "Throg, you mentioned you were Captain of the Assembly's personal guard and left due to heartache. May I ask what happened?"

Throg twirled his goatee and his eyes narrowed. "Sure. I haven't spoken of it in a while. I loved Bianca's sister, Samantha. She was ambitious, and a captain just wouldn't do, though I sensed her passion for me. She chose to marry a man of a prominent family instead. I decided to take a break, and realized how the woods had become healing for me. You'll understand one day."

The girls emerged from their bathroom in a wave of perfume and sparkling gowns.

"Jumping Manticores," Stuart whispered, his eyes wide. "Wow, Riley, you sure are dazzling."

"Hold on a second" said Max, feigning concern. "Did you see some girls named Shelby, Riley, Emily, and Morgana in there?"

The girls beamed and blushed, stunning in their resplendent dresses.

Emily wore a gown of light blue with silver scrollwork along the hem, the needlework accented with glittering diamonds the size of teardrops. Her bodice was laced tightly, and gorgeous sleeves draped to the ground. Turquoise forget-me-nots hung in her caramel hair, accented by a single white rose.

Riley's blonde locks cascaded across her shoulders and down to her rosy pink ball gown. It was embroidered with golden roses and rubies that sparkled in the firelight. A gorgeous ruby headband shone brilliantly among her honey locks. She swept the gown back and curtseyed.

Morgana preened in a midnight blue ball gown. Black lace, etched with silver, covered the dress, and sapphires gleamed as if stars. Her eyes had been painted a lovely shade of beryl, matching her fierce, warm gaze.

Zach's eyes were glued to her, and she blushed. He swallowed hard, unable to turn away.

Shelby emerged last, her raven hair braided and twirled up behind her head, where gold flower barrettes held it in place. Small daisies dotted the braids. She wore a luscious rusty orange gown. Brilliant yellow and aurous accents rose from the bottom up, swirling like flames. They hit her waist, each tendril ending in a shining topaz gem.

Max gaped at her.

"Well, we did spy them earlier," said Riley in response to Max. "They must have walked off with the group of boys who were just in here before."

They all snickered and admired their lush attire.

Bianca poked her head in the door. "Ready, Kin?"

"Yep, Auntie," Shelby answered for them, and they exited to the hallway.

Max sidled over beside her and smiled.

Zach slid next to Morgana as they walked through the stone doorway. "You are gorgeous, milady."

"Thank you, sir. You're not half-bad looking, yourself."

The Assembly lined the hallway just outside the door, garbed in extravagant accoutrements. Each wore colors that would make a peacock envious. Long gowns adorned the women, glittering with gems and metallic threads. Rings of emeralds, diamonds, sapphires, rubies, and other blazoning gems adorned their slender, gloved fingers. Necklaces hung around their thin, elegant throats.

The men of the Assembly were as handsome as the women were gorgeous. Their coats and slacks fit them well. Each man had a single gold ring on his right hand with the symbol of the Aulic Assembly on it—an armillary sphere. The men bowed and smiled.

"You all look lovely," said Elita to them, akin to a doting mother. She rested a palm on Emily's shoulder before proceeding.

They sauntered down the hallway to a large, scarlet double door, their shoes clacking on the stone. Macklin swung it open to a cavernous ballroom.

CHAPTER 48

The people at the packed tables rose and cheered, and everyone clapped as the Kin entered. The vaulted dome hovered almost a hundred feet high. Alabaster columns supported the painted ceiling, engraved with scenes of ancient texts. The floor stretched forward with dark marble, highlighted with black and white stone. A pattern sprawled across the ground, more like a mural than a checkered floor.

The artwork, Shelby realized with surprise, gleamed of the night sky. She gaped at a shooting star emblazoned with gold and silver as she walked over it.

They passed a table occupied by a bandaged Milo and the Stonecoats, and another dozen tables seated with the Battleswine. The newly appointed General Gunther's head bulged out of a black leather tuxedo and oversized dotted bowtie. Blunderbuss stood clapping with the Centurions. His pinstripe suit further elongated his tall and gangly figure.

They strode forward until they reached Lord Achernar's table. Musicians and balladeers populated the ballroom and played wonderful tunes, their fabulous music floating to the highest point in the chamber and bouncing off chandeliers of crystal and gold.

"Three cheers for the Kin," cried out Barrick from a table that featured Sculptor, Cumber, Boozer, Vilaborg, and Healer Beekman.

Simon zoomed up to Shelby in a dapper blue suit. "They gave my father a light sentence—three years confinement to his chambers—and he's been dismissed from the army. And I get to visit a lot!"

She knelt down and hugged him. "That's wonderful. We put in a good word with Bianca for him." She rustled his hair.

Just as they were about to sit, the doors to the ballroom opened and the cheers subsided. In walked Drake, his hands clasped behind his back. Murmurs flared up from the crowd, only to quiet a moment later as the Leshy held up his hand.

"Normally, I do not leave my forest." His voice echoed across the enormous chamber. "But, I have come to give my thanks to the Kin and their brave companions." He scanned the crowd, and his green eyes glittered when they landed on Morgana. "And to bring a family back together."

Loud barking came from outside, and a dog bounded into the room. Shelby gaped at the enormous dog, which resembled a large German Sheppard.

"Otis!" cried Morgana. Otis raced to her, and she knelt and wrapped her arms around him. "Oh, thank you, Drake! Thank you so very much!"

Drake approached and laid a hand on Morgana's shoulder, and spoke with her in a quiet voice.

Shelby frowned and turned to Zach. "What's he saying? Do you know?"

Tears slipped down Morgana's rosy cheeks.

"I think he just told her that her father is gone," whispered Zach.

Once Drake departed, Zach left Shelby to help Morgana to her feet. Zach must have said something to her, because she nodded and smiled, then took his hand.

With Otis by her side, she returned to the rest of the Kin. "My father is dead, but he would be proud to know what we've accomplished, and that Meridia is free once more."

Shelby agreed. "Your father was a brave man, Morgana. He will never be forgotten."

"Thank you."

They sat down at the capacious round table. Waiters suited in white emerged with trays of dazzling platters. Copious amounts of honey-coated shrimp, truffle-fried squid, orange-infused duck, lemon-laced poultry, and seasoned steak tips soon adorned the table. The air was thick with the scent of mouthwatering spices.

Shelby drank it in. The splendor of the chamber, the magnificence of the people—all of it was hers to enjoy.

Morgana chatted as Otis gorged from a bowl beside her. Shelby was glad to see her doing better.

She relaxed and let her gloved hand find Max's beneath the table. Tomorrow, she'd be strong. Tomorrow, she could face her fears. Tonight was a night for celebration.

The Kin talked amongst one another as they ate. They swilled fine wines, ales, and juices amid the clamoring voices and sweet music. A bard sang of the Kin's heroics as he danced from table to table.

Max turned and smiled at Shelby. His hazel eyes shone, and she laughed.

CHAPTER 49

Byron Pardow writhed in his bed. The room was freezing, the darkness murkier than usual. Red-faced demons crowed over him as he moaned.

The mattress dissipated as a fog emerged.

He rose to his knees and rubbed the ground, then pulled his hand up from the mud and stared at the wet dirt on his fingers.

"You are a pathetic man. You couldn't even hold your job, you useless slob." The distorted voice of his ex-wife, Samantha, barked out from the emptiness.

"P-please, Sam, I did my best. I l-loved you," he cried out in anguish.

"Liar!" the Samantha-creature screamed. "Liar, liar, liar, liar," echoed several venomous voices.

The figure approached him out of the mist, the sounds of its bare feet squishing in the mud as it came into view. The Samantha-creature had a pale green complexion. Her tawny teeth formed a morbid smile. She was his ex-wife, but disfigured, wearing long black hair stringy and splotched with moss.

"I am so happy without you. You are a deadbeat loser. I hope you rot," the Samantha-creature said with disdain.

The red-faced goblins accompanied her, dancing all around him. "Byron the deadbeat loser. Deadbeat loser," they chanted in malevolent whispers.

"P-please leave me alone. Leave me be," he begged from his knees, his mud-splattered body trembling.

"I did leave you alone." The Samantha-creature then cackled as the demons continued their chants of, "Deadbeat, loser, liar, deadbeat, loser, liar."

A broad shadow loomed behind the demons as the sun rose behind them. The head of a massive lion peered down on them with a broiling countenance. Its crown sat perched on the body of a dark stallion. Hefty tiger claws protruded in front. The creature was the most brilliant thing Byron had ever seen.

"What is it? What is it? What is it?" the demons chanted in a whisper.

"I am the dream-eater, Baku." He lifted his head and roared, rearing on his hind legs. Lightning flashed, illuminating his white mane, and thunder crackled from above.

The Samantha-creature discharged a shrill cry of terror as Baku swooped in and gorged her and the demons in one sickening crunch. Baku swallowed them whole, and suddenly, Byron stopped trembling in fear and anguish.

He remained on his knees, his body immobilized as the ground transformed into a groomed lawn, the sun toasty and welcoming.

Baku strode forward regally and licked his lips, and halted in front of Byron.

"Wh-who a-are y-you?"

"I am Baku, the dream-eater."

Byron stood up. "B-Baku?"

"Your daughter has been deficient of a father. You are blessed to have a Kin as your child. Go to her. You are liberated of these hellions. I am full."

"Y-yes, of course. Thank you."

"I am the dream-eater. I am finished here." Baku whirled and vanished into the woods.

Byron grew fatigued and slouched closer to the scent of the crisp sod. His eyelids weighty, he sprawled out on the fluffy green and nodded off.

He roused in his bed, deluged in sweat. Sleep was a welcome respite, and this time, it had been dreamless.

Outside his door, the kitchen light seeped in. With no volume, his television illuminated the room in a flickering glow. The program showed Lucas Denon joyfully playing an acoustic set on stage.

Byron exhaled, grasped a towel, and dried himself off. He shuffled out the door on wobbly knees, shielding his eyes from the sudden light as he lumbered toward the kitchen.

Shelby sat at the table, quietly drinking tea. Her black hair was braided and there was something different about her. No longer did she look young. Her shoulders were squared, her lips tight, and her gaze exhausted.

His eyes welled as he approached her. His daughter was beautiful.

"Oh, Shelby." Wet tears spilled down his face.

She continued sipping her tea.

"Baby, I am so sorry. I love you so much... so, so much."

Shelby's eyes watered and she rose from the table. "I forgive you, Daddy."

Byron swept her into his embrace and held her tightly. Heartache sped through him. The pain he'd caused her would never happen again. He swore it, his voice quivering. "Never again, my little darling. Never again. Daddy is here."

They held each other for several minutes, swaying back and forth.

CHAPTER 50

The monitor peered upon the home of Shelby, but the image distorted out of view. The dark figure hissed in front of the screen and slammed his fist on the console.

"The mentors have clogged the channel," he barked as he fiddled with a switch. A Nightlander soldier scowled next to him.

The door leading into the chamber slid open and a woman marched in. Her obsidian leather suit squeaked as she strode across the dark, enormous hall carved from black stone. A few torches guttered in their braziers, casting a wicked light across the room.

"Master Hideux, the sinister Kin are ready," she said, tossing her hair aside. She smirked and rested a hand on her hip.

"Excellent, Samantha. I will inform Father." Hideux's black spiked hair stood rigid, and he glared back at the six flickering screens with blood red eyes. "The Kin resume school on Earth soon." He lit a pipe and inhaled, and a fiendish sneer curled on his pale lips. "Let's send them a homecoming gift, shall we?"

Behind Samantha appeared six figures covered in shadow. One stepped forward, a raven-haired girl with eyes blacker than a shark's, and an expression equally lifeless.

GLOSSARY

ATLASERIA - A magnificent, modern city that existed on medieval Earth, where the Canary Islands now stand. It was destroyed by Biskara in a massive tsunami known as The Great Deluge.

THE AULIC ASSEMBLY - The governing body of Meridia, who report to their king, Lord Achernar. Current members are Bianca Saddler, Macklin Morrow, Rowan Letty, Elita Ezmer, Satchel Spool and Brock Fergus. They have psychic links to the Kin, and are the only beings able to operate the Silver Sphere.

AXEL THROG - The former captain of the Aulic Assembly's private guard; he has now chosen a life in solitude as a forester due to heartache... until....

AZIMUTH - A planet, part of the Eridanus constellation in the southern hemisphere, 200 light years from Earth, where the Atlaserians on Earth had fled to for a new beginning.

AZIMUTH CODE - The code Azimuth lives by, where advanced weaponry (blasters, bombs, planes) are illegal due to the massive loss of life and nature caused by these weapons in previous wars. Only the United Forces are allowed to use such armaments, and only to defend the planet in extreme circumstances.

BANE - The surly leader of a mercenary gang the Kin encounter in Vixen.

BATTLESWINE - A ferocious warrior race that holds the head of a boar, and are allies to Meridia.

BAKU - The Dream-eater, a supernatural being that devours dreams and nightmares and is *usually* indifferent toward mankind.

BISKARA - An ancient, powerful demon.

BLUNDERBUSS - The affable leader of the Centurions.

BOGMEN - A furry band of mercenaries that roams the forests on Azimuth.

BRODEUR - A kind, old thief with many tales.

THE CARK WOODS - A dark, haunted forest in western Meridia.

THE CENTURIONS - A ragtag band of soldiers, smugglers and thieves.

CETUS - Milo's second in command of the Stonecoats.

CHUD - A chewy substance made from the roots of Druids, which travelers eat on the road in Meridia.

COOGLE - The main form of currency on Azimuth.

DIRE CONFLICT - A popular virtual video game the soldiers of Meridia like to play.

DISEMBOWELERS - Terrible beasts trained by the Nightlanders into their army.

THE FOMALHAUT - A starship in the United Forces that harbors, by law, the only advanced weaponry to defend Azimuth, including the potent Star Darts fleet.

FORNAX - A habitable moon near Azimuth, where they hold universal games every two years.

THE FUGUES - The magical guardians of the Silver Sphere, they appear as several sets of beautiful eyes, and have strong psychic contact with certain Kin. However, they cannot stray too long from the Sphere, or they perish.

GENERAL CORNELIUS KRUPP - The veteran leader of the Battleswine.

GRAY-CLOAKS - Shrouded demons that usually exist deep in the Cark woods, but start to migrate to the outer limits as Malefic gains power.

GREEN-TEETH - A zombie-like race that inhabits the Cark woods.

GUNTHER WERRA - The massive Battleswine who is General Krupp's loyal field commander.

HIDEUX KAKOS - One of Biskara's former mortal sons who started the first Great War on Azimuth, and now dwells on the celestial plane.

HOROLOGIUM - The celestial headquarters of the Truth Seekers.

INTERCEPTORS - Meridian soldiers entrusted with meeting guests that arrive through the mobile portal on Azimuth.

THE KIN - Children born with psychic links to the Aulic Assembly, and when they pass through the mobile portal, they age and inherit the abilities of their links. Current members are Shelby Pardow, Zach Ryder, Max Tuttle, Emily Lawson, Riley Upchurch, and Stuart Lesser.

KIN LINKS WITH THE AULIC ASSEMBLY

Shelby Pardow - Bianca Saddler

Zach Ryder - Brock Fergus

Emily Lawson - Elita Ezmer

Max Tuttle - Macklin Morrow

Riley Upchurch - Rowan Letty

Stuart Lesser - Satchel Spool

LESHY - Forest spirits that protect the woods and its animals.

LUCAS DENON - Once a famous rock musician and poet on Earth, he is now a Truth Seeker.

MALEFIC CACOETHES - The evil, mortal spawn of Biskara.

MANTICORE - A near-extinct, powerful beast that lives deep in the woods in Meridia. It has the body of a red lion, and a head similar to a man, with three rows of sharp teeth and a trumpet-like voice.

MERACUSE - The capitol of Meridia.

MERIDIA - The dominant country on Azimuth, founded by the Atlaserians soon after they arrived.

MENTOR - A person trained in magic, science, history, and combat in the Meridian Army. Very few pass the rigorous training to become a Mentor.

MILO MORGANTE - The courageous leader of the Stonecoats and considered to be the most powerful human warrior on Azimuth.

THE MOBILE PORTAL - An instrument that teleports objects and people from other planets. It can only be used in certain locations.

MORGANA SUNDER - A young citizen from the village Chapton, which is attacked by Malefic and his Nightlanders.

NICK CASEY - A college student on Earth who rescues Emily Lawson, and unknowingly becomes a celestial soldier.

THE NIGHTLANDERS - Malefic's mortal, evil army.

PEGASI - Large birds with the head of a horse that roost on the Eridanus River.

PRESAGE - The wise Mentor that greets the Kin soon after arriving on Azimuth.

THE SCUTTLEBUTT - A tavern in the town of Vixen.

THE SILVER SPHERE - A magical armillary device created by the Truth Seekers, which can deliver the precise celestial coordinates of the demon Biskara. Only the Aulic Assembly can operate the Sphere. Upon death, the Kin inherit the Assembly's ability to utilize the Silver Sphere.

SIMON CROAN - A Meridian interceptor's young son who is captured by the Nightlanders.

THE SPANGENHELM - A hidden, secret cabin, discovered by bandits and the like, that harbors weapons, goods and clothes. Any item taken must be replenished at a later date, with additional items as payment. It is the one thing bandits and thieves in Meridia honor.

THE STONECOATS - An elite club of soldiers with a long history.

THE TRUTH SEEKERS - The celestial protectors of the universe; they cannot enter the mortal plane.

TUSKARIANS - Citizens of the country Tuska, a stout warrior race.

VIXEN - An entertainment village in Meridia, complete with gambling, mercenaries, games, goods, shops, and other services.

WALTER DEMPSEY - The benevolent curator of the Rutherford B. Hayes Library who unknowingly accompanies Shelby through the mobile portal to Azimuth.

WINTRESS THE CHANNELLER - The kind, psychic shopkeeper in Vixen who is an ally of Meridia.

WISHPOOSH – Man-eating beasts that resemble giant beavers and usually nest in the Invunche Lake. They do not stray far from the water.

ZUMBAKI – A cannibal tribe that resides near the Cark woods.

ACKNOWLEDGEMENTS

It takes a village to raise a book. This one was nurtured from its first page. I must express gratitude first and foremost to my amazing wife Jenna, for her support, dreams and enthusiasm, and all of my family on both sides of the country.

To the early wave of those brave beta readers and editors that helped shape my vision: my wise literary coach Timothy Staveteig, and my first editor, the outstanding Kira McFadden. And to my friends for their essential feedback and encouragement: Alex Mueck, Jeff Raymond, Peter Winther, Caroline Correa, Justin Hopper, Kevin Martin, Megan Jacobs, Elyse Luray, Susan Dishell, Marina Gigante, Mallory Rock, Meaghan Mikos, David Bushell, J.P Henreaux, J Cooper, David Binstock, Dennis Blair, Jeannie Fontana, and Zach Sklar.

To my publisher, Evolved Publishing, and all the wonderful minds there, including the owners, Dave Lane and D.T Conklin, as well as Kimberly Kinrade, Emlyn Chand and the rest of the shining authors, editors and artists in our EP family — the ultimate writers support group.

To the uber talented Mallory Rock for bringing my dreams, visions and characters to life as, well, the *complete* art director for *The Silver Sphere*.

To publicist Jeff Raymond and movie producer Peter Winther, my close friends and partners on the film development side, for all their guidance, coffee talk, feedback, and creative sessions next to the fire pit.

To one of my best friends, Kevin Martin, for his support and permission to use his incredible music on Mallory's awesome book trailers.

To my senior editor at Evolved Publishing, Dave Lane, who is the bar all editors should be held up against.

To Margaret Riley, Whitney Lee and Virginia Monseau, for critiques with a trained eye that were much needed.

To Alex Mueck, a friend who always believed in me, nudged me along, and encouraged me at all times.

For me, this was, and is, the perfect village to raise a book.

ABOUT THE AUTHOR

Michael has been writing since first setting pencil to steno pad at age 8. A year later, he began developing the world of his current series-in-progress, and even created the first title, *The Silver Sphere*.

Despite his frequent escapes into parallel worlds, he roots himself firmly in his very real family and community. When not pacing the yard maniacally after every few pages of writing, he spends as much time as possible hanging out with his studly young son, and with his inspirational wife, Jenna. He also coaches several local youth sports teams in Beverly Hills, and alternates between yelling at his two crazy Corgis and hiking with his trained German Shepherd.

Michael encourages you to join him in his favorite fantasy worlds, from *Lord of the Rings* to the creations of C.S. Lewis, Ann McCaffrey and Terry Brooks.

For more, please see his website at www.TheSilverSphere.org, or stop by and say hello on his Facebook page at /AuthorMichaelDadich, or tweet him at @MichaelDadich.

WHAT'S NEXT?

Enjoy one of Michael's short stories, *The Cistern Mission*, coming from Evolved Publishing in December 2012, in *Pathways (A Young Adult Anthology)*. And of course, watch for *The Sinister Kin*, the sequel to *The Silver Sphere*, in late 2013.

MORE FROM EVOLVED PUBLISHING

EULOGY by D.T. Conklin
This dark, epic fantasy novel is available at Amazon.

~~~~~

"They'll stand amongst the corpses of the beloved." That's what he said at the end, though I never considered myself one of the beloved, not at the beginning. I was simply a terrified woman then, but now... now I understand. Maybe I wish I didn't.

Void take me, this is so demon-damned hard.

In the beginning, he loved me. Irony, it twists and twirls like a lover's song, but this is hardly a lover's tale. It's one of blades and blood. I wish I could've seen it sooner, but that would've been too easy. I wouldn't have learned to love him.

~~~~~

5-Star Review: "Conklin writes with a poet's flair, using minimal words to deliver maximum dramatic impact. Visceral, shocking, and deeply imaginative, *Eulogy* pushes to the edge . . . and then dives right over it. An unapologetic, no-holds-barred descent into madness—yet there is method in it. Readers with the fortitude to take the plunge stand to be rewarded with what may go down as one of the most ambitious, redefining forays into epic fantasy of all time." – Eldon Thompson, Author of *The Divine Talisman*

5-Star Review: "Some epic fantasies are straightforward tales of magic and adventure, where a band of heroes fights and defeats an evil overlord. *Eulogy* is not such a tale. Conklin's book overflows with magic and adventure, but the book is a puzzle – a maze of secrets and wonders, implications and hidden meanings. A treat for readers who love a challenge!" – Tom Crosshill, Nebula-nominated Author

5-Star Review: "Conklin manages to write a book that is at once recognizable as fantasy but at the same time wholly his own. There are the escapists conventions: swords, battles, beautiful women, and magic, but it's this last one, magic, where the genre is subverted in the best way possible. In the world of *Eulogy*, the system of magic is reality-bending, and as such functions on a philosophical and psychological level, posing existential questions while swords flash in the foreground. I don't want to scare away readers who are in it for the adventure. There is always that, too, from personal quests to wars that sweep across the whole landscape. I just want to point out that there is something beyond the surface, and for readers like myself, who come to the fantasy genre only rarely, it's pleasant to find a book that successfully explores the deeper side of things while remaining thoroughly entertaining." – Zach Powers "wordist"

5-Star Review: "Conklin has written one of those books that gets in to your brain and whispers to you anytime you aren't reading it. The adventure is very much your own for with his characters, Conklin draws from the reader the magic they didn't realize they were bringing with them. Like most stories the overarching battle is good against evil, the characters each must face the darkness and demons that lie inside the soul of anyone who loves, hates, strives, and suffers. Some win. Some lose." – MJ Kaufmann "~MAJK~"

DEAD RADIANCE
(A Valkyrie Novel – Book 1)
This romantic YA fantasy adventure featuring Valkyries and Norse Gods is now available at Amazon.

~~~~~

That day I knew for sure. I'd lost control of my tears then. They fell in huge, mocking drops. I stared at Joshua through those bitter tears, my heart missing beats as I tried to remember to breathe.

I finally knew what the glow meant.

I was a freak and Joshua was going to die.

~~~~~

Bryn Halbrook had always seen the glow. But it is only when her best friend dies that she discovers the meaning of those beautiful golden auras — Death. Alone, lost in the foster system, she struggles to understand who she is and why she was cursed with the ability to see the soon-to-be-dead.

The new foster kid, Aidan, isn't helping any. Mr. Perfect seems to fit in no matter what, making her feel even more pathetic. But when his affections turn to her, Bryn finds him hard to resist. Impossible, actually. A mystery himself, Aidan disappears, leaving behind a broken heart and a mysterious book that suggests Bryn might not be entirely human.

Bryn stands at the threshold of a journey of discovery. Will destiny help her find herself, find her purpose and her place in a world in which she'd never belonged?

FORBIDDEN MIND
(Forbidden #1)
This romantic YA paranormal adventure, featuring teenagers with extraordinary powers, is now available at Amazon.
Winner of 2011 Forward National Literature Award (Drama: 2nd Place)

~~~~~

Sam thinks she's months away from freedom. After spending her life in a secret school, rented out to the rich and powerful as a paranormal spy, she is ready to head to college like any normal eighteen-year-old.

Only Sam isn't normal. She reads minds. And just before her big going-away party, she links to the mind of a young man who changes everything.

Drake wasn't raised as a 'Rent-A-Kid.' He was kidnapped and taken there by force. But his exceptional physical strength and powers of mind control make him very dangerous, especially to Sam.

When they meet, Sam is forced to face the truth of her situation, and to acknowledge that not all is as it seems in her picture-perfect world. For what awaits her on her eighteenth birthday isn't a trip to college, but an unexpected nightmare from which she may not be able to escape.

To survive, they must work together.

But will their powers be enough to save them before it's too late?

FARSIGHTED
(Farsighted #1)
This romantic YA fantasy adventure is now available at Amazon.
Multiple Award Winner

~~~~~

Alex Kosmitoras's life has never been easy. The only other student who will talk to him is the school bully, his parents are dead broke and insanely overprotective, and to complicate matters even more, he's blind. Just when he thinks he'll never have a shot at a normal life, an enticing new girl comes to their small Midwest town all the way from India. Simmi is smart, nice, and actually wants to be friends with Alex. Plus she smells like an Almond Joy bar. Sophomore year might not be so bad after all.

Unfortunately, Alex is in store for another new arrival—an unexpected and often embarrassing ability to "see" the future. Try as he may, Alex is unable to ignore his visions, especially when they suggest Simmi is in mortal danger. With the help of the mysterious psychic next door and friends who come bearing gifts of their own, Alex embarks on his journey to change the future.

RECOMMENDED READING FROM EVOLVED PUBLISHING

CHILDREN'S PICTURE BOOKS

THE BIRD BRAIN BOOKS by Emlyn Chand:
Honey the Hero
Davey the Detective
Poppy the Proud
Tommy Goes Trick-or-Treating
Courtney Saves Christmas
Vicky Finds a Valentine

I'd Rather Be Riding My Bike by Eric Pinder

HISTORICAL FANTASY / ROMANCE

Sunrise & Nightfall by Kimberly Kinrade and Dmytry Karpov
Blood of the Fallen by Kimberly Kinrade and Dmytry Karpov
Tears of the Fallen by Kimberly Kinrade and Dmytry Karpov
Flight of the Fallen by Kimberly Kinrade and Dmytry Karpov

HISTORICAL FICTION

Circles by Ruby Standing Deer
Spirals by Ruby Standing Deer

LITERARY FICTION

Torn Together by Emlyn Chand
Hannah's Voice by Robb Grindstaff
Jellicle Girl by Stevie Mikayne
Weight of Earth by Stevie Mikayne

LOWER GRADE

THE THREE LOST KIDS – Special Edition Illustrated - by Kimberly Kinrade:
Lexie World
Bella World
Maddie World

THE THREE LOST KIDS – CHAPTER BOOKS by Kimberly Kinrade:
The Death of the Sugar Fairy
The Christmas Curse
Cupid's Capture

MEMOIR

And Then It Rained: Lessons for Life by Megan Morrison

MYSTERY

Hot Sinatra by Axel Howerton

ROMANCE / EROTICA

Skinny-Dipping at Dawn by Darby Davenport
One Word and I'm Yours by Daring Davenport
Her Twisted Pleasures by Amelia James
Secret Storm by Amelia James
Tell Me You Want Me by Amelia James
The Devil Made Me Do It by Amelia James

SCI-FI / FANTASY

Eulogy by D.T. Conklin

SHORT STORY ANTHOLOGIES

FROM THE EDITORS AT EVOLVED PUBLISHING:
Evolution: Vol. 1 (A Short Story Collection)
Evolution: Vol. 2 (A Short Story Collection)
Pathways (A Young Adult Anthology)

SUSPENSE / THRILLER

Forgive Me, Alex by Lane Diamond
The Devil's Bane by Lane Diamond

YOUNG ADULT

Dead Chaos by T.G. Ayer
Dead Embers by T.G. Ayer
Dead Radiance by T.G. Ayer
Skin Deep by T.G. Ayer
Farsighted by Emlyn Chand
Open Heart by Emlyn Chand
Pitch by Emlyn Chand
Silver Sphere by Michael Dadich
Ring Binder by Ranee Dillon
Forbidden Mind by Kimberly Kinrade
Forbidden Fire by Kimberly Kinrade
Forbidden Life by Kimberly Kinrade
Desert Rice by Angela Scott
Survivor Roundup by Angela Scott
Wanted: Dead or Undead by Angela Scott

CPSIA information can be obtained at www.ICGtesting.com
Printed in the USA
BVOC010916031212

307132BV00003BA/5/P